THE JAGUAR
PRINCESS

CLARE BELL

TOR
fantasy ®

A TOM DOHERTY ASSOCIATES BOOK
NEW YORK

This is a work of fiction. All the characters and events portrayed in this book are fictitious, and any resemblance to real people or events is purely coincidental.

THE JAGUAR PRINCESS

Copyright © 1993 by Clare Bell

Cover art by Jody A. Lee

Edited by James R. Frenkel

A Tor Book
Published by Tom Doherty Associates, Inc.
175 Fifth Avenue
New York, N.Y. 10010

Tor® is a registered trademark of Tom Doherty Associates, Inc.

ISBN: 0-812-51516-1
Library of Congress Catalog Card Number: 93-25920

First edition: October 1993
First mass market edition: September 1994

Printed in the United States of America

0 9 8 7 6 5 4 3 2 1

DEDICATION

To my brother, David Weston Steward,
kindred spirit and saver of cats,
fellow wayfarer on the long, strange
journey.

ACKNOWLEDGMENTS

Dorothy Bradley, whose travels and interest in ancient Mexico gave me the idea. (She also loaned me a ton of reference books.)

To Francis Gillmore, whose books, *The Flute of the Smoking Mirror* and *The King Danced in the Marketplace* inspired me.

To Jane Yolen, who said this was not a short story.

To members of the Wordshop 1991; Kevin Anderson, Michael Berch, Dan'l Danehy-Oakes, Avis Minger, Gary Shockley and Lori Ann White.

And to M. Coleman Easton, who knew I had to write this, and made me do it.

1

IN THE AZTEC year Three Reed, in the age of the Earthquake Sun, a six-year-old girl named Mixcatl sat in a
barge threading its way through the waterways of Tenochtitlán. She glowered at the passing reflections and
tugged angrily at the slave yoke about her neck. Leather
thongs hobbled her ankles and wrists. Her hands had
been tied in front, where she could chew on the length
between her wrists when the overseer wasn't looking.
She was making little progress in freeing herself; the
leather was tough.

Scowling and wincing with pain, she felt the sides of
her neck above the wooden yoke, where the flesh was raw
and full of splinters. A crude and clumsy thing, the collar
was made of two Y-forked pieces, lashed together to form
a tight diamond-shaped opening for her neck and two
handles that stuck out over her shoulders.

Mixcatl knew well what those handles were used for.
She had been dragged from the jobbing lot where slaves
were collected for transport to market. The collar handles
made it easier for the slave traders to seize slaves and
shove them into the market boat.

Reaching up awkwardly with her bound hands, the
girl touched one side of her neck and remembered. She

had resisted being put in the boat, fighting, struggling, screaming. Finally two strong men lifted her by the handles on her collar and let her hang with her toes barely touching the ground while others loaded the remaining slaves.

When she was finally let down, the slave traders put her in the only place available, a small space up front by a ragged old man. Ignoring him, she hugged her dirty knees and stared out at the peaks that rose above the thatched and tiled roofs of the island city.

She didn't want to think about what lay ahead for her. Aztec warriors had overrun her eastern jungle village when she was barely three. Tears of rage burned her eyes when she remembered how she was torn from the arms of her grandmother by an Aztec soldier, forced to march with a gang of other captured children and sold as booty in a squalid town. Each time she was bought, her owner found her unsatisfactory and sold her again. Each time, her life had gotten worse.

Now she was here, along with other unwanted slaves that the merchant was getting rid of in Tenochtitlán. From her experience in being sold, she knew that these sorts of slaves were useless for anything except being killed as offerings at a temple.

Her gloomy thoughts were interrupted when the ragged old man beside her spoke a few words of the eastern tongue used in her village. This startled the girl out of her sullen retreat, though at first she continued to ignore him. He kept speaking to her until at last she looked at him.

He was elderly and fragile, probably too sickly to labor, the girl thought, staring away again. If he was not bought as an offering, he would probably die soon anyway. His collar hung loosely about his wrinkled neck and his bony wrists were bound in front of him. His head was bald, he had only a few peglike teeth and a dirty-yellow beard that straggled down onto his sunken chest, but there was a kind expression in his watery eyes.

The journey was long and slow, for the barge had to be poled through the canals. Often the slave boat had to wait for other craft to pass or for a logjam of barges and canoes to clear. At first, there was nothing to look at except adobe houses that lined the muddy banks of the canal and the floating crop-gardens of the outskirts. Finding no interest in these, the girl stared at waterweed swirling past the square prow of the barge and nursed her hurt.

As the old slave spoke to her in a mix of the village language and the Aztec tongue, Nahuatl, she understood, even though she refused to answer. He was trying to cheer her up by telling her what he knew of the city.

Soon the sights he was pointing out became more interesting. Rows of adobe huts gradually gave way to more massive buildings and open plazas. Where there had been only the drab clothing of farmers and laborers, now she saw brilliant flashes of color from the costumes of people gathering in the plazas.

"And that is the Snake Wall, and beyond, the Temple of the Sun," said the old slave in his raspy voice, pointing to a gleaming stepped pyramid that looked to Mixcatl like a mountain. The boat slowed as it rounded a sharp corner and another building came into view on the opposite bank. It seemed to lie along the canal for a great distance, dazzling the slaves with its white walls. Brightly hued banners hung between its square columns, and painted carvings decorated panels at the corners. Though in height the building was no match for the Temple of the Sun or any other of the stepped pyramids in the temple precinct, it made an impressive sight.

"That is the king's palace," said the old slave to Mixcatl. "Our ruler lives there. He has beautiful gardens and surrounds himself with animals and rare birds. Listen, you can hear them if you are quiet."

But Mixcatl was already silent, leaning forward to catch the sounds. She heard the noises of her homeland, the raucous cries of jungle birds and the screeching of parrots. They made her feel tense and excited. She dug her nails into the wooden side of the boat. She could smell animals as well as birds. Monkeys, coatis, ocelots. And even from this distance, over the stone walls, she caught the sharp scent of a jaguar, trapped and pacing within the walls.

She leaned over the side of the boat, trembling with dread and longing. It was always so when she caught the smells of jungle animals, especially the big cat. She had known them from the time she had lain in her cradle as an infant. The scents drifted in through the windows and doors of her grandmother's hut. And her grandmother had shown her the different animals that made those smells. She glanced back at the old slave. No. He couldn't smell them. He was like all the other people, even the ones in her village. They couldn't smell anything except food cooking.

The boat glided down the canal and the animal odors faded out. The old man was talking again and Mixcatl only half heard him. But some shift in his voice caught and held her attention.

"This is but a rumor among slaves," he said, his voice quieter than before. "The king's palace lies not far from the market where we are being taken. It is said that if you are about to be bought and you run away, the king will give you protection if you can touch the walls of his house. Do you understand me, child?"

Mixcatl stared at him, clawed the yoke around her neck. "Not a slave?" she croaked out in the words of her own tongue. The old man nodded, then winced as he was poked from behind by an overseer. He did not point but instead fixed his eyes on the walls of the palace that were starting to slip away behind the boat.

"If I were not so old, I would try it," he whispered.

Mixcatl sat beside him, looking straight ahead. If she concentrated, she could still catch the lingering scent of the king's menagerie. If she escaped, the odors could guide her.

To be away from these hard hands and loud voices. Could she ever find a life without them?

So far her life had been short and harsh. She had worked first in a brickyard, scooping adobe clay into molds in the hot sun. Several decorative and rebellious handprints on the top of a brick had earned her a severe beating and a change of ownership.

Then came the turkey farm, where she lugged grain and water to the gabbling flock and cleaned manure from pens. She still remembered how noisy the birds were, especially when she was around them. They seemed to hate her smell, for they would chase her and try to peck her. One day, cornered and frightened, she had lashed out, belting a pullet with a half-full grain sack and breaking its neck.

If she managed to get free, where would she go? Back to her village and her grandmother? She had been taken so far away that she could never find the way back. And even if she found the village again, would her grandmother still be alive?

A burning sob pushed up her throat past her collar. Awkwardly, because his wrists were tied, the old man laid a hand on her shoulder. They sat together as the boat swung around the last corner, turning into the stone quays of the market.

Mixcatl stood on the edge of the market plaza, her back to the canal, the leather hobbles stretched between her ankles. The stone of the plaza swayed beneath her as though she were still on the market boat. The swirl of noise, color and sound added to her disorientation. As the other slaves were unloaded, she became lost in a forest of legs and feet. She jumped in fright as a macaw screamed from its cage in a stall near the quay.

She felt a touch on her shoulder and looked up into the eyes of the old man. Despite his bound wrists, he managed to guide her out of the milling mass of slaves, then stooped down beside her. His voice was a raspy whisper, but she found it soothing. While the slave merchants were distracted with the task of unloading their merchandise, the old man talked to Mixcatl in a mixture of Nahuatl and her own tongue, helping her make sense of the rioting colors and shapes about her.

His voice and his gentle manner calmed her. Across from the quay stood small mounds in colors of red, green and orange. When Mixcatl blinked away the tears that blurred her vision, she could see that the hills were mountains of fruit and vegetables, more than she had ever seen in her life. There were smooth-skinned melons and pebble-skinned squashes, mounds of yams, cassava and other root crops, along with stacked baskets of tomatoes and beans.

A spicy tang tickled her nose and she saw the dried, wine-red shapes of peppers tied in bunches hanging from the awning of a nearby stall. A muddy wet odor drew her gaze to squat, clay-sealed baskets filled with live fish from the lake. Saliva filled her mouth at the hot-griddle smell of baking tortillas.

A warning touch drew her back from her fascination with the marketplace. The slave merchants were assembling the captives in several ragged lines before marching them across the market plaza. Mixcatl stepped into place, but her eyes still roved the market and the old man's voice droned on above her head.

Mountains of pots were piled opposite the produce,

stacked so high that the weight had broken some of those underneath. Mantles made of cloth so white that it seemed to gleam lay atop colorful tapestries and sashes. Carved jade flashed in the sunlight as it was turned in eager hands. Shimmering quetzal plumes escaped their bundles and fluttered over the edges of woven baskets.

"Do you see that man?" the old slave asked, extending his bound hands toward a richly dressed figure who stood on a red stone block. Mixcatl stared, squinting. She thought at first that the figure was a statue, for he stood so still in his richly dyed blue mantle. Then she saw his head turn and sunlight flashed on his chestpiece of beaten gold.

"He is the Lord of the Market," the old slave said. "He enforces fair trading. If a seller cheats or makes false measures, he judges and punishes."

Mixcatl looked at the Lord of the Market, who stood like a statue guarding the plaza. He held a carved staff with a fan of feathers bound to the top and had a stern hook-nosed face. Would he judge slaves, Mixcatl wondered. If she tried to run, would she be dragged before him and then be beaten to death?

With hoarse shouts, the slave merchants prodded the captives into a slow shuffle across the plaza. They straggled past piles of rolled mats that gave off a dry reedy odor, past stacks of thick paper made from the beaten bark of fig trees and covered with fine white clay. In the stall next to the paper-seller, a scribe dipped a brush into a paintpot and started to make the first stroke of color on a page. Mixcatl was fascinated, but she had to move along with the other slaves.

Glancing at the old man, she recalled what he had said to her on the market boat, about the king's palace and how escaped slaves could gain their freedom once they touched its walls. She remembered the scents of the king's animals and grew frightened because she could no longer find them amid the many odors of the market-place.

The slaves passed a group of people doing a festival dance, men in embroidered loincloths with elaborate knots and tailpieces, women in gaily patterned skirts. The drum pattered, a flute skirled a piping melody and the dancers' feet tripped a light step while the slaves shuffled by.

Beyond the dancers was another stone block, this one larger and shaped in the form of a pyramid base. On the platform sat six men in white mantles, all with the stern expression Mixcatl had seen on the face of the Market Lord. The old slave told her that these men were lawgivers and judges. Before the six judges stood three warriors with spears who guarded a man whose hands were bound together before him with thongs. He pleaded, shouted and covered his face with his bound hands, but the judges paid him no heed. They spoke only briefly and the man was hauled away by the three spearbearers. Mixcatl averted her eyes. What had he done, she wondered. Was he a thief or an escaped slave?

Again she thought about the king's palace. What would those dazzling walls feel like beneath her palm? They would be warm with sunlight and the feeling of freedom. But she had lost the scent that might guide her there. Her spirits started a plunge into despair, but halted as she caught another smell.

An animal smell. Her nostrils flared, her head came up. Images of ocelots and monkeys leaped about in her mind. But the odor had a deadness and dryness to it. There was only the scent of skin and hair, nothing of the live creature within.

The odor came from beneath a large canopy, raised on poles. In the warm shade beneath the tent lay a mound of stiff flattened animal hides. The group of slaves halted, waiting for another gang to catch up. Mixcatl took advantage of the opportunity to study the stall and its contents. The empty feet of the hides still bore claws and the snarling heads had lost their eyes.

Apart from the large pile of varied animal skins lay a smaller stack of softer furs. On top of these finer pelts lay a yellow-gold one with black spots in a rosette pattern. A man in the embroidered mantle and feathered headpiece of a noble was handling the skin, feeling the fur. A strange rage seized Mixcatl. She bared her teeth, would have flung herself at the purchaser but for the old slave's bound hands that held her collar. She twisted herself sideways but could not escape his grip.

Still struggling, driven by an anger she did not understand, Mixcatl turned back for one last glare at the man about to buy the jaguar skin. A strange drumming began in her head and something seemed to leap about inside her mind and then out. Her stubby child-fingers stiffened, curled. One of her tethered hands drew back in a sharp raking motion.

The paw of the jaguar pelt twisted in its buyer's grip, pulled itself through the noble's hand, scoring his palm with its dangling claws. The man jumped back with a cry, startling others who had gathered about the stack of pelts. People gathered into a knot around him, gabbling like turkeys. He shouted in Nahuatl, seized the hide-seller, smearing him with the blood from his open palm.

From the corner of her eye Mixcatl saw spearbearers come running up as the Lord of the Market descended from his plinth, then walked to the pile of hides while the young noble clenched his bleeding hand. Fear had whitened his face beneath the bronze skin.

And then she was poked from behind and made to move on, leaving the tumult and the shouting behind. One last glance over her shoulder let her see the Lord of the Market picking up the jaguar skin. It flopped limply, but the noble would not buy it. He turned and stalked away.

She felt strangely dizzy and had to be lifted onto the selling platform when the slaves reached it. The fingertips of her right hand tingled. She wondered if in some strange way she had hurt the man who was buying the jaguar skin. Had her anger made him bleed?

"An arrogant son of powerful men, who blames others for his own clumsiness," said the old slave softly. "Even a dead jaguar has claws."

Mixcatl lifted her head, stood up straight, though her fingers still tingled beneath the nails. Her head cleared. There were fewer market scents in the air about her and she was on the edge of the stone dais so that the sweat and stink of the other slaves blew away in the wind. She focused on trying to find the guide smell, the one that might lead her to freedom.

So intent was her concentration that she didn't notice the overseer who had come up behind her. She only caught a glimpse of a scowling face before she was dealt a slap on the side of the head.

"Stop that grimacing," he scolded in Nahuatl. "I can't sell you if you look like an animal."

With tears stinging the edges of her eyes, she huddled close to the old slave and buried her face against him.

"You must stand away from me now," he said gently. "There are buyers coming."

Mixcatl sniffled away her remaining tears and did as he told her.

The sun crept westward behind the girl, throwing her shadow and those of the few remaining slaves along the square flagstones of the plaza. She could see herself, looking like a stretched black ghost in company with others atop the platform. She curled her stumpy fingers, making talons on the shadow hands.

And then a man walked up and bought the old man, who was still standing next to her. The transaction was abrupt, with little haggling. The buyer paid the low asking price of three cloth mantles, then motioned the old man down from the platform.

He held back just long enough to say a few words of farewell to Mixcatl. "Do not sorrow, little one. You knew me only for a day. It is not a bad life that lies ahead of me, for the one who buys me looks like a kind man."

Mixcatl stared at the old slave, then away. He looked relieved, almost happy, and she suddenly hated him for his good fortune. She resisted the temptation to look at him once again in order to remember him. Why should she? He had only known her one day. But as the slap of his footsteps faded, the image of his face stayed in her memory.

She bowed her head and stared sullenly at her feet. They were short, wide and without an arch. Her toes were too short and spread too far apart. But she knew how fast she could run. If she got a chance.

The sun beat on her naked back. Thirst began to daze her. None of the slaves had been given water for fear that they might choose to relieve themselves on the selling platform. A poke between the shoulders brought her out of her daze, made her stare down at the two men arguing in front of her. One was the chief slave merchant, the other a stocky man in white cloak and gold arm-rings. She had learned enough Nahuatl to understand the gist of their conversation.

"Not even one mantle for her?" the slave merchant whined.

"She is ugly, ill-tempered. She is fit only to carry ashes from the hearth. How old is she?"

"Six or seven, although she is as strong and heavy as a child of ten. And though she looks feebleminded, she is teachable. She already understands our speech." The customer only grunted as the slave merchant continued in a wheedling tone, ''You must also consider the costs of transport. She was brought all the way from the eastern jungles . . .''

''Then you might as well have left her there. No one will trade even the most ragged mantle for such a slave.'' He took a dirty leather pouch and shook its contents into his hand. ''Cocoa beans. The entire pouch for her.''

''I will be mocked for accepting such a price,'' the slaver complained.

''You deserve mockery for bringing such poor goods,'' sneered the other man. ''Shall I summon the Lord of the Market?''

The slave merchant narrowed his eyes at the prospective buyer, then squinted up at Mixcatl. She felt a hot angry lump grow in her throat just above her collarbone. She wanted the slave merchant to refuse the purchase and send the man on his way, preferably with a kick.

''Loose the hobbles about her ankles so I can see how she walks. And untie her wrists so I can see that her arms and hands are not crippled.''

The slave merchant gestured at his helper, who undid the knots that linked Mixcatl's wrists together, whipped the thongs from around the girl's ankles and paraded her back and forth on the selling platform before the customer. She tried to limp or drag her feet. The idea of being sold to this man made her shudder.

But the man was already gesturing acceptance and the slave merchant was taking the pouch of cocoa beans. Mixcatl grimaced, searching again for the scent of the king's menagerie. For an instant she caught only market smells, but a breeze, gusting from behind her, brought traces of the animal and bird odors she had caught while passing the king's house. Just a trace, but enough to give her direction.

With a bound she was down from the stone platform

and running through the market, her heels smarting from the impact. From the corner of her eye she saw the purchaser try to snatch back his pouch of cocoa beans, but the slave merchant jumped out of reach, crying, "You bought her, you catch her!"

With a roar of dismay, Mixcatl's new owner gave chase. She glanced back and saw that his big belly hung out over his knotted loincloth, but his arms and legs were heavily muscled. The girl fled as fast as she could, slamming the calluses on her feet against the paving. Panic peeled her lips back against her teeth and people in her path jumped out of her way.

She gasped, heard her pursuer coming closer. She cut the corner as she scuttled around a stack of melons, sending the fruit bouncing and rolling into his path. She heard a wet crunch, dared a look behind and saw that he had put his foot through a large rotten melon and was dancing about on one leg, trying to shake it off.

Grinning, Mixcatl flashed away, but soon the pounding of feet behind told her she hadn't lost him. He was coming fast, with long strides. She tried all the tricks she knew from the games of her jungle childhood and panic helped her invent new ones. She careened into baskets of loose parrot feathers, sending them billowing into the air to form a madly swirling curtain between her and her pursuer.

She bounded over rows of stacked jars, landed in the midst of ceramic pots, sending them clattering. She knocked down stall awnings, set caged birds screeching, squashed a tomato underfoot and then ran across stacks of gleaming white mantles, leaving dirty tomato footprints.

The shouting of outraged vendors mixed with the raucous laughter from people thronging the market as Mixcatl hurtled past them. To her surprise and relief, none joined in the effort to catch her. Laughter and havoc rolled around Mixcatl, carrying her like a wave until at last she broke free of the market and sprinted across the open plaza. The smell was growing stronger in her nostrils and she imagined that she could hear the cries of the birds in the king's menagerie. But heavy panting and shouting behind told of her purchaser's tenacity.

The collar bound Mixcatl's throat, not letting her breathe as deeply as she needed to. Now she was running along the canal, whipping around one corner, streaking for the next. Ahead of her, above the roofs of surrounding buildings, she could see the shimmer of white walls. Hope leaped in her, blinded her with grateful tears as she scurried around the last corner, thinking how it would feel to slap her hand against that wall and come away free.

She didn't see the flower-seller until the last instant, when she tried to leap aside. The startled woman did the same and down they both went in a multicolored tumble of petals, bouquets and baskets. Shaking, Mixcatl scrambled free, her eyes darting frantically in the search for a footbridge across the canal to the king's house. She had seen one in the moment before she collided. She sighted the bridge once more and launched herself for it just as her pursuer rounded the corner and startled the disoriented flower-seller into jumping in the canal.

The long run and the collision had cost Mixcatl her speed. Her legs were wobbly and each movement seemed impossibly slow. She ran wide of the footbridge, nearly went past it, but caught a stone pillar in one hand and flung herself onto the bridge. Panting grunts sounded close behind her. There was the sound of air whistling through woven reeds and a yell of triumph that made her jump as if a whip had cracked behind her.

The wall loomed just ahead, barely a handstretch away. Mixcatl leaped, both hands extended, chest heaving and sobbing. She would be free, she could go back to her village and find her grandmother . . .

And then a rattan barrier came down between Mixcatl and the gleaming white wall. She landed hard on stomach and elbows, tried to thrust her hand beneath the edge of the rattan, scrabbling and stretching for the wall. So close, so close, but now beyond her reach. She screamed and threw herself against the inside of the heavy basket that had been clapped down on top of her. Again she thrust outward with her free arm, but her captor stamped on the rim of the basket, pinning and bruising her arm until the pain forced her to pull it back inside.

Mixcatl raked the rattan with her fingernails, attacked with her teeth until her mouth bled. The taste of her own blood drove her into a frenzy. Her vision went red, then white. She writhed on her back, kicking, scratching, tearing. Her voice became stronger, more piercing. New strength expanded her arms, flowed down to reshape her hands. She yowled, splintered rattan with fingers that seemed to have curved and sharpened into claws.

But the rattan would not yield. She felt her captor bouncing on top of the basket, trying to squash her down. The white fire of rage consumed her and then, at its peak, froze and shattered, leaving only blackness.

The first sensation to return was pain, from her bleeding lip, torn fingers and bruised arm. The next was her sense of smell. Hot pavement, the weedy stink of the canal, the anxious sweaty smells of people gathered about her. Dizzily she sat up, found that both her hands and feet were hobbled. She had been moved across the canal from the palace wall to prevent any sudden lunge for freedom.

The basket that had trapped her lay on its side. A man with a spear, his hair bound up in a warrior's tail and wearing the robes of an official, stooped, peering into the basket. Others did the same, although none touched it.

The man who had bought her stood by, looking red-faced and triumphant, holding a rope knotted to her collar. There was an odd wariness in his eyes and he stood as far away from her as the rope would allow.

Mixcatl pushed herself up on her hands, peered into the basket. The heavy rattan was splintered, in some places bitten through.

The official got up, faced Mixcatl's new owner. "She didn't touch the palace wall?"

"I swear she didn't reach it," the man replied. "I had her under the basket before she got close." He extended a hand to the drenched flower-seller who was gathering up what remained of her scattered merchandise. "That woman is my witness."

"I'll be a witness that you stole my best basket!" the flower-seller shouted, her grimace and wizened face making her look like an enraged monkey. "Look how the brat has ripped the inside!"

"Old liar. It was worn and broken," the man sneered, then jerked Mixcatl's rope, pulling the girl to her feet. A bitter sob welled up in Mixcatl's throat as she remembered how close she had come to freedom. With the hobbles, she had no chance, except to fling herself into the canal and drown.

"You will pay, greasy thief." The flower-seller shook a fist in the man's face. "The Lord of the Market will have you tried by the Court of Six and stoned."

With a contemptuous laugh the man pushed the flower-seller aside and began to drag Mixcatl away through the crowd that had gathered to watch the pursuit and capture. She stumbled after him, head bowed, trying not to think of what her new life would be like. Something inside made her wonder how she had managed to damage the basket, for she knew it was stout and strong, not old, as her captor claimed.

She resented how the crowd seemed to part as if mak-

ing way for her new master. Then she glanced up and
realized that the people ahead were not stepping aside for
him but for someone else coming the other way. The
crowd thinned, letting three barechested warriors
through.

To Mixcatl's astonishment, they seized the man who
had bought her and held him until two more people arrived. The first was the slave merchant, angry and shaking. He waved his fingers in the man's face, but before he
could speak, there came the flap of a slate-blue cloak and
a flash of gold as the Lord of the Market came through the
crowd.

He set his plumed staff firmly on the flagstones and
turned his stern gaze to Mixcatl's new master. "You are
accused of trading with goods of false worth," he said,
holding up the leather pouch of cocoa beans.

The man paled, started to back away, but the guardsmen held him firmly.

The Lord of the Market shook a brown bean into his
hand, held it between thumb and forefinger and squashed
it flat. "Wax mixed with amaranth dough," he said.

"Honorable one, I did not know. I accepted the beans
in barter earlier today. Had I known . . ."

The slave merchant began to shout and other vendors
in the crowd began to boo and jeer. Several cried out that
they knew this man and that it was not the first time he
had tried to pass off counterfeit cocoa beans.

"You are sentenced to be tried by the Court of Six,"
said the Lord of the Market. "Your purchase is to be
surrendered." He turned on his heel and walked away.

The guardsmen marched after him with the counter-
feiter between them, followed by the angry old flower-
seller, still berating him shrilly about her damaged
basket.

The slave merchant took the rope tied to Mixcatl's
collar, but she could see he did not look pleased.

"All that time and effort wasted without a real sale," he complained. He glowered at the girl as he led her back to the selling platform, and she heard him muttering that he would rather drop her in the canal than haul her back to the jobbing lot in his boat if she were not bought by the day's end.

"That would be a waste of one who is strong in body and spirit," said a light voice above Mixcatl's head. She turned, stared up at a young man with cropped black hair, a dark purple mantle with embroidered golden stars and a thin, ascetic-looking face.

"She is a young wildcat, better drowned than sold. I will be the one dragged before the law courts if she escapes from you and runs wild again."

"I am a tutor at the priests' school. We need a sturdy young slave to draw water and carry out slopjars."

The slave merchant only growled and spat. Mixcatl felt her eyes widen. She measured the new arrival, wondered how fast he could run.

"I will give you two cotton mantles for her," the young tutor said. "They are not new, but freshly washed." He brought out a bundle from beneath his cloak.

The slave merchant looked relieved. "Done," he said, with only a quick glance at the contents. "Take her and go quickly. I warn you, you will only have yourself to blame if she wrecks your kitchens and runs wild among your pupils."

He placed the rope end in the young man's hand. Mixcatl studied her second new owner of the day. She balanced on her toes, wondered if she could jerk the rope from his hand and make a second run. She felt weary, heard her stomach growl. Freedom seemed suddenly less attractive than food. At least eating would give her time to think.

The young man knotted the rope about his wrist, ending any chance of losing his grip to a sharp jerk. He gave Mixcatl a keen look. "I don't like tethering a child, but until we're out of the market, it will help you resist any temptation."

Thinking of hot corn tortillas baking on a stone griddle, Mixcatl put aside her thoughts of freedom, bowed her head and followed her master.

2

IN THE SUNRISE direction from the Aztec city of Tenochtitlán lay a city-state called Texcoco. It stood on the eastern
shore of Lake Texcoco, the swampy, shallow body of
water surrounding the Aztec capital. Independently ruled
by an allied tribe called the Chichimecs, Texcoco had
long been a flourishing trade center. Wise Coyote, Texcoco's *tlatoani* or Revered Speaker-King, saw that his city
could not compete with the Aztecs' military strength.
Instead he had entered into an alliance with them and
concentrated on making Texcoco the capital of art and
learning for the Aztec Empire.

In addition to his estates in the city itself, Wise Coyote
owned lands at Tezcotzinco, in the hills above the lake.
Here he had built a palace of sapphire-blue stone and
surrounded it with gardens full of rare and exotic flowers.
Whenever he tired of life in the city, he retreated to Tezcotzinco.

Today he had come to the gardens to bathe. A fresh
wind blew between the hills, but the sun was strong and
warm on Wise Coyote's back as he pulled his knotted
mantle off over his head. He laid the cloak on the grassy
bank beside his turquoise headband, loincloth and blue
sandals, then waded into a pool that nestled among the
rocks.

Had the pool been formed naturally from the gathering of mountain streams, the king would have dipped quickly and shivered back into his clothing. Human hands and the will of the tlatoani himself had changed the form of the hills and the flow of the streams. Now water gathered behind stone dams, trickled into shallow collecting basins and ran along troughs of sun-warmed rock until it spilled into the bathing pool.

Wise Coyote lay back on his elbows, his head and shoulders in the sunlight, the rest of his body in the water's soothing caress as it made its way to the outflow and cascaded down into the channels and pools below. Idly, he lifted a foot and touched the center one of three stone frogs who sat by the poolside. He'd had them made, half in jest, as a present for his queen. The frogs represented the cities of the Triple Alliance in the Valley of Mexico. The two on the outside were the cities of Tlacopan and his own city of Texcoco. The center frog, and the one with the most severe goggle-eyed stare (at least it seemed so to Wise Coyote) was the Aztec city of Tenochtitlán, the self-declared center of the world.

In a moment of irreverence, he slapped the sole of his foot against the frog's stone face. If the tlatoani of Tenochtitlán saw these and knew what they were, he would have demanded why the center frog had not been made larger than the others. Wise Coyote frowned, then caught the image of his own face frowning back at him from among the ripples in the bathing pool. Some nobles at his court in Texcoco had flattered him, saying that he resembled the Aztec ruler, Hue Hue Ilhuicamina, but it was not true. Wise Coyote's eyes were too deepset, his nose not blunt or broad enough, his face too finely sculpted to meet the standards of ideal Aztec beauty as personified by the features of Ilhuicamina. And his eyes were too wide open and there was a touch of fear in them, for his day of birth had been One-Deer.

Some whispered that he did not have the face of a warrior, or that he had no heart to face the blood sacrifices made to Hummingbird on the Left. He smiled a little sadly to himself as he touched the scars that laced his arms and chest. He remembered pain from the strike of the obsidian-edged sword and the stab of the spearhead. For a man said to be lacking the heart and face of a warrior, he mused, he had done well. And war had not yet cut from him the thing that it had severed from so many—the gentleness of soul that kept the man within the warrior.

Perhaps that is a quality neither needed nor wanted in these times, Wise Coyote thought to himself as he climbed from the pool and let the morning sun dry the water from his skin.

He had dressed and was walking along the path to the shaded patio of his palace when he saw a boy coming to meet him. Wise Coyote opened his arms and his mantle to embrace Huetzin, his son by his favored concubine, the woman with the golden skin.

Twelve-year-old Huetzìn, with his gift for working stone, was the happiest of Wise Coyote's children, singing and running everywhere he went. But today his feet dragged and his face looked anxious. The carving in his hand that he usually would hold up proudly he grasped low in a fist held by his side.

Wise Coyote stooped beside the boy, looked up into the lad's downcast eyes. He lifted the hand and saw in the cupped palm a songbird carved from jade.

"And what song does this bird sing," the king of Texcoco gently teased his son. "Does he celebrate the loveliness of my gardens, or of your mother's beauty?"

"No, lord father."

Wise Coyote, hearing the tremble in the boy's voice, tipped his son's chin up. "Then it is of anger and grief he sings. Tell me."

"It is your heir, the Prodigious Son," the boy cried. "My mother sent me to speak to you. Oh, lord father, I am afraid."

The king felt his heart sink within him, although he tried not to let his face stiffen. If his eldest son by his queen Ant Flower had met with mishap or illness, it would not have been Huetzin who would have been summoned to tell him. He waited, letting the young craftsman tell his story.

"I finished this bird yesterday morning and thought it so beautiful that I would make it a gift to my half brother. I took it to his palace and laid it in his hand."

"And he found it flawed?"

"No, he was delighted and spoke of my skill. But then he put the bird aside and asked why I did not take more interest in weapons and fighting. I spoke of my admiration for the honors he had won in war and he showed me his storehouse of weapons."

"Storehouse?"

"Oh, yes," said Huetzin. "Many rooms, all filled with *macuahuitl* swords edged with black glass, arrows tipped with green, well-made bows and throwing spears." The boy paused for breath. "And there were so many warriors at his court, lord father! I saw them walking about in jaguar skins and eagle feathers and fighting each other on the training fields." His face darkened. "They said things about you I didn't like, so I took the bird away and went to my mother. She sent me to you."

"What words did they say?" asked Wise Coyote mildly.

"That the Prodigy would make a better tlatoani than you. And the Prodigy just laughed when I said I didn't believe it."

The boy knelt, laid his hands in the dirt and kissed his dusty fingertips in the gesture of respect. Wise Coyote straightened, his hands on his son's shoulders. He wondered how much credence to place in the tale. Huetzin was too young and too guileless to lie. Much of his story must be true, although certain exaggerations might have been encouraged by the golden-skinned woman who was Huetzin's mother. It was not the first time a concubine had attempted to displace a son of the legitimate wife so that her own children might succeed.

With an ugly tickle of fear and bitterness within him, Wise Coyote knew he had let the Prodigy go too long without attention or discipline. How long had it been since he had visited the prince?

The young man whose battlefield exploits had won him the name of the Prodigy had been eager to leave his father's court and build his own. And Wise Coyote had let him go too soon, perhaps out of indifference, perhaps out of reticence.

Wise Coyote knew that some nobles at Texcoco saw him as one who turned away from the blood sacrifices, one too gentle and tame to be tlatoani. Had the Prodigy learned to despise his father and had his independence tempted him to a premature challenge? Wise Coyote ran his fingers along the wound-scars of his forearm. He had bought his reed-woven throne with blood as well as wisdom. The Prodigy might need to taste both.

"It is good that you told me what is happening," he said to the young craftsman, "but think no more about it. Return to your jade-shaping, for it creates beauty that outlives the scheming of men." He clasped Huetzin's fingers about the carving and sent him running down the path, the bird held high between his hands.

Wise Coyote wished that all his sons were like Huetzin, so that they crafted materials or ideas into new and beautiful forms. But at least one son had to be taught to craft the affairs of war and state so that Texcoco would have a tlatoani after Wise Coyote had grown too feeble. If none were worthy, the Aztec Ilhuicamina might move to place his own seed onto the reed throne and bind Texcoco so tightly to him that it became no more than a precinct of Tenochtitlán.

In learning the craft of rulership, a young man might taste power, a drink more heady than *octli,* the fermented sap of the maguey. Wise Coyote remembered all the times he had sipped it and of the bitterness that came after. He turned and went into the shadowed portico of his palace.

In his private chamber, he sat in silence, then summoned spies he had once used against enemies. Now he was sending them against one of his own house. He told the spies nothing of Huetzin's story, only that they were to go secretly to the Prodigy's palace and report everything they saw. Perhaps the story had exaggerated the threat of rebellion and he would only have to give his son a severe reprimand. As he sat in the shaded dark of his chamber, he feared that would not be all . . .

On the same afternoon in Tenochtitlán, Mixcatl continued her journey from the marketplace, through many streets and across canals. Though her new owner held tightly to her rope, he spoke to her in a friendly manner, as if he were a companion rather than a master. His name in Nahuatl, he told her, was Three-House Speaking Quail. Mixcatl could only offer the single short name that she bore, for she had no idea what her birth-sign had been.

"Perhaps a diviner-priest would be able to discover it," said Speaking Quail thoughtfully. "As a slave, you don't need an elaborate name. What you have will do. But without your sign of birth, how are you to know what fate the gods have prepared?"

Privately, Mixcatl thought she probably didn't want to know, but she didn't want to anger Three-House Speaking Quail by saying the thought aloud.

She was unsure of her ultimate destination. Speaking Quail had mentioned that he was a tutor in a school, but when she asked him where they were going, he used the Nahuatl word *calmecac*. To Mixcatl, who was still learning to piece together words in the Aztec tongue, the word meant only "a row of houses." Her spirits rose. Perhaps Speaking Quail's house was one in the row and she was to be his personal slave. She didn't mind that, for he was well-meaning if a little distracted.

As they drew closer to their destination, Speaking Quail became worried and began muttering to himself. "I wonder if I should just slip you in and feed you from my ration," he said. "Maguey Thorn sent me to the market for chilies and here I return with a slave-child. Not that I fear her," he added, lifting his chin and sending a defiant look into the twilight descending about the city. "After all, she is only the matron."

Mixcatl peered into the dusk. The building ahead did not look like a row of private houses. It was much larger and had no window openings that looked out on the street. From within came the raucous shouts of young boys and the gruff reprimands of older men. The main entrance was draped with a lightly woven cloth hung with copper bells. Mixcatl noted that Speaking Quail held the cloth aside to minimize the jingling as he motioned her through.

"My quarters are down the hall," he said, pointing with his chin, and headed for them with a scurry resembling the quail of his namesake. Mixcatl shrugged her shoulders and followed.

Before they reached his sanctum within the calmecac, a large woman emerged from a side corridor, arms folded and scowling.

"Where are my chilies, Speaking Quail? And what is that street urchin doing tagging after you?"

Speaking Quail proffered a package that he'd been

carrying inside his mantle. The woman took it, sniffed it and grumbled a bit, but evidently the chilies were strong enough to please her. She wore an old *huipil* blouse, a loose short-sleeved garment pulled on over the wearer's head. It was dirtied with kitchen stains. Her wraparound skirt fell to her knees.

"And this little gutter-lizard?" she demanded, folding arms that were well muscled from grinding corn to make tortillas.

"Please, Maguey Thorn. She was being ill treated in the market square. I thought I would buy her and give her to the school. You have often complained about having too much work." To Mixcatl, he said, "This is Ten-Earthquake Maguey Thorn, our matron at the calmecac."

Ten-Earthquake Maguey Thorn appeared to fit her name. She was a wide, powerful figure, with a round fat face and braids bound around her head so that the ends stuck out over her forehead like two horns. She brought an unlit brazier, ignited it, placed it in a wall niche, then scowled down at Mixcatl.

"She looks strong enough. But that face! No, Speaking Quail. This is unacceptable. She looks like one of those demon images from the jungle."

Mixcatl felt her spirits begin to sag. Was she to be returned to the slave market after all? "I do many things," she said in her halting Nahuatl. "Grind corn, make tortillas, wash clothes. Anything you need help, I do."

Maguey Thorn started to shake her head with its double chins, but something seemed to stop her. "Speaking Quail, we will discuss this in the morning," she said. "The child is hungry and tired. Make her up a bed of rushes while I see if there are any tortillas that the students haven't eaten. And give her a bath."

Before obeying Maguey Thorn, Speaking Quail removed the yoked collar Mixcatl had worn to market and used a salve to dress the festering splinters on her neck. Maguey Thorn watched, her fists planted on her wide hips. Her presence seemed to make Speaking Quail nervous and overly talkative. Several times he told Mixcatl that he was only taking the collar off because it would slow her down in her work, but the girl suspected his words were really meant for the matron.

After the collar was off, Speaking Quail gave Mixcatl a weary pat on the shoulder and showed her to a small room. He supplied her with two pots of tepid water and a peeled soapstone root, which made a lather when rubbed. When she had cleansed herself and washed the market grime from her cropped hair, Speaking Quail gave her a clean cloth to tie about her waist as a makeshift skirt and a rough fiber mantle to wrap about her for warmth on the rush bed. Maguey Thorn brought tortillas and a steaming bowl of squash stewed with tomatoes and peppers.

Maguey Thorn handed Speaking Quail the food, then departed, her skirts rustling. Mixcatl's mouth watered at the aroma of the squash and spicy sauce. She took the bowl from Speaking Quail, held it between her hands and inhaled the steamy vapors, then scooped up the stew with freshly made tortillas. She ate until her belly was comfortably full and her eyelids drooping. She stumbled to the rush bed, wrapped herself in the mantle and instantly fell asleep.

The following morning Speaking Quail presented Mixcatl once again to Ten-Earthquake Maguey Thorn. Yawning, the girl blinked in the light of dawn spilling into the calmecac's courtyard as the matron examined her.

"She is sturdy and more willing than some of the prettier slaves I have seen," Maguey Thorn admitted. "But, Speaking Quail, the head priest will see her presence as a baleful influence on the students. I cannot have her grinding corn or preparing food that would go into the mouths of the boys here. After all, we do not even know her birth-sign. And if the fathers should object, well . . ." She trailed off, shaking her head.

Mixcatl stood with her shoulders hunched, looking at the ground. She tried not to hate Maguey Thorn, or Speaking Quail either. He had meant well, but he really didn't have the authority to buy her or to bring her to the school. She should have known and not let her hopes rise too far.

"Isn't there some task she could perform that would not bring her into direct contact with the boys?" asked Speaking Quail.

Maguey Thorn considered this. "Well, I need someone to collect kitchen leavings and put them out for the refuse boat. And empty latrine jars. My girls turn up their noses at such work. It would be good to have someone I didn't have to beat and shout at to get the work done." She folded her stout forearms over the breast of her huipil and studied Mixcatl with sharp black eyes. "She doesn't look as if she will be too clever for the task."

"She understands what you tell her," said Speaking Quail.

"All the better if she is backward. She will have no thoughts of bettering herself and will need no schooling. All right, Speaking Quail. We'll try her out for a while. But any sign of balkiness or temper and back to the market she goes."

Mixcatl raised her head, barely daring to breathe. Would they let her stay after all? Carrying slopjars might not be the most pleasant task, but anything was better than being sold again and possibly falling into the hands of someone like the man who had tried to buy her with counterfeit cocoa beans. She shuddered inwardly every time she thought of him.

She put the memory aside and listened, for Maguey

Thorn was addressing her directly. The matron spoke slowly and too loudly, choosing simple words meant for a very young child. For a moment Mixcatl rebelled inwardly. Her features might be brutish, but she knew there was nothing wrong with her wit. But that same wit told her to retain the mantle of dullness that Maguey Thorn had thrown upon her. She was suddenly glad that her tongue still stumbled over Nahuatl and that her shock of black hair had been only roughly cropped by her previous owner and now tumbled forward to hide her eyes. She didn't want Maguey Thorn to look too deeply into them.

The matron turned to Speaking Quail. "She is to stay out of the courtyard and the rooms where the priests are teaching their classes. She may enter their quarters only to empty the refuse jars." Abruptly she turned to Mixcatl and explained it all again in a way that made the girl want to squirm with impatience. "Do you understand?"

Mixcatl nodded. After giving her another once-over and a final harrumph, Maguey Thorn led Mixcatl to an open room with a large raised firepit that served as the kitchen. Speaking Quail departed with a wave.

"That young man should get married and have children of his own instead of bringing me waifs like you," said the matron as she handed Mixcatl a small bowl of maize porridge, dished a larger one out for herself and plumped down on her mat. Mixcatl made no answer, for she was sure Maguey Thorn was speaking to her out of habit rather than of any expectations of a reply. The porridge was flavored with sage, making it surprisingly tasty. Even though she had eaten the previous night, Mixcatl gobbled it down eagerly, wishing there was more.

She then set about the tasks she had been given, learning them quickly over the next few days. At first she labored about the hearth and courtyard, directed by scrub-girls and kitchen drudges. To her fell the lowly job of gathering up scraps and squashed or spoiled vegetables that had been rejected as unfit for the cookpot. She scraped them from the floor with her hands, dodging the quick steps and impatient tongues of the cooks.

"Out of my way, you little garbage-gathering toad!" came the shrill words and a wooden spoon would descend on her shoulders or back. Mixcatl would scuttle out of their way, cramming her handfuls in the slopjar she carried or, if a morsel was not too dirtied or bruised, into her mouth.

When she wasn't working or scavenging about the kitchen, she made the rounds of the calmecac's living quarters. She took the vessels that served teachers and students as chamber pots, emptying them into larger jars and carrying those to the canalside in back of the school. If there were no other tasks to be done, Maguey Thorn would summon her to help with the wash.

Elbow-deep in soaproot suds, Maguey Thorn became more relaxed and talkative, exchanging banter with her girls over the ceramic washpots and giving Mixcatl an occasional word. Maguey Thorn would not allow the slave girl to wash or rinse the clothes, nor could she touch them when clean. Instead Mixcatl brought armloads of soiled loincloths and mantles, some white, some beautifully embroidered with brilliant colors and patterns.

"Ah, those priests," Maguey Thorn sighed to herself, as she held up one emerald-green cloak that had been stained with sweat and streaks of an oily black grime. "They don't appreciate how much work goes into keeping them properly dressed, they don't." She plumped the garment into the washpot, squeezed it and scrubbed the folds together. "One wearing and it's a mess. Between that black body paint they smear themselves with and the oil from their hair, well!" She pummeled the garment so vigorously that Mixcatl thought she might tear it to shreds and grumbled, "Religious penance, they call it.

Well, it's just an excuse to be filthy, that's what I think. I can't believe that the gods appreciate stinking tousled mops.'' She snorted and pulled the mantle out, dripping and somehow intact, and even appreciably cleaner.

Mixcatl, who had not yet seen any of the priests or their students, became curious, but she knew she dare not ask Maguey Thorn any questions. When one of the other girls ventured a comment, the matron became gruff, saying that it was not the business of servants to gossip about their betters. "And don't you go blabbing about what I said," she added, lifting one lather-covered fist at the hapless drudge. Grinning to herself, Mixcatl dumped another load into the washpot and went to retrieve more. She remained curious about the priests and their students, hoping to catch a glimpse of them as she went about her tasks.

Late one morning, she was returning a scrubbed out chamber pot to the priests' quarters when she caught sight of a tall, black-smeared figure striding along the hallway. Quickly she ducked out of sight, but her eyes followed the priest. He wore an elaborately knotted loincloth with a tailpiece. His mantle, knotted over one shoulder, was made of orange, red and white squares sewn together. He wore gold ear ornaments and wrist rings that stood out against his paint-blackened skin. A wild mass of uncut and unbrushed hair spilled back from his forehead. Mixcatl wrinkled her nose at the stink wafting back from him. There was the acrid reek of the body paint mixed with the smell of oily hair, and underlying it, the scent of dried blood.

As the slap of the priest's sandals died away, Mixcatl crept from her hiding place, shivering a little. She wished her sense of smell were not so acute. She sensed that the priest had killed something recently. Whether it was an animal, bird or a human, she didn't want to know.

Quickly she returned the pot to its place and hurried away.

Later in the afternoon, she got her first glimpse of the calmecac's students through the curtained door leading into the center courtyard of the school. They were all boys, ranging in age from about eight to those in their upper teens. They sat, crowded together in the courtyard while the priest-tutor conducted lessons. They wore white mantles edged with red or brown, and squirmed on their mats while they listened. The teacher knelt with a length of fig-bark paper unfolded on his lap and followed the images painted on it with his forefinger as he recited. Mixcatl suddenly wished she could be seated among the boys, for ever since she had seen the folded books in the marketplace, she wanted to know more about the odd little pictures in them.

A slave girl had no business even thinking about joining a class made up of nobles' sons. Putting the thought aside, she went back to work.

3

WISE COYOTE WAITED at Tezcotzinco until the spies returned from the Prodigy's palace with their report. "The Prodigy is boasting that he will be a great tlatoani," said the spies. "Weapons gleam on the walls and he talks of conquest. When the Prodigy becomes the Great Chichimec, Texcoco will rise again to its former glory."

Wise Coyote grew more unhappy as he listened. Aspiring to kingship before the reigning tlatoani had grown too old was a crime of treason, to be punished by death. Wise Coyote paid the spies well and sent them away. Then he summoned his queen, Ant Flower, and told her of the prince's indiscretion.

"Dear one of the honest eyes," he said, using his favorite name for her, "I wish I did not have to tell you what I must do now."

"He is a young man, and young men brag. I'm sure he intends no treason," answered Ant Flower gaily, but he saw that she was trembling.

"And do young men gather armies and speak of their father's weakness?" Wise Coyote asked sternly. "The people know the penalty for treason. If they see that the prince goes unpunished, they will know that I deal two kinds of justice; one for my sons and one for my people."

Ant Flower turned from him and buried her face in her hands. "My previous two sons died for your justice. One for adultery and the other for coupling with a man. The Prodigy is the last, for I am too old to bear more. He is my only son. He cannot die."

Wise Coyote turned his wife to him, drew her hands from her tear-streaked face. "And he is the son of the woman I love the most."

"Then scold him for his pridefulness and strip him of his honors, but do not stain this marriage with a third death."

Wise Coyote tilted her chin up to him as he had done with Huetzin. "Do you think that if I went to his palace he would kneel humbly at my feet? Not after all those boasts he has made before his warriors. Hands would reach for those weapons on the walls and either he or I would die. And so would everything I have tried to make here in Texcoco."

"There must be another path," Ant Flower cried. "I do not want to lose my son or my husband."

Wise Coyote clasped his wife to him. Ant Flower was a small woman, and he taller than most men, so that her head lay beneath his chin as he held her. But her eyes, when she looked at him, were deep and utterly clear, even while brightened by the tears of grief. And when those honest eyes saw and judged, Wise Coyote wondered how he would fare in the judgment.

"There is another path," he said softly into her hair. "The Prodigy's crime is against the Triple Alliance as well as Texcoco. I will summon the other two kings of the Alliance and hand over the case to them. It is the right thing to do. I cannot be an impartial judge."

Ant Flower closed her eyes. "Then you would hand your son's fate to the Aztec Hue Hue Ilhuicamina. The tlatoani of Tlacopan is merely a pawn of Tenochtitlán."

Wise Coyote tried to soothe her. "Ilhuicamina is severe, but at heart a good man. I fought by his side on many a campaign. He too has seen rebellion among his sons and knows how to deal with it.''

And inwardly he thought, *Ilhuicamina is involved in this whether or not I wish him to be. If my Prodigy is not punished, he will challenge Tenochtitlán. If I come to open war with my son and I am killed, Ilhuicamina will annex Texcoco. If the Prodigy is killed, there will be no tlatoani after me, the kingship will lie open and Ilhuicamina will see that it is filled in his favor.*

The Ilhuicamina he had fought with, sharing hardship as well as victory, had been a good man. But something had changed Ilhuicamina, making him fearful on the inside and harder on the outside. Was it the years of drought, when prayers to the gods had brought nothing but dust and fire in the earth? Ilhuicamina had sworn that those times would never come again, for he would keep the Aztec sun and war god, Hummingbird on the Left, well fed with sacrificial blood.

Do I know Ilhuicamina, Wise Coyote asked himself. *Can I trust him to find a balance between firmness and compassion? Or has his service to Hummingbird twisted him? Whatever I fear does not matter. Ilhuicamina will come.*

He sent messengers to the two rulers of Tlacopan and Tenochtitlán, asking them to Texcoco. He also sent a message to his warrior-son to prepare a welcoming feast for them at his palace, though he did not tell the prince the reason for their visit.

Several days later, Wise Coyote greeted the two other kings as they came ashore from the royal dugouts they had used to cross the lake. Ilhuicamina was resplendent in a plumed headpiece and a mantle of iridescent quetzal feathers that shone and shimmered like the sun on chips of obsidian. He also wore the turquoise-blue coronet that was the symbol of the Speaker-King. The king of Tlacopan was old, wizened and wore more somber garments.

Next to Ilhuicamina, he resembled a rock dove beside a phoenix.

Wise Coyote took the two kings to Texcoco and sat them down on the judgment seats in his great hall. Set into the arm of each seat was a human skull, positioned so that each king could lay his hand on it and speak what words he thought just. Wise Coyote did not take his seat among them. Instead he said, "Remember that the prince is still young and has gained skill in war and not wisdom. Chastise him as is just but show him no leniency because I am his father."

Then he stood in his hall and heard the kings call the witnesses one by one. The witnesses came in secret for fear that someone would take their names for later vengeance. Wise Coyote's young son Huetzin was brought to testify, holding the same jade songbird that he had offered his half brother. The concubine with the golden skin spoke, as did the queen Ant Flower. Wise Coyote gave his own account of what he had heard from Huetzin.

After all the witnesses had departed as secretly as they had come, Ilhuicamina rose and stretched. The judgment throne, though beautiful, made the occupant's back stiff.

"Have you made your decision?" Wise Coyote asked.

Ilhuicamina swept his quetzal-feather mantle about his shoulders and stood on the stone dias near the throne so that he would not have to look up to the king of Texcoco.

"You summoned me for this purpose and have given the case over into my hands," Ilhuicamina answered him. "You have removed yourself from it. Now go to your gardens at Tezcotzinco and wait until I come."

The tlatoani of Tlacopan said nothing, merely bobbed his head in agreement with Ilhuicamina.

Wise Coyote's mouth felt dry. Not even to know his son's fate once it had been decided! He started to protest, then fell silent. It was his bidding that had brought the two kings to his judgment hall. If he tried to interfere now, Ilhuicamina's easily ignited wrath might fall on him. He bowed his head and went to Tezcotzinco.

He walked the paths of his garden, bathed his feet in its pools, but could find no pleasure in its beauty. For a day and a night, he roamed the palace halls and garden paths, refusing to eat or sleep, listening for the tread of sandals that would bring him the news of his son's fate. He knew that if the Prodigy died so would Ant Flower's love for her husband.

At last guardsmen came to him to announce that the king of Tenochtitlán had arrived. The king of Tlacopan had gone home, for there was no need for him to come. Wise Coyote met Ilhuicamina on the shaded portico of his palace, offered him greeting and refreshment.

"In trying this case, I recalled the times when my own sons spoke of war and rebellion," Ilhuicamina began. "The young wolves must challenge the old, for it is their nature. Even so, young men often make more war with their tongues than with their obsidian swords."

Wise Coyote listened, growing hopeful. Perhaps Ilhuicamina knew the meaning of mercy.

"But, of course, I had something else to do with my snapping cubs. If they wanted a taste of war, why not let them have it? At the edge of my empire where their bloodthirstiness could buy me new lands and peoples."

"So you want to send my son to extend the territories of the Triple Alliance? But have you not taken all the lands and peoples you can control? If the empire could still expand, why then does the Prodigy have to win his manhood by challenging me?"

Ilhuicamina laughed. "Well are you named, tlatoani of Texcoco. It is true that the empire is spread as far as supply lines can reach. The young no longer have the opportunity to prove themselves in true war. That is why I bring you this."

With one hand Ilhuicamina reached beneath his mantle and drew out a garland of magnolia. The blooms were crushed, broken, and the string stained with red.

"I went to the feast prepared for me at your son's palace and an excellent repast it was," he said, rubbing his belly with the other hand. "I went up to the prince to offer my thanks and to place a wreath about his neck. The garland was too large and thus I drew it tighter and tighter . . ."

Wise Coyote cradled the flowered garrote that Ilhuicamina had used to kill the Prodigy. Tears stung his eyes.

"Did you not know what I wanted from you?" he cried aloud.

"Tenderness? Mercy?" Ilhuicamina's voice was mocking. "Does mercy keep the Fifth Sun in the heavens? Does mercy strengthen Hummingbird on the Left in his war with the demons of the moon? What use is tenderness when the earth burns and hunger clenches the belly?"

"Once, you knew," Wise Coyote whispered, dripping tears on the broken flowers.

"Once," Ilhuicamina answered. "But those were the days when you let yourself be driven from the throne of Texcoco and were known as the Hungry-Coyote-of-the-Hills."

"So a man must be hard," said Wise Coyote bitterly. "But remember this, Ilhuicamina. The hardest wood comes not from the live tree, but the dead one that has dried beneath the sun."

The tlatoani of Tenochtitlán shrugged his shoulders beneath his shimmering quetzal-feather robe. His eyes turned to flint as he answered, "You could have kept the judgment for yourself."

Wise Coyote made no answer to those words. There

could be none. He became acutely aware of Ilhuicamina's gaze on him.

"Have you completed the plans for the water channel from Chaultapec to Tenochtitlán?" Ilhuicamina asked.

For a moment Wise Coyote's anger flared. How could this man come to him after killing his son and then demand an accounting of him as a taskmaster would demand of a craftsman? He was not bound to the building project; he had offered to perform it as a favor to Ilhuicamina and to demonstrate that his engineering skills had a use beyond creating pleasure pools and gardens.

Then reason cooled his anger, although he wasn't sure that the timidity of the Deer had not crept in. He would build the aqueduct for the people of Tenochtitlán, not for Ilhuicamina. It would be shortsighted of him to punish the thirsty population of that city for its ruler's lack of compassion.

Quietly he said, "Yes, the plans are done. The work will begin on the day of Five-House."

Ilhuicamina's eyes brightened. "It will be wonderful to see good fresh water rush into the city and spew up out of a fountain. The prices demanded by those who sell water by the jug are burdensome to my people and so they must mix it with the bilge of Lake Texcoco. Your name will be greatly praised."

Wise Coyote said nothing, wondering if it was indeed greatness of heart or the Deer's cowardice that had shaped his reply.

As Ilhuicamina turned away, he added, "I will expect you in Tenochtitlán for the sacrifices to Hummingbird on the Left. After you have had sufficient time to mourn, of course."

"I am grateful for such favor," Wise Coyote muttered beneath his breath as Ilhuicamina and his retinue departed from the palace.

He went to his chamber and sat alone, running the

bloodstained garland through his fingers. He was no stranger to those means by which kings sought and held their power. Had he not sent Horned Mask, Ant Flower's previous husband, to his death in the War of Flowers so that he might marry the lovely girl and make her his queen? Hadn't he pursued the Tepcanecan tyrant Maxtla into the round steambath house, where Maxtla had taken refuge, dragged him out, cut the heart from his body and lifted it as a sacrifice to the gods of war?

Who was he to speak of mercy?

Perhaps it is that Ilhuicamina is more honest in his cruelty than I am.

And Wise Coyote bowed his head and mourned bitterly, not only for his son, but for Ilhuicamina and himself as well.

Two years passed and Mixcatl continued to live in the calmecac, doing the simple tasks that she had been given. Though Maguey Thorn still grumbled about her appearance, the matron was grudgingly satisfied with her work. There was no more talk about selling her.

Summer had come again and the day was bright and hot. Eight-year-old Mixcatl, her hands still wet from the morning's wash, stepped into the courtyard. Her head was still full of Maguey Thorn's banter and she didn't stop to see if the courtyard was clear before she entered.

Immediately she saw her mistake. A class was in session, listening to their teacher-priest recite from a fanfolded book that spilled across his lap. He was speaking so loudly that the noise had covered up the sound of the copper bells on the door flap, and Mixcatl thought she might slip back through without being heard. As soon as she took a step in that direction, the priest's voice sank down to a sibilant whisper as he dramatized his recitation.

Instead of trying to leave as she had come, and risk

the betraying noise of the copper bells, the girl slipped along the inner wall of the courtyard and crouched behind a ceramic pot containing an agave plant. The teachers often plucked its spines to punish lazy or disobedient students. Mixcatl hoped that the boys would all be on their best behavior so that their teacher would not need to visit the agave.

From her refuge behind the pot, Mixcatl could see the end of the sacred book as it sprawled from the priest's lap like a great flattened python. Unlike a python, the manuscript was formed in segments, each stiff page bound to the next so that the entire text stretched out in a long strip. With her sharp eyes, she could make out some of the larger figures. Fascinated, she leaned out as far as she could from behind the agave without risking discovery, and squinted across the distance at the codex. The shapes of warriors and kings, dressed in elaborate costumes and headdresses, marched across the page. She saw the form of a temple split by an arrow, then flames curling up about a bundle of reeds.

What did the figures mean? What story did they tell? She was consumed by a desire to know. And a memory came to her of an old hand, veined and wrinkled, dipping a brush into a pot of color and drawing elaborate figures with curls and scrolls. She squeezed her eyes shut. The brush made other figures, fantastic creatures, footprints, jaguar tracks. Jaguar tracks. The number six, shown by a jaguar's pawprint with the pad and the five toes. She remembered counting on her own palm and fingers. It seemed so distant, like a dream or someone else's life.

She opened her eyes. The priest's voice was rising again as his forefinger followed the pictures on the page.

"We sing the pictures of the book," he chanted. "We sing the sacred hymns. The story of the One-Prince, Plumed Serpent. The story of his disgrace at the hands of Smoking Mirror, Tezcatlipoca."

After the priest had sung or chanted a phrase, he made the boys sing after him, either in unison or one at a time, until they had memorized the words. Thus the recitation went very slowly, but Mixcatl never grew bored. Though she knew nothing of Plumed Serpent or Smoking Mirror, the sound of their names sent chills down her back. They seemed to resonate with something buried deep inside her, something she had not known was there.

She hunched behind the agave, shivering. The priest sang and the boys chanted after him. Even though she did not understand all of the Nahuatl, the words stayed in Mixcatl's ears and she knew she would remember them long after the priest's voice had faded. The priest sang:

> They say that the One-Prince, Plumed Serpent, was
>   much beloved by his people.
> They say that love made others jealous
> The magicians of the city became jealous
> The greatest of the magicians was Tezcatlipoca, Smok-
>   ing Mirror
> He tried to change the people's love for Plumed Serpent
> He tried to make Plumed Serpent do evil things
> But Plumed Serpent would not do them.

Mixcatl listened to the hymn, caught up both in the cadence of its chant and by the images in the book. She thought she could see ties between the pictures and the words. Wasn't that undulating form a serpent covered with plumes? And there was the shape of a mountain. She strained to see better, wishing that she could sit with the boys. The story went on:

> Smoking Mirror decided to deceive Plumed Serpent
> He gave him the fermented juice of the agave so that he
>   became drunk

He gave him a beautiful woman and said, take your
   pleasure
And the prince took his pleasure and then slept.
But when Plumed Serpent woke, he saw that the
   woman was his sister and that he was disgraced
He was disgraced by Smoking Mirror's trickery
He was disgraced by his own lechery and drunkenness.

He bowed his head and said, "I can no longer rule the
city."

In his grief and anger, he seized Smoking Mirror
Lifted him high and cast him into the sea
High over the mountains into the sea.
And as Smoking Mirror fell, he changed
His skin became spotted, his hands and feet grew
   claws.

Mixcatl leaned forward from her hiding place behind
the agave. The priest's forefinger was resting on a figure
that was half spotted cat, half man. Tezcatlipoca, Smoking Mirror. His tail curled up in defiance, his mouth was
open, showing teeth. He bore a feathered shield and
above his cat ears, an elaborate headdress.

Though the hymn portrayed Tezcatlipoca as evil,
Mixcatl was fascinated by his image. She remembered
the incident in the marketplace, the jaguar skin, her
hands curling into claws and her arm moving with a
sharp raking motion. And how the skin had jerked in the
hands of its purchaser, wounding him.

About her the hymn continued:

Smoking Mirror's cry became a roar as he fell into the
   sea
He became a jaguar
Whose spotted coat symbolizes the stars of the night
   sky

He did not die in the sea
For he was a jaguar and jaguars can swim
He came ashore and crept into the jungle
And he lives among us even now.

Silence fell as the priest's voice halted. Mixcatl suddenly came back to herself. Drawn by the image of Tezcatlipoca, she had emerged from behind the agave. Now, with a shock, she realized she was standing in the open and that the eyes of the priest and all his students were fastened on her.

And then she realized that the black-smeared figure was that of Speaking Quail and the eyes looking at her held wonder as well as annoyance.

Booing and jeering broke out among the boys. Some scrambled to their feet, fists lifted to strike the impudent slave girl who would dare spy on their class. Mixcatl shielded her face with her forearms as the blows began to fall.

"No!" cried another voice, stronger and deeper than the high-pitched shouting of the boys around her. She peeked out between her fingers. It wasn't Speaking Quail, for he stood on his teacher's mat, trying to quiet the remains of his class. No, this was one of the students, an older boy, with a sidelock of brown hair falling past one ear and a face that might easily assume a grin. Right now his eyebrows were drawn together over his nose as he glared at his schoolmates. Sullenly they withdrew.

Mixcatl began to tremble. Soon the noise would bring Maguey Thorn into the courtyard. Hadn't the matron told her explicitly not to enter the presence of the priests or their students? Now she would be beaten and dragged back to the slave market to be sold. She flung herself on her knees, bending her head down into the dust to beg for mercy. But the boy caught hold of her wrists so that she could only bow her head down before him and kneel, shaking, in his grip.

"They won't hurt you," he said. "I won't let them and I'm stronger than they are. Why did you sneak in here?"

But Mixcatl, terrified, couldn't answer. She heard the slap of a priest's sandals, caught the scent of black body-paint.

"Let her go, Six-Wind," Three-House Speaking Quail said softly, then raised his voice. "And the rest of you, put away your fists and grimaces, for your victim is one beloved of Tezcatlipoca. Six-Wind was right to stop you."

Speaking Quail went to the courtyard entrance, thrust his head between the belled strands. Mixcatl saw him peer back and forth, as if to make sure the way was clear for her. He drew the hanging aside so carefully that the curtain made little noise. She scurried past, then stopped to look back at him with wide eyes. As she hastened along the corridor, she could still hear the voices as the priest admonished his class.

"Are you turkey pullets that you rise gabbling and threatening when a harmless creature comes into your midst? A scholar should let nothing disturb his studies. And a noble should take no pride in raising his hand against a slave."

Mixcatl gave a huge sigh from her place in the corridor. The way Three-House Speaking Quail shamed the boys would prevent them from bragging about the incident or mentioning it to Maguey Thorn. She hoped so. But this was a Speaking Quail that she had never seen, calm and self-possessed, instead of the nervous little man who went about dodging the burly matron. Perhaps the hymn had given him strength.

And what had he meant when he said that she was one "beloved of Tezcatlipoca"? The thought made her flush and shiver at the same time. The image of the dancing jaguar was so beautiful that she ached to see it again, yet the hymn said he was evil. Did that mean that she also was evil? The thought saddened her as she went about collecting kitchen scraps and emptying refuse pots, but she could not forget what she had seen.

As evening drew on and she heard the students gathering for the last meal of the day, she hid behind a wall and trembled, fearful that someone would tell what happened in the courtyard that morning. Although the boys chattered as they ate, there was no mention of the courtyard incident. She hoped that they would soon forget it.

But one, however, did not.

The following day, she was withdrawing from the empty students' quarters with pots to empty. As she backed out the door, she felt someone behind her and spun, nearly spilling the pots' contents on a pair of sandaled feet.

The boy Six-Wind stood before her, his legs apart, his fists pressing his mantle against his hips, his head cocked. "You!" he said. "The little pisspot carrier."

Mixcatl began to back away from him.

"I won't hurt you. I didn't before, remember?" He paused. "Can you answer or are you dumb?"

Mixcatl drew the back of her hand across her mouth. Her tongue was dry. "I can answer," she croaked in Nahuatl.

"That's better," said Six-Wind. Mixcatl saw that he had an open, pleasant face when not scowling. "I thought you might have some wit to your tongue when I saw you peering at the book."

Mixcatl's mouth fell open. "Maguey Thorn. Please, don't tell. She will whip me. Sell me."

"Old Earthquake Bosom is busy in the kitchens," said Six-Wind, a mischievous glint in his hazel eyes. Even in her fright, Mixcatl couldn't help a nervous giggle at Six-Wind's name for the matron. It described her perfectly.

The boy took Mixcatl by the wrist and led her to a small chamber nearby. For a minute she resisted, but his grip was too strong and she feared any commotion would bring the priests or Maguey Thorn down upon the two of them.

"I'm not going to hurt you," Six-Wind said, a touch of impatience in his voice. "I just want to know what happened yesterday morning."

"Why do you talk about that? Why do you pull me in here?" Mixcatl protested as he pushed her down on a mat, for the room was empty except for hangings and mats. "The other boys forgot it. Why can't you?"

"Who kept you from getting beaten?" Six-Wind whispered. "If they'd all gone for you, a whipping from Maguey Thorn would have felt like the touch of a feather in comparison. Sit up and stop whimpering."

Mixcatl shook the hair out of her eyes, sat back on her heels. "What do you want?" She tried to keep her voice from trembling. She knew that sometimes boys, even ones as young as Six-Wind, took girls into closed rooms and did things said to be shameful.

For a minute Six-Wind stared at her, then tipped his head back in laughter. She knew he had read the suspicion in her solemn little face.

"You think I want you for *that*? Gods no, although I don't think you're as ugly as some say."

She waited.

"Why did you sneak into the courtyard and hide behind the agave pot?" Six-Wind asked. "You put yourself in danger, you know. Slaves aren't supposed to see the religious books. You were lucky the teacher was Three-House Speaking Quail or else you might be back at the slave market right now, being sold for sacrifice."

Another pang of fear went through Mixcatl, but instead of starting another bout of trembling, it made her bristle. This boy wasn't her owner and had no right to frighten her with threats of being sold. She retorted in her best Nahuatl, then folded her arms defiantly, unafraid of his words or blows.

Six-Wind only laughed again. "What a little fighting cat you are! I almost would have liked a scrap in the courtyard, just to see what would have happened."

Some of Mixcatl's anger evaporated and she stopped pursing her lips at him. He was too easygoing to be malicious. "I didn't mean to do anything bad," she replied. "I thought that the courtyard would be empty. Then once I was there, I was afraid that the door curtain would ring if I went out, so I hid."

"Well, you were lucky you didn't get close enough to really see the texts or hear the chant. That's why Speaking Quail let you go, you know. It's not just because he's kind."

Mixcatl felt her temper start to burn. She knew that she would be safer if she kept quiet, but the truth pushed itself out. She had seen the text and heard the songs. Her face might be ill formed, but her eyes were sharp and her ears keen. And she remembered all she saw and heard. It was something to be proud of, especially when there was little else. Six-Wind's assumption stung that pride.

"I *did* see the book," she blurted.

Six-Wind put a hand across her mouth. His palm tasted salty and she could feel the calluses against her lips.

"No you didn't," he said gently. "You were halfway across the courtyard, in back of the class. You couldn't have seen anything."

"I did!" Mixcatl hissed.

"You're crazy, girl. A hawk could not have seen the figures from that distance. And you only caught a quick glimpse."

"I saw them. A temple falling over. An arrow coming down."

"You didn't," said Six-Wind.

Mixcatl stuck out her chin. "I did."

"Prove it," the boy challenged.

Mixcatl stood up. Again came the memory of a veined hand holding a brush and from the tip came swirls of color and shape. She had no brush or paper, but a stick and the damp earth by the canal bank might serve. Her heart beat fast. This might get her into trouble, but the danger seemed to fade before a burning hot desire to show this mocking boy that she was more than a dull-witted slave.

"I *will* prove it," she said.

This time she led the way, walking swiftly through the corridors of the school, carrying her chamber pots in a businesslike manner, but anyone who passed could see that her eyes glittered. She was glad no one came by. Behind her Six-Wind walked, keeping his distance so that it wouldn't appear that he was accompanying her.

She went to the canalside behind the school, emptied the pots in the big jars, then ran down the canal and ducked behind a clump of creosote bushes. A short time later Six-Wind crept around the wall, looked both ways and scurried over to her hiding place. He knelt, flinging his mantle over his shoulder to keep it out of the dirt.

Mixcatl cleared a space on the ground, brushing away the leaf litter with the palm of her hand. The sandy clay beneath was moist. Wrinkling her nose at Six-Wind, Mixcatl snapped a dry twig off the creosote bush. Holding it between her stubby fingers, she pressed the end into the dirt and drew a slanted line. Then another that met it. And several more, parallel to the first.

"You are making a house, such as little children draw. And you aren't even making it right, for you have tipped it up on one corner," said Six-Wind scornfully.

Mixcatl made another face at him and kept drawing. She added more lines, the pillars of a temple. Then she added the curving outlines and jagged tips of flames encircling the overturned temple.

She looked at Six-Wind. He had turned white. "The glyph for the taking of a city," he muttered.

She bent her brows at him. What was a glyph?

"What you just did. The figure painted in the book," he said, inadvertently admitting that her drawing had indeed reproduced the figure.

Mixcatl felt flushed with success. She cleared more ground and began another drawing. She could see the next figure in her head, its forms and colors as clear as if the page were lying before her. She hardly even had to guide her hand, for it seemed to follow her eyes as she traced the image in her mind.

The shape was a pretty one, resembling a pot with odd tassels hanging from the top on two sides and one tacked onto the bottom, as if the pot was suspended in midair. She made the cross in the middle, then two parallel stripes that curved to follow the outline of the pot. Then an odd scroll emerging from the top of the pot like a plume of steam. There was only one problem. She didn't know what she had drawn. It was too pretty to be a piece of crockery and there was no fire shown beneath to make the pot boil.

Another snap from the creosote bush drew Mixcatl's attention away from her drawing. Six-Wind was doing something funny. He had plucked a small sharp twig and was trying to stab his finger with it. He managed to draw blood and squeezed the finger so that a bright red drop beaded on his skin. Then he lifted his face, closed his eyes and muttered something beneath his breath.

"The sign for the number beyond counting," he said and took up a leaf from the ground and pressed his finger so that blood fell on the leaf. Then, boylike, he put the finger in his mouth and gave Mixcatl such a strange stare that it frightened her more than anything else he had done.

"How do you know these glyphs? Where did you learn them?" he demanded.

"I never learned anything. I don't know what glyphs are. All I know are the pictures I saw this morning." Mixcatl paused. "Why did you hurt your finger?"

"Glyphs are pictures that remind us how to sing the sacred hymns. When we see the temple overturned and burning, we chant of the fall of a city."

"And this?" Mixcatl put her stubby finger next to the other figure she had drawn. "Does this mean a pot that boils without fire?"

"No. It is *xiquipilli,* the sign for the number that can't be counted." He stared at her. "I have studied these figures myself and still can only draw their outlines. But you have seen them only once from a distance and yet here they are. And in as much detail as if they had been done by one who studied them for more years than you have lived!" He sucked his finger again, though his eyes never left Mixcatl.

"Why did you hurt yourself?" she asked again.

Six-Wind took his finger from his mouth. "We are taught to shed blood whenever we pray to the gods for protection from evil spirits and witches."

Mixcatl was baffled. "What is a witch?" she asked and Six-Wind told her. A witch had strange abilities and used them to hurt others.

"Am I one of those bad people?" she asked.

Six-Wind stared at her again. His mouth formed an uncertain smile, but his eyes were still wide and round. "I do not know what you are. But I do know one thing and that is you must never let anyone know you can draw these pictures."

He put out his sandal to scuff away the figures. She

stopped him, feeling a lump rise in her throat. How could her drawings be evil? Yet they had made Six-Wind afraid. He had prayed and drawn blood from his finger.

"Not even Speaking Quail?" she asked.

"No one." The boy swept the earth with his sandal, wiping away the intricate drawings. "I must go now—the gong is ringing for another class. And you must go back to your work."

Mixcatl grabbed Six-Wind's mantle as he rose to leave. "Why did Speaking Quail say that I was one beloved of Smoking Mirror. Does Smoking Mirror help . . . witches?"

"No. He protects slaves," Six-Wind said. He snatched up the leaf with his blood on it and was gone.

Crouching low, he scurried from the creosote bush back into the calmecac, leaving Mixcatl alone with the bare ground. She knew she could do her drawings again, exactly as she had the first time. But she shivered. Perhaps it was best to do what Six-Wind said. She hoped the boy wouldn't change his mind and tell any of the priests. Again she bowed her head and went about her duties.

4

CLOUDS MOVED SWIFTLY across sapphire-blue sky as Wise Coyote stood in a hollow between two hills at Tezcotzinco. A little grass-covered mound lay at his feet, where he had buried the magnolia garland. The Prodigy had been buried two years ago on the same day, beneath the stones of his palace courtyard. The palace now stood empty, awaiting the next heir of Texcoco.

There will be none, Wise Coyote reminded himself bitterly. *Though I have other wives, they are concubines and their sons may not inherit the office of Speaker-King. Even if Ant Flower has not grown too old to bear another child, her grief has turned her from me.*

The cloud shadows on the grass chased one another up and down the hillside. Wise Coyote had stayed long enough, but he could not make himself leave. This place felt right to him. The wind from the lake cooled his forehead, the noise from the palace and the lower gardens was diminished by distance. Wildflowers rippled down the hillsides into the hollow, and to one side a swift stream ran.

Wise Coyote wondered if his grief would ease if he stayed here long enough. Perhaps the wind would steal the misery and toss it away into the sky. Or the sun would warm it until it dwindled and diminished, like a pool of evaporating water.

This place feels sacred, he thought. *But not to any of the gods of blood and fire. It is too quiet for them. Perhaps here is where I might find the faith I have sought—in Tloque Nahaque.*

He resolved then that he would build a temple in this vale to the God of the Near and By. A small simple structure, to be laid out with his own hands. Each stone would be set reverently, without the noise and clamor that accompanied construction projects. At the decision, he smiled wryly at himself.

Men rage at the death of their sons; women weep. And I will mourn as I always have, by building.

He caught sight of another shadow on the grass, turned and saw his son, fourteen-year-old Huetzin.

"I followed you up the path, lord father," the boy stammered. "Please don't be angry."

Wise Coyote opened his arms, but his son did not run to his embrace. A weak feeling in his legs made Wise Coyote sink until he knelt on the ground. After the Prodigy died, all his sons had come to fear their father. His lips wanted to form the words he knew were a lie. *It was Ilhuicamina who killed your half brother, Huetzin, not me.*

The boy knelt down before Wise Coyote, trembling. "If I displease you, lord father, will I also be killed? That is what my brothers say."

Wise Coyote felt as though a spear of ice had gone through him, but he only closed his eyes and said, "If you feared you would die because you displeased me, why did you follow me up the path?"

The boy grew more frightened and Wise Coyote thought he would jump up and flee. But he stayed and looked his father in the face. "You are sad. It is hard to be alone when you are sad. I thought I would go with you . . . even if you had me killed for daring."

Again Wise Coyote held out his arms and this time Huetzin came into his embrace. He held the boy closely, stroking his hair. "Where is the little carved bird you made so long ago?" he asked gently.

"I broke it. I smashed it between two stones. There must have been an evil spirit inside it to have caused so much trouble."

Wise Coyote held Huetzin by the shoulders. "The trouble was not caused by your carving or the words you spoke. If you would please me, carve another."

"But it won't be the same, lord father. Every piece I make is different."

"Because you are so gifted. I am grateful for your talent and so should you be. Only those who have no art except boasting and warmaking are cursed with king-ship."

"That is not true," said the boy softly. "You are tlatoani."

Wise Coyote cursed his glibness and his sarcasm. The boy was not trying to flatter him, he only spoke what he knew.

"I saw you studying the ground as if you planned to build," Huetzin said.

"I am thinking of a temple. Just a small one."

"To your gentle god?"

"Yes," said Wise Coyote, thinking that this was one of the few times that the word "gentle" had not been meant as an insult.

Huetzin looked up at him eagerly. "I will carve something for your temple, if you wish. Tell me what your gentle god looks like."

"You may carve any image you wish," said Wise Coyote. "The Lord of the Near and By is invisible to human eyes."

Huetzin looked puzzled. "He has no image, like the

rain god Tlaloc? He carries no symbols, such as Smoking Mirror? He is a strange god, father."

A strange god, perhaps, for a strange man, thought Wise Coyote. Aloud, he said, "Perhaps you will worship with me. There will be no blood shed in my small temple to Tloque Nahaque."

"No sacrifices?"

"Just flowers."

Huetzin smiled. "It will be nicer than watching the rites of other gods. But I thought all divine ones needed blood to live, father."

"A few do not. There is Quetzalcoatl, the Plumed Serpent. And Tloque Nahaque." Wise Coyote got to his feet. "The best offering to those gods is the work of your hands and mind."

"I will go and think about what to carve," Huetzin said, his eyes shining. Wise Coyote imagined that the boy was already sculpting in his mind, drawing shape from stone. He knew how much joy came from artistry, for he had the same feeling himself when he drew out plans for a building project or wrote a hymn to Tloque Nahaque.

Wistfully he watched Huetzin run away down the path. He envied the boy the freedom to create, uninterrupted by the duties or griefs of kingship. Then he walked through the grass and stooped at the spot where he would lay the cornerstone of his temple.

The day after she had made the drawings for Six-Wind, Mixcatl arose early, collected the pisspots from the rooms and carried them out to the slopjars in back of the school. As she finished dumping the last one, she heard the dip of a barge pole. She turned to see the refuse barge sliding along the stone dock built alongside the canal.

Usually she didn't see the boat. When she did, it was manned by a grumpy old man. This morning a boy stood amidst the squat clay refuse jars, the barge pole in his hands. Mixcatl immediately compared him with Six-Wind. While the young scholar was sturdy and direct, this boatboy seemed lanky and easygoing. He was much taller than Six-Wind, dark, bony and unkempt. A shock of tangled hair nearly covered his eyes, which seemed to watch Mixcatl with a languid amusement. He wore a ragged loincloth and ratty sandals, but what she noticed immediately about him was the black mark on the right half of his upper lip.

As the barge scraped the dock, the boy jumped off and moored it. Despite his thin frame and sleepy eyes, he showed a surprising lightness and grace in his movements. And strength too, for he heaved up the slop vessels belonging to the calmecac and dumped them into the squat containers aboard the barge.

Mixcatl had always wondered what happened to the night soil and garbage in the clay jars she put out on the quay.

"Where do you take this?" she asked, shading her eyes against the midmorning sun as she squinted at him.

"To the floating gardens, the *chinampas*, where farmers put it on dung piles. When it is well rotted, they put it on the corn." The boy cocked his head, his wide mouth spreading in a grin. "What is your name? Are you a student in the calmecac?"

Mixcatl gave a little sigh, wishing that she could be. "No. I am a slave."

The boatboy shrugged his shoulders as if that didn't matter and Mixcatl felt a growing friendliness toward him. She asked a few more questions and learned that the old man she had seen before was the boy's grandfather, who had become too feeble to pole the boat and dump the refuse. The boy's name was Latosl, and, like Mixcatl, he had no other name, nor did he have a birth-sign.

"What happened to your face?" she asked with child-like directness and tapped the right side of her upper lip.

"This?" said Latosl as he let down an empty jar and touched the black mark. The expression on his face and the slight hesitation in his movement made Mixcatl realize she had spoken heedlessly.

"I'm sorry," she said. "I didn't mean to be rude."

"I was born with it." He squatted down so that Mixcatl could examine his face. At first Mixcatl thought that it was a raised birthmark, of the type she had seen on other children. When she looked, she saw that it was a black area of skin, no different in texture from the coppery skin of Latosl's cheek.

"I won't tease you about it," Mixcatl said solemnly. "I know how it feels to be made fun of. People think I am ugly."

Latosl paused in his work and eyed her. "People don't speak to a night-soil hauler either. But I don't care. Anyway, you are not ugly. A bit different, perhaps." His face darkened and his hand made a sweeping motion toward the calmecac and its surroundings. "*They* are the ugly ones."

Mixcatl protested, thinking of Speaking Quail and Six-Wind. When she tried to tell Latosl, he waved her away impatiently and there was a look on his face as if he had said more than he should have.

He leaped back aboard the barge and pushed off, leaving Mixcatl with unanswered questions. Who were the "ugly ones" and what did he mean by those words? She shrugged as she scrubbed out the empty containers and returned them to their places. She should not worry about what Latosl said. He was only a barge boy, after all, and she had other things to think about.

Even though Mixcatl thought she had dismissed Latosl from her mind, she found herself on the stone quay behind the school when the barge pulled in the following morning. She watched as he poled the boat, admiring and envying his skill. His copper skin glowed in the brilliant sunlight. His limbs were sinewy and he moved with a controlled grace that seemed unusual for one of his age or class.

The black mark on his upper lip reminded her of the black patch on a puma's muzzle just behind the whiskers. The way he moved and his graceful spareness made Mixcatl think of the long-legged cat of the mountains. The Aztecs called the puma Red Dog, as if they had no interest in distinguishing the wily and secretive animal from their own yapping curs. Mixcatl felt her lip curl in scorn. Her own language had a better name for the puma, the right name, the one the cat would answer to.

And then she caught herself. How did she know these things? The only time she had seen a live puma was in the marketplace, in a cage. The imprisoned beast was starved and mangy, not at all like the animal in the wild. There were more images in Mixcatl's head of beasts she knew she had never seen; the red-gold coat of the puma, the spotted rosettes of the jaguar, the blue-gray of the jaguarundi, the markings of the ocelot. Where had they come from, she wondered, and as she pondered, Latosl sprang out of the refuse barge.

"So, you are here again," said the boatboy with a grin as he dumped the first slop jar.

"Can I help you?" Mixcatl asked.

"You look strong. Try lifting that one." Latosl pointed to a smaller clay vessel at the end of the row. Mixcatl seized the jar and hoisted it, carried it to the end of the quay and put one foot on the barge.

"Ai, no! It's not moored," Latosl yelped in dismay, but Mixcatl was already straddling a widening gap between boat and quay. She had managed to shove the jar aboard, but the distance was too great now for her to jump back to the dock or scramble onto the barge. Her legs would only spread so wide. Latosl was trying to counter the barge's drift with his pole, but the boat was heavy and stubborn. With a dismayed cry, Mixcatl fell into the canal.

She went right down to the bottom, her toes sinking in among the cold slimy waterweed. With a panicked kick, she launched herself to the surface, gasped a breath and sank again. This time she flailed and kicked, fighting to stay afloat, but it was no use. She felt herself being dragged under again, her mouth filling with water, drowning her scream.

Something bumped her. Something straight, smooth and growing right out of the water like a tree. Latosl's barge pole. She grabbed it, hugged it and struggled to climb hand over hand out of the water, or at least to the surface, where she could regain her breath.

The pole started to slant and Mixcatl clung with all her strength, shuddering with a fear she did not understand. The pole ground against the boat's hull. She felt herself being lifted, squinted out of one closed eye and saw the boatboy dragging the pole and her over the side of the barge. At last she felt his hands close about her arms and she was swung onto the deck.

She collapsed and lay in a sodden puddle, giving thanks for the dry deck, the warm sunlight and the air that entered so easily into her lungs instead of choking and drowning her. While she rested, she felt Latosl poling his boat back to the quay, for it had drifted quite a distance in the sluggish current of the canal.

When the dugout hull grated against the stone, she lifted her head, peering toward the calmecac. Had anyone seen? Had anyone heard? Would Maguey Thorn come bustling out to seize her by the ear and drag her inside, scolding her and threatening to sell her?

Mixcatl held her breath for a long time, but the calmecac didn't stir. They were all busy.

"Hey." She started as Latosl tapped her back. She

turned, wiping wet hair from her eyes. His shock of hair hid his eyes, but his mouth was frowning. "You scared me. You went right down and I thought you weren't coming up again. Why didn't you say that you couldn't swim?"

"I didn't know," Mixcatl said, still shaking as she watched the swirling canal. "I've never been in water, except for baths."

"Never been in . . ." Latosl rolled his eyes in disbelief. "By Tlaloc's slimy green hair, I've never heard of a canal-side brat who couldn't swim." He got out, moored the barge securely and finished his task while Mixcatl wrung scummy canal water from her clothes and pulled strands of waterweed from her hair.

Latosl paused before tipping the last jar. "You know, you could have gotten me in a lot of trouble, girl. If you had drowned, those calmecac people of yours would have fined my family or even made me a slave to pay for your loss."

"You didn't tie up your boat," Mixcatl retorted.

"I never do," Latosl replied. "I just hop off, dump the jars and pole away again. It's much faster that way." He squatted on the deck, long slender arms wrapped about bony knees, and fixed Mixcatl with an odd, intense gaze. "Why can't you swim?"

"I don't know how."

"Someone should teach you," said the boatboy. "You can't live here in Tenochtitlán without knowing. It is too easy to fall into a canal." He paused. "Maybe I can teach you."

She stared at him, still squeezing water out of a corner of her garment.

"Think about it," said Latosl, swinging back aboard the barge.

How odd he is, thought Mixcatl, as the shape of the

barge dwindled downstream. *Not at all like Six-Wind, but nice in a different way.*

She stood on the dock, letting the breeze and the sun dry her clothes. When most of the dampness was gone, she gathered up her pots and went back inside.

During the next few years Mixcatl was kept too busy by her duties to do much more than exchange a few words with the boatboy when he came. Even if she had the time, she used it to draw figures in the dust, for the images she had seen in the sacred book clamored to be recreated. Mixcatl was careful not to enter the school's courtyard at all, even when she knew it was empty. She used other, more circuitous routes to make her way about the calmecac. She caught only brief glimpses of Six-Wind and he was always at the center of a throng of laughing, shouting boys.

But his words stayed in her mind. She was strangely gifted, she knew that. And she had already used that power to harm. Was she, as he had said, a witch? And the skill in her hands and her eyes that brought back the wonderful images in the sacred book; was that bad? She went about with her head bowed and a tight feeling in her throat. Once she had thought that good and bad meant little to her and that it would be as easy for her to harm someone as to please them. But remembering Six-Wind's fear and the way he had withdrawn from her brought a lump into her throat.

When Mixcatl was ten, the head priest of the calmecac, an old man called Two-Rabbit Cactus Eagle, fell ill. Suddenly the atmosphere of the school seemed to change. The boys no longer went about in noisy shouting groups, but quietly, shepherded by the priests. Instead of classes, there were sessions of praying, and at night, strange bustlings up and down the corridors.

Mixcatl had never seen Cactus Eagle. Maguey Thorn

told her that he was a man so old that scraggly gray hairs had sprouted from his chin. He knew all that went on in the calmecac, even down to the doings of the drudges and the slaves. He even knew about her, Mixcatl was told. If he had not given his consent for her to stay, it would not have mattered what Maguey Thorn or Speaking Quail thought about her.

From the sadness that fell over the school, Mixcatl knew that Cactus Eagle was valued by everyone there. Even Maguey Thorn, who was the first to spread a juicy piece of gossip about anyone, spoke of him with nothing but respect. And the sadness deepened as the old man grew worse.

At night Mixcatl watched through the belled curtain by the light of a bonfire as priests and students together knelt in the courtyard. They prayed fervently and shed their own blood in sacrifice, using agave thorns to pierce their fingers, earlobes and lips. Mixcatl could smell the blood, mixed with the odors of sweat and black body-paint. As the praying grew more frenzied, some slashed their palms with obsidian blades and made cuts on their arms so that the blood ran freely and dripped into bowls carved from lava. Mixcatl had watched without feeling more than a slight tinge of revulsion, for she was no stranger to the sight of wounds and bleeding. When the supplicants set the vessels into the fire, she shivered and crept away, unable to bear the acrid smell of burning blood.

She retreated to the kitchen, with its great raised firepit. No one was there, for they were all at the old man's side or in the courtyard, praying. The fire had died down to coals and Mixcatl knelt on the adobe brick, warmed by the heat radiating through. She stared at the glowing embers as if in a trance. Then she noticed that the great tiles that surrounded the firepit were blackened by soot. A few twigs lay near her feet, spilled from the kindling used to light the fire that morning. Mixcatl's hand groped among them and picked one up.

She looked at the twig, then touched its end to the sooty tile. It made a mark, for the tile was of fired white clay. Idly she drew a squiggle, then a few lines that crossed each other, but they dissatisfied her and she rubbed them out. In her mind the images of the sacred book still flickered, begging to come out. She knew that despite her sharp memory, she could not keep all of the details. Some had already started to fade.

A tear started at the corner of her eye. If she did not re-create the figures, she would lose them and there was little chance she would be able to see the book again.

She took another twig, one that had a sharper point than the first and could make a finer line. The figure she wanted most to make was that of Smoking Mirror. How wonderful he had looked, with his crest of plumes, his feathered cape and his jaguar claws. And the great roar he gave, shown by the sound scrolls issuing from his open mouth. Yes, he was there in her head. And she felt he would die and wither if he were not set free.

With her tongue clamped between her teeth, Mixcatl bent over a soot-blackened tile. She drew his head and body, the spotted arms with wristlets, the elaborate knotting of the loincloth. She drew his clawed feet, and then, beneath one foot, the shape of a strange shining circle, ornamented and patterned. Speaking scrolls also emerged from the disk, as if it too had a voice.

As she made Smoking Mirror, her heart beat faster. How beautiful he was. How could he be evil? She went back to the head and frowned. How did the headdress go? And how did it fit about the jaguar ears? There were so many bands and curls and plumes and drapes and she couldn't remember how they all fit together. She tried, but it didn't look quite right. But it had been years since she'd glimpsed the picture and all the details weren't there.

She leaned over the drawing, feeling tears of frustration well up in her eyes. He must be perfect. He must! But her attempts to repair the headdress only smudged it. She tried to scrape up more soot from the hearth and sprinkle it over the bad lines, but she lost a few good ones as well. With trembling fingers, she made the eyes, but they seemed to glare at her, accusing her for her clumsiness.

She backed away, a teardrop spilling down her face to land on another tile, making a gray splotch. Six-Wind was wrong. She didn't have any great talent. She had failed to make Smoking Mirror as he should be. Angrily she snapped her scribe stick in two. She was just an infant, scratching in the dust as she had done long ago at her village. For an instant she wanted to wipe out the drawing, but something in the figure forbade it. Instead, she turned and ran from the hearthside to her small room with its bed of rushes. She flung herself down and wept in a way she never had before, not even when she had been abused as a slave. At last, still sobbing, she fell asleep.

She was woken by shrill cries that rang along the hallway. Sitting up, she wiped crusted tears from her face. Howls and lamentations were coming from the kitchen.

"It is an omen," one voice cried. "Cactus Eagle is not yet in his shroud, yet the image of the Mocker appears, graven on our very hearth! One-Death is among us!"

Another voice joined the clamor. "Send for the high priest who oversees all the calmecacs. Only his magic is strong enough to stand against this!"

And then came a voice that Mixcatl recognized as Speaking Quail. "Wait. Is it not possible that this has another explanation? The image is the same as in the sacred book I use to teach the boys."

"But what young whelp could have drawn this? It is by a masterful hand. No, Speaking Quail. There is more at work here than the skill of a scribe. Do you see how it is done among the soot of the hearth? What better place to strike at a household than at the place of the life-giving fire?"

"That may be," said Speaking Quail firmly, but quietly. "Yet I will question my students. Until we rule out a human agency, we should not invoke a divine one. Cover the tile so that the women may prepare the morning meal without seeing or disturbing the image."

In her room nearby, Mixcatl heard the voices and huddled, her arms about her knees. She noticed a black smear of soot on her hand and quickly wiped it off. She remembered her drawing. Was it that which frightened them so? Smudged and muddled as it was?

She got to her feet, meaning to creep out of her room before the priests left their discovery at the hearthside. But she was too late. She heard the slap-slap of sandals behind her. She couldn't help a quick glance back and she caught Speaking Quail's eye. She saw his eyes widen and his step falter for just a beat before he matched pace with the other priests. She feared that just then he had recalled her long-ago intrusion into his class and her heart thudded with fear. If he connected the incident with Smoking Mirror on the hearth, she would be killed for sacrilege.

Quickly she began her duties. How could anyone even begin to think that a lowly dull little slopjar carrier had anything to do with the image on the hearth? And why were they all so upset by it, badly done as it was? She tossed her head, flipping her black bangs from her eyes. She should have rubbed it out, destroyed it. Even now, she could run into the kitchen and sweep her hand across the tile.

But she knew she couldn't do that either. She had

made the image. She could not bring herself to obliterate it. And what if someone caught her in the act? Then they would know without a doubt. The best thing she could do now was go about her regular routine and keep her hands from trembling too much.

There were few pots to empty. Students and teachers alike had spent the night in the courtyard, praying. Now they were clustered about Cactus Eagle's quarters, wailing and lamenting. The sound carried through the whole school. Mixcatl bit her lip. Did this mean that the old man was dead? Had she hastened his death by making a drawing whose power she didn't understand? Or by making it badly?

As she came out of a side hallway, she heard someone running. It was Six-Wind. His hair was disheveled and his loincloth dingy and stained. With a moan, she ducked back, but it was too late. He had seen her. In a few steps he was on her, grasping her arm in a hard grip, taking the pots from her and dropping them carelessly in a corner.

"Speaking Quail wants you. Hurry!"

He hustled her along the corridor, ducking out of sight when the slap of sandals or the murmur of voices warned that someone else was near. But there were few such incidents and they reached a larger chamber which held only one sleeping mat and a low lapdesk with pots of color beside it. There was also a rattan shelf that held more of the folded texts.

"Bring her in here," said Speaking Quail. "Away from the curtain, for those passing can see through."

With trepidation, Mixcatl looked up at him. His face was gentle, but haggard and weary from his night of vigilance. Multiple gashes across the backs of his forearms were crusted with scabs and a few still oozed.

He knelt before Mixcatl and stared deeply into her eyes. "Child, Cactus Eagle died last night. This morning an image of the Black Tezcatlipoca was found on the hearthstones. Many believe it is an evil thing and the sight of it has caused even more grief than Cactus Eagle's passing. Six-Wind has given me an explanation I can hardly believe, but he has always been truthful.''

Mixcatl looked at Six-Wind out of the corner of one eye.

''Remember, I warned you,'' the boy hissed back at her.

''Is it true, as he says? Do you have the skill to make such images? And to remember them exactly even though seasons have passed?''

Again she glanced at Six-Wind. If she played dumb, the boy's story would crumble. He was the only one who had seen her make the other figures under the creosote bush long ago. And he had wiped them out with his sandal.

At her silence, Speaking Quail turned to Six-Wind. ''Boy,'' he said mildly, but there was a graveness that brought out a new severity in his features, ''if this is an untruth, then you have disgraced yourself. A priest may not twist words wrongfully, nor may he take advantage of a time of sorrow to draw attention to himself. If your accusation against this slave is false, you will be expelled from the school and your father notified.''

Beneath his bronze, the boy flushed and then went pale. Mixcatl could only guess what it had cost him to dare tell his story to any of the priests, even one as gentle as the scholarly Speaking Quail.

Again she hesitated. She could keep herself safe, at the price of Six-Wind's future. But it was he who had kept the other boys from attacking her in the courtyard and it was he who understood, even though he was frightened. Perhaps Speaking Quail might also understand.

She lifted her head to Speaking Quail and, with a

mixture of pride and dread, answered, "Six-Wind is truthful. I made the picture on the tile."

She felt Speaking Quail's hands start to tremble as they slid from her shoulders. He picked up her wrist, stared at her stubby fingers with their grimy nails. Carefully he held her thumb, scraped a little of the black from beneath her nail with his own and sniffed the residue.

"Soot," he said. "But that does not complete the proof."

Six-Wind bent down and picked up one of Speaking Quail's brushes, offered it to Mixcatl. "This will," he said, pointing at the fig-bark paper spread across the low desk.

Mixcatl crouched before it, dipped the brush and held it over the paper. Again the sacred text was spread before her and its figures came to life in her mind. She dare not do Smoking Mirror; he was too dangerous. Instead she painted the undulating serpent decked with plumes.

Before she had even finished, Speaking Quail took down a book from the shelf, opened it on the mat and spread before her the same page she had glimpsed that day in the courtyard. He laid the two figures side by side. Except for the fact that the girl's drawing was done in a single color of brown paint and the figure in the book was brightly hued, the two were similar. Mixcatl could see some flaws in her painting, but Speaking Quail reacted in amazement.

"Where did you learn this? Were you given schooling?"

Mixcatl shook her head. The only thing she remembered was the veined hand laying brushstrokes on rough paper. She didn't know who that hand even belonged to. Her grandmother?

"I bought you," said Speaking Quail, running a hand distractedly through his tangled hair. "I have responsibility for you. But if I had known . . . why didn't you tell me?"

Mixcatl had no answer. Until she saw the book, she herself hadn't known. But would Speaking Quail believe that?

"Well, one thing is clear. We must bring the truth into the open. Cactus Eagle's funeral rites will not be marred by rumors that an evil sign appeared out of nowhere to disturb his journey to the underworld."

Mixcatl looked up at him. Dare she ask the question that had been troubling her since she heard of the old man's death? "Did my picture make him die?"

"No, child. He was very old. Everyone knew that his end would come soon, although they did not want to accept it." A corner of Speaking Quail's mouth twitched. "But because of that, we still have a problem. I don't believe that what you did harmed him or will cast any evil influences over his spirit, but there are other priests who would be quick to see otherwise."

"If we are the only ones who know, then why tell the others?" asked Six-Wind.

Speaking Quail pointed to the brush that Mixcatl still held. "Because such an extraordinary talent and memory is a gift that can not lie unused. And it will not, even if she has to scratch in the dirt outside. Do I speak the truth, little scribe?"

Mixcatl closed her eyes. She knew that she could not keep from drawing any more than she could stop breathing or eating or making water. Slowly she nodded.

"Will you go before an assembly of the calmecac and show them the truth behind the tile-painting?" Speaking Quail asked the girl. Again she nodded.

Six-Wind had been looking more and more worried as Speaking Quail questioned Mixcatl. "Honorable teacher, won't they just kill her?" he burst out. "Even if the priests believe that the work is by her hand, they might argue that some evil influence possessed her.''

''There is that chance,'' agreed Speaking Quail. ''But by the same token it could be said that such a child might be blessed by the gods. Was it not Plumed Serpent himself who brought us the art of setting down the sacred hymns and histories in books? Should we kill a slave-child for having that art? No. That is how I will argue.''

''You are a teacher of literature, not oratory,'' said Six-Wind softly.

''My tongue is not as quick nor as flowery as that of some, but it will serve.'' Speaking Quail gave Mixcatl and Six-Wind a tired smile. ''Besides, if the judgment goes against her, I will suffer too. I brought her among us.''

Six-Wind took a shaky breath, then straightened his shoulders. ''I'll stand by you. If any teacher has made me see what is right, it has been you, Speaking Quail.''

The tutor clapped him on the shoulder and Mixcatl could see that the boy's allegiance made his eyes shine brighter. She felt a sudden surge of hope. With two such friends beside her, perhaps she had a chance.

''I think you should be apprenticed to the priests who keep records,'' said Speaking Quail to Mixcatl. ''They can teach you far more about the art of glyph-painting than I or anyone else here.''

Her heart began to beat fast. To be among others who had the same talent and who would share it with her. It seemed like a dream beyond anything she could hope for.

But she also felt a new hunger. To know about those figures in the sacred books and what they meant. To know the stories behind the names. The questions came so rapidly she could not sort them out.

''Please,'' she blurted awkwardly. ''Tell me more about Smoking Mirror.''

Speaking Quail glanced at Six-Wind. ''I have done this girl an injustice,'' he said. ''Assuming she was dull witted, I didn't think she needed the kind of schooling that is the right of every child in Tenochtitlán, whether slave or freeborn. All right, little scribe, listen and I will tell you."

He took a seat on his mat and Mixcatl crouched nearby, hugging her knees. He told legends and sang hymns about Smoking Mirror, who was the Mocker, the Trickster, the capricious god who would raise men's fortunes on a whim and then cast them down again. Tezcatlipoca was the Black One, whose birth-sign was One-Death, yet he was also the god of youth and the protector of slaves.

In these myths, he appeared not only as the dancing jaguar that so fascinated Mixcatl, but as a human warrior who fought with other gods and against them. And he could suffer and bleed. One tale told of how he had sinned against the gods and in punishment had been trapped by the knife god Tecpatl within an enclosure of blood-red obsidian blades. When Tezcatlipoca tried to escape, the knife god caught and held him by the foot. Tezcatlipoca wrenched himself free, but left his foot behind. The severed foot was replaced by a smoking mirror that gave the god his name.

Speaking Quail got out the book with Smoking Mirror's image and showed Mixcatl how the god's sandaled human foot projected beneath the pad and claws of the jaguar. There was no foot on the other leg. Instead the jaguar claws rested atop the disk that had smoke-gray curls emanating from its surface.

She frowned. She had drawn him as a jaguar, not a human cloaked in a jaguar skin. To her he was still the jaguar that danced atop the smoking mirror.

When she said that to Speaking Quail, he stopped and stroked his beardless chin.

"Some of the scholars who have studied the most ancient records say that Smoking Mirror's original name was Tepeyolotli, the divine jaguar called Heart-of-the-Mountain.''

The name stirred something inside Mixcatl. She had heard it before, or something similar. Where? When?

She realized that Speaking Quail's form had fallen into shadow and Six-Wind had silently departed. Stiffly she uncurled and felt a yawn stretch her mouth. Evening had fallen, unheeded by either of them. Mixcatl was too caught up in listening and Speaking Quail in the telling.

He stirred, as if waking from a trance. "Off to your room now," he said, getting to his feet. "And don't worry about tomorrow. It is in the hands of the one I've been telling you about, and I think that he smiles on you, child.''

Mixcatl scurried to her room, curled up on her bed of rushes. She whispered "Heart-of-the-Mountain" to herself several times. Then slowly she drifted into sleep.

Early the next morning, Six-Wind knelt by Mixcatl's side and shook her shoulder.

"Speaking Quail has asked for an assembly of the whole school," the boy said as Mixcatl blinked and sat up. "They are already together in the courtyard. Hurry!"

She straightened her skirt, rumpled by sleep, and drew her mantle about her shoulders, for the morning was cold. The boy led her down the corridor and then out through the belled curtain.

All the priests were waiting, arrayed in their black bodypaint and richly colored cloaks. Gold arm- and wristbands shimmered in the early sunlight. A few wore gold lip plugs or earlobe disks. The students huddled together in small groups of boys their own age. They fidgeted and laughed nervously, but soon fell quiet under a glower from one of the priests.

Mixcatl looked anxiously for Speaking Quail and found him sitting apart from the others. He too was covered in black, his hair oily and tousled, his cheeks fiercely striped, but his face was somehow still gentle. And in one corner of the courtyard, surrounded by chests and lying upon cloaks even more magnificent than the ones the priests wore, was a bundle about the size of a man lying on his side with his legs drawn up. The bound and shrouded corpse of Cactus Eagle would also be a witness to whatever judgment was made here.

Eyes fastened on Mixcatl as she came into the courtyard with Six Wind. Their gazes held wonder, disbelief, grief, rage and hatred. Mixcatl knew she had been invisible to the priests and teachers at the school, just another one of the nameless workers and slaves that kept the school running. Now she had become visible, as if someone had turned over a rock and found something uniquely evil or wonderful underneath.

Speaking Quail beckoned her to his side. She stood, fingers twined together, her eyes unfocused so that she stared out at the black and bronze faces without really seeing them. Wishing she could become a statue or a block of stone, she stood still while Speaking Quail told the priests and their students how the image of Smoking Mirror had come onto the hearth tile.

When he finished, the priests and boys looked at each other in shock. Eyes narrowed, lips curled.

"Let the slave bitch be sacrificed to the god whose image she made," cried one voice.

"Spill her blood here before the corpse of Cactus Eagle, that his spirit may see that the evil has been cleansed from its path," another shouted.

"Take her to the Mocker's temple and bend her backwards over the altar stone. If she wishes to serve Smoking Mirror, she may give him her heart."

Mixcatl clamped her teeth together and held her lips rigid so that they would not tremble. At last the cries and threats died away, as if those who made them had courage enough to shout, but not to act. Speaking Quail rose to speak.

"Have I come mistakenly to the wrong gathering?" he asked mildly. "I thought I was among students and scholars who valued learning more than vengeance. Perhaps I have made a wrong turn and come to the school of those reckless ones who are trained only for war."

Mixcatl watched out of the corner of her eye while Speaking Quail paused. Grumbles and mutters came from the priests, then some reluctant shaking of heads.

"Ah, so we remember who we are. That is better," said Speaking Quail. "Remember Plumed Serpent, who is the patron god of this calmecac. Would he act so toward a slave? And would Cactus Eagle, if he still lived?"

A few gazes turned downward in shame, both among the students and their teachers.

"One of the things we strive for here is the mastery of the scribe's art. You know how difficult and painstaking a task it is and how students struggle to make the simplest figures. We try to produce artists with the skill needed to copy the sacred books, and as we all know, very few succeed." Speaking Quail paused. "Why then should we turn with hatred on such talent when it appears among us?"

"Would you keep her here, Speaking Quail?" asked another priest roughly. "The calmecac is not for slaves or for girl-children."

"No. She will go where she is needed. To the priests who keep the records and the sacred calendar."

Murmurs broke out in the courtyard, some agreeing, others shaking their heads. Mixcatl could see fingers touching blades of obsidian taken from their sashes.

Suddenly Six-Wind got up from his place, breathing hard. "If you kill her, I will not stay at this school. Better to be a warrior or even a ditch digger than a priest who kills because he is jealous of a slave girl's pictures!"

At the looks that passed across the priests' faces, Mix-catl knew that Six-Wind had struck home. Even with his rough boy's words, he had made them face the truth. Yes, they were jealous. All of them. And now they knew it and were ashamed.

"Very well, Speaking Quail," said the elderly priest who had objected to girl-children being in the school. "Take her to the priests of the calendar, if they will have her. But she will not stay here. There is a strangeness about her that has already shown its influence among the students," and here he glanced meaningfully at Six-Wind.

Mixcatl stood stiffly until the last of the priests had left the courtyard. She felt a touch on her shoulder and released her rigid muscles too soon so that she collapsed against Speaking Quail.

"It is over, child," he said steadying her. "And we have won at least the first battle."

Mixcatl felt tears burning in her eyes, but she held them back. "The priests of the calendar," she choked. "Will they take me?"

"They would be fools not to, once I show them your drawings." Speaking Quail smiled at her. "And they are not fools."

He turned to Six-Wind. "Young man, those were hard words, but they needed to be said. I am grateful."

Six-Wind tilted his chin up, but Mixcatl could see that he was biting his lip. He had endangered his future, per-haps even his life, for her sake.

The words did not come easily to her lips, but she said them. "I am grateful too, Six-Wind."

"Well, gratitude doesn't fill stomachs," said the boy awkwardly. "All this has made me hungry. I wonder if we can talk old Earthquake Bosom out of some stew and tortillas?"

Mixcatl followed him to the kitchen.

5

EVENING HAD COME to the palace of Tezcotzinco. A moist breeze blew through the window while a shaft of fading sunlight illuminated the low table where Wise Coyote knelt. Before him lay a large sheet of varnished bark-fiber paper containing a hand-drawn map of Lake Texcoco's northwestern shore with the island and causeways of Tenochtitlán. From the glyph that marked Chaultapec, the Spring of the Grasshopper, a red line ran down to a point near the lake. The line marked the section of the aqueduct that had already been completed. It had taken four years of planning, measuring, trenching and masonry to bring the project this far.

Wise Coyote sighed to himself, remembering the site where he had promised to build a temple to his gentle god. The place still lay undisturbed, for the Chaultapec aqueduct had consumed all the time he could spare from his duties as Speaker-King.

Yet he did not protest or resent the demands of the project, for he enjoyed the tasks of engineering. It gave him great satisfaction to reshape the earth to the needs of men. He had done so on a lesser scale with the dams and reservoirs at Tezcotzinco and now he was well on the way to achieving his greatest triumph—two massive stone troughs that would carry fresh water into the center of Tenochtitlán. He knew that he was building his own memorial, for long after his death men would point to the aqueduct and speak his name.

The first segment had been easy, for it was a straight downhill run from the high springs of Chaultapec to the lakeshore. The next section troubled him. He studied a lightly drawn blue line that showed the projected routing.

Should he stick with his original plan and run the trough along an existing causeway to Tenochtitlán or change it and strike out boldly across the lake? The latter idea would be more difficult, but it would provide a straighter run. And if he threw a dike across the lake to support the aqueduct, it could serve a double purpose by preventing brackish water from the west and south portions of the lake from contaminating the fresh water in the north.

He dipped his brush in dark-blue ink and bent over the map. A smile came across his face as he extended the line straight out across the lake. How the building-masters would cry out with dismay when they saw his plan. It couldn't be done, they would cry. They always told him that his schemes were impossible and then they worked as hard as possible to carry them out.

When his revision was complete, he rinsed his brush and laid it aside. The light would soon be too dim to work by. Besides, he had done enough and sitting cross-legged, bending over the low table, had made his back stiff. He got to his feet, stretching. Having eaten an early supper at his worktable, he was now free to do as he wished for the rest of the evening.

He decided to treat himself to a session in his library, considering questions about religion that had long troubled him.

The library at Tezcotzinco was a museum as well, for in addition to scrolls, tablets and codices, there were ancient polychrome potsherds, pieces of bas-relief limestone carvings, statuettes and other artifacts. Wise Coyote had gathered them during his travels. At first, when he was younger, his collection was random—he took what appeared most beautiful or whatever provided interesting information about its ancient creators. In recent years, the collection had taken on a new theme, reflecting Wise Coyote's search into the beginnings of Aztec beliefs.

Here, beneath the torches burning in their niches, stood the crumbling pillars of warrior-gods from the Toltec city of Tula, carved sun-disk calendars from the great vanished ceremonial center of Teotihuacán, and Oaxacan stelae covered with corpselike figures whose outflung arms and legs made them appear to be dancing.

The soft jingle of bells as the door cloth was pulled aside took Wise Coyote's attention from his artifacts. He looked around in annoyance, for he had not wanted to be disturbed, but when he saw that the visitor was his son Huetzin, he held out his arms in welcome.

"I thought you would be in the library," said Huetzin. He had grown since the day when he had come to Wise Coyote with a little bird carved from stone and the unwitting tale that had cost his half brother's life. Now he was a dark, slender, delicate youth of sixteen, with his mother's eyes and the deft fingers of a craftsman.

Wise Coyote could guess why he had come. Huetzin often came to gaze at or handle the pieces in the library museum. He was very careful and respectful, so Wise Coyote let him do what he wished. He knew that Huetzin was studying the various styles and techniques used in those works in order to develop and expand his own. He was still working on a way to express Wise Coyote's idea of the gentle God of the Near and By.

"I am sorry that the building of Tloque Nahaque's temple had to be postponed," he said with a shy smile, "but it does give me more time to try some new ideas."

"How can one make an image of a god who has no form?" Wise Coyote asked quizzically, then added, "Never mind. If there is a way, Huetzin, you will find it."

He embraced his son, then together they walked about the library.

He watched as Huetzin's gaze strayed along the shelves lit by torchlight, past the carvings of the feathered serpent Quetzalcoatl, past images of old gods and spirits, until they came to rest on one figure, set alone from the others.

It was a freestanding jade figurine of a man holding what looked like a large infant up in front of him. The statuette was about two handspans high. The figure's head was large for its body and shaped like a block with the corners only slightly rounded. Long, narrow ears had been carved at the sides of the head. The hair had either been depicted in a stylized manner or the figure wore a tight-fitting cap. The nose was flat and spread, the eyes were holes shaped like the sharp-ended oval of a pumpkin seed beneath high-arched brows. The chin was strong, but the mouth was so strongly bowed and pursed that the face looked petulant.

The infant, if that's what it was, looked even stranger. The body, though small, was not proportioned exactly like a baby's. The neck was thicker, the arms and legs stouter, making the small figure look like a sexless obese little adult. It had a bald, square head that was cleft at the top. The slanted eyes were narrowed ovals, slightly crossed, like the eyes of a great cat. Beneath the flattened nose lay the mouth, the upper lip thick and hoop-shaped, the corners drawn down in a snarl or cry. The gums showed a prominent alveolar ridge and were nearly toothless except for two tiny sharp fangs.

Huetzin reached for the piece, then checked his hand, as if its strangeness had made him think twice about touching it.

"That one is new," he remarked. "Where did you get it, Father?"

"It was brought to me by a merchant friend of mine, a *pochteca* who trades in the eastern jungles."

"How ugly, yet how well crafted," Huetzin said.

Wise Coyote nodded agreement. That had been his first reaction upon seeing the statuette.

"A master hand has done this," said Huetzin, picking up the statue. "Look how the carver has used curves and form to make the image look as if it is about to move. And it appears larger than it really is. I would give much if I could carve such powerful lines!" Huetzin ran his finger along the arm of the figurine. "But I would not waste my skill on making repulsive babies."

"I too do not find the piece beautiful," said Wise Coyote. "I was considering placing it in my storage-house, but each time I look at it, I find myself more intrigued."

Huetzin turned his head to stare at his father, his brows raised.

"You know that I have long sought the beginnings of our religion," said Wise Coyote. "Left-Handed Hummingbird is not the first god and the last. Nor is Quetzalcoatl, for all that the Feathered Serpent is a much worthier lord. Even Tlaloc is not the most ancient. There is a tradition that lies behind them all and I am determined to seek it out."

"Why, father?"

Wise Coyote surprised himself by his answer. "Because, if there is true power in our beliefs, it lies beyond the legends and bloody steps of the temples. I have sought all my life for a god that I don't have to force myself to worship. Yet I still hunger for the divine, Huetzin."

"Tloque Nahaque—"

"Is only a misty dream, a slender hope that I can fall

back on if I cannot find the truth," Wise Coyote interrupted, more sharply than he intended. There was a short silence, then he smiled down at his son. "Sometimes I think it is not a good thing for a man to become too wise. If I had kept my ignorance, I could have worshipped the gods of Texcoco without question. Do not become too wise, Huetzin. The price is heresy."

"Someone must have wisdom," Huetzin said. "Should I be sorry or glad that it is you, Father?"

"Both, perhaps," said Wise Coyote softly, thinking of Ilhuicamina. He shook off his moodiness.

Huetzin was studying the statuette. "There is an odd catlike look about both faces," he said. "Especially the small figure's. The mouth reminds me of the jowls of a puma or jaguar when the beast is snarling. I have sculpted those cats, trying to catch the right expression, but it is very difficult." He paused, tapping the figurine. "This artist could have done it."

"So then, my conjecture might be right," said Wise Coyote.

Huetzin looked surprised.

"In the eastern jungles, there are legends about an ancient people who existed long before any of the tribes we have now. They were said to have great power, so they were known as the Olmeca or Magicians. They worshipped the jaguar and it was said that there were those among them who were half jaguar, half man." He paused. "I think this statuette represents a Magician holding up a child born from the union of human and jaguar. Your impression helps support my idea."

"But what has this to do with your search for the divine?" asked Huetzin.

"I read many tablets and books while I was thinking about my temple to Tloque Nahaque. One very old one said that my God of the Near and By is an aspect of our Tezcatlipoca. As you know, Tezcatlipoca often appears in the form of a giant jaguar called Tepeyolotli, Heart-of-the-Mountain.'' Wise Coyote spread his hands. ''That cannot be an accident.''

''So you think that your gentle god had his origins in this?'' Huetzin tapped the figurine.

''Yes, and there is more. If there is a key to the divine, it rests in the hands of these lost people. If they indeed had the powers that legend says, then perhaps they were more than just men. Perhaps they were the first gods. Perhaps it is from the Magicians that Tezcatlipoca and Tloque Nahaque are descended.''

Huetzin looked puzzled and Wise Coyote knew why. The statuette was alien and frightening in its ferocity. How could the idea of a gentle god have arisen from such unpromising beginnings?

Wise Coyote watched his son replace the figurine in its place. He thought about sharing one more thing with Huetzin—the thought that the statuette, grotesque as it was, represented reality—that the jaguar-people had really existed.

Why else would their legends have been preserved after so long a time? Why else would their powers still be spoken of in respectful tones by the people who still lived in the eastern jungles? Why would the image of the jaguar have continued as a strong undercurrent in Aztec religion, emerging in Tepeyolotli, Heart-of-the-Mountain?

Wise Coyote had to confess that the statuette's appearance chilled him. The idea that Tloque Nahaque might have his beginning in this shook him deeply.

But the path to the divine can never be straight or easy, he thought, as he extinguished the torches and followed Huetzin from the library.

Several days later, while presiding at his court in Texcoco, Wise Coyote heard the cries of nobles as an old tale-teller was led through their ranks.

"Aagh! How he stinks. Bring him through quickly, quickly!"

"What does the tlatoani want with such as this? It is the fourth time that he has brought such wretches to Texcoco."

The Speaker-King rose from where he was sitting on his reed *icpalli*, a legless wickerwork chair. He went into a side chamber to meet his visitor.

Ordering refreshment to be brought, he greeted the old man, then took a place across from him. From a tangle of matted gray-white hair and scraggly beard, two sharp eyes peered out at him. Wise Coyote felt his hopes lift. Too often had he admitted old wanderers into his chambers only to find that the revelations they had promised were empty senile cackles or repetitions of legends that Wise Coyote already knew. This one might be different.

"Word has gone out that you wish to know about the ways of the Magicians of the eastern jungle," the old man said.

Wise Coyote leaned forward eagerly. He studied the man's features, wondering if he perhaps saw a trace of the pursed mouth, the elongated eyes of the statuette. He decided that it must be his imagination. "Speak what you know," he said softly.

The gaze on him was steady, with a depth that made him feel uncomfortable despite the difference in status between him and the old man.

"Once I was a scholar, just as you," his visitor began. "Now I am a wanderer and a tale-teller. I seek out stories that are worthy of being joined to lives and lives that are worthy of being joined to stories. Some stories and lives should join, some should not." He winked. "This is a warning, noble tlatoani."

Inwardly Wise Coyote groaned. Another one who wandered not only with his feet, but in his head. "I am not seeking stories," he said, trying to keep from expressing his impatience.

"Is not all truth a tale and all tales expressions of truth? Some stories you can listen to and then go back to your life, but some you cannot. What is your intent, Wise One of Texcoco."

The tlatoani bit back a sharp reply. It was not just impertinence in the old man's words. He was asking if Wise Coyote intended to act on the knowledge he would be given or whether he would just write it in a manuscript and store it in his library.

He felt as if he were taking a step over a strange threshold as he said, "My life is filled with disquiet. If what you tell me opens a new path, I will follow it."

Again the old man was quiet, measuring him, reading him. Could the tale-teller sense the hunger in him that had grown almost desperate? He had to find a new hope; a new power before the mania of Hummingbird on the Left consumed Ilhuicamina, who had once been his friend.

"Is my search too late?" he whispered, more to himself than the old tale-teller. "Have all the Magicians and their ways died out? If so, Hummingbird rises unopposed and we are lost."

"No," said his visitor, in a tone much deeper and stronger than Wise Coyote had heard him use. "You are not lost to Tenochtitlán. If you believe and if you aid the ones in whom the ancient blood flows."

"Who?" Wise Coyote looked up from his reverie, startled that the old man had answered.

"They are called the Jaguar's Children, tlatoani, and I will tell you their story."

And so Wise Coyote settled on his mat like a child before his teacher and the old tale-teller wove his tapestry of words.

Long ago, before ages were counted in the cycle of

New Fires, a people arose in the jungle country near the eastern seacoast. At first their ways were no different from the scattered bands of half-savage dwellers about them; they hunted animals, grubbed in the ground for roots, gathered plants and roamed endlessly as did the ancestors of the Aztec, Chichimec and others. But a change came upon them. No one really knew where it came from, but it was said that it was at that time that the gods first descended to walk among men in the form of jaguars.

From the union of earthly human and divine cat came children with the flesh of both and powers that gained them the name of Magicians. These children became the first kings among their people. They built the first pyramid towers and ceremonial centers, began the cycle of ritual about which life was built and gave to the world two great gifts, the writing of glyphs and the creation of the calendar.

For age upon age, kings with jaguar blood ascended to the onyx thrones of their ancestors, yet there were times when they fled the pyramid towers to take on jaguar shape and run wild in the forest. It was a conflict within that started the downfall of the Magicians but the cause remained hidden. Even so, it started many cracks that weakened the edifice of this first empire until it began to crumble. Invasions from outside ended the rule of the jaguar kings and the people went back to a simple forest life.

But those with the heritage of the great cat did not disappear. Though widely scattered and weakened, they kept contact with each other, bred to keep the sacred blood alive and watched with growing dismay as the Aztecs washed over the lands that had once been theirs, bringing with them a god whose demands for blood horrified even those who had been born of the predator.

"The Jaguar's Children still exist," said the old man,

as Wise Coyote leaned back on his hands. "And they are as devoted as you are to checking the rise of Tenochtitlán's bloody god."

"Then tell me where they are," said Wise Coyote, growing excited. "I must meet with their leaders, make an alliance."

The old tale-teller shifted to ease his stiff back. "I do not know where they are, tlatoani. Even if I did, you would not be able to find them by seeking. You must wait until they send word to you."

"How long will that be?" Wise Coyote asked as the old man started to get to his feet. "And how will I know that the message comes from them instead of from enemies who might wish to deceive me?"

"They will send you a sign that only you can interpret," said the old man, arranging his robes about him. "I am grateful for the refreshments and the kindness you have showed me, but I must be on my way."

Wise Coyote was filled with questions, but he kept them to himself as he personally showed the old tale-teller out of a side entrance to the palace so that he would not have to endure the insults of the nobles. He also gave the old man gifts of cloth and food.

When he returned to his chambers, he felt dizzy with warring doubt and hope, as if he were again a youth, embarking for the first time on life. Now the ones for whom he searched had a name. The Jaguar's Children. The doubter in him said that the old tale-teller was as much a fake as all the others, but something else in him wanted to believe. All he could do now was to wait and hope that when the sign came from the Jaguar's Children, he would have the wit to recognize it and the courage to act.

Mixcatl soon knew that Speaking Quail's challenge and Six-Wind's words had persuaded or perhaps shamed the administrators of the calmecac into setting aside the punishment they had intended for her.

Several days after the special assembly in the school, Speaking Quail again brought the girl into his quarters. She saw Six-Wind sitting cross-legged on a mat. Across from him, seated on an icpalli, was a plump middle-aged man in fine robes.

"Master of Scribes," said Speaking Quail, "this is the girl I told you about."

Mixcatl edged cautiously toward the master-scribe, feeling shy and confused. Then she caught a scent that made her eyes widen—the smell of paints, ink and brushes hung about the man. She lost her shyness and came forward eagerly. From the corner of her eye she could see the scrolls that Speaking Quail had shown the Master of Scribes. They contained samples of her work.

"She is young, as you say, but definitely gifted," said the Master of Scribes to Speaking Quail. "We have not taken many girl-children as apprentices, though there have been a few." He stroked his beardless chin. "There is also the matter of her religious instruction. As I understand you, she has next to none. This is most unusual, even for a slave-child. Such a lack is a serious matter."

Speaking Quail answered, "She was not taught religion because she was thought to be backward. Since that is clearly wrong, we at the calmecac are at fault. I propose to tutor her personally. It will not take long to make up the deficiency. I have found that she is a very rapid learner."

"Would she continue to stay with you during that time?"

"Regretfully, no. There has been too much disruption and controversy surrounding her. I ask that you make a place for her in the House of Scribes. During the first year, your apprentices learn to make the blank books that are used for the records. While she is engaged in that task, she can also be coming to me for religious instruction."

Mixcatl held her breath as she watched the master-scribe consider Speaking Quail's proposal. She had wanted to speak out for herself, but sensed that it would be better if she stayed quiet.

At last the Master of Scribes seemed to have reached a decision. "I think such an arrangement could work and would benefit the House of Scribes. I must discuss this with my superiors, but I feel they will agree."

He turned to Mixcatl. "So you wish to be a glyph-painter, do you, child?" He stroked his chin again, then looked at Speaking Quail. "You realize, scholar, that the life of a scribe-painter is a difficult, exacting one. I will not hide the fact from you or the child. At the upper levels, great demands are made on our artists and those who cannot meet the challenge are punished severely, even killed."

Mixcatl saw the teacher's face pale slightly. Was he going to turn away the possibility because he thought it too hard or dangerous for her? No! There was nothing else to put in its place. She could not stay in the calmecac and the only other alternative was to be sold once again. Solemnly she said, "Speaking Quail, do not be afraid. I am strong enough to bear any punishment and I am not afraid of being killed. I want to be a glyph-painter. Let me go to the House of Scribes."

"Little one," began the scholar, drawing her to him. "Do you understand the choice you are making?"

"Yes," answered Mixcatl. Turning to the Master of Scribes, she said defiantly, "I will paint so well that you will not need to punish me or kill me."

"Well, she is certainly not too timid," said the Master of Scribes, jovially. "Or too modest. Actually, Speaking Quail, I think she will do very well. The punishments are for lazy or untalented painters and she, I think, is neither."

"Will you take her then?" asked Speaking Quail. "There will be no price asked. I ask only that you treat her as you do your other apprentices. If you do, I am sure you will be rewarded."

"When can you bring her?"

"Three days after we receive word from your superiors. We will need to get a replacement . . . and"—his gaze strayed briefly to Six-Wind—"we would like to give her a little time to say farewell."

The Master of Scribes said he understood perfectly and rose to leave. Mixcatl, still dazed by happiness and the wonderful odor of paints and brushes, ran to Speaking Quail and hugged him. As she buried her head against the sweet scent of his robe, a tightness came into her throat. He had been so good to her when he didn't have to be. He had fought to give her a place and a life.

She fumbled, trying to say words of gratitude, but none would come. Finally she said awkwardly, "You have done so much for me, Speaking Quail. I wish I could do something for you."

Gently the scholar disengaged Mixcatl's arms. "You will be living in the House of Scribes, but returning each day to me for religious instruction. You will please me by learning your lessons well." He paused, smiled gently. "And you will have a good life, child. That is all the reward I need."

"Even after that time is over, I will not forget you—or Six-Wind either," she said turning to the boy, who still sat, somewhat awkwardly, across from Speaking Quail. Another child might have blushed or ducked his head, but the young scholar quietly extended his hand to Mixcatl. It was a gesture that freemen and noblemen used with each other, never with peasants or slaves. Mixcatl knew that and grasped his hand carefully. His palm was dry and warm.

"I hope that the Master of Scribes will give you your

freedom," he said solemnly. "You deserve more than the life of a slave."

"For now I will be happy as a slave who paints," Mixcatl answered.

Six-Wind's face broke into a roguish smile. "I will miss you, little slopjar carrier. Perhaps I can visit you in the House of Scribes. Maybe when I am older and have my own household, I can buy you and free you, if the Master of Scribes hasn't done it by then. I mean it," he said intently and Mixcatl found herself looking deep into his eyes. "Well, farewell, at least for now," the boy said, getting up. "I have classes to attend." He disappeared through the door hangings.

Mixcatl, feeling a bit overwhelmed, took refuge in her duties. Backing toward the door, she told Speaking Quail that she had pots to empty.

"Do not become too fond of that work," the scholar said. "You have only three more days of it."

"Who will buy the new slave? You?"

Speaking Quail laughed. "Maguey Thorn will send anyone but me, I imagine. Go do your pots."

She scuttled away.

Mixcatl told her news to the boatboy Latosl when he came by in the refuse barge.

"So I will be living in the House of Scribes," she ended proudly. "Have you seen it?"

Latosl said that he had. It was a large grand-looking building near the palace of the Speaker-King himself. "But I'll still be able to see you," he added. "Even those people have dung jars and they need someone to empty them."

Mixcatl wasn't so sure, but she said that she would try to be out on the canalside when Latosl's boat came by. "I will be able to tell it is you before I see you," she teased, referring to the pungent odor that hung about the barge and wafted ahead to announce its coming.

"Speaking of the barge, there is one thing I should do before you leave," said Latosl.

"What?"

"Teach you to swim. I am sure that the Master of Scribes would not want the career of such a talented pupil to be cut short by drowning in the canal."

Mixcatl agreed and said that she would be out on the quay early the following morning. Latosl said that if she wasn't, the consequences would serve her right. She grinned, thinking about how much fun it would be to go with him and paddle about in a cool stream. If she learned quickly, she might even be able to show off her skill to Six-Wind before she left the calmecac!

The following morning was not all that she had anticipated. Latosl came when promised, and picked her up. The morning was as golden and warm as she had hoped and no one noticed that she was gone. Even the boat ride itself was enjoyable, for there were no dung jars yet aboard and Latosl had scrubbed away most of the stink.

But when they reached the quiet backwater and Latosl started his instruction, Mixcatl discovered one unanticipated and frustrating fact. Her body would not float.

She was not afraid to put her face in the water or even to open her eyes underneath. She was not stiff and tense either, but totally relaxed. Yet every time she leaned back with Latosl's hand underneath to steady her, she sank like a boulder and had to stand up spluttering.

"I don't understand," the boatboy said. "Everyone floats. What did you do? Eat stones for breakfast?"

Mixcatl considered the possibility that Maguey Thorn's tortillas had the density of flattened rock, but as she had not yet eaten that morning, she couldn't blame the contents of her stomach. She tried again, attempting to lie straight in the water instead of bending in the middle. Nothing helped. She went down like a stone statue.

Latosl tried to hold her up and found himself struggling. "Why are you so heavy?" he asked. "You are not fat. Even if you were, you should be light in water."

By drifting around on his back, Latosl showed her how it was supposed to work. "Try to push me down," he said, "and see, I pop right back up again. When I take a deep breath, I float even better. Try that."

Mixcatl gave a huge inhalation, but even the deepest breath could not overcome her inherent tendency to sink. At last she gave up and sat in the shallow water, gritting her teeth in frustration.

"Everybody floats," said Latosl again.

"Maybe slaves don't," she said crossly.

"Everybody does. Even animals. I've seen dogs and even turkeys. They squawk and gabble, but they float."

"Everyone does except me. Why?"

Latosl spread his hands. Worldly as he was, he'd had no experience with anything like this. "Maybe you should ask a healer," he said at last.

"Why? I'm not sick."

"But you don't float when other people do. Maybe that's a kind of sickness."

Mixcatl thought about that. "I don't think so," she said slowly. "And I don't think that a healer would know about this." She got out of the stream and wrung water from her garments. "I should go back, Latosl. Anyway, a scribe doesn't need to swim."

As the barge glided back down the stream, Mixcatl sat on the peeling wooden deck and puzzled over the strange difference that seemed to set her apart. People floated. Animals floated. But she couldn't, no matter how hard she tried. Did that mean that she was made of something different than the people and animals around her? She sighed unhappily at the thought.

Well, even if she was made of different stuff, it should not matter to the people in the House of Scribes. At least she hoped that it wouldn't.

"Well, if you fall into a canal, I'll be there to fish you out," said Latosl, trying to be helpful.

The breeze was pleasant and the sun warm all the way back to the calmecac, but Mixcatl found that she was too distracted to enjoy them. What was she? she wondered. Would she ever find out?

She stared at the water gliding by and tried to lose herself in the green depths of the canal. She didn't even feel the bump when the barge came to rest at the quay.

Two days later, word came from the House of Scribes that the arrangement proposed by Speaking Quail had been approved. The tutor intercepted her while she was making her morning rounds and she jumped so high with joy that she almost dropped her pots. Her excitement chased away the dismay of learning that she could not swim. What did that matter now? Her hopes and wishes had come true. She was going to be a glyph-painter!

"This news comes at an auspicious time," said Speaking Quail. "This is the seventh day of Xochitl, the Month of Flowers. It is honored by weavers, painters and, of course, scribes." He paused. "Since you have no calendar name, you might consider adopting Seven-Flower."

"What do you mean by a 'calendar name'?" Mixcatl asked, puzzled.

"I keep forgetting that you have had no Aztec schooling," said Speaking Quail, with a mild touch of impatience. "Did your people have no way of reckoning the passage of days?"

Mixcatl tried to reach back in her mind, but everything was too fuzzy. She had been so young when she had been taken from her village. Slowly she answered, "I think they did, but it was . . . different."

"Well, here the calendar is very important. So much so that we name ourselves by our day of birth. Of course, since more than one child is born on each day, we have personal names as well. My full name is Three-House Speaking Quail, since I was born on the third day of the month called Calli, or House. Come to my study and I will explain."

As she settled herself on the mats in his chamber and listened attentively, he explained the Aztec calendar and how it worked. There were actually two calendars, one based on the solar year and used for secular purposes; the other, more important, was the *tonalpoualli,* the sacred or divinatory calendar. Aztec children were named for their day of birth as reckoned by the tonalpoualli.

The divinatory calendar was made up of twenty months, with names such as Wind, House, Lizard, Flower, Rabbit, Earthquake and others. Each month had thirteen days, with each day being designated by the month's name followed by the day number. He gave the examples that she already knew. Maguey Thorn, the matron, had been born on Ten-Earthquake. Cactus Eagle, the deceased elder, had been born on Two-Rabbit.

The combination of the thirteen numbers and twenty month-signs gave a series of 260 days, which formed the sacred year.

"When the gods decide that a child will come down to us on a specific day," said Speaking Quail, "the sign of that day will govern him until he dies. His fate is laid out for him and nothing he does may alter it." He gave more examples while she listened, pointing out that the signs could be baleful as well as benevolent. For instance, a child born under the sign Four-Dog would be rich and prosperous. The sign One-Jaguar condemned its possessor to die as a prisoner of war.

"Sometimes we try to avoid the worst signs by waiting several days after a child is born before naming him," Speaking Quail explained. "And sometimes by hard work, dedication and devotion, a person might escape the fate decreed by the signs."

"What about someone like me, who has no sign?" Mixcatl asked.

"You must either discover it or accept that your fate is unknown. Perhaps by adopting a favorable sign, you may be able to influence the portents of the tonalpoualli." He put his chin on his hand as if thinking and then said, "Certainly you would be more comfortable among your peers if you did so. There would be the expense of a ceremony, but I feel that our school should bear it."

Mixcatl heard his words with mixed feelings. Almost the only thing she had retained was her name. Now she was being asked to give it up, or at least preface it with an Aztec one. It was hard to imagine responding to "Seven-Flower."

"I will take the calendar name to please you and to make it easier to enter the House of Scribes," she said at last.

"You are not comfortable with the idea. Well, you do not need to decide now. You have a few days to think about it. Perhaps there is another sign that would be more appropriate. If so, I can help you to find one."

"I will think about it. Thank you, Speaking Quail," she said solemnly. The thought of a new name as well as a new life made her feel anxious, but she knew that she had to accept both if she wanted to fulfill her dream of becoming a glyph-painter.

A day later, she and Speaking Quail explored various signs and their meanings, deciding at last that Seven-Flower was, after all, the most suitable. A diviner-priest from a nearby temple was called and asked to confirm the choice and give the blessings of the gods. He sacrificed a turkey that Speaking Quail provided. Mixcatl herself only had to be there briefly and was not required to witness the offering.

Within a second day, as Seven-Flower Mixcatl, she bid farewell to the calmecac and was escorted to the House of Scribes to begin her new life.

6

An early morning breeze blew in through the stone window of the House of Scribes, stirring the cloaks of the slave-scribes as they slept. Wrapped in her new mantle, Mixcatl woke up on her rush mat, thinking she was still in the calmecac. Then she remembered that the school was no longer her home. She groped along her mat and found the rest of her clothes; short skirt, loose sleeveless blouse. All were made of undyed cotton cloth, as was proper for the dress of a slave-apprentice. To Mixcatl, who had worn nothing but rough maguey-fiber cloth in the calmecac, the garments seemed the height of luxury.

She put on her new clothes and went to the window. The sky over Tenochtitlán was rose and gray, with a storm lowering to the east over Lake Texcoco. She could smell rain in the air and hoped that she would be allowed outside so she could feel the heavy drops splash down onto her face. She stayed at the sill, leaning on her elbows and looking out over the city. To the other apprentices and scribes she answered to the name Seven-Flower, but had not given up thinking of herself as Mixcatl.

The House of Scribes lay within the complex of buildings used by the priests who kept the records and the calendar. It had three levels, thus raising it above most of

the other buildings that only had one or two. The slaves
lived on the highest level and it made Mixcatl breathless
to look down from the window onto the rooftops of the
city. She could see the twin pyramids of Left-Handed
Hummingbird and the rain god Tlaloc, their peaks rising
above the wall enclosing their sacred precinct. The house
of the Speaker-King, built of whitewashed stone, glowed
cream and pink in the early dawn. She could see into the
courtyards of other noble houses and could even catch a
glimpse of the calmecac.

Other slaves were starting to yawn and stretch. Mixcatl went with them down to the hall adjoining the
kitchen, where she was given a bowl of corn porridge
flavored with sage. As was customary, she ate with her
fingers, then washed her hands and prepared herself for
her first day at the House of Scribes.

She hoped she would be given paper and brushes, but
instead she was taken down to a covered courtyard with
a group of younger or newer slaves and put to the task of
making paper. The Master of Scribes wanted every new
apprentice to understand the complete process of creating
a pictographic manuscript, from making the folded pa-
perboard to the last flourish on the glyphs.

Although disappointed that she couldn't start painting immediately, Mixcatl soon became interested in the
method used to produce the blank fan-folded sheets that
made up a book. The process began with bark from a wild
fig tree, brought to the House of Scribes by merchants
who traded outside the city. The bark was soaked in stone
troughs, then placed on wooden planks and beaten into
flat sheets.

The work was harder than the tasks she had done at
the calmecac. After a noon meal she went to her sleeping
mat with aching arms and shoulders. She woke from the
midday sleep groggy and cross, not wanting to walk to
the calmecac, where Speaking Quail waited to give her

the first lesson in her instruction about the Aztec faith. Rubbing her arms and trying not to envy the other apprentices who stayed indoors and busied themselves with lighter tasks, she put on a rush raincape, sandals, and set out for the calmecac.

Speaking Quail met her at the courtyard entrance and guided her inside to his study. When she had shaken her wet hair out of her eyes, she settled herself on a mat and looked at the teacher with anticipation.

"You must understand," began Speaking Quail, a little awkwardly, "that I usually teach rhetoric and the art of composition. There are others who teach religion and who do it much better."

Mixcatl tilted her head to one side, looking at him gravely as he continued, "However, none of the religious teachers have the flexibility, nor the sympathy, to fit their instruction to your needs. For that reason, and because I feel responsible for your situation, I have chosen to teach you myself." He paused. "It will be a new experience for both of us, I imagine. I hope it will be a pleasant one. You note that I do not have an agave plant within my quarters. I feel I will not need to use the thorns."

He winked as Mixcatl allowed herself a chuckle.

"First," he said, "tell me what you have already observed and we will see if we can build upon that."

Carefully Mixcatl told him what she had seen and interpreted about the Aztec religion. She told him of the priest she had passed in the halls whose oily hair and stale blood smell had repulsed her. She spoke about the bloodletting rituals she had observed, from Six-Wind pricking his finger to the priests and tutors who gashed their bodies during the vigil for Two-Rabbit Cactus Eagle. She spoke of the text she had overheard when she had inadvertently come into the courtyard, the story about Plumed Serpent and his downfall at the hands of Tezcatlipoca, Smoking Mirror. She left nothing out, speaking honestly of her reactions and feelings to what she had seen.

"I have only pieces," she said to Speaking Quail, looking at him directly. "Some of them frighten me and make me feel sad. Perhaps if you tell me more, I will feel better."

A troubled look came into her teacher's face. "If you are seeking comfort by learning our religion," he said softly, "you will find little. It is difficult, even harsh, and I would do you no favor by trying to soften it. The knowledge that you must absorb before you can train as a glyphpainter is not easy to understand or accept, especially for you."

Mixcatl swallowed. "Because I am a slave?"

"Because you are an outsider who is starting instruction late in childhood. And because you will soon be a woman." He hesitated. "There are goddesses, rituals and ceremonies set aside for women. At first I thought of sending you to a priestess, for their doctrines are less demanding." He sighed. "I decided not to, because although you are still young, you already show a sharpness of mind that could place you beside my older students. Watering down your course of instruction would not prepare you for the demands made by the House of Scribes."

Though Mixcatl understood his words, she sensed an uneasiness that lay beneath them. Softly she said, "Speaking Quail, are you afraid of what you must teach me?"

His eyes widened in surprise, then closed briefly. "To be honest with you, yes."

"Why?"

"Because you have come to me . . . unspoiled . . . as none of my other students have been. It is only your foreign background and the mistaken assumption that you were backward and fit only for menial tasks that has kept you from being forced to follow our religion." He paused. "Have you noticed that none of the boys in my classes ever ask questions?"

Mixcatl shook her head.

"They listen, recite and learn by heart. That is all that is asked of them. The agave thorns are for the restless, the disobedient or the slow, but not for the questioners. In this school there are none."

"You forgot Six-Wind," said Mixcatl, and watched a smile creep onto Speaking Quail's face.

Six-Wind is not our typical student. His family comes from Texcoco and has affiliations with that royal family. But your point is valid. There are a few students who question or doubt, but most do not, because they have been punished to discourage it."

"Why?" asked Mixcatl again.

"That is a question that I am not really qualified to discuss in depth. Perhaps we will approach it again toward the end of our lessons."

"You are teaching me differently from the other students, aren't you?"

Speaking Quail gave her a gentle smile that had a touch of sadness in it. "Yes, I am. The uncritical way we usually teach would not work with you. Not just because you are stubborn, but because you have somehow learned to think for yourself, something rare, and, as you already know, dangerous." He paused. "My method is one my superiors would not look kindly upon, so I ask that we keep these discussions between ourselves."

"I promise," she answered. "You will let me ask questions?"

"Some," agreed Speaking Quail. "Now then, we had best begin."

Using pictographic texts to illustrate his teaching, he began describing the world as he understood it. There were four worlds, or "suns," before this one, he said. In each world humankind appeared, only to be wiped out by catastrophe at the end. The present world was that of the Fifth Sun. The previous sun was the Water Sun, whose age had ended in a cataclysmic flood. The present age was the Earthquake Sun, which had begun on the date One-Earthquake. It would end when earthquakes destroyed the land. The Monsters of Twilight, the Tzitzmime, who hide behind the western sky and await the final hour, would then swarm out and devour all who remained.

He spoke the text in high Nahuatl, using the book only to prompt his memory. Despite the gloom and grimness of the revelations, Mixcatl found a certain lyric beauty in the words themselves, as if the very language used to depict the death and destruction of the world had rebelled and spoke secretly of beauty and hope.

Speaking Quail showed Mixcatl a cross-shaped glyph he called "ollin." This, he said, represented the Aztec picture of the world. The uppermost bar of the equal-armed cross represented the east while north stood to the right, west below and south on the left. Tenochtitlán, the capital, stood exactly in the center of the cross.

Mixcatl realized that this map might hold the answer to a question that had puzzled her ever since she had begun to hear about Aztec gods.

"Is that why your sun god is called Hummingbird on the Left?" she asked.

"A good question," Speaking Quail replied. "The literal translation of Hummingbird's full Nahuatl name means 'the reborn warrior from the south.' We believe that warriors who fall in battle are reborn as hummingbirds. South is represented by the left bar of the glyph 'ollin,' thus his title." He smiled. "You are running ahead of me, little scholar. You will hear more of Hummingbird in future lessons. This one is ended and you should return to the House of Scribes before you are missed at the evening meal."

Thanking him, she dressed once again in her rush cape and left the calmecac.

Each morning at the House of Scribes, Mixcatl worked making paper, pounding the fibrous fig-tree bark on a board set across her knees. The beater was a scored stone lashed into a forked stick. She learned how to use beaters with coarser or finer scoring to control the texture of the paper, and when she had mastered that, she was shown how to mix and apply the chalky varnish that stiffened and smoothed the sheets. Great care was needed at every step of the process, or else the paper would be too rough for the artist's brush. Often the instructor stripped Mixcatl's sheet from her board and told her to begin again.

Her days fell into a routine of rising early, eating sage-flavored porridge, then laboring in the courtyard until the noon meal. After eating, everyone slept away the hottest and most humid part of the day before resuming work. For the other students this was a time for visiting or light tasks. For Mixcatl, it meant a walk back to the calmecac so that Speaking Quail could continue her religious instruction.

"Now I will tell you of the origins of our world and the gods in it," Speaking Quail said as Mixcatl shed her raincloak and settled herself on the mat.

Showing her the glyphs on the book in his lap, he told of how, at the world's beginning, the Earth-Father and the Sky-Mother gave birth to all the gods and how they came to the ancient Toltec city of Teotihuacán where they lit an enormous brazier. In those days there was no sun and the sky was twilight from one horizon to the other. During the gathering, a little god who was covered with boils plunged into the brazier as a sacrifice and emerged as the blazing disk of the sun. But, though the sun was wondrous in its brightness, it could not move. Only when the gods sacrificed themselves, giving their lives to feed the sun, did it gather strength and began its present path across the heavens.

Mixcatl sat in a daze, her imagination filled by images of the solar disk rising from flames and the gods spilling their blood to nourish the newborn sun.

"Each day, the task begun at the sun's birth must be continued or else the sun will falter in its course and cast the world into darkness," Speaking Quail recited solemnly. "Every day we must feed the sun with its food, 'the precious water,' the *chalchiuatl*, human blood. We exist so that the blood that runs within us can nourish the sun. That is our first and most sacred duty. And what is true for the sun is true for everything else; the earth, the sky, the rains, and all else in the world. Nothing is born, nothing endures, without sacrifice."

Mixcatl listened. Was this dependence on blood sacrifice spoken of by her own people? She felt echoes of things that sounded familiar, yet there were also jarring discords. She didn't know. She had been taken too early, before her disparate early memories could coalesce into a whole. At least now she was beginning to understand why Six-Wind had dripped blood from his finger onto a leaf when he feared she was a witch, and why the priests in the calmecac had gashed their breasts and arms during rites for Cactus Eagle.

"Nothing is born, nothing endures, without sacrifice," she recited gravely after Speaking Quail.

"To fail in that duty betrays the gods and all of mankind."

She swallowed and spoke the words after her teacher.

"May I ask a question," she said as she watched Speaking Quail studying his text and preparing himself to interpret more of the glyphs written upon it.

Speaking Quail nodded.

"Even if you know sacrifice is necessary, isn't it difficult to kill another person? To do that, wouldn't you have to hate them or look down upon them? How would you feel if you had to sacrifice me?"

The teacher clasped his hands and was silent for a short time. "You have asked me the most difficult question of all and one that still wars with my deepest feelings. Some priests delight in bloodhunger and look upon a victim as an enemy to be slain. I disagree. To me a sacrifice is a messenger to the gods and as such is cloaked with divine dignity. To me there is no dislike or bloodlust between sacrificer and victim. Both are joined in a unity beyond fear or hatred.

"When a true warrior takes a prisoner for sacrifice, he says, 'Here is my well-beloved son.' And the captive, if he understands, replies, 'Here is my well-beloved father.' "

"So both are joined together to prevent the ending of the world." Mixcatl ended for him. She paused, knitting her brows as she looked at her teacher. "I think I understand, but it is difficult."

"As difficult as it would be for one friend to see another die on the altar," answered the teacher softly.

He fell silent, letting Mixcatl wrestle with what she had learned. She knew that sacrifice was a subject that few except the chosen nobles and clergy had to think deeply about, although everyone had to accept it as part of life. She sensed that had she been given the usual education of an Aztec girl, she would have never been allowed to think about such things, only to accept them unquestioningly. In a way, such an education would have been easier. But Speaking Quail was right when he said that sort of learning would never satisfy her.

She came out of her daze, for he had begun to speak once again.

"Let me connect this with something we learned in our previous lesson," he said. "Do you recall the representation of the world embodied in the glyph 'ollin,' or movement?''

She nodded as he showed her the cross-shaped glyph in the text.

''Each of the four directions rules one of the signs we spoke of previously. Acatl, or Reed, belongs to the east; Tecpatl, or Flint Knife, belongs to the north; Calli, or House, to the west; Tochtli, or Rabbit, to the south. Remember that east is the upper limb of the cross and you will have little difficulty orienting yourself.

''Because of the way the sacred calendar is constructed, a year can only begin on a day that has one of those four signs. Since each sign can have thirteen days, the combination of thirteen and four yields fifty-two possible beginnings to the year. Thus time as we understand it is bound together in fifty-two-year bundles.''

''At the end of that period, a great fear falls upon everyone, for as we watch the sun set on the last day of the last year of the 'bundle,' we do not know whether it will rise again.''

Mixcatl shivered and moved closer as he spoke in a voice filled with uncertainty and dread. In her imagination she felt as though she had moved back through time to that last day and stood watching.

''In the evening, the red flickers of fires go out one by one, as the order comes to quench them and darkness floods the land. People throw away their possessions to prepare for the end of the world and weep in terror with their families. In the night, anxious crowds gather on the slopes of the great snow-capped mountain above Tenochtitlán. The priests, standing and shivering at the peak, watch the cluster of stars called the Seven Warriors as they rise toward the zenith. Will the stars go on and the world continue? Or will they halt and the monsters who wait behind the twilight come swarming out?

''A sky-watching priest lifts his arm as the constellation nears its height. A prisoner is bent back over a stone altar. With the downstroke of the priest's arm, so comes the downstrike of the flint knife, opening the victim's breast so that the 'precious water' spurts forth. And in the raw mouth of the wound, the priests spin the firestick until flame leaps up. At the sight and sound of the miracle, the people shout with joy. Messengers light torches to rekindle the cold hearths and run to every part of the valley with the message of life renewed.

"Again the world has escaped its doom, redeemed by the sacrifice and the flames of the New Fire. The monsters stay imprisoned behind the sky, and at dawn, a new sun rises."

Mixcatl had to shake herself free of the vision, so compelling were Speaking Quail's words. And when she turned to him, she saw that he was not reciting from the text; he had put the book aside.

"I was there on the mountain slopes as a child, and I will never forget the cold dread that numbed me so deeply that even my father's arms could not bring the warmth back into my bones," the teacher said. "When I saw the New Fire and knew the world had been spared, I vowed then to become a priest and spend my life serving the gods." He paused, reflectively. "Unless I am blessed with many more years than most men, I will not see the next 'binding of years.' Perhaps that will be a blessing, for I think my heart may burst with dread if I must face it again."

In the silence that followed, Mixcatl cupped her chin on her palm. She was young; she would probably live to see the next "binding of years." Would the world end then, or would another New Fire spring from the breast of a slain sacrifice to rescue the world once again?

Another thought troubled her. Why had she not heard of this before? Had her grandmother, or even her lost mother, ever spoken to her of the world or its ways? Try as she might, she could not remember anything except the green jungle and the grunting cough of jaguars that roamed the night. She had been too young to recall anything as complex as a religion.

The lesson was ended. She bade farewell to Speaking Quail and returned to the House of Scribes.

After Mixcatl could produce well-made sheets of thick, boardlike paper, she learned how to stick them together in strips that were so long that they often reached across the courtyard. All the blank books that the apprentices were working on had to lie parallel to each other, or else they would cross and stick together. Once the strips were dry, each was carefully fan-folded into a large package that could be tucked under the arm for carrying or placed on a shelf for storage.

All this took time. Many thirteen-day stretches passed and Mixcatl learned the sequence of signs by naming them as she lived through each day they governed.

Sometimes she had visits from Six-Wind, who told her the latest gossip of the calmecac, and what he was learning. Sometimes, if she could get out on the quay that fronted the canal, she could see Latosl and exchange a few words with him as he emptied the slopjars and the night-soil baskets into the clay bins on his boat.

Most often, however, her days were filled with work and thoughts of what she had learned from Speaking Quail the previous day. Her ties to the calmecac, her absorption in learning and her promise to Speaking Quail kept her at a distance from her fellow apprentices. All were youths older than she and, despite the stated policy of taking girls if they were exceptional, there were no other young women. The few female students who had previously entered were now at a high level and fairly inaccessible to a young apprentice. When Mixcatl was older and had completed her religious education, the Master of Scribes promised, she would meet some of her sister scribes. For now, she would have to be content in knowing that they existed.

Her progress satisfied the Master of Scribes, for when he questioned her to see how well she had learned the gods, sacrifices and prayers, her answers pleased him. Her instruction at the calmecac was to continue, but she had shown enough dedication so that her provisional status was changed to full acceptance.

Relieved that one hurdle had been cleared, Mixcatl still felt troubled. She knew she had satisfied the Master of Scribes by concealing her feelings about what she was learning. By now she had become familiar with the primary figures of the religion. It was Tlaloc, the grotesque-faced rain god, who sent the clouds to water crops. Xipe Totec, the Flayed One, symbolized the renewal of the earth in fresh growth. Coatlicue, She-of-the-Serpent-Skirt, was celebrated as mother of innumerable gods. Tezcatlipoca, Smoking Mirror, who took on the fascinating aspect of a dancing jaguar, played his part as guardian of death and youth. Indeed, he was starting to rise above the rest of the pantheon to challenge the deity that the Aztecs worshipped above all others—Hummingbird on the Left.

Within the confusing and often contradictory jumble of gods, rituals and prayers lay a message that bothered Mixcatl more as she approached the age of twelve. It was that individuality meant nothing in the scheme of things and that the primary emotion was dread. Humanity was crushed beneath the weight of the gods and the stars, imprisoned by the signs and forced to give an ever-widening river of blood so that the threatened universe might totter precariously from one instant to the next.

While she accepted the Aztec faith in fearful obedience, part of her rebelled. Try as she would, she could not suppress the feelings. Perhaps it was the strangeness in her, the unnamed thing she sometimes felt circling within, that could not bear the picture of such a world. It made her want to beg Speaking Quail to say this was not reality, that the world in truth was not so desperate and fragile after all.

It also made her wonder what would happen if someone was brave or foolish enough to withhold the sacrifice, to refuse to bring the knife down upon the victim's chest, and see then if the sun faltered or the world ended. To ask such a question was unthinkable, even of Speaking Quail. Such doubts were far too dangerous when the possibility of the world's ending hung in the balance. She herself might not have the courage to make that challenge when the moment came.

And even if those doubts were right, speaking them now would destroy everything she had gained and ruin her chance to create a life as a glyph-painter.

So she kept those thoughts in a secluded place in her mind and kept quiet, but she couldn't help wondering if anyone else shared them.

Mixcatl began to think that she would spend her life preparing empty pages for other artists to fill. She was almost startled when the day arrived when she and the other slave-apprentices were shepherded into a large room and given small pieces from blank books that had been judged unfit for any other use except practice.

Her brush was a twig with the ends chewed and her ink was watery, but Mixcatl eagerly set to the first exercise in glyph-drawing. She found it much too easy and finished long before the rest.

She soon discovered that the scribe's skill demanded more than artistic ability. Each complex tiny figure had to be drawn to exacting standards according to certain rules. Figures of men, animals or gods were always shown facing left or right. A figure's head was always a third of its height, even if that convention distorted true proportions. Variations or mistakes were not tolerated. Even practice paper was in short supply and not to be wasted. Students were admonished to look at a figure until they could draw it in their heads before trying to transfer the lines to paper.

Mixcatl found the task easier than did most other students, for she had the ability to keep images in her mind and draw from them, the way she had drawn Tezcatlipoca from memory. But she had to struggle to control her brush, so that the lines would not wander. Other students who were careless or who could not control their strokes were punished or dropped from the class. Mixcatl saw them later, making paper in the courtyard. They would either be sold or would spend all their lives devoted to tasks requiring less skill. Mixcatl vowed that she would not be among them and bent her head over her practice sheet.

In each figure, every tiny little detail was important, for the shape and decoration of face decoration, headdress, shield sandals or garments gave important information about the warrior, king or god being shown. Even colors were symbols and the artist had to be sure to get the hue and shade exact or readers would misinterpret the picture's meaning.

Once a line was down, it could not be removed by erasing or smearing. Anyone who tried had the back of his hands pricked by agave thorns. Though Mixcatl did not like the punishment, she never thought it unusually cruel, for she had become accustomed to the infliction of wounds as chastisement and it was no worse that what students received at the calmecac.

Quickly she learned how to place figures on the page in relation to each other, how to proportion them properly and how to make the blue speech scrolls that symbolized words issuing from their mouths. She executed and memorized the simple glyphs for things like trees, mountains, and then more complex ones for city names and the titles of nobles or warriors.

The rainy season, then the hot season, came and went while Mixcatl spent her days crouched over her practice board or performing some task in the shaded courtyard.

As the complexity of the drawing assignments increased, the number of slaves in the class diminished as more found that they were not able to meet the exacting demands of the art. For those who continued, like Mixcatl, tasks became harder and punishments more severe for those who failed.

When the scribes in training were given their first blank books instead of practice sheets, it was both a time of joy and dread. At last Mixcatl had a surface worthy of her skill, a well-varnished smoothness that wouldn't drag at her brush tip or pull her hand astray. Eagerly she applied herself, the paint flowing evenly from her brush, the lines controlled, the proportions proper. But even while she was buried in the act of creation, she could not help but hear another student moaning in fear because he had blotted or marred his work and the teacher would beat the offending hand with a thorn whip.

Mixcatl knew that scribes at the upper levels were punished severely, even killed, if they made a mistake on an important document. Though she resented the atmosphere of fear created by this severity, she accepted its necessity. If scribes did not take the utmost care in making the figures, or if they allowed variations to creep in, the books would soon become unreadable and thus useless. Dread of pain or even the loss of one's life might be a cruel motivation, but it had worked. As complex as the figures were, they could be read by anyone who had been given the proper training in interpretation.

And perhaps she gave little thought to the severity of

the punishment because she was convinced she would never receive it. Her eye was sharp, her hand steady, her brushstrokes sure. She could see an entire figure in her head and project it onto the paper so that her brush only had to trace over lines that seemed already drawn.

This gift put her far ahead of the others and soon the teacher accepted her skill, placing her in an advanced class of experienced scribes who were learning the finer points of the art. She was also given her first real assignment, a listing of tribute collected from a newly conquered area. Carefully she made the pictures of the items she was told to draw, such as mantles, blankets, strings of jade beads, shields, warrior costumes and tropical birds—all goods that the conquered town had been forced to yield.

Other assignments followed, each more difficult and longer than the last. Mixcatl worked eagerly, but carefully, completing each one without flaw. Soon she had made a strong reputation for herself as a gifted apprentice. The Master of Scribes declared that he was well pleased and moved her up in rank to become a scribe's assistant and then a full-fledged glyph-painter with all rights and responsibilities of a trained artist. It was an honor, for at thirteen, she was one of the youngest ever admitted as a fully trained scribe.

Toward the beginning of her fourteenth year, she was brought in to work with some of the best glyph-painters on a series of books commissioned by the Speaker-King himself. They were to comprise a history of all the lands of the Aztec Empire, a project that the older scribes said would take the most careful and exacting work over the span of many years.

Mixcatl was sitting in a room on the top floor with the other scribes assigned to work on the document, painting by the light of a torch made of strips from twisted resin-filled pine. Outside, thunder rumbled and rain sluiced down on the city. She sat near the window, for she enjoyed the sound of the rain, although she was careful not to let any raindrops spatter onto her page.

Propped up nearby were several old yellowed texts that she was using as sources. One of the benefits of working as a scribe was the ability to interpret as well as copy. Often she put her brush aside to pore over the ancient glyphs.

One text showed the origin of Hummingbird on the Left. Speaking Quail had made sure she had memorized the legend. As she read the text, she remembered his words.

She touched the figure of Hummingbird's mother, Coatlicue, She-of-the-Serpent-Skirt. Surrounding the goddess were tiny figures of children she had already borne, the many stellar gods called the Four Hundred of the South. Again Coatlicue was shown, now sweeping the steps of a temple and looking up as a fluffy ball of feathers containing the soul of a recently slain warrior descended from the sky. Coatlicue placed the ball of feathers in her bosom, unknowingly impregnating herself.

Mixcatl paused in her study, deciding that she would be wary of any little fluff balls that might happen to float her way. Although this only seemed to happen to goddesses; mortal women only bore children after lying with a man.

Coatlicue's other offspring, finding her to be inexplicably with child, grew angry and swarmed upon her, demanding her death. At their approach, the child within her womb spoke out, telling his mother not to fear. From her swollen belly he leaped forth, already fully grown and armed with shield and snake-headed club, which turned into a thunderbolt to incinerate all who stood in his way. He turned on his siblings and drove them away, just as the rising sun chases away the night and dims the light of the stars.

Mixcatl frowned as she studied the figure of Hummingbird. She wasn't particularly fond of him, but she had to reproduce him accurately for the new text. He was shown as a striding warrior with a blue and white striped face, lifting his snake-headed weapon to drive away his brothers and sisters. His helmet was in the form of a hummingbird, the long beak sticking out over his forehead to form a visor. He had the arched Aztec nose and a grim, implacable expression.

Carefully she painted his figure on the new page, then added in the rest of the glyphs containing the legend.

Across the room an older scribe sighed, stretched, rubbed his back and returned to his task. The work was going much more slowly than anticipated, for the history was very difficult and complex. Several books had already been rejected as imperfect and the artists demoted or punished. It was said that the Speaker-King was starting to grow impatient with the House of Scribes.

Mixcatl worked as fast and as well as she could, but the project crept on at an agonizingly slow pace. Different artists came and went, although she, thankfully, was left alone.

As she put the final touches on the glyphs of Hummingbird's legend, the doorhanging was pulled aside and the Master of Scribes entered, followed by an old man with a bald pate ringed by curly white hair. He had a high bulging forehead and a scraggly yellow-gray beard.

When Mixcatl caught sight of the old man's face, it reminded her of someone she had seen before. He had the same small flattened nose, the same type of high forehead, thinning curls and sparse beard as the kind elderly slave who had ridden with her aboard the market boat to Tenochtitlán.

Staring harder, she felt a sense of disappointment.

No. This old man might share some features of the one who had taken pity on her that day, but he was not the same man. His throat was wattled like the neck skin of an iguana. His lips were fuller and bowed much like her own. His eyes were lighter in color, the gray-brown of fired clay.

He was close enough in appearance to the man in Mixcatl's memory that she assumed he would be gentle and kind, the way the other had been.

The Master of Scribes motioned to get everybody's attention, then presented the newcomer. "This is Nine-Lizard Iguana Tongue. He has been given to us by the house of Tlacopan to aid us in completing the history for our Speaker-King. I ask you to make him welcome."

Mixcatl watched as Nine-Lizard Iguana Tongue's gaze traveled over the group, appraising them. As he looked her way, his eyes lingered and a little line appeared between his brows. Somehow that wasn't the expression she had expected to see when he looked at her. Instead of being mild and kind, his gaze was sharp and critical.

She heard him ask the Master of Scribes about her and heard the expected answer. The old man grunted and shrugged his shoulders. Mixcatl felt her face warm. Was he worried about the prospect of working with a young woman? Did he fear her work would not be good enough? Well, he would soon think otherwise. The Master of Scribes had already judged her productions to be better than many of the more experienced artists.

"Please use my calendar name," said Nine-Lizard to the group. "I prefer it, as you might expect. Now, show me the history and how far you have come with it."

Mixcatl's eyebrows rose. For a slave newly introduced into the group, Nine-Lizard was behaving as if he had been asked to take charge of it. Perhaps he had, although that would be unusual. She watched him as he examined the completed portions, ordering them all to be placed before him and going over them with an expert eye. Though his manner was polite, his commands were firm and there was a look in his eye that said that slave or not, he was accustomed to being heard and obeyed.

"Who did this section?" he asked, tapping on a page with a yellowed fingernail. Mixcatl saw that it was one of hers. He motioned her forward with a crisp gesture. Lifting his head, he squinted at her. He tapped the page again. "This will have to be done over."

Mixcatl's mouth fell open. The Master of Scribes had already passed this work as acceptable for the history. What right did this old slave have to tell her it must be done again?

"Your proportions are wrong," said Nine-Lizard Iguana Tongue. "There is no point in wasting paint on pretty brushstrokes if you do not draw your figures correctly. The head should be one-third of the figure's height."

"They are almost one-third," she answered.

"Almost is not exactly," said the old man.

Mixcatl dug her fingernails into her palms. What right had he to criticize her so openly, to disgrace her before the others? Up to now everyone had accepted her as an equal, treated her work with respect and often used it as an example.

"Look," he commanded, and to Mixcatl's horror, he took a brush, dipped it in brown paint and drew the same figure that Mixcatl had already done right next to hers and on top of some others. She clenched her fist, ground her teeth in anger. Now he had deliberately ruined her page, forcing her to do it over. And all the while he was gabbling on, completely oblivious to the outrage, using her work as if it were just practice paper and she a total beginner.

He might want to be called by his calendar name, but to her he would be Iguana Tongue.

Yet she could not help but be impressed with the swiftness of his brushstrokes and the simple beauty of his lines. He used fewer strokes than other artists and his figures came out looking much cleaner and more alive. There was a certain grace and uniqueness to his work that made it unmistakably his.

For the first time in her life, Mixcatl faced a talent greater than hers. She burned with envy. Forgetting herself, she said, "Teach me this! Teach me to paint as you do."

It came out as a demand, almost a shout. Heads lifted, turned.

"Young woman," said Nine-Lizard mildly, "I would concentrate on learning the basics of proportion before you aspire to anything greater." He tore off a blank section of her page and handed it to her, indicating that she was to use it for exercises in figure-drawing.

Her face flaming, Mixcatl took the board on her lap and dipped her brush.

"I will inspect your work later, Seven-Flower. If it is satisfactory, you may resume your former task."

She controlled her impulse to dump a paintpot on top of his thinning curls. "Old Iguana Tongue," she muttered as she began to draw.

She gained some small consolation from seeing Nine-Lizard Iguana Tongue find flaws in the work of other artists and set them to practicing as he had done with her. One or two he had shaken his head sorrowfully over and asked them to leave the room. Well, at least I am not among them, Mixcatl thought to herself.

She eyed him as he circled the room, hands behind his back. She took malicious pleasure in noting that his robe was soiled and a dab of paint had come onto his cheek. The wattles in his neck made him resemble the beast he was named after and he shook them often as he paced between the sweating artists.

At last, he stopped beside Mixcatl. Silently she lifted her board for his inspection.

"Better," he said, "but you still tend to make the head too small. Measure and mark before you begin. That will aid you."

"But men and beasts do not have heads so large," she said, her frustration making her dare to argue. "If they did, their necks would break."

She expected Nine-Lizard to scold, but instead he chuckled. "That is observant of you, Seven-Flower. But you are not here to paint the world as you see it. You are here to produce documents that people can read."

Mixcatl pouted. "If I am such a bad artist, why was I chosen to work on the Speaker-King's history?"

"Because even with your flaws, you are among the best of those here," said Nine-Lizard. "Even though the Master of Scribes means well, the art of scribing here in Tenochtitlán is starting to languish. Work such as this would not be accepted at Tlacopan or Texcoco. Certainly not at Texcoco. Wise Coyote will not accept anything but the best work for his library."

"Who is Wise Coyote?" Mixcatl asked.

"He is the ruler of our neighboring state across the lake. A wise man, an artist and a scholar. Would that our own Speaker-King was more like him," he added in a softer voice so that only Mixcatl could hear, then he moved away.

To her disgust, Mixcatl found that she had to spend several days doing exercises before Nine-Lizard would let her work on the new book again.

"You think I am too hard on you, eh?" he remarked, his knees creaking as he stooped beside her. "No need to speak; I can see it in your face."

Mixcatl grimaced. "Everyone else liked my work."

"I have much sharper eyes than anyone else," said Nine-Lizard. "And you have keen eyes too; I can see it in the way you look at things. You must take that sharpness in your eyes and put it into your brush."

She shook her head. "I do not understand what you are saying."

"You will, in time," he answered. He examined her work, muttering to himself. "How I wish I had been brought in earlier. There has been too much praise, too little demand. They have let you get away with scribbling not fit for decorating pots!"

Mixcatl, stung, curled her hands the way she had done in the marketplace years ago and hissed, "Then show me how to do it right, old Iguana Tongue!"

"Oho! So I am Iguana Tongue after all," said Nine-Lizard. "Very well, I will show you." Almost savagely he grabbed her brush, swirled it in the paintpot and sent it sweeping across the smooth plate of the codex. Figures rose from the paper as if blooming there and the bare lines seemed to fill themselves in with color in Mixcatl's mind. She quailed before the sheer power of his artistry, despairing that she could ever match it.

His fury exhausted, Nine-Lizard lifted the brush from the page and stared coolly down at Mixcatl. "So then," he said softly.

"Teach me," Mixcatl choked. "I will not argue, not ever again."

Nine-Lizard snorted. "I doubt that. You are a strong-willed creature, Seven-Flower Mixcatl. I will hear the name Iguana Tongue in my ear many times before I have finished teaching you."

He turned away, stooping beside some other artist to comment on his work. Mixcatl, her head swimming, continued her drawings. In the midst of her dying anger and frustration, she found a little ember of promise. He would teach her. She was good enough so that he would spend the time and the effort needed. He was right. She had not been pushed and stretched as her ability deserved.

Once again she touched her brush to the paper on her board. She looked at the figures he had drawn and realized that he had left the sheet for her instead of taking it with him as he usually did when illustrating points for other artists.

Old Iguana Tongue, I will be worthy of you, she promised, to both Nine-Lizard and herself.

7

IN THE YEAR Eight House a procession of white-robed priests and nobles wound up the path to Chaultapec, the Hill of the Grasshopper. Wise Coyote peered out from behind the hangings of his litter, then clutched the side rails to keep from sliding as a bearer stumbled on the muddy trail. Ahead he could see the palanquin of Il-huicamina, larger and grander than his own, but clumsier and bulkier. It lurched as the men who carried it fought to keep their footing.

Wise Coyote sighed and braced himself against another jolt. He would much rather have walked, but Il-huicamina had insisted on honoring him. Turning in his seat, he looked back down the slope to Lake Texcoco and the city of Tenochtitlán. How it had expanded, even in his own lifetime! Once a poor village on a snake-infested island, the Aztec capital now covered great tracts of re-claimed land in the lake. Seven great causeways linked it to the mainland, where the metropolis was starting to spread along the lakeshore.

But the lack of potable water had slowed the city's growth and threatened to choke it from within. Now, with the opening of the aqueduct from the springs of Chaultapec Hill to the city's heart, fresh water would be available to all.

Wise Coyote sighed. Eight years of his life. Eight years of sweating over plans by torchlight, laboring with his crews to dig the trenches and set the stones, of struggling to dike the lake and run the aqueduct across. Eight years, so filled with work and urgency that he had nearly forgotten his son's death at Ilhuicamina's hands. Perhaps the Aztec Speaker-King had done him a favor.

Soon the litters halted. The spring's seepage made the way slick and difficult. As Wise Coyote climbed down from his seat, he glanced to one side and saw a group of yoked prisoners flanked by guards. Those were Ilhuicamina's contribution to the celebration, captive warriors intended for sacrifice.

He looked away, though he kept his face expressionless so that no one looking would see his distaste. There were enough whispers already about, saying that the tlatoani of Texcoco had no stomach for death.

He had begun to wonder if they were right. He had been raised to believe in the bloodhunger of the gods and the power of human sacrifice. When hunger stalked the land or drought blighted the fields, sacrifice was proper and the victims themselves died rejoicing. When Tlaloc demanded a child's life in payment for the first rainfall, a young girl was cast into a cistern, a practice that Wise Coyote viewed as necessary. But with the rise of Ilhuicamina's Hummingbird on the Left, sacrifices were made in such numbers that their power was squandered.

Wise Coyote wondered how and when the captives would die. Ilhuicamina hadn't told him.

Ilhuicamina's litter tried to proceed, but the steep muddy path at last forced the Aztec Speaker-King to descend. Wise Coyote muttered a little prayer to the rain god Tlaloc, grateful that Chaultapec had forced the great Ilhuicamina to touch the earth with his sandals.

With his retinue about him, Wise Coyote climbed the hill to the spring. His throat caught when he came to a turning along the path and saw the aqueduct. The twin channels gleamed with dew in the morning light, making it seem like a work of gods rather than men.

The stone troughs waited, new, and still empty. Chaultapec's waters still flowed down their natural course, but only a small dike of rocks and sod now diverted the spring from the aqueduct.

Wise Coyote joined the crowd of celebrants gathering at the head of the twin channels. He passed plumed nobles wearing gold nose and ear-plugs, and elaborately knotted loincloths with embroidered tailpieces. Their capes billowed out in swirls of fiery color. Among them, looking like the shadows of demons in their greasy black body-paint and tangled hair, were the priests of Hummingbird.

Ilhuicamina turned, his feather-fan headdress shimmering in emerald and aqua as it caught the morning light. The harshness of his features was eased for a moment by a smile.

Wise Coyote glanced at Aztec warriors who were unyoking the captives and assembling them near the first section of the aqueduct. He knew the victims were from Tlaxcala, a city-state Ilhuicamina had recently subdued. The warriors held their swords. The sun flashed on the glass-sharp edges of obsidian chips set into the wooden shafts. Some trick of the light, or Wise Coyote's mind, painted the sword-edges crimson.

He knew it was an illusion, yet his stomach clenched. For an instant, the tlatoani of Texcoco thought of asking Ilhuicamina to send the captives away. The celebration was for him, wasn't it? He should be able to have what he wanted. Or what he did not want.

He imagined the shocked stares of the priests if he should make his request. How the whispers and mutters would run through the crowd, building into cries of outrage! And Ilhuicamina, swayed, could easily forget his gratitude for the building of Chaultapec.

Sacrifice the captives, then, Wise Coyote thought angrily. *Kill them and be done with it.*

But Ilhuicamina made no move to order the sacrifice. No signal made the warriors lift their swords. Instead he offered his fellow king a wooden staff, richly carved and polished.

"You shall send the lifeblood to my city," he said.

As Wise Coyote opened his hand for the staff, he saw the warriors lean close to the captives, their arm muscles swelling as they hefted their weapons. The gaze of the doomed Tlaxcalans went from Ilhuicamina . . . to him.

And in Ilhuicamina's eyes, there was mockery behind the praise. Too late, Wise Coyote knew that he had been tricked, maneuvered into a task he hated. Some action or word from him would trigger the sacrifice. And even if he knew exactly which, he could not avoid performing it.

His fingers closed on the staff. The captives did not die. He turned, carrying the staff to the dike. One thrust and shove would break the temporary earth dam, sending the water leaping into the aqueduct. He lifted the staff, listened to the shouts of praise from the crowd, felt a heart-tearing mixture of pride and dread. The captives did not die.

Ihuicamina raised his arms in rapture to the sun. "Hummingbird on the Left, drink deeply so that my city might quench its thirst."

Wise Coyote hoped Ilhuicamina's words would end the Tlaxcalan's lives, but the warriors still waited, their eyes on him.

With a grunt that was more a muffled cry of despair, Wise Coyote plunged his staff into the dike. He wrenched it back and forth, making a mortal wound that tore open as water burst forth. It splashed his robe and leaped into the first of the twin channels.

As the spring water started on its downhill race to Tenochtitlán, a fierce yell broke out from Ilhuicamina's warriors. With raised swords, they drove their captives downhill alongside of the stone troughs, ahead of the flow. The obsidian blades fell upon the necks of the victims. Men died as they ran, their bodies falling into the channels, their blood mixing with the rushing water.

The cascade swept the corpses along or shoved them up and over the lip of the channel, where they tumbled headless upon the ground.

Ilhuicamina clenched his raised fists, his face distorted in a rictus of mixed joy and fear. "Drink the life of the sons of Tlaxcala, that they may never again defy us."

When the last crimson-streaked Tlaxcalan prisoner had toppled into the channels, Ilhuicamina looked around eagerly as if he wanted more blood for his god. For one sickening instant, Wise Coyote thought that Ilhuicamina would choose more sacrifices from his own men or even from Wise Coyote's own retinue.

The instant passed. Wise Coyote shook himself and wondered if the moment had taken place only in his imagination. No one, even the Aztec ruler, could make such a capricious demand. And the tlatoani of Tenochtitlán was not a complete madman.

Not yet, thought Wise Coyote.

Ilhuicamina lowered his fists. "The god is well pleased. Now nothing can stop Tenochtitlán's march to greatness." He turned to Wise Coyote, offered his open hand. "This is the man whose wisdom and skill have given us this aqueduct. Let me hear praise for the Engineer of Texcoco. He has subdued the mighty lake itself to bring water to the empire's heart."

A roaring cheer went up as Wise Coyote came forward, lifting the clay-stained wooden crowbar. The cheers ringing in his ears lifted him up and warmed his spirit, but there was a place, deep in his gut, that stayed cold.

He made a short speech, accepting the praise and gifts offered him as creator and director of the construction project. He brought forth other men, architects, masons, foremen and laborers, and spoke of their part in the building so that they might receive their due. When he was finished, Ilhuicamina spoke once again.

"As much as we need the effort of brilliant men, so too do we need the favor of the gods. Today we have fed them with the blood of our enemies, but the campaign against Tlaxcala is over. The rebel state is subdued, but the gods still hunger." Brows lowered, Ilhuicamina swept his gaze across the crowd. "How shall we feed them? If we deny them blood and hearts, then the foundations of the world will tremble and the empire will fall."

Ilhuicamina paused, letting the full impact of his words fall upon the crowd. Wise Coyote ground his teeth, knowing and resenting Ilhuicamina's gift for oratory. Well he deserved the title Speaker-King. Wise Coyote envied him, for although he himself used words well, he could not generate the emotional fervor that hypnotized crowds the way Ilhuicamina did.

"We have plenty of young warriors who are eager for battle," Ilhuicamina continued. "I will give them what they seek. Every three moons, I will declare a War of Flowers against an allied state. The young can wet their blades in combat while providing captives whose hearts will feed the gods."

He announced that the first Flower-War would take place against Tlacopan. Wise Coyote, fearing that Ilhuicamina might choose Texcoco for the "honor," felt relieved. Flower-Wars were nothing new. They were formally arranged battles between otherwise friendly states. By fighting in a War of Flowers, young men might vent their energies in battle without challenging the borders or rulers of the states within the Aztec Empire. Those who won received glory, while those who lost were sacrificed.

Yet dismay mingled with relief and turned the place in Wise Coyote's gut colder than ever. A new series of Flower-Wars would provide an endless stream of victims for Hummingbird on the left. There were instances in which a battle begun as a Flower-War turned into a real war, especially against states within the Alliance who still flaunted their independence from Tenochtitlán. Their rulers died "accidentally" on the battlefield and the Aztecs mourned the tragedy and then cheerfully annexed their lands.

What did Ilhuicamina have in mind for Texcoco? Though the Aztec Speaker-King professed great friendship for Wise Coyote, Texcoco's relative independence and reluctance to raise a temple to Hummingbird on the Left was a thorn in the Aztec's side. Favors to Tenochtitlán—such as building this aqueduct—might hold off Aztec rapaciousness for a few years. But Wise Coyote knew that Texcoco could not long withstand the pressure from its powerful neighbor across the lake.

The thought of having a temple to Hummingbird on the Left in his own city, perhaps right outside his palace, made Wise Coyote sick at heart. To see the blood running down those steps every day and to smell the same stink that pervaded Tenochtitlán—no! He would die before allowing such an abomination.

And if Ilhuicamina does declare a Flower-War against Texcoco, you might very well die, King-With-a-Deer's-Heart, he scolded himself as he walked back to his litter and prepared to mount.

It was late at Tezcotzinco and Wise Coyote had already gone to his sleeping mat. He was woken by the soft rustle of door hangings and the tread of feet. Instantly, as he came alert, his hand sought the dagger that lay beside his wooden headrest.

"Father?" came the voice of Huetzin. "Your guard let me through. A man has come to see you. I said it was late and tried to turn him away, but he said you would understand when you saw this."

Wise Coyote took his fingers from the dagger and sat up, blinking in the light of a torch that a servant was fixing in a bracket on the wall. He brought his gaze to the cloth-wrapped package between Huetzin's hands. When he took it in his own, the weight of it was more than he expected. Unwinding the wrapping, he caught a glimpse of green serpentine. Another statuette.

Quickly he freed the figurine of its wrappings and held it up in the firelight. At first he had expected another figure like the one he already had in the library, but this one was very different. Instead of a standing figure shown in a symmetric formal style, the shape was much more fluid, showing the figure in a half-kneeling position, forearms resting on thighs and head thrown back so that the face tilted up.

The head itself was oblong in shape, with a high-domed crown. The face was strange, a blend of human and great cat, as if a human was shown wearing a jaguar mask. The nose, lips and jaw especially suggested the cat.

Wise Coyote thought that the figure was indeed wearing a mask, for he pointed out a definite border between the cat face and the rest of the head. It was Huetzin, with his sculptor's eye, who saw that the area that Wise Coyote had called a mask was in actuality recessed from the rest of the head, indicating that instead of being covered, skin was being pulled back from the face, exposing the cat features underneath.

On the forehead were strange wiggly lines which ran together, suggesting blood vessels that had been exposed by flaying. It was not a pleasant realization and gave Wise Coyote a chill in that vulnerable place in his gut.

"So, do you understand what this statue means and will you see the man who brought it?" Huetzin asked.

Wise Coyote thought about his conversation with the old tale-teller and the promise that the Jaguar's Children would send him a sign. Was this it? Certainly the theme of a blending of man and jaguar could not be coincidence.

"Show him in to my private quarters." Wise Coyote pulled a fresh robe over his head and splashed his face with water from a bronze bowl. He went into the adjoining room, asking Huetzin to come with him.

The servants were escorting in his late-night guest. The caller was an elderly man, though not as decrepit as the ancient tale-teller. Wise Coyote could tell at once from his dress that he was a slave and from the pigment stains on his hands that he was a scribe.

The old man greeted the king respectfully and introduced himself. "I am Nine-Lizard, glyph-painter of Tlacopan, currently residing in Tenochtitlán." His head had a crown of curls surrounding a high-domed shiny pate that gleamed in the firelight. Wisps of beard curled around his chin as if trying to hide a plump, homely face. Wise Coyote noticed that there were certain resemblances between the old man's features and those of the statue in the library. The same high vertical forehead, squashed nose and bowed pursed lips were there, though in less grotesque form. On the statue the face had looked austere and forbidding. The echo of it in the old scribe's visage only added a touch of pleasant homeliness.

"Are you of the Jaguar's Children?" Wise Coyote asked, trying not to let his eagerness or his trepidation show.

"I have had my associations with them, tlatoani," the old scribe replied. His eyes seemed to twinkle with amusement, but behind them, Wise Coyote sensed a wariness.

"You are a slave, as stains on your hands show." Wise Coyote leaned forward. "You have risked much to come here. A slave who leaves his assigned duties can be accused of escaping and then slain. Why have you come to me?"

"Because I have heard that the tlatoani of Texcoco seeks allies in his opposition to Tenochtitlán."

"Then they will join me?" Wise Coyote felt a surge of hope.

Nine-Lizard held up his hand. "I am no longer a member of the Jaguar's Children—I cannot speak for them. I have come on behalf of another."

"Who?"

"A young slave girl, presently in the House of Scribes. She was taken in from a calmecac when events exposed a great talent for painting and copying. I believe she has other gifts as well, but those gifts, if revealed, may endanger her life. I would advise you to take an interest in this young scribe, for she may help you find the path that you have been seeking."

Wise Coyote asked more questions, but the old scribe Nine-Lizard, though respectful, would say little else.

At last, frustrated, Wise Coyote said, "Why do you speak in riddles and shadows? I could offer better help if I knew more about the girl and these people who call themselves the Jaguar's Children."

"I am practicing caution, as are they," Nine-Lizard replied. "You know yourself that dealings with the royal houses of Tenochtitlán, Tlacopan and even your honored house of Texcoco have been very dangerous for those whose talents may brand them wrongly as enemies. No. I have given you enough information that you may act if you choose. What you do will tell the truth of your intent." He paused. "The girl's name is Seven-Flower Mix-catl."

Wise Coyote felt as if he were being subjected to a test that would determine if he were worthy to have dealings with the Jaguar's Children. To be told that he would have to first be judged by the nature of his actions irritated and dismayed him. After all, it was he who was offering these unknown people aid. As king, he had power and resources that they would need.

He put those feelings aside, for he sensed that royal impatience would carry no weight with the old slave-scribe. The old man had already ignored the veiled threat that he could be executed for leaving the House of Scribes without leave from his masters.

He knows that I will not punish him, thought Wise Coyote. *I am too curious about the girl.*

Aloud, he said, "If you were worried about this young woman, why did you not bring her with you? I can offer refuge at Tezcotzinco."

"She has been set to work on a special history for Hue Hue Ilhuicamina, who would be displeased if that task was interrupted. No, tlatoani. Because of that . . . and other complications as well, it is best to leave her in the House of Scribes. You can keep watch on her from a distance—that is something you nobles are very good at doing."

You are too polite, old scribbler, thought Wise Coyote. *You do not say that I can depend on my spies.*

Nine-Lizard rose to take his leave. "Keep the little figurine I gave you. It will have a use."

"To tell you the truth, old man, it is not something I would choose for myself. The flayed face and the atmosphere that surrounds the piece makes me look upon any contact with the Jaguar's Children with uneasiness. I will think long and hard before I make any move. I want to be sure of what I am stepping into."

The old man smiled benevolently at him. "Good. That is why I gave it to you."

He would say no more, but asked instead to be escorted out. To Wise Coyote's surprise, he would not accept the usual gifts that the tlatoani offered his visitors, but went away empty-handed into the night.

Restless and wakeful, Wise Coyote studied the strange figurine by lamplight. It was late in the evening before he could put it aside and turn once again to his sleeping mat.

8

LATER IN THE year, the tlatoani of Texcoco visited Tenochtitlán. He came in response to a request for his presence
at an elaborate new religious ceremony honoring Hummingbird on the Left. It was an invitation he accepted
unwillingly.

After the sacrifices and ceremonies, the Aztec
Speaker-King gave a feast in his palace. As an invited
guest, Wise Coyote could have partaken of the many
delicacies and the entertainment, but instead he chose to
eat alone in the rooms provided for him. The events of the
day lay heavily on him. He needed time in solitude.

Ilhuicamina had thoughtfully given him apartments
on the side of the palace away from the temples, but the
blood stench hung in the air all over the city. Wise Coyote
had been tempted to return home, but he knew that such
a gesture would be taken as a slight. Even his dining
alone tonight would cause gossip at Ilhuicamina's court,
but Wise Coyote resigned himself to that. He couldn't
face the thought of sitting among the warriors and nobles, listening to jests and laughter while images of the
day's slaughter still haunted him.

*Never again would he attend an offering to Hummingbird
on the Left!* He had come out of politeness. No, the truth

was that he had come in hope of salvaging the rags of friendship that remained between himself and Ilhuicamina after their bond had been torn by the Prodigy's death.

But now, although he swore he would never again set foot on those blood-slick temple steps, the ceremony seized his mind, as if he were being forced to witness it again.

Tenochtitlán's streets and plazas were filled with flowers, music and festival. As Wise Coyote rode in a litter to the ceremonial center of the city, the beat of a great drum overwhelmed the noise of celebration.

The drum seemed to echo his own heartbeat, slow and heavy. The sacrifice at the opening of the aqueduct had hardened him. After that, he thought, nothing could make him feel more wretched. But his heart knew better.

The tlatoani of Texcoco glanced out through the hangings that hid him from view. The city's great central plaza was overflowing with people dressed in colorful finery and decked with flowers. He felt the litter slow as he passed through the crowds.

The palanquin seemed to jolt along, as it had during the muddy climb to Chaultapec's spring.

It must be my imagination. The bearers would not stumble on the smooth pavement.

He squashed his impulse to get out and walk. Besides having to contend with the throng, he would be standing in the shadow of the twin stepped pyramids that dominated the plaza. The one on the right he could bear to look at; it had been newly raised to the Toltec rain god Tlaloc. The other honored Hummingbird on the Left.

Ilhuicamina had manipulated him into giving the order that had cut down Hummingbird's victims at Chaultapec. It was that outrage, not just the number of prisoners or the way they died.

So he tried to tell his pounding heart and grinding gut, even while he strove to draw serenity across his face.

At last his litter arrived, coming to a halt behind Il-huicamina's at the foot of Hummingbird's pyramid.

Ilhuicamina had descended from his palanquin and was climbing the steep stairs. His footsteps were impatient, carrying him ahead of his escort of priests and courtiers. As Wise Coyote mounted the stone staircase in the Aztec's wake, he saw, amid the crowd, a file of men all dressed in simple white loincloths. The line ran from the base of the temple itself, across the plaza until it was lost to sight among the other buildings of the city.

He felt the sweat prickle beneath the band of his turquoise coronet and knew it wasn't just from the exertion of climbing the pyramid's staircase in the hot noon sun.

He wanted the file to be a line of worshippers, eager to make their devotions to Hummingbird. He did not want to see that their necks were yoked, their hands bound and their eyes dull with fright.

His heart no longer beat to the rhythm of the drum. It was fast, frantic, nearly closing his throat. His earlier thought, that the number of sacrifices did not matter, now seemed to mock him.

He was ready, but not for this. Not for a whole river of victims who stood ten abreast, flowing from the depths of the city to the foot of the temple . . .

No! This was not devotion. This was a frenzy bordering on madness, and an obscenity in which he should have no part.

He hastened his steps to the summit, determined to speak to the man who still called himself a friend. At the top he was blocked from Ihuicamina by the sheer press of bodies about the Speaker-King. His protest was swallowed in the roar of adulation from the crowd massed below. He could only watch, mute, as the Aztec turned to the throng and lifted his hands.

Ilhuicamina's magnificent feather-fan headdress of emerald quetzal feathers, beaten gold and precious stones shimmered as he tilted his head back to face the noon sun. Sweat ran down the planes of his upturned face. The king of Texcoco, rocked with horrors, shuddered with yet another: that the Aztec would blind himself by staring too long at the sun.

Emotion stilled Wise Coyote's tongue for an instant too long. His attempt to speak was drowned by the beginning of the Speaker-King's rant.

"Hummingbird on the Left! Never again will you hunger! Never again will you thirst!" Ilhuicamina thundered at the sky, clenching his hands. "The previous rulers of this city neglected you and in return you struck with drought and famine. Never again shall this happen, for the city of Tenochtitlán shall be a fountain from which the gods may drink forever!"

A black-smeared priest with wildly tangled hair handed Ilhuicamina an obsidian knife. With a push they sent a captive stumbling up the steps. Others on the steep stairway hastened the victim upward, for he was so numbed by fright that his eyes stared at nothing and his knees buckled. He crawled up the last few steps.

Ilhuicamina turned to Wise Coyote with a triumphant smile and for an instant the tlatoani of Texcoco thought that the knife would be handed to him to do the killing. With a swirl of embroidered robes and swish of feathers, the Aztec ruler turned toward the altar.

The sacrifice staggered to the top and was met by wild-eyed priests who bent him back over the sacrificial stone. Ilhuicamina plunged the knife into the heaving breast.

Wise Coyote closed his eyes, but he could not shut his ears to the sounds of tearing flesh and breaking bone that told him that the heart was being taken from the corpse.

Streams of blood splashed on the flagstones and began their cascade down the steps of the temple.

Ilhuicamina called for another blessed one to ascend, met the victim on the top step and killed him where he stood, letting the body tumble down. He then handed the knife back to the priests, evidently tiring of the effort involved in killing. Wise Coyote wished that the sacrificing would end, but foresaw what must follow. Victim after victim stumbled, was shoved or dragged up the slick steps to be bent back over the altar stone and slain.

The king of Texcoco felt sick with disgust. He cursed again the servility of the Deer's heart that had brought him here. It made him accept his son's death at Ilhuicamina's hands without rebelling and had made him embark on the construction of an aqueduct to bring water to those masses whose upturned faces now shone with bloodlust.

The deaths continued, though the manner of the killings varied. Some victims gave their hearts, to be burned in a lava bowl on the altar to Hummingbird on the Left. Some were flayed and their skin worn by priests in honor of the dread Xipe Totec. Some of the black-smeared priests danced around costumed in the fresh skins while others set fire to a great paper snake wound around a pole.

Wise Coyote watched with a growing revulsion and anger that showed only in his clenched fists, hidden beneath his robe. He knew that Xipe Totec was not one of the original Aztec gods. Nor did the flayed god appear in the traditions of his own people, the Chichimecs. It was an import from the savage Zapotecs to the south and deserved no place among the sacred Aztec rites.

The savagery and frenzy of this new rite were probably what appealed to Ilhuicamina, Wise Coyote thought in dismay. He wanted desperately to leave, but could not. If he showed his revulsion by descending from the temple, it would be seen by others as a sign of weakness and, even worse, disloyalty.

He had endured the rest of that day by distancing all thoughts and sensations from his brain, and putting a mask of indifference on his face. He had used his body as a refuge, turning away from the evil outside, hiding behind his eyes like a coward.

And now, as he sat in his quarters at Ilhuicamina's palace, he remembered and was bitterly ashamed.

Could I not have done something to stop it?

He laughed, then cursed himself for a fool as he put aside his turquoise coronet and tried to eat. He remained on the throne of Texcoco only under Ilhuicamina's sufferance and by the ties of a family friendship. Trying to interfere with Ilhuicamina's religious ceremonies would earn him disfavor, perhaps even death. Texcoco might flaunt its independence, but it was a state of scholars and philosophers and would never stand up to the might of the Aztecs.

It is not death itself I fear, but what will happen to my people, he thought, staring without appetite at the tamale between his fingers. It was stuffed with that greatest and rarest of Aztec delicacies, the flesh of hairless dogs. He returned it to the dish. *Were I not king, I would stand up against these excesses. Or do these excuses come from the heart of the Deer, whose sign has followed me since birth?*

A hand drew the doorhanging aside, making Wise Coyote turn his head sharply. At the sight of Ilhuicamina, his throat tightened. He dropped his gaze, following the custom that no one, even the highest nobles, could look Ilhuicamina in the face while at court. At first he thought that the Aztec had come to upbraid him for not joining the feast, but the pensive expression on Ilhuicamina's face told him otherwise.

"Look up, look up," the Aztec ruler said impatiently. "That custom I keep only for those who would otherwise use me to gain their desires. You I count as exempt. Will you accept the company of your old friend?" Ilhuicamina asked, seating himself on the mat beside Wise Coyote. "Here. I have brought two cups of *chocolatl*."

Wise Coyote inhaled the steamy bitter aroma of cacao frothed with vanilla. He sipped, marveling at the fact that Ilhuicamina had served him with his own two hands.

"I see you have wearied of the feast." Ilhuicamina arranged his cloak about him and crossed his legs. He had put aside the ceremonial garb and plumes of the morning, though he still wore gold arm- and wristbands, ear and lip plugs. "I too am beginning to find it oppressive. The laughter is too loud, the jests too stale."

And the meat might not be to your taste tonight, Wise Coyote thought, knowing that roasted flesh from the thighs of sacrificial victims was probably among the dishes being served in the banquet hall.

"Perhaps you are thinking too hard about other things to enjoy the feast," Wise Coyote said cautiously. "If you wish to share your worries, I will listen."

A smile widened the impassive planes of the Aztec's face. "What a prize I have in the prince of Texcoco!" he exclaimed. "Not only are you wise in the ways of the world, but also in the things that trouble my heart. Yet you are younger than I. How did a stripling gain so much wisdom?"

By living through great trouble. By carrying my father's body to his pyre with my own hands and setting it alight. By living as a fugitive in the hills for most of my life, Wise Coyote thought.

He gave no indication that he recognized Ilhuicamina's words as the false flattery they were. "I do not know where my wisdom comes from," he said smoothly. "Take it as a gift from the gods and unburden yourself."

Ilhuicamina fell silent for a while, staring at the

murky surface of his cup of chocolatl. "Do you know," he said, "I remember the faces of the blessed ones I sacrificed today. I have never had a good memory for faces, yet those are etched in my memory as if they were my sons." He swirled his drink and Wise Coyote noticed the deep shadows under his eyes.

He cannot sleep. That is why he comes to me.

"The priests of Left-Handed Hummingbird keep saying that the victims should die in ecstacy, but ever since I have wielded the altar knife, I have seen only grimaces of fear that would dishearten the most resolute of men. Of course I am more determined than most, since I always kill them without hesitation, but the victims today seemed more reluctant." Ilhuicamina tipped up his cup, drinking in great swallows.

"Is it possible that these captives were not previously informed of the reason for their deaths?" Wise Coyote asked. "After all, they were Tlaxcalan and do not speak our dialect."

"By the green hair of Tlaloc, I never thought of that." Ilhuicamina raised his eyebrows. "That must be the reason, of course. I shall order the priests to have interpreters available for the captives of any nation so that they will know they are dying gloriously to feed Hummingbird on the Left."

I wonder how many will take comfort in knowing, thought Wise Coyote. He too had the images of faces engraved in his memory and the echoes of screams still resounded in his ears.

He looked at the lines about Ilhuicamina's mouth, the hard planes of the cheeks, slicked with sweat although the night was cool.

"What else troubles you, my friend?"

Ilhuicamina's eyes, when he lifted his gaze, were haunted. "Do you think I gave Hummingbird enough sacrifices?"

Wise Coyote had to clench his teeth together to keep from retching. Enough! He remembered the river of victims that had wound through the plaza and into the city, the killing that had gone on until late in the evening, the heavy odor of blood that still fouled the air of the city. Enough!

"I think you have been most generous," he managed to say, and hated himself for it.

"I could get more," said Ilhuicamina, in the tones of a small child trying to please his teacher. Then he struck his fist on the matting. "I vowed that Hummingbird on the Left would never have reason to turn from us again. My predecessors were mangy curs. Their stinginess cursed us with the years of want."

Wise Coyote drew a deep breath. If he confined his answers to mindless agreement, he would help bring about a future where the temple steps would be washed with blood day after day. If, on the other hand, he used friendship and influence to reason with his fellow ruler, he might be able to turn Ilhuicamina aside from such a course. But he would have to use the utmost tact and delicacy.

"My brother king," he said. "You have praised me, but you yourself are a man of great learning and wisdom. You have surrounded yourself with scholars who study the stars, the weather, and all other happenings in this world."

He saw that he had made a good opening. The Aztec ruler sat up straighter and expanded his chest.

"Use of that wisdom in explaining the world can exist side by side with reverence," Wise Coyote continued. "In fact, it complements devoutness. Any simpleminded fool can worship without understanding, but when an educated man understands and still worships, then that is a rare gift and the gods value it greatly."

"Yes, that is true," said Ilhuicamina, nodding with his chin on his hand.

"We can use wisdom to explore the nature of the gods as seen by our ancestors, who wrote the sacred texts. Those men recognized that the giving of life to the gods was the most sacred act they could perform. As befits a unique gift, they reserved the 'precious water' for the most special and auspicious occasions."

Ilhuicamina interrupted, "Did the gods not consider our ancestors to be mean and niggardly in their offerings? Were those rulers and their people not punished?"

"No," answered Wise Coyote. "The texts say nothing of divine displeasure. Crops were fruitful; people flourished. There were offerings of animals, fruits or flowers. The few victims who gave their lives each year were more than enough."

"Are you suggesting that I return to those ways?" The Aztec's brow wrinkled beneath the band of his royal blue coronet. Wise Coyote plunged on, feeling a coldness on the skin of his chest, as if an obsidian sword blade were touching him there.

"I am only saying that Hummingbird's thirst may not be as great as you assume," Wise Coyote said earnestly.

"The priests tell me that he is always thirsty. He has always been thirsty. The drought came because he was left unsatisfied."

I have learned that priests tell you what will benefit them, not their god. Wise Coyote left the thought unspoken. Instead he said, "If that is true, how then did our ancestors flourish, grow their crops and build cities?"

"Are you sure that they went unpunished?" Ilhuicamina asked.

"I will show you the sacred texts and you can read the truth for yourself."

"Perhaps the gods become thirstier as they age," Ilhuicamina grumbled to himself, but Wise Coyote could see that he did not accept his own argument.

He pressed on. "Would it not relieve your heart to discover that Hummingbird is not so demanding as you fear? That he does not really need the blood of the many that you have generously given and he is not angry because you cannot give more?"

There. He had said it. If Ilhuicamina were to condemn him for heresy, it would be now. Perhaps his position as creator of the aqueduct that Tenochtitlán so badly needed would save him from the Aztec's capricious wrath.

For an instant the Aztec king looked at him doubtfully, but then a look of wonder came across Ilhuicamina's face, making his expression as radiant as a child's. "The god has not been angry with us? Oh, how wonderful it would be if that were really true. Then I could sleep and not feel so afraid."

"Why can't it be true?" asked Wise Coyote gently, putting a hand on his friend's shoulder, yet inside he had to fight to overcome feelings of outrage and anger. He knew he would have little sleep tonight after having witnessed a river of people meet their deaths on the temple steps. Why should Ilhuicamina expect an untroubled sleep?

"Why can't it be true?" the Aztec whispered, staring ahead at nothing. "Oh, to be freed from this burden. A part of me sickens of endless war and temple-building, although I would have no one know it but you."

"Listen to the part of your heart that speaks so." Wise Coyote chose his words with care, praying that he had at last found a way to reach his friend. He sensed that Ilhuicamina was standing on the threshold of a new turn in his life, a new freedom and joy for himself and perhaps for his people.

And then something mean and petty, born of long-held grief, rose up in Wise Coyote.

Why should he know happiness? He killed my son!

The words that might have helped Ilhuicamina cross the threshold, throw off the bonds of fear that bound him to his god, remained unspoken. There was only silence between the two men. Wise Coyote saw the moment of enlightenment slip away, then the doors of fear slammed shut again, locking Ilhuicamina's soul behind them.

"No. I dare not even dream of the possibility. I must keep Hummingbird on the Left sated or all will crumble. I must root out any weakness that keeps me from that duty. Do not tempt me, old friend. Tenochtitlán cannot become another scholar's paradise like your Texcoco."

Wise Coyote tried again, using other lines of reasoning. He spoke of the original reason for human sacrifice. Its power came from its gravity and rarity, he said. To pile bodies before the altar like sticks of cordwood only cheapened the value of such offerings. Like any man overfed on sumptuous dishes, the god's palate would surely grow jaded.

He also pointed out that the grotesque flaying rites of Xipe Totec were not part of the original Toltec or Aztec religions at all, but were imported from the savage Zapotecs of the south.

It made no difference to Ilhuicamina. Wise Coyote heard his own voice grow hollow in his ears. All the wisdom and reason in the world could not sway a man driven by consuming dread of the divinities he was forced to serve.

Perhaps the Aztecs had come too far on the path of blood and fire to turn from it now. The subject peoples and even the states of the Triple Alliance seethed with resentment against the Aztecs. Ilhuicamina spoke the truth, bitter as it was. If he halted the wars of conquest and the taking of sacrificial victims, the entire Aztec edifice might well crumble or Ilhuicamina would be overthrown by the powerful priesthood and the warrior class.

Yet Wise Coyote was haunted by the feeling that if he had found the right words, Ilhuicamina could have found the right ways. The greatest restraint on the Aztec was not the threat from priests or warriors but his own gut-consuming dread of the god he had been raised to serve.

He found Ilhuicamina eyeing him narrowly and wondered if the Aztec resented him for waving such an impossible temptation or despised him for his weakness in not being able to tolerate this new version of sacrifice on such a mass scale.

And today's slaughter, Wise Coyote thought in despair, *is only the beginning.*

"I will leave you now," said Ilhuicamina, draining his cup. "Your words and a draught of octli will help me sleep." He rose, bid Wise Coyote good evening, then disappeared through the doorhanging.

The king of Texcoco stared numbly at the tapestry, still swinging from Ilhuicamina's passage.

If I had truly cared, if I had spoken to him out of the fullness of my heart, I might have eased his terror so that his wisdom could come forth, Wise Coyote thought. *Instead I let myself become distracted by hate. I wanted him to suffer and bleed, like the victims he has slain. Like my son. Oh gods, it was such a little weakness, yet such a great one!*

With a sigh, he lay down upon his mat. As drowsiness numbed his mind, he wondered how long the Aztec state would be able to sustain Ilhuicamina's increasing demand for victims.

Remember, thought Wise Coyote, recalling the blood-splashed image of Hummingbird on the Left and addressing it directly in his thoughts. *You took two pairs of sandals when you left home as a young warrior. One to stride forth in victory, the other to return in defeat. You are wearing the first pair now, but the time will come when you must change to the second.*

9

THE WARMTH OF the morning sun tempted Mixcatl to leave her quarters in the House of Scribes and go down into the courtyard. She decided not to.

The throat-choking odor of burned blood hung like a shroud over the city. To the other scribes and apprentices, the stink was disturbing and annoying. To Mixcatl, with her acute sense of smell, the odor was a torment.

The first day of the ceremony, she stood with the other apprentices, who craned their heads out of the large upper window of the House of Scribes, watching the crowds that filled the streets, and the line of victims that marched up Hummingbird's pyramid to the altar at the top. The House, though within the walls of the temple precinct, was distant enough from the pyramid so that the young apprentices could not see the details of slaughter. They had to make do with imagination, but for Mixcatl, the black plume rising like smoke from a volcano spoke not only of endless death but of terror so intense as to bring on madness.

She could not stay among the other slaves at the window, but fled to an inner room, her hands over her nose, her body shaking so badly that she staggered. Sick and sweating, she fell onto a pallet, buried her nose in the reedy smell of matting and tried to gain control of herself. She raged at the strangeness within her that she knew was at the root of the attack, the same strangeness that had made her draw a dancing jaguar on a soot-blackened tile in the calmecac and had made a spotted pelt in the marketplace come to life and wound its buyer.

And now it had betrayed her by making her feel panicked and nauseated by the smell of mass offerings. She had fought long and hard to push away all the revulsion she had felt for this aspect of the religion, and finally, she felt, she had won. She believed what Speaking Quail had taught her. Sacrifice preserved the world from the disaster that threatened to fall upon it at any moment. Nothing was born, nothing endured, without the gift of the 'precious water' from the human breast.

Yet she, because of the strangeness within her, could not bear the way that the world had to be. At that realization, she despaired and wept, soaking the matting through with tears. How could she continue in the House of Scribes now that all the apprentices knew her weakness? How would Speaking Quail react when he discovered her failure?

The soft sound of a door flap opening made Mixcatl cower. Surely a report of her behavior had reached the Master of Scribes. Now he was coming to upbraid her, to demand that she be dragged to the marketplace and unceremoniously sold.

Unable to bear the tension of not knowing who had entered, she lifted her tear-slick face from her hands. Her eyes widened. It was not the Master of Scribes at all, but her tutor and gadfly, Nine-Lizard Iguana Tongue.

At the sight of him, she felt both relief and dismay. Since their first encounter after his arrival, she had met the challenge that he offered, struggling to bring her drawings up to his standards. As he predicted, sharp words had often been exchanged between them. After her initial frustration, Mixcatl had begun to feel the exhilaration of having her ability stretched and worked by a teacher worthy of her best effort.

"I saw you go flying past my chamber, Seven-Flower, and I thought I'd better see what was happening," said Nine-Lizard as he let the door flap drop behind him. "What is all this about, hey?"

Mixcatl was strongly tempted to tell him to take his iguana's neck and tongue somewhere else, but she caught a fresh wave of the burned-blood scent on the air that Nine-Lizard had let into the room. Queasiness and despair overwhelmed her once again.

In the midst of her retching sobs, she felt a cool dry hand touch her arm. An open deerskin bag was put into her hand and guided to her face. She inhaled the aromas of spicy herbs and mountain flowers, finding that it helped to banish both sickness and terror.

She breathed gratefully, trying to keep her tears from falling on the brushed deerskin and making stains. Then, as the worst of the feeling dissipated, she found that she could hold the open bag beneath her chin so that she could speak while still inhaling the perfume of its contents.

"I do not know what is the matter with me," she said at last. "I was standing at the window, watching the ceremony, although I could not really see it since the pyramid is too far away. When the smell came, it filled up my mind with horrible things. I did not even think. I just ran away."

With fear starting to thin her voice, she said, "Everybody saw me. They will all think I hate the ceremony. I tried hard with Speaking Quail. I believe what he taught me, I really do. But when the Master of Scribes hears what I did, I will be thrown out."

"I do not think so," said Nine-Lizard gently.

"But I am a troublemaker. I lose my temper and call

you names. I try to paint differently than I should. And when the priests do good things, like burning hearts to keep the sun in the sky, I run away from the smell.''

She faltered, for at the phrase ''good things,'' Nine-Lizard had let a grimace cross his face.

''Oooh,'' she breathed. ''You do not like it either!''

The old scribe looked a little discomfited, as if he had not meant to reveal his feelings. He looked away.

''I saw your face,'' said Mixcatl.

Gruffly, Nine-Lizard replied, ''All right. It is true. It is not just the smell I dislike. I find these events excessively bloody. That is why I spent the day in my quarters instead of down in the plaza with the other scribes.''

''The Master of Scribes let you stay away?''

''He allows me certain privileges because of my skill. You have shown evidence of similar ability, so he will not throw you out.''

Mixcatl felt a little better, but she was curious how he had known what was the matter with her and what to bring.

''I had prepared the herbs for myself,'' the old man said, but he refused to let Mixcatl return the bag. ''No, I am not so sensitive to the smell as I used to be. Keep it.''

She sat beside him in silence for a while, feeling confused. He had shown a side of himself she had never seen before, a kind, caring grandfatherly side. Yet he had also revealed the same sort of distaste for the Aztec rituals that she had struggled so hard to overcome.

''Nine-Lizard,'' she said, solemnly, her chin on her knees. ''I am puzzled by something.''

''Ask it, then.''

''If the sacrifices of the ceremonies are good and necessary, as Speaking Quail has taught me, how can anyone dislike them? Yet you do, and I do not think you are a bad man. My stomach does not like them either and it is not usually a bad stomach.''

"I think your stomach has more sense in it than most men's heads," answered Nine-Lizard, with one of his rare sharp grins.

"But if the world will end without the giving of blood," Mixcatl began, then faltered. She knew it was dangerous to bring her doubts into the open, even to someone who seemed to share them. And the fact that he did seem to share them made speaking with him even more dangerous than ever.

He seemed to sense her uneasiness, for he made a move as if to get up and leave the mat.

"Please do not go, Nine-Lizard," Mixcatl said softly.

He sighed. "You are troubled, aren't you? By all rights, I should not stay and speak to you of such things, but my conscience is forcing me." He took a breath. "Seven-Flower Mixcatl, what Speaking Quail is teaching you is the prevalent belief, but that does not mean it is the only one."

"I know that there are other gods besides Hummingbird on the Left," Mixcatl said. "But they all demand blood."

"Some do not. When you are handed crumbling manuscripts to copy, you will see references to older gods and older ways. Do not turn your back on these stories as many priests and scribes do now. Read and understand them and then you may see that the Aztec religion is not the only path open to you."

"I have to learn what Speaking Quail teaches me or I can not become a scribe," she answered.

"Learn the texts then, but do not let their words rule you or plunge your thoughts into gloom. You deserve better than that," he added, with a peculiar intent look in his eyes. Then he gathered his robes together, saying that he had work to do in his chamber. Mixcatl might keep the bag of herbs and return it to him once the bothersome scent had been blown away by the winds sweeping down from the peaks about the city.

10

EARLY THE FOLLOWING morning, Wise Coyote prepared to leave his guest quarters at Ilhuicamina's palace and return home across the lake. He was looking forward to walking in Tezcotzinco's gardens and breathing the fresh wind from the hills. Though the event honoring Hummingbird was supposed to be a celebration, the spectacle of mass sacrifices seemed to have cast a heavy gloom over Tenochtitlán. Even Ilhuicamina seemed sobered by what he had done. Perhaps he would think twice about doing it again, Wise Coyote thought, as he directed servants to pack his feathered cloaks and gold ear and lip plugs.

He did not welcome the interruption when a servant lifted the door flap to tell him that he had a visitor. He had a good idea who it was. At Nine-Lizard's suggestion, he had sent spies to watch the House of Scribes and had arranged so that the old scribe could send word to him via these agents.

Everyone cleared the room so that the king could speak alone with his spy, who had brought a message from Nine-Lizard. At first Wise Coyote was annoyed, for nothing momentous had happened. Mixcatl, the young apprentice that Nine-Lizard had spoken about, would be leaving the House of Scribes later that morning on an errand. If the king was to see the girl for himself without letting anyone know his interest, he should disguise himself and wait at the small side-entrance to the House.

After directing his servants to resume packing without him, he exchanged his royal finery for a simple maguey-fiber loincloth, a plain mantle and rope sandals. He always had these garments with him, for he frequently adopted disguises and mixed with the crowds. Doing so had enabled him to learn much more about what people expected and wanted of a king, helping him to rule wisely.

Smearing stain on himself to darken the bronze of his skin he removed his gold ear plugs and chose a wide-brimmed hat to shade his face. Wise Coyote made sure no servants saw him as he slipped out of his quarters in the palace and down to the plaza outside.

Pressing close to the dew-moistened side of the wall surrounding the complex that included the House of Scribes, Wise Coyote watched the small side-entrance through which the girl would probably come. From his position he could also cover the main gate, although it was used for ceremonial purposes. It was unlikely that a young slave-scribe would pass that way.

The sun was touching the top of the wall when Wise Coyote heard the sound of bare feet on flagstones. He drew back as someone came out of the side entrance.

The girl was young, but she had none of the delicacy or childish vulnerability that Wise Coyote had seen in other girl-children. She was taller than he expected, broader through the shoulders than the hips. Her arms, beneath the sleeves of her huipil blouse, had the length and power of a man's, yet her limbs were smooth and well shaped. Her hands were wide and her fingers short and blunt.

Yet it was her face that captured and held his attention. At first he thought her ugly, for she was far from the Aztec standard of female beauty. Her forehead was high instead of slanted back, the bridge of her nose dished in instead of straight. The space between the base of her nose and her upper lip was swallowed up by the strongly bowed shape of her mouth. Her head was entirely the wrong shape, rectangular and blocky, like the head of the Olmec figure who was carrying the jaguar-baby in the composite greenstone statuette.

With a shock, Wise Coyote realized that her face indeed echoed that of the Olmec image. But how different her visage was from the half-feral, half-idiot blank-eyed gaze of the Olmec figurine. Although the proportions of her face were the same—short nose, full jaw, high forehead, squared flattened ears and arched brows—her features combined to form an impression of intelligence and an exotic uniqueness that unexpectedly became beauty.

Perhaps it was her eyes, Wise Coyote decided. Hers had the same narrowed slanting form as the statuette's, but the figure's eyes were shallow pits, dug in the greenstone, empty of anything except perhaps a coldness that chilled the heart. The girl's eyes were a rich brown, with amber flecks that caught and danced in the sunlight as she turned her head.

Or perhaps her mouth. Her lips were full and as strongly bowed as the figurine's, but they had none of the imperious petulance carved on the mouth of the statuette. Instead her own character had shaped them, so that their shape spoke of patience, determination and a sense of humor. At the same time, the swell of her lower lip resembled the curve in the outthrust petal of a flower, and Wise Coyote found himself wondering if it would have the same silken feel against his own lips.

The thought and the sudden reaction it produced startled Wise Coyote. No, this Mixcatl was yet a child, he told himself. He had come here to learn what clues she might give that would aid his search for a true power to stand against the bloody might of the Aztecs, not to indulge in lustful fantasies.

He had spent so much time in thought that the girl had gone though the entrance and was far down the stone walkway that led to the canals. Scolding himself under his breath for becoming distracted, he prepared to leave his hiding place in the shadow cast by the wall.

He halted at the sight of a group of boys who crept onto the path after the girl had turned a corner. He saw quickly that the children had set one of their number on watch and this sentinel now beckoned his compatriots to follow. They moved stealthily, like hunters after prey. Some carried sticks.

Wise Coyote frowned and stroked his chin. He had thought he was the only one intending to shadow the young apprentice. It surprised him to find that she was being trailed by others, even if they were just children.

What were the boys after, he wondered. Was this a game of simple childish persecution or an indication of something more sinister?

His first instinct was to intercede and disperse the band, but he knew that such action and resulting ruckus would only alert the girl to his presence. No, better let the boys continue their hunt, although he would try to get between them and their quarry.

When the boys had passed, Wise Coyote heard the soft slap of someone running barefoot. As he hid again, he saw a wiry long-limbed youth appear from a different direction. The boy was running as fast as he could, yet trying to stay quiet. His eyes, beneath a wild shock of hair, were angry and his jaw set. On his upper lip was an odd black patch. The water stains on his ragged loincloth and the dried mud on his legs told Wise Coyote that the boy was probably one of the waterfront people of the city.

The youth slowed for an instant, as if afraid of getting too close, then cautiously ran on.

Wise Coyote scowled, puzzled and annoyed. What was this canal boy up to? Was he on an errand of his own, or with the others, or running to aid the girl?

Silently he slipped from the concealment of the wall's shadow and followed.

Morning in Tenochtitlán was dazzling and the sun sparked off the canals, turning the muddy depths gold. Mixcatl, walking back from the open-air market where she had finished her errand, wanted to stop on the canal bank and enjoy her surroundings.

She halted once, thinking she had lost the children who were following her. Perhaps at last she could stand at the canalside without being molested. Perhaps she could smell, see and experience the city with all the depth of her senses, and capture part of it as a picture in her mind. She doubted that she would ever paint that picture, for it was too different from the formalized figures used by the glyph-painters and record-keepers in the House of Scribes.

The sound of sandals against pavement, hoarse shouts and the clack of sticks jolted her from her reverie and sent her hurrying on, eyes tearing, teeth grinding with anger. The boys from the calmecac. It was a market holiday and they had escaped their teachers. What better sport on a beautiful sunny morning than to gather in packs like wolves and descend upon the enemy they hated most?

It had been years since she left the calmecac, but its students remembered the incident with the tile picture and the ensuing uproar. They had made a point of teasing or harassing her whenever they could.

Perhaps they were preparing for their role later in life, the girl thought.

She knew that Six-Wind still attended the calmecac. He came to see Mixcatl and often walked with her on errands to provide her some protection from his schoolmates. Today he was not here and she was fair prey for the other boys. Even though time had passed, the hatred was slow to die. It had been kept alive by certain priest-tutors in the school who had lost face when Mixcatl was given to the House of Scribes instead of being sacrificed.

She pulled her robe more tightly about her shoulders and walked faster. The matron in charge of the younger slave-scribes had sent her to buy chilies today and she had a string of them. Now all she had to do was reach the House of Scribes before the boys caught up with her. She thought about breaking into a run, for she knew her fleetness. No. That would only encourage them to chase her. And even if she could outdistance them, her pride rebelled at running away.

So she kept her step even though she trembled all over with fear and a growing rage that frightened her almost as much as did the boys themselves.

Then came the taunts.

Slave, slave, ugliest one beneath the sun
All you are fit for is emptying dung.

Mixcatl huddled beneath her cloak and increased her pace. A quick look back told her there were five tormentors, ranging in age from eight to fourteen. She was fourteen and strong for her age, but as a slave, she dare not strike out against them.

Slave, slave, you must obey this
Open your mouth to receive our . . .

Shuddering, Mixcatl covered her ears and walked on but the slap of sandals was all about her. Her tormentors capered around her like demons. She turned sharply from the canal, hoping to shake them off, but they stayed with her. A stone hit her back. A stick was thrust between her ankles, tripping her. She stumbled and walked on, holding tightly to the string of chilies.

Now she was in an area of rich houses, whose walls and courtyards formed a maze. She saw at once that she had made a mistake and tried to get back to the canal, but the boys blocked her at every turn, singing their chant and slapping their sticks against their hands.

And then, suddenly, she was trapped in a small courtyard. She looked over the boys' heads, hoping to spot some passersby, but away from the canal the pavements were deserted.

Until now, fear and self-control had kept her mute. In a choked voice she shouted, "Go away! I must bring back these chilies."

The boys laughed and the oldest one said, "That will wait. We have another task for you. Kneel down."

Mixcatl hunched her shoulders, glaring at him. He looked like all the others, copper faces flushed, lips drawn back in glee. Their hands were white at the knuckles, tight about their sticks.

A sharp shout drew Mixcatl's attention to another boy who ran into the courtyard. Latosl!

"Leave her alone!" Latosl's black-marked lip curled. "Nobleman's spawn! Filth from the dung jar of a calmecac!"

The boatboy rushed at the oldest of Mixcatl's tormentors, arms flung wide, mouth snarling, hair flying. As he attacked, she tried to dodge between three others who were starting to encircle her. Hands jerked her back.

Wiry and strong, Latosl was a match for one boy, but not two. Mixcatl caught only glimpses of his battle as she struggled against her own captors. Her last glance caught him belly-down on the plaza with two boys astride him.

One bounced fiercely on Latosl's rump while the other leaned forward, two hands pressing a heavy stick across the back of Latosl's neck.

A blow struck the back of the girl's legs, making her crumple forward onto her knees. The chilies slid from her fingers. Hands seized her hair, jerking her head back. Other hands pulled her arms up behind her. A sandal stepped on her leg behind the heel, grinding the top of her foot into the pavement.

The oldest boy came up to her, stood over her. He was so close that her chin brushed the fabric of his loincloth. He stared down at her, eyes slitted, nostrils flared, tongue caressing his lower lip.

"Open your mouth," he said.

Mixcatl clenched her teeth. An odd rippling passed across her vision, distorting the boy's face for an instant. An instant of panic followed the sweep of anger. Something was going to happen. Something terrible.

"Do not do this," she begged, and sensed that she was pleading not only for herself but for their sakes as well. "Smoking Mirror will curse you."

The youth struck her face. "Open, pisspot."

Another boy kicked her in the ribs while a third jerked her head far back. Mixcatl clamped her jaws harder, then lifted her lips to bare her teeth. The ripples washed through her vision at the same rate as the waves of anger sweeping through her.

The oldest youth pushed the butt of his stick against the girl's jaw. "Open or I will break your teeth."

The ripples became faster, deeper, devouring the color in her vision. Fury grew in Mixcatl, leaping about inside her, seeking a place to go. She remembered how her rage had animated a jaguar pelt and how the claws had raked its buyer. But there was no pelt here; these enemies wore only cotton loincloths.

With no escape, the rage raced around inside her

body, rushing forward into her face, her eyes, her defiantly clamped jaws. Latosl's choked yelling resounded in her ear. Her wrists began to burn and itch in the grasp of the youth behind her. The end of the stick tapped against her teeth, hit again, harder.

She twisted her wrists against her captor's grip. The burning intensified. And then the skin on her arms seemed to break and release a slippery fluid that let her wrists turn in the hands of her captor.

From a place dim and far away behind the pulsing of her rage, she heard the boy who held her arms cry out in dismay, "Ai! The filth bleeds! Her skin is coming off!"

Now the burning and itching was in her mouth, in the very roots of her teeth and in the bones of her jaws. Her sight blurred as her face was wrenched by a pulling sensation. It was in her back teeth now, lifting them up, higher in the jaw, drawing them to a tongue-scraping sharpness.

She yanked her wrists free. As she drew her arms up, she felt her hands curl. Now panic added to her rage, for she did not know what was happening to her.

The savage triumph in the boy's face above her crumpled into uncertainty, then fright. At the sight of his contorted features, an entirely new emotion seized her, a savage rejoicing at the smell and sight of human fear. As she grinned, she felt the points of her front teeth slide past her lower lip.

Above her was the youth, still frozen by terror and disbelief. She no longer saw his face. Her gaze narrowed to the pulsing patch of copper skin at his throat.

Curling her body in a way she had never been able to do before, she launched herself up at him, head turning, teeth seeking the throb of life at the throat, hands raking down with nails grown strangely long and curved, catching in cloth, tearing . . .

Her enemy fell away, shrieking. Sticks descended on

Mixcatl, striking her head, her shoulders, her back. She lunged after the others, stumbling because her legs no longer worked the way they had.

The colors in her vision bleached to faded hues, dominated by blacks, whites and edges, making her sharply aware of every move going on around her. To one side the boat-boy sprawled, held down by the youths on top of him. Her sense of smell, already acute, sharpened until the odors flooding her nose threatened to wipe out thoughts of anything else. The itching and tingling sensation moved up her arms, making her scratch and tear her skin even as she lunged at her tormentors.

. The boys fled, leaving the half-choked boat-boy and the youth who had fainted. Her fallen tormentor lay on his front, his arms outflung. Bent over in a strange crouch, she circled back and went down beside him on hands and feet. She reached to turn him over, but her arm no longer moved in the way she was used to. Dexterity was fading from her hands, her thumb and fingers stubbornly lying together so that she could only make pawing motions. She had to hook her nails into the boy's clothing to drag him over. The cotton cloth tore and fell away.

Attracted by the sight and smell of warm flesh, she sniffed along his belly and then an ancient instinct came and she bared her teeth for the bite into his gut.

Something made her lift her head and stare into the boy's face, now made relaxed and childlike by the faint that had come over him. It raised a feeling of disquiet and she moved away from the body, staring out over the canal. She had seen something once, a vision that danced in gold and fire. A vision she wanted to capture and keep. With these new eyes, she could no longer see the beauty, and something locked away inside her felt the loss and mourned.

What came from her mouth was not the cry of a young girl but a thundering growl that seemed to reverberate off

the walls. A part of her spirit felt trapped, frightened.
Moving on hands and feet, she began to circle at a rapid
pace, so fast that everything blurred before her eyes.

Suddenly she was seized by a feeling of weariness so
deep and overwhelming that her head fell until her nose
was near the ground. She staggered and toppled, landing
heavily on her side. The almost unbearable intensity of
her smell sense faded, the itching and burning in her skin
ended and color returned to her vision before darkness
closed down around her.

Wise Coyote ran down the path that led to the courtyard,
listening to the sound of the children's shrieks. He had
forgotten how fast children could run when hunting
down and tormenting an enemy. Or perhaps Mixcatl's
visit to the market without being attacked had made him
relax his guard, thinking that the youngsters had given
up.

Raising a fist, he charged in, yelling, but he saw that
something else had put the boys to flight before he arrived. A diminishing clatter of sandals told him that most
of the gang had gotten beyond his reach. Three figures
were left, two down, one still moving.

One was the canal brat he had seen earlier. The boy lay
on his stomach, his head turned away, a stick still lying
across his neck. He was gasping, as if he had been choked
nearly to insensibility. Wise Coyote stooped beside the
half-strangled boy, took the stick off his neck and rolled
him over. He could do nothing else except leave him
alone to gather his breath.

Another youth lay on his back nearby, thighs gashed,
loincloth torn. Over him crouched the girl. Wise Coyote
could not see her face, but the way she held her body and
moved her limbs made him think of a great cat, an animal that had somehow become trapped inside a human
form.

Or was her form entirely human? Her torso seemed to have deepened, lengthened, pulling apart the ties of her skirt. Her limbs had become more powerful and massive, stretching the sleeves of her blouse. Her entire figure seemed to have become larger.

No. It was his imagination. It was the glare of the sun on the pavement and the fear beating through him. He took a step closer and saw something else. The copper of her skin was shadowed by an indistinct darkness, especially on her arms.

He watched as she lowered her face to the fallen youth's loins and then his belly. Was it a distortion in his vision caused by fear, or had her face taken on not only the feral grimace of a beast but the very lines of an animal's skull? Her lip drew back, exposing teeth that gleamed and seemed to grow longer, but her hair fell across her face, curtaining off his view.

Wise Coyote was already fighting off feelings of unreality, but he felt a stab of pure horror when he heard the growling and coughing sounds coming from her. The flash of sunlight on teeth told him that she was about to savage her prey before his eyes.

With the canal boy's harsh gasping still in his ears, Wise Coyote rose into an attack crouch, his hand starting toward the dagger in the hipband of his loincloth.

Before he could draw the dagger, she lifted her head and seemed to study her victim's face. As if in revulsion, she turned away, stared out at the canal. She shivered, threw back her head and gave a mixture of roaring and wailing, with an anguish so deep it tore at the heart.

Beside her victim she circled and then abruptly fell on her side. With a shudder and sigh she was still.

Wise Coyote eased his weight from one foot to the next. What would happen next? There were no other people nearby; they were all in the major plazas for the market. He took a step toward the girl, trying not to imagine how she might suddenly rise up and turn on him.

Behind him, the canal boy sat up, coughing. The boy on the ground lay still. Beside him was Mixcatl, motionless on her side. No. Wise Coyote looked again. She was moving—shrinking—like something damp drying in the sun. Perhaps the unknown change was reversing itself. In another few steps he was sure. The animal grimace was gone, the lines of her face once again the same as they had been when he watched her leaving the House of Scribes.

He bent first beside the young male victim, whose eyes were fluttering. Quickly he dragged the boy aside, into the shelter of an oleander bush. The youth had been raked along both thighs, but other than that and the ripped loincloth, he had suffered no injury except fright.

He patted the boy's cheeks, none too gently. From a distance he had heard the puerile chant and its message of degradation. With a sudden jerk the youth came awake.

"No! Keep her away!" His voice cracked to a whisper. His eyes were wild in remembered terror.

"May your mouth be filled with your own filthy water," Wise Coyote hissed at him. "The gods have dealt you punishment. May you find a lie to explain your disfigurement that your teachers will believe. Be gone!"

Shuddering, the youth got to his feet, took one look at the girl, still motionless on the pavement, and fled.

Wise Coyote turned to the canal boy, hoping for some explanation, but the boy was still in the midst of a coughing fit.

With a deep sigh, the king wiped his hands on his robe and carefully approached Mixcatl. Now she looked normal again—she could have been a young slave who had passed out in the growing heat and had crumpled to the ground. For an instant Wise Coyote's mind played tricks on him, making him wonder if he had really imagined the incident that had just taken place.

Carefully he knelt beside her, slipping his fingers between the hot moist skin of her arm and the sun-warmed pavement in order to feel the wrist pulse. He found it, fast and strong, but lost count when he saw something strange. On both forearms her skin had split deeply and peeled back, leaving a raw area. In the red and oozing flesh, he saw an odd stubble, like the hairs on a shaven head. Fighting a surge of alarm and revulsion, he studied her face, struck again by the way her features echoed those of the Olmec statuette. Yet there was something else that reminded him of the jaguar-baby that the Olmec figure was holding. He couldn't tell what, but some obscure impulse made him put his other hand on her head, feeling in her hair. The jaguar-infant in the composite statuette had been depicted with a definite cleft in the skull. No doubt that was symbolic or iconographic, not the true representation of a living being.

He was still telling himself that even as his fingers felt beneath her hair, traveling over the bones of her head, and slipped into a strange indentation that split the crown of her head so that her skull was slightly double-domed. Hidden beneath her hair, the malformation was not something that would be visible to mar her appearance, but it was definitely present.

So the statuette wasn't just a flight of morbid fancy, he thought, feeling cold, despite the sunlight spilling into the plaza. As he finished the pulse count and pulled his hand away, her skin broke like a water blister, a piece of it coming away on his fingertips.

Repulsed despite his sympathy for the girl, he shook his hand as if he had touched something filthy, then wiped his fingers on his robe. He wondered if he had perhaps pressed too hard in his haste and somehow injured the girl's wrist. No. Skin didn't break like that unless it was blistered, burned or diseased. He had spent enough time among his healers, watching them tend the sick, to know that this was not normal.

Disquieted, he bent over, trying to examine Mixcatl without touching her again. Curiosity won out over caution, if only for an instant. Folding his hand in the fabric of his robe, Wise Coyote lifted Mixcatl's left hand, seeing that the raw area, with its odd growth of stubbled hair, extended all the way around her forearm. A band of thin, whitened skin—her own, Wise Coyote thought, with another jolt of horror—hung loose about her wrist like a macabre bracelet.

Part of his mind screamed that she was a demon or one accursed by the gods, perhaps even a black deity. Another part sought for a rational explanation. Was this the strange peeling away of skin shown on the Olmec statuette?

A sound behind the king warned that the canal boy had recovered enough to get to his feet. Wise Coyote turned to meet him, but instead of attacking, the youth tried to drop down on his knees beside Mixcatl. Wise Coyote seized him and held him away.

"She wounded the other boy. Do not go near her."

The boy ignored the warning, then called out as Wise Coyote tried to restrain him, "Mixcatl!" The girl stirred weakly in response.

"What? You know her name?" Wise Coyote said in surprise.

The youth looked at him with astonishment and suspicion. His breathing was still hoarse. "How do you know who she is? Who are you?"

"One who does not like to see anyone mistreated," answered Wise Coyote mildly. "What is your name?"

"You didn't give me yours," the boy retorted, but he shrank a little under Wise Coyote's glower. "All right. Latosl."

"Those boys were choking you. Did you attempt to interfere?"

The boy squinted at Wise Coyote, the black-marked side of his lip drawn up. A bruise showed along the side of his chin where his jaw had been shoved against the pavement. He nodded, rubbing the bruise.

Wise Coyote studied him, a suspicion growing. As an apprentice in the House of Scribes, Mixcatl rarely went outside it. He himself would not have known of her departure unless word had come from Nine-Lizard via his own spy. How could a scruffy canal brat have gotten the same information? And that gang of boys?

"They found her by watching me," Latosl confessed after some questioning.

"And how did you know she would be leaving the House of Scribes?"

"I talk with her on the dock when I come by to dump the jars. We are friends."

The answer came too quickly and glibly for Wise Coyote's taste. Even though he and the boy seemed to be on the same side, the youth was evasive and tricky. He grabbed Latosl's upper arm.

"You know more than you are telling," he said, watching the boy's face. "Someone sent you to watch her."

Latosl couldn't meet Wise Coyote's gaze. "Yes," he said softly.

"Who?"

"I do not know."

Wise Coyote shook him.

"I swear. I hear only a voice. I never see a face."

"Someone must come and give you money for your services."

"No." Latosl shook his head.

"If you are not paid, why then do you do it?"

Latosl gave an odd little smile. "You would not believe the reason."

Try as he might, Wise Coyote could get nothing more out of the boy. At last he said, "We waste time chattering. We must move the girl away from here, for her own good and for that of others."

"The House of Scribes is too far and we will surely be noticed," said Latosl. "If we load her on my boat, I will return her to the House."

Wise Coyote was suspicious, but he couldn't think of any other alternative, so he agreed.

Wise Coyote stripped off his cloak and used it to make a sling to carry the girl. The boy took the front, since he knew where he was going. Wise Coyote, clad only in his loincloth, grasped the rear.

By Quetzalcoatl's feathers, she's heavy!

The boatboy moved with surprising speed, despite the weight of his burden. Wise Coyote was sweating and beginning to wonder if they were carrying a human body or a stone statue. He also felt a sense of trepidation. Here he was, following a lower-class youth through the city. Did the boy have any idea that his fellow stretcher-bearer was the king of Texcoco?

The morning only grew hotter as the two neared the canal. Wise Coyote had expected at least a market boat or peasant's dugout; when he saw the old refuse barge, he groaned.

"Help me get Mixcatl aboard," said the boy coldly. "Then go."

Wise Coyote was tempted to do just that, for the stink of the barge, the boat boy's rude manner and the girl's peeling skin all repelled him. He wanted to go and cleanse himself in a steambath and make offerings to ward off any malign influence.

The boatboy helped him lower Mixcatl to the decked-over bow. Wise Coyote arranged his cloak to form a pallet and pillow for her. She was still deeply asleep.

The boatboy scrambled along the barge, casting off ropes, then halted before he let go of the last one, expecting Wise Coyote to jump off.

The king felt irritated. He had given up his cloak, been thoroughly frightened by the incident he had witnessed, endured Latosl's rudeness and was now being dismissed. He had learned a little, but it had only served to mystify him further. And Latosl wouldn't give him any more answers.

For an instant, he was tempted to reveal his status and demand that the boatboy explain everything. Then, inwardly, he laughed at his foolishness. He didn't have a shred of proof to back up his claim to royalty.

He jumped down and stood on the dock. Somehow even proving that he was tlatoani of Texcoco would not impress this strong-willed youth. He would probably have to throw Latosl into the canal a few times to get any more answers and this might attract attention that he didn't want.

The boat began to drift away from the bank, swinging outward in the sluggish current.

The boatboy waved at him and called, "Do not worry about Mixcatl. She will be fine."

Wise Coyote stood on the quay, the sun beating down on his bare shoulders, for he had left his cloak on the boat. Inside the band of his loincloth was a small pouch of cocoa beans, enough to buy another cheap garment for the walk back to his quarters in the palace. With a shrug, he turned toward the marketplace.

The same evening that he returned to his retreat at Tezcotzinco, Wise Coyote studied the two serpentine statuettes that stood on the window ledge where he had left them. He kept his hands together behind his back, fearing to touch either figure. If the tradition they represented had true power, they might be dangerous. He trembled a little inside, recalling how the skin on Mixcatl's wrist had loosened and then fallen away beneath his fingers.

Again he wiped his fingertips on his tunic, an act that had become an obsession in the few days since he had returned from Tenochtitlán. His fears of witchcraft had so far been shown unnecessary; neither he nor anyone in his household had suffered any illness or accident. But his fingers could not forget the strange feel of the girl's flesh as it split and tore, and the bracelet of sloughed-away skin that hung about her flayed wrist.

He looked hard at the statuette on the right, the single form of a jaguar-man, the figure Nine-Lizard had given him. It gleamed in the sun's light. He remembered when he had last talked about it with his sculptor son. Yes, Huetzin was right. The image was flayed. The carver had sculpted definite lines that showed a boundary between human skin and jaguar flesh. The jaguar part was recessed, showing that the skin had once overlaid it. Wise Coyote could clearly see the skin rolling away over the crown of the head, resembling a hood being drawn back. A tendril of skin curled down, meeting and blending with the line of a still-human ear. Exposed blood vessels writhed like snakes from the figure's temples and across the scribed muscle fibers on its breast.

It was easy not to see such features in shadow, but in daylight they stood forth almost obscenely. As the girl's skinless flesh had shown in the full sun of the courtyard.

The flaying on the figure was a depiction of reality—Wise Coyote knew that now from what had happened to Mixcatl. What about the rest of the figurine; the paws, the face which showed the human nose broadening into the muzzle of a great cat, the upper lip splitting, the forehead and cheekbones reshaping themselves?

Wise Coyote felt cold. The statuette itself was almost

a caricature, a grotesque, a joke. But if it meant that living flesh would change in this way, it became sinister. And how far would the transformation go?

He narrowed his eyes. He had seen many things that men called magic; appearances of gods in human form, portents, signs, events. And he had even accepted them as real in a detached way, even though his sharp eyes saw through the charades of the priests. This was a different sort of reality, like the sting of peppers or the warning buzz of a rattlesnake's tail. It slapped you across the face with a truth you couldn't deny.

And if Mixcatl was the being depicted in the statuette, then the traditions of the Olmec Magicians were true and the power behind them was real.

He had managed to trace the origins of Tloque Nahaque, his gentle god, to Tepeyolotli, Heart-of-the-Mountain, the divine jaguar. Tepeyolotli was only an Aztec name for a divinity that had been worshipped by the Magicians.

Wise Coyote had spent most of his life wishing for a god that was not just part of a hopeful human imagination. Could it be that he had found what he sought?

And if he had found the trail that led to the divine in the form of Tepeyolotli, would the Jaguar be any less bloodthirsty than Hummingbird on the Left?

He suddenly wanted to fling the image to the floor and shatter it.

11

IN THE HOUSE of Scribes, Mixcatl sat cross-legged, working on a section of the history commissioned by the Speaker-King, Ilhuicamina. She had recently been given her own chamber in which to work. Sunlight flooded in through large windows, giving her plenty of illumination. This change had been made, the Master of Scribes had told her, so that she might paint without interruption.

The change in quarters had taken place shortly after Latosl had returned her to the House of Scribes on his boat. The memory of that day was curiously hazy and dreamlike. She recalled going to the market, purchasing a string of chilies, then being cornered and tormented by the boys. She remembered the helpless rage that possessed her then, and even the strange pulling sensations in her face and her teeth, but after that, everything was murky. She hadn't regained full awareness until she had awakened on Latosl's refuse barge as it pulled into the canalside dock at the House of Scribes. Nine-Lizard had gone down, carried her up to her chamber, put a damp compress on her forehead and salve on the raw areas on her arms and wrists.

The flesh on those areas was still tight and pink,

though Nine-Lizard said that the markings would soon fade. He had tried to reassure her, saying that the strange skin-peeling was probably due to her foreign heritage. He knew something about such illnesses. They might be uncomfortable, but never life-threatening. Anything beyond that he would not say, although Mixcatl suspected he knew more.

That incident and the one before, when she had fled from a roomful of apprentices because she was unable to bear the odor of sacrifice, had reemphasized her strange difference from the others.

Although she had privacy within her own rooms, to enter and leave she had to pass by other chambers belonging to officials and high-ranking scribes. Somehow there was always someone present, and she often had a sense of being watched.

Today, however, that feeling had receded. The sun, brilliant and warm, shone on the page, making the colors so intense that they seemed to glow. With her paintpots and brushes about her and the half-finished book unfolded across her lap, Mixcatl lost herself in the contentment of painting.

From the old books she used as references, she had learned much about history as well as glyph-making. The Aztecs, according to the texts, were descendants of an older and even more glorious race called the Toltecs. The time of the Toltecs had been a golden age, where learning, religion, and most of all, art and craftsmanship, reached great heights. The Aztecs were the direct inheritors of this tradition and they strove to surpass the accomplishments of their distinguished ancestors. Reverence for the Toltec heritage was expressed in the Nahuatl language, for an artist of exceptional skill was honored by being called "tolteca."

After the fall of the Toltecs, the people who were to become the Aztecs went to live on the island of Aztlan, from which they took their name. In a cave on the shore, they found a statue of Hummingbird on the Left. Hummingbird promised the Aztecs that they were destined to rule the world and all its riches and commanded them to wander until they found a homeland.

From memory, Mixcatl drew the figures of the original four tribal Aztec chiefs who left Aztlan. Above their heads, she made the symbols for each tribe. Three of the chiefs carried journey sacks. On the back of the fourth, she drew in a small figure that represented the image of Hummingbird, for the Aztecs had carried the god throughout their wanderings. Underneath the four chiefs, she painted in a line of footprints, indicating their long journey.

She paused between glyphs and looked down along the stiff sheets that composed the book. She and Nine-Lizard had done most of it. There had been a time when Nine-Lizard's work was clearly better, but now her glyphs matched his in quality. She knew that a careful eye could distinguish her work, for she had developed a certain style and flourish in her figures that gave them a distinct signature.

She dipped her brush into a bowl of sepia, then drew it across the chalky varnished surface of the page. Shifting from practice sheets to prepared pages had been a struggle, for the chalky texture caught the brush tip, making it go in directions the painter did not intend and ruining the figure. Or a hair of the brush pulled out and stuck in the wet paint. Mistakes such as these were faults for which a scribe could be punished, often severely.

Mixcatl had already earned unwanted attention for her individual style. Tradition and, to some extent, practicality dictated that the pictures should be drawn exactly the same each time they were made. Something in Mixcatl rebelled at making each line in a glyph an exact reproduction of another scribe's work. For a while she had forced herself to do it, but the figures came out looking dead and boring. Finally she had let herself go a little, putting her own signature on everything she drew. Her figures were as legible or more so than most and her rate of production higher, so that the masters of the House of Scribes let her eccentricities pass as long as they did not veer too far from the standard.

Recently the master-scribes had allowed her to select which glyphs she could use in cases when there were none already established. She enjoyed the challenge and had grown quite good at it. The trick was to pick combinations of pictures that, when read aloud, sounded like the words one wished to say. There was no established figure for the city of Quauhitlán, but she could break up the city's name into two words that did have glyphs: "quauhitl," which meant *tree*, and "tlantli," which meant *teeth*. A glyph of a tree with a set of teeth in its trunk represented the sound of the city's name.

Not only was she good at constructing combinations of glyphs to fit new expressions required in the history, she could also decipher constructions created by ancient scribes, whose work was often so convoluted and esoteric that even the masters couldn't figure out what they meant.

Mixcatl smiled with pleasure as she painted. She never thought she would find her place in the world, but somehow, she had. Here, among priests and scholars, she didn't have to worry about her appearance and her ability raised her above the level of her slave class. The life she had might not be perfect, for there were still questions about her own nature that troubled her. But compared with the fate that might have fallen on her, this was paradise indeed.

She worked until the level in her paint and inkpots became low. Discovering that she had no water to mix new colors, she took up a pitcher and went to fill it.

As she reached to pull aside the door flap, her hand halted. An odor filled her nose, a smell that made her think of deep shadowed jungle and the flash of sunlight on the back of a great spotted cat. The jaguar scent was musky, seductive. In her mind the image of the prowling jaguar stopped, fixed her with eyes of molten gold and called to her in a voice that she could not disobey.

She plunged ahead, as if the door flap covered a portal into the jaguar's world. But it only led to the hallway and her clumsy rush carried her right through the hanging and into someone passing by.

Mixcatl drew back in dismay, even though the compelling scent still filled her nose. She had stumbled into a young priest wearing a jaguar skin as part of his regalia. It was a new pelt, freshly skinned and tanned. The cat's spirit still lingered within it, calling to her.

"Clumsy slave wench! Are you blind?" the skin's wearer raged. "I have spent the morning in rites of purification only to be fouled by your touch. Now I will be forced to repeat the ceremony."

Trying to shake off the scent's influence, Mixcatl stooped to pick up her pitcher, which, thankfully, had not broken.

"Insolent girl! Reply when you are spoken to."

Slowly she straightened, deciding to tell as much of the truth as possible. "I could not see you as I came through the hanging. I was going to fill my pitcher to mix paints."

From the corner of her eye, she could see heads craning out of nearby doorways. People were being drawn by the priest's sharp voice. Mixcatl thought of just scuttling away, but a part of her burned with anger. She was no ordinary slave to be abused so. She was a scribe and an artist.

"Let me pass," she said keeping her voice level.

The young cleric blocked her. "You did not use the proper form of address to a priest."

Her answer came in a low voice. "You do not deserve it."

She glared at him, feeling the anger start to churn in her body. Her hands curled, the way they had at the marketplace long ago. The pulling sensation began in her teeth, the way it had a few days ago in the courtyard.

His face contorted by rage, the priest seized Mixcatl's hair and tried to fling her to his feet. She resisted and she could see that the strength she showed surprised him. Her anger grew. She wrestled to control it as she glared at the young cleric, for she remembered what had happened when the boys from the calmecac had trapped and teased her.

She half wished, half feared that the transformation would overtake her once again. The beast spirit was already awake and circling within her, as if her body was a cage with a door ready to be opened.

The young priest jerked hard at her hair, trying to drag her down. The door to the cage opened. The spirit did not seize her own flesh to work its changes. Instead she felt it extend from her into the spotted pelt on the priest's shoulders.

The jaguar skin billowed and lifted. The hanging head snapped up, fire in its eye sockets. The dangling tail twitched and lashed.

"Hummingbird on the Left, help me!" the priest shrieked, loosing Mixcatl's hair. "Sorcery!"

Too caught up in rage to back off, Mixcatl brought her curled hand down twice and each time the dangling claws of the jaguar pelt raked skin.

The priest tore the writhing pelt off as if it had been on fire. Plumes and gold ornaments fell with it, but the terrified priest took no notice.

"Sorcery!" he cried, pointing a shaking finger at Mixcatl. "You saw. Slay her! Burn her!"

The girl flung her hair back from her face. She trembled with the effort of suppressing her fear and anger so that the thing she had unleashed would return to her before it could do more damage. The jaguar skin slumped into a dead pile on the floor.

The commotion brought other scholars and scribes out of their chambers. With a twinge of despair, Mixcatl saw the Master of Scribes coming down the hallway, his arms folded across his white robe, his shaved head gleaming.

"You saw!" cried the priest again, turning to people whose heads had been poking out of doorways. Some heads nodded, others shook slowly in disbelief. From the corner of her eye, Mixcatl saw Nine-Lizard making his way through the crowd gathering in the hallway.

Suddenly the young priest yanked a knife from his belt and ran at Mixcatl. "Left-Handed Hummingbird demands that we kill those who give themselves to demons!" he shouted.

As quick as he was, Nine-Lizard was faster. The lifted arm was seized and jerked back. The blade clattered to the floor. The jaguar pelt, which had billowed up again when the jolt of fear went through Mixcatl, collapsed again.

Half crouching from her effort to guard against the knife, Mixcatl looked up at the scene before her. Nine-Lizard still had a grip on the young priest, whose arm was still high in the air.

"Young man," said the old scribe mildly, "perhaps the intensity of your devotions has left you a bit fevered."

The priest struggled to free himself, but Mixcatl saw that Nine-Lizard had a strong grip for an elder.

"Get your hands off me, slave filth," the young priest spat. "Who are you to keep me from killing the demon-possessed?"

"I am a scribe-painter, as is the girl you stumbled into. I am sure she meant no harm. She could not see you through the hangings in the doorway."

"She is a sorcerer. She sent devils into my jaguar skin cloak!"

The Master of Scribes had come up behind the two figures. He cleared his throat deliberately and loudly. "This is a house of learning," he said in a gruff voice, "not a school for warriors. Nine-Lizard Iguana Tongue, let the priest go."

The old man released his grip, but Mixcatl noticed that he put his foot on the priest's fallen knife.

"Master of Scribes," she said, "I was coming out of my chambers and I stumbled into the noble sir."

The priest glared at Mixcatl and repeated his accusation. The Master of Scribes scowled and scratched his bald pate. "And then?" he asked the young cleric.

"I grew angry and seized her by the hair, as I had every right to do. And then she whispered spells and I felt my jaguar cloak moving on my back. See how it clawed me?" He showed the Master of Scribes a set of scratches on his ribs.

Mixcatl felt an indignant anger welling up inside her. The priest was lying on that point. She had whispered no spells—she didn't know any.

"Is that the skin?" asked the Master of Scribes, and requested Nine-Lizard get it for the priest.

Nine-Lizard stooped down stiffly to pick up the pelt, but before he lifted it, he shot a quick glance at Mixcatl to be sure that she had control of herself. He gave it to the Master of Scribes.

"Here," the master-scribe said, offering the cast-off pelt to its wearer. The skin hung limp and heavy across his arm.

"No! I will get another that has not been bewitched."

"As you wish," said the Master of Scribes. "But they

are expensive and I am sure that your head priest will want to know why you discarded it."

The young priest glowered at Nine-Lizard and Mixcatl. The Master of Scribes held the skin out once again, saying, "Touch it and tell me if there is anything in it besides skin and fur."

Fearfully the young priest tapped the jaguar skin, but when it stayed limp, he reluctantly accepted it with a last fearful glance at Mixcatl.

"Say what you will," he growled, "but she is a sorcerer and must die on Hummingbird's altar."

The master-scribe's face darkened. "If you kill her, you will have to answer to representatives of the Speaker-King. He will want to know why the scribe working on his specially commissioned history was not able to complete it."

At the mention of Ilhuicamina, the young priest paled, then flushed. "It is he who demands greater fervor from us in driving out those who are accursed. And she is one." He looked around at the assembled people. "You all saw what happened."

"A strong wind often blows down these hallways," said Nine-Lizard smoothly. "Many a gust has been mistaken for the work of spirits."

Mixcatl followed the priest's gaze around the circle of faces, hoping that they would believe Nine-Lizard. She cursed herself for letting her temper get away from her and the youth for his arrogance. She saw the questioning glances exchanged and knew that even though most people would accept Nine-Lizard's explanation, there would be those who knew what they had seen. And in the gazes that were turned on her, she saw the hard glitter of suspicion.

"Go fill your water jug and finish mixing your paints, Seven-Flower," the Master of Scribes told Mixcatl. "Ilhuicamina wants no interruptions in your work."

Gripping the handle of her pitcher, Mixcatl walked past the people, down the hallway. Behind her, she heard Nine-Lizard and others soothing the priest. But she knew the affair was far from being over. Too many questions would be asked. And what if it happened again? Many other people who came to the House of Scribes also wore jaguar skins as emblems of their office and rank. Mixcatl didn't like the practice, but she accepted and understood it.

She filled her jug and went back hoping she could lose herself in her work. Soon she was caught up in the making of glyphs, but the contentment she had felt that morning was gone.

In the library at Tezcotzinco, Wise Coyote stared at the two statuettes, now standing side by side on their own shelf. He remembered Nine-Lizard's words when the old scribe had brought him the second one.

I have placed my foot on the threshold, he thought. *Do I wish to go beyond?*

The pieces of ancient art in his collection seemed to regard him silently. He turned to a great stone disk bearing the Plumed Serpent. How he had searched for a sign that said that Quetzalcoatl's powers were real. But all he could find was evidence that Plumed Serpent was an ancient and revered king.

Will I be thought of as a god when I am dust, thought Wise Coyote. *Will men turn their faces to the image of a coyote and embellish the story of my life until it becomes legend?*

He wandered around the library, admitting at last to the sorrow that tore his heart. He let his gaze travel along the collection, many pieces from many palaces and times, all with their message of the divine.

Why can I not believe? Wise Coyote cried and nearly shouted aloud.

And then, as he turned back, his gaze fell upon the

two statues, the Olmec holding the jaguar-baby and the were-jaguar caught in the instant of change. No. It was not true that he had no faith. Had he been given the choice, he would never have wished that these Olmec figurines, out of all the other images he had gathered in his life, would be the ones to prove true. Now he believed, and was afraid.

He could end it here. He could forget what he had seen and drop his plan to have Nine-Lizard Iguana Tongue "stolen" and brought to Tezcotzinco.

And then he would have to stand alone against the city across the lake.

The mysterious people of the Jaguar might prove uncertain allies, but submission to Hummingbird on the Left was worse.

Abruptly he walked from the library, summoned his most trusted warriors and gave them instructions. Then he went into his gardens to wait.

The old man was waiting for him in an audience hall the following morning. Wise Coyote wasted no time with greetings or chatter.

"I see that you took my advice," said the old scribe, rubbing a bruise on his leathery arm. "I really thought I was being abducted by slave stealers until I saw the hills of Texcoco. Next time, please send someone with a little less enthusiasm or I will not last for more than one or two more encounters."

Wise Coyote felt a twinge of regret that he had to use such methods, but it was the scribe himself who suggested it.

"My apologies," he said curtly, "but haste required it."

"It is well. I needed to see you. Mixcatl has become a prisoner in the House of Scribes. When the history that she and I are working on is completed, I fear she will be put to death."

Wise Coyote leaned forward in his icpalli. "Why? Did someone else witness the attack on the boy from the calmecac? Was that boatboy a spy in disguise?" He halted, thinking that his words might be a complete mystery to Nine-Lizard, since the old man probably didn't know about the incident.

"I know in part what happened that day," said the scribe, fixing the king with a steady gaze that Wise Coyote found unsettling. "When Seven-Flower Mixcatl returned to the House of Scribes, she confided in me, although she did not understand what had happened to her. No. The imprisonment stems from another incident involving a young priest wearing a jaguar skin."

Wise Coyote listened as Nine-Lizard related the events that had taken place when the girl had stumbled into the young cleric, who was visiting the House of Scribes on an official errand.

"I tried to smooth things over," said Nine-Lizard with a sigh, "but too many people witnessed the incident. Charges of sorcery are being whispered against her and she has been made captive, supposedly for her own protection."

The old man's voice fell silent and Wise Coyote found that he could hear the sound of his own breathing. His icpalli creaked as he shifted his weight.

"Glyph-painter, I have never believed in sorcery, yet what I saw that morning in the plaza has no explanation," he said quietly, then dropped his voice to a whisper. "Who is this girl? Why is such strangeness visited on her?"

"The only ones who can answer that, tlatoani, are the Jaguar's Children."

"Then send word to them," said the king impatiently.

"I have done so. They do not reply."

"Why not?"

Wise Coyote watched as Nine-Lizard took a deep breath and looked at the floor, his shoulders bowed as if he were remembering some old and deep shame. "They have turned their backs on me. It was an ancient crime and done in the recklessness of youth; I cannot tell you more."

The king stared at the old man and drew his cloak about his shoulders.

"You are the last hope she has," said Nine-Lizard. "The priests of Hummingbird will soon clamor for her death on the altar."

"Why does it matter so much to you? Are there not other apprentice scribes who are worthy of your tutoring? Why this girl?"

He saw Nine-Lizard clench his gnarled old fists and look up into empty space as if challenging an enemy. "The Jaguar's Children refuse to accept my word. Even I doubted at first, but there have been too many strange happenings that cannot be explained away. She is the incarnation of Tepeyolotli, Heart-of-the-Mountain, the one they have been waiting for through a thousand New Fires."

Wise Coyote felt his heart beat fast in mixed dread and hope. Could this scribe girl indeed be what Nine-Lizard had implied, a descendant of the Olmec Magicians and an incarnation of the Jaguar? Could she lead him to the path he most sought or stand with him against the might of Tenochtitlán?

"Does the young woman know her heritage?"

"No, and she must be taught quickly or the powers that she has may become dangerous," said Nine-Lizard. "Take her into your court, tlatoani, and take me as well. She will need someone to guide and teach her, and I, even with my poor skills, may be able to provide what she needs."

"Once you advised me not to bring her to Tezcotzinco. What has changed your mind?"

"I will not lie to you, prince of Texcoco. Bringing Mixcatl to your court will have its own dangers. Indeed, if I find a way to return her to the Jaguar's Children, her stay with you should, I pray, be short."

The king knitted his brows. At first he had been eager to offer sanctuary to a gifted scribe who might be endangered by the priests of Left-Handed Hummingbird, but now . . .

He found it difficult to say the next words. "I confess some trepidation. After seeing what happened when the girl became enraged by teasing . . ."

"You fear she will actually become a great cat and you will have to cage her," said Nine-Lizard. "In truth, I do not know if she can complete the transformation yet. I hope that my presence may prevent that from happening before she is ready."

"There is also the history that you and she are preparing for Ilhuicamina."

Nine-Lizard stroked his curly beard. "Your library here is well known. Perhaps the document might be improved if we were to have access to your records as well as to those in the capital."

"Someone will have to convince Ilhuicamina," said Wise Coyote. Inwardly he winced, knowing who that someone would be. And Tenochtitlán's ruler hadn't been very willing to listen to him lately. No matter. He would have to try. For his own sake as well as the girl's.

He summoned the men who had "stolen" Nine-Lizard and bade them to return him to the House of Scribes. And to handle him with more respect.

Then Wise Coyote went into his quarters to plan his own trip to Tenochtitlán.

* * *

Wise Coyote's reception at Ilhuicamina's palace was somewhat different than he had anticipated. Instead of being made to wait while the Aztec finished other business, he was ushered into Ilhuicamina's private suite of chambers and told that the Aztec would cut his business short to dine early that evening with him.

The tlatoani of Texcoco was at once delighted and yet wary. Ilhuicamina would not treat him so unless the Aztec wanted something and he wondered, with trepidation, what that favor might be. In a side-chamber within the Aztec's living quarters, Wise Coyote prepared himself for the occasion, taking out the simple gold lip plug that he usually wore to keep the hole punched beneath the margin of his lower lip from closing. In its place, he inserted a much more ornate one with several finely wrought pieces and dangling chains held together with gold wire.

He put on his finest loincloth and richest cape, then put patterns on his face with a pottery stamp dipped in dark-brown paint. He bound up his hair into the honored warrior's tail, then put on a gold pectoral, anklets and wristlets. And last of all, he settled his turquoise coronet on his head.

He was seated first, in a cushioned icpalli before the table. Even the customary screen would be taken away so that Wise Coyote might share the Speaker-King's presence as well as the luxurious repast set before him.

Servants gave him a mug filled with chocolatl frothed with vanilla, and offered him one of the same gold straws that Ilhuicamina used.

Ilhuicamina came in, looking as majestic as ever in an embroidered turquoise cape, edged with scarlet and held with a worked-gold clasp. He too wore the blue coronet, with a tail of shimmering green quetzal and parrot feathers.

"That Snake Woman of mine," he said, complaining

about the male official who managed domestic affairs for the Aztec state. He plumped down in his wicker seat across from Wise Coyote, his cape billowing over the back. "How he bores me with his endless talk of trade and taxes! Well, I do not have to be bothered with it, but I wish he would learn that I do not even want to hear about the petty details." He leaned forward, inhaling steamy aromas as richly dressed woman-servants brought in various dishes.

"Ah, a favorite of mine!" said Ilhuicamina, catching hold of a plate of rolled pancakes before the servant had placed it on the table. "You must have some of this, my esteemed friend. The pancakes are stuffed with the most delectable filling, stewed tadpoles and cactus worms."

The first time Wise Coyote had faced this formidable dish of traditional Aztec cuisine, he had balked, but he had found the stuffed pancakes surprisingly tasty, even if a tadpole or two seemed to wriggle in his mouth. This appetizer was followed by a spicy dish of prickly-pear fruit steamed with fish roe, and frogs with green chilies. The less exotic items included roast wild pork and pheasant from the hills.

Wise Coyote made the best of the opportunity. Even his own palace kitchen in Texcoco could not come up with as many and as varied a selection of dainties as was laid before the king of Tenochtitlán. Knowing that Ilhuicamina gave greater respect to those whose bellies were as capacious as his, Wise Coyote ate out of duty as well as enjoyment, but he did not indulge to excess, for he wanted to keep his mind clear.

Throughout the meal, Ilhuicamina alternated enthusiastic remarks about the food with grumbles about his Snake Woman. "I think I will ask the Council of Commanders to choose me a new Snake Woman," Ilhuicamina said, as Wise Coyote was settling back into his icpalli and wiping his lips with a wetted cotton cloth.

"Does the present one not govern ably and well?" asked Wise Coyote, who knew the man by reputation, although not by acquaintance.

"He has the mind of a merchant and great enthusiasm for petty details. He is annoyingly lacking in fervor for the tasks I consider most important, such as the building of new temples in the conquered cities of my empire." Ilhuicamina took an impatient swig of his chocolatl and splashed the drink on his face. Wise Coyote glanced away as the Aztec swore and ordered servants to clean him up.

Wise Coyote's heart sank, for he knew what Ilhuicamina was about to ask of him. His engineering skills had been praised ever since the opening of the Chaultapec aqueduct. Who else would Ilhuicamina choose to supervise a large-scale building project?

"Hummingbird deserves to have only the most glorious temples raised to him. You, among all men, have the gifts to serve him well."

"I am deeply honored by your faith in me. Which city is to be honored by Hummingbird's first shrine outside Tenochtitlán?" Wise Coyote forced himself to ask.

"I have considered that question carefully. Since, naturally, you will want to make modifications as you build, the site should be close to your own source of stone. And, so that the project will not interfere unduly with your duties, I have ordered that it be located within your own city of Texcoco."

Wise Coyote felt a flash of bitter hatred, but he kept his expression smooth. *He knows how the rites of Hummingbird sicken me. And he dares to imply that Texcoco stands among the list of the conquered, even though his armies have not yet set foot on my lands.*

He took a sip of his own drink and replied, trying to sound unconcerned. "I believe you have made allowances for my convenience that are really not necessary."

Ilhuicamina smiled, but there was a hard look in his

eyes that told Wise Coyote that he knew exactly what he was doing. *Careful. You are within his grip. Lose your temper now and you will be crushed. Play along with him, but do not make it too easy.*

"Before we proceed further, I have a request to make of you." Wise Coyote felt the tightness of the muscles between his shoulders and wished he had a slave to massage them. "The favor is but a small one. There are two excellent glyph-painters in your House of Scribes. I wish to have them at my court. One came recently from Tlacopan. The other is a gifted apprentice."

Ilhuicamina pursed his lips, then picked his teeth. "The scribe Nine-Lizard Iguana Tongue and his apprentice are working on a history that I commissioned. Could you not take two others?"

"The history could be completed at Texcoco," said Wise Coyote, using his silkiest tones. "If those scribes also had the use of my library, it would improve the accuracy of their work."

"Do not let me catch you sticking in anything about your Tloque Nahaque," Ilhuicamina said petulantly, then slapped Wise Coyote's shoulder and laughed. "None of your scholar-gods for my kingdom of warriors."

"I would not dream of doing any such thing," said Wise Coyote. "May I have the two scribes?"

Ilhuicamina grumbled to himself, rubbing his chin. "There was something about that apprentice—Snake Woman was too lazy to look into it so I had another official inquire. Oh, yes, now I remember. Some incident with a young cleric. There were accusations involving the bewitchment of a jaguar skin." He frowned.

Wise Coyote waited, forcing himself to breathe evenly. He had no idea that the incident with the young priest had traveled this far up in Aztec officialdom.

"The priests of Hummingbird wanted to have the offender sacrificed," Ilhuicamina said with a yawn. "In fact I intend to give my permission once the history is complete."

"I have no interest in the life of a glyph-painter," said Wise Coyote, trying to sound indifferent. "But I need the talents of both scribes, for the history and for research of my own."

"Because it is you, I agree," said Ilhuicamina, putting his arms behind his head. "But remember, the girl has been accused of sorcery. If I hear rumors of such doings at your court, I will be greatly displeased." He sat forward, his eyes gleaming with eagerness. "Now, about the temple to Hummingbird."

Wise Coyote wet his lips. He had secured the two scribes and perhaps had bought the girl's life, but was it worth the price Ilhuicamina was asking him to pay?

It makes no difference. If I do not agree now, Ilhuicamina will force me and give no favors in return.

Taking a breath Wise Coyote began, "In choosing a site, I must bear in mind considerations other than a supply of stone."

"Yes. The devoutness of the workers who will labor and the people who will worship is most important. I am told that the city of Texcoco eagerly awaits Hummingbird on the Left. Who am I to deny the hunger of your people?"

Especially when I have resisted bringing his bloody abomination into my city. And well he knows that.

"My request is that of one friend to another," said Ilhuicamina, picking up his glazed mug of chocolatl. "Let it remain so."

"I will be honored to undertake the task." Wise Coyote picked up his mug, but the drink had become suddenly bitter on his tongue.

Ilhuicamina clapped his hands to summon a servant. "Enough! I tire of talk. Let there be drums, juggling and well-fleshed women to dance for us. Friends should enjoy themselves, prince of Texcoco!''

Wise Coyote leaned back against the stuffed pillows of his icpalli. He had wrested a small compromise from the prospect of utter defeat. The girl Seven-Flower Mixcatl and the old man Nine-Lizard Iguana Tongue would soon be on their way to the palace at Tezcotzinco. Soon he would know more about the mystery that was beginning to ensnare him, but the prospect left a chill in his gut that could not be warmed by draughts of agave wine. Nine-Lizard had spoken of dangers and he had already seen for himself that the old man's words were not just senile babblings.

And the specter of a blood-washed shrine to the Aztec sun god standing nearly on his doorstep in Texcoco was a nightmare that had already begun to haunt him.

What have I done, he thought, fighting to keep despair from showing on his face. Slumping back into his icpalli, he forced himself to watch the dancing girls.

12

A BOAT CAME at night to take the two glyph-painters from the House of Scribes across the lake. Mixcatl had already been told by Nine-Lizard where she was going and why. When the touch came on her shoulder she woke quickly and, without asking any questions, took up the bundle in which her brushes, paints and blank books were packed. Silently she bid farewell to the House of Scribes and followed Nine-Lizard down the stone steps into the night-damp air.

She thought that they would embark at once, for she saw the shape of a waiting craft lying in at the dock near the House of Scribes. Instead, Nine-Lizard led her away from the quay, across a plaza and into the courtyard of a large house. A man hailed him, he answered and the door flap was pulled back, allowing them to enter.

"Do not let the girl touch anything," a voice said, and as the speaker came forward, Mixcatl saw that he was robed as a healer. "Have her walk on these mats and bring her into this chamber."

Though puzzled and a little angered, Mixcatl followed Nine-Lizard as he crossed the mats and entered a small room, brightly lit with torches. It too was floored with mats.

The healer and an assistant came in behind Mixcatl and Nine-Lizard.

"Remove your garments, both of you," said the assistant gruffly to Nine-Lizard.

The old scribe narrowed his eyes. Clearly he had not expected this. Mixcatl felt her uncertainty and irritation grow into anger. "What is this? Are we being stripped like some common slave at market, so your master may see more clearly what he is getting?"

"My master, Wise Coyote, has requested that you and your companion be examined and found free of disease or infirmity before embarking for Texcoco," the healer said calmly.

Mixcatl felt Nine-Lizard's hand, warm and callused, on her shoulder. "What he asks is reasonable," he said softly. "Wise Coyote knows what happened to you that morning in the city. He just wants to make sure that you do not have an illness you could give to others. They will do us no harm."

Slowly Mixcatl began to untie the shoulder knot of her cloak. The marks on her arms and hands were fading, but still distinct. She wondered if the healer would scowl at her because of the disfigurement.

Her hands trembled a little on the hem of her huipil blouse as she began to pull it off over her head. When she was younger, she had run about barechested and unconcerned, but now she was aware of her young breasts. She understood why the examination had to be done, but she found herself resenting the fact that as a female slave, she was allowed less modesty than she would have if freeborn.

Out of politeness, Nine-Lizard turned away. The healer's expression was pleasant, but she still found it difficult to undo the ties of her short skirt and let it fall about her ankles.

Once all her garments were off, the healer went over

her briskly and efficiently, but gently. He did raise his eyebrows at the marks. He felt the shape of her head, muttering to himself uneasily. Opening her mouth, he felt her teeth gingerly, as if expecting them to be sharp, then dictated to his assistant, who was scratching down some crude glyphs on a piece of fig-bark paper.

"These marks on her arms," the healer said to Nine-Lizard. "How did she acquire them? It does not look like the result of wounding or burning."

"It is a condition of the skin that occurs periodically in her family. It is not contagious. I can say nothing else about it," the old scribe answered. From the tone of his voice and the expression on his face, Mixcatl knew that Nine-Lizard was stating the truth, or as much of the truth as he could. But she sensed that there was more that he knew, but could not or would not reveal. It was the same look that had come across his features when she lay in her chamber and begged him to tell her what had happened to her.

"I cannot tell you now, for I am not certain," he had said then, smoothing her sweaty forehead. "If I tell you my fears, it will only worry you, and I may be wrong. No. It is better that we wait and see what happens."

And she'd had to be content with that.

Although the healer treated her with courtesy, he made his examination much more thorough than she would have liked. Soon the coolness of the air on her unclothed skin and the discomfort of having an unfamiliar man touching her body made her wish for the ordeal to be over. She couldn't help wondering, half resentfully, if Wise Coyote would have to be subjected to the same sort of intensive scrutiny before he was allowed to meet her!

The healer finished and spoke over his shoulder to his assistant. Then, while Mixcatl was dressing, the healer went over Nine-Lizard, speaking his findings to the assistant, who jotted them down as best he could.

Finally the healer finished and washed his hands in a bowl of agave suds.

"Let it be stated that I have examined the glyph-painters Nine-Lizard Iguana Tongue and Seven-Flower Mixcatl. To the extent of my skill and knowledge I affirm that they are free of any fevers, agues, wastings or other ailments that could pose a danger to the House of Texcoco." He nodded to Nine-Lizard, who was still dressing. "The boat awaits you. You may go."

Mixcatl followed Nine-Lizard back past the House of Scribes to the waiting craft. Torchlight gleamed on the polished sides of the canoe and on the backs of the men who paddled it. The wind from Lake Texcoco made the firebrands flutter and sent a chill through Mixcatl, huddling beneath her cloak, clutching her bundle. There were three passengers to be picked up, herself, Nine-Lizard and an escort from Ilhuicamina's court, who was to oversee the transport of the partially completed history from the House of Scribes to Wise Coyote's palace at Tezcotzinco.

Who was Wise Coyote? Mixcatl had heard only a little about him from Nine-Lizard. The old man described the ruler of Texcoco as a wise and scholarly man. She was still not entirely sure why the king would want her at his palace, although she suspected that the incident with the priest and the jaguar skin had much to do with it. She did not think her life would change—after all, she was still a slave and moving from one master to another would not change that.

She thought of Six-Wind, the boy at the calmecac who had promised that when he came of age he would buy her and set her free. He had been at least three or four years older than she and by now must have gained manhood.

Where was he now? She couldn't remember when he had last seen her. Perhaps he had found prettier girls and regretted that hasty promise. Perhaps he had told himself that he need not honor a vow made to a slave. Or he had just forgotten.

Nine-Lizard sat beside Mixcatl, and when the boat left the shelter of the canals for the open lake, he wrapped a portion of his cloak around her. Neither spoke, for the escort was sitting just in front. And even if he hadn't been there, she would have remained quiet. To the questions she wanted to ask, she knew that Nine-Lizard would have no answer.

She listened to the soft splash as the paddles were dipped and the liquid gurgle as they were drawn back and up again. With every stroke, she felt the boat pull forward. She could hardly believe she was finally leaving Tenochtitlán. During the last few days she had become a guarded prisoner in her chamber, under suspicion of sorcery and threatened by death. Frightened as she was, she had kept painting, for only by losing herself in work could she keep calm.

Now the danger was behind her and growing more distant with every paddlestroke. She had no idea why the king of Texcoco had bargained for her safety, but she was too grateful to question. Texcoco would be a refuge for her and Nine-Lizard, where they could work on the history in peace.

Even as she pictured the life to come, it was overlaid with images from the day in the plaza when the schoolboys tormented her and the later incident with the youthful priest. Would things like that happen in Wise Coyote's house? Mixcatl knew she had left a part of the danger behind, but another part she could not be rid of. It traveled with her, inside her. And she sensed that it had only begun to awake and grow.

She hoped that Wise Coyote did not wear a jaguar skin

and then weariness overwhelmed her and she sank into slumber.

Mixcatl peered up through the mists of sleep at the thin gray dawn that hung over the lake. The dugout was no longer moving forward, but rocking and bumping. Knuckling her eyes, she saw that the boat was moored at a stone dock at the base of a steep hillside. Nine-Lizard rose, took her arm and helped her out.

After a night on the canoe, Mixcatl found herself weaving and staggering along the stone dock, and when she saw the stairway cut into the sharp slope, she feared she would be too dizzy to climb it. Determinedly she shook away the giddy feeling and mounted the steps, Nine-Lizard behind her. Her legs were aching from the long climb before they were halfway up. The rising dawn turned the damp stone pink and touched the clouds to the west with fiery orange.

At last they reached the top, where a flagstoned walkway led between little pools and waterfalls. Spring water ran in glazed troughs from pool to pool and fed the luxuriant gardens that had been planted. The flowery scent and the humming of the bees about the dew-moist blossoms got into Mixcatl's head and made her dizzy.

And then came another smell, one that made her widen her eyes and lift her chin. What it was, she didn't know, at least she could not have spoken it. In her mind however, the scent raised shadows—fleet shadows with long legs and strange crowns of horns. The thoughts made her hunch her shoulders and change her gait, so that she walked with a slow, measured step.

"There are animals here," she said to Nine-Lizard. He glanced at her with an odd look, as if the tone of her voice had changed. She felt strangely dreamy, yet alert and intensely excited. "Take me to see them!"

Nine-Lizard only muttered under his breath, then took

Mixcatl's arm and hurried her along the path. "I did not think that our host indulged in the princely habit of keeping tame deer on the palace grounds," he grumbled. "I hope he will take my advice and pen them, or move them elsewhere."

The musky scent in the damp morning air intoxicated Mixcatl. The thought came into her head that, if she struggled, she could probably escape Nine-Lizard. She felt strong enough to overpower him. Once she was free, her nose would lead her to the source of the scent.

Even as she tensed to wrench herself loose, the odor faded in her nostrils and a part of her mind flashed a warning at her. Turn against Nine-Lizard? Her friend, teacher and mentor? He had kept the angered priest from plunging a knife into her that day in the House of Scribes.

The shock of what she had wanted to do drove the thoughts away. A breeze blew in her face, damp with the wind from Lake Texcoco. She drank it in, letting it cleanse the strange feeling from her mind.

Another flight of stone steps and then another walkway brought them to the palace of Tezcotzinco.

It was a handsome edifice, made of sapphire-colored blue and green stone, inlaid with mosaic tile. It was built into the side of a hill, so that it had more than the usual two or three levels. Mixcatl noticed that several of the little streams which tumbled down the hill had been redirected to run underneath the palace's foundations and emerge in covered troughs.

Here the escort that Ilhuicamina had sent with them departed, to be received in a manner worthy of his status and class. The two slave-scribes were taken in through an unobtrusive side-entrance by servants. They were received by a man who introduced himself as an assistant estate manager. His job was to look after the small staff of slaves and servants who maintained Tezcotzinco when the king was not in residence.

He showed the two slave-scribes to a large, airy chamber that looked out over the lower gardens. A partition was set up to separate Mixcatl's sleeping mat from Nine-Lizard's, but otherwise, they shared quarters.

The assistant estate manager informed them that Wise Coyote would not be arriving for many days, as he had business in his capital city. They were to make themselves at home and continue their work on the document for Ilhuicamina. If they needed or wanted anything, they could make a request of a servant, who would then convey the message to him.

Mixcatl, who had been needing to relieve herself, noticed that there was no pot available for the purpose. When at last she asked a servant, she was shown to a small chamber, almost a niche in the rock walls of the palace. The little room was narrow but deep, curtained off for privacy. Mixcatl expected to find a vessel akin to the pisspots she had emptied while in the calmecac, but instead she found only a low stone slab with a hole in it. From the hole came rushing and gurgling sounds that dismayed her. When she did peer through, she saw a stream of water running beneath the hole.

Why Wise Coyote had made a stream run under his house, she did not know, but when she used the hole for its apparent purpose, she realized that the swiftly running current swept everything away so that there was no remaining smell. Another trickle of water to one side continually filled a stone basin and drained down into a channel on the floor. There was an empty bowl she could use to dip and rinse with as well as drying cloths hung on pegs.

What a clever man Wise Coyote was, she thought. With a little room one could go to there was no need for chamberpots which stank or, worse yet, overturned and spilled their noisome contents unless they were quickly emptied. She wondered if there were other little chambers for other rooms in the palace. How nice it must be for Wise Coyote's servants, not to have to collect all the pisspots and go outside to dump them.

She told Nine-Lizard of her discovery and he inspected the water room, nodding, although he declined to make use of it. Then the two ate breakfast served to them on a turquoise-inlaid tray. After that, they began work on the history.

Though painting the document was absorbing, Mixcatl occasionally grew weary and needed time away from her paints and brushes. She asked for permission to go beyond the confines of her quarters. The assistant estate manager sent word that she might explore the gardens and the palace, as long as she did not enter any rooms or go too far from her quarters. She soon realized that, apart from herself, Nine-Lizard and the resident staff of servants, the palace was empty.

She decided that the absence of anyone else at Tezcotzinco was connected with the examination she and Nine-Lizard had undergone before crossing the lake. In addition, she had a feeling that the assistant estate manager had been directed to keep a close watch on them through the servants. Even if the healer had passed the two newcomers as being free from sickness, Wise Coyote might keep them away from the rest of his household until he was certain.

How long would he keep them alone, she wondered. She enjoyed the simple life of rising early, breakfasting, then painting glyphs all morning and taking walks after lunch. But there was something about the isolation here and the sense of being observed that made her feel unsettled. She wanted Wise Coyote to return, so that she could see for herself what sort of man he was.

One day in the early afternoon, Mixcatl was strolling the blue-tiled hallways of the palace near the library when she heard the echoing slap of sandals on stone. She thought at first that a servant might be approaching, although they seldom went near this part of the house. She quickly decided that it was not a servant. The loud ringing steps spoke of confidence, as if the one approaching knew he had a perfect right to be there.

Perhaps it was Wise Coyote himself, returning unannounced to see how his scribes were doing. She halted, feeling frightened as the steps grew nearer. Perhaps she should run back to her room. He might not appreciate her wandering around his palace. If he wanted to visit her, he would do so. She shouldn't thrust herself in his way. After all, as Nine-Lizard had told her, he was the ruler of Texcoco.

As these thoughts went through her head, a young man came around the corner, swinging his arms and singing to himself. He was tall, but not broad of chest like a warrior. Instead he had a graceful slimness like a dancer or a runner and a bounce to his step that went with his engaging smile. He wore a cloak and loincloth of dark jade-green, with a matching headband. On his hands and thighs were smears of an odd green dust and Mixcatl could see some on his clothes as well. He looked as if he might have come from a craftsman's workshop.

It was too late to duck around a corner. He had seen her and was coming toward her. Well, if this was Wise Coyote, she would get her chance to meet him. She did not fall to her knees as she had seen others do when approached by one of noble status. She only bowed her head, as was proper, so she would not look him in the face.

"Look up, child." His voice was light with happiness, but resonant and strong. "The sun is pouring in the window and the dust motes are dancing. It is too beautiful a day to cast your eyes down."

"Are you Wise Coyote?" Mixcatl peered up at him.

"No. I am one of his many sons. It is said that I resemble him greatly. I am Huetzin."

She studied the newcomer's face and decided that if Wise Coyote was similar to his son in appearance and manner, she would like him. Huetzin's face was slightly long, his complexion dark, his eyes deepset. In another, such features might have given a gloomy or moody impression, but there was a certain luminosity of spirit that lighted the young man's face.

"You must be one of the two scribe-painters that father told me about," said Huetzin. "Are you enjoying life at Tezcotzinco?"

"Very much," answered Mixcatl politely, and added, "it is nice not to have to empty pisspots."

Huetzin laughed. "Of all the things to praise about Tezcotzinco, and you choose that. Well, I will tell you a secret. Father hated emptying pots too, so he built those little water rooms. I didn't like them when I was small—I nearly fell through the hole." Shaking his head, he chuckled to himself.

"I would like to meet your father. Will he come soon?"

"I think so. He sent me word that I could come and use the library. That means he is satisfied that it is safe to let you have contact with others of his household."

"He seems to be a wise and cautious man."

"Yes. His practice of keeping newcomers to the household separated from the rest has saved us from several plagues that swept through the courts of other kings. Neither he nor I understand why the method works, but it does."

"Why haven't I seen you before this?" Mixcatl asked.

"I do not stay here. I have a workshop close to the palace grounds and I sleep in a small shelter nearby. It is not the life of luxury pictured for a king's son, but I have what I want."

Mixcatl wanted to know what that was.

"Why, the same thing as you have been given, young scribe. The freedom to work at my art without being disturbed."

It was easy to talk to Huetzin, with his smile and his open manner. She soon learned that he was a stone-worker and a sculptor. As a king's son, he did not have to work, but he enjoyed doing statuary for temples and creating pieces from his own inspiration. It was not enough to live on, but Wise Coyote kindly supplied the difference.

"Would you like to come into the library? I am sure my father would not mind," the youth said, drawing aside one edge of a doorhanging.

To Mixcatl, a library was a chamber where scholars stored and read sacred texts. When she followed Huetzin into the room, she saw many bound-up manuscripts on shelves. Pieces of artwork and sculpture stood on the floor or rested on pedestals or special brackets.

She quickly saw that Huetzin had not come to study the books, but to draw inspiration from the figurines and bas-relief carvings of Wise Coyote's collection. He handled each piece with reverence and care, studying it closely before replacing it on the shelf. Some he took over to the windows, where a rich yellow sunlight was streaming through.

"These are all images of gods and spirits from times long past," he said to Mixcatl. "Some were lost; others now make up our present religion. My father seeks in them the beginnings of a god he can worship without getting blood on his hands." Huetzin's face turned pensive as he turned away from the window. "And I seek to create an image of a god that has no form. Perhaps, as some say, it is a foolish task."

Mixcatl did not understand Huetzin's words, but she felt in them something similar to longings that she had known, but could not yet put into words. As she let her eyes travel along the shelves of beautifully wrought or carved objects, her gaze came to rest on two that stood slightly apart from the rest. One was a composite figure of a broad-shouldered and deep-jawed man holding the figure of a grotesque baby. The other was a single figure, not stiffly upright but down on one knee, with head and hands raised. Looking closer, she saw that the hands looked more like paws and the face was a strange blend of human and great cat.

An odd feeling like a shiver ran down her back as she looked at them, yet she felt a compulsion to pick them up, touch and study each one in turn. There were strange echoes of familiarity in both, as if she had once known what they meant, but had somehow forgotten. Feeling her heart start to hammer in her chest, she quickly moved away.

For an instant she had forgotten Huetzin. Now, as she sent a glance toward him, she saw a questioning look on his face and his mouth moving in words that he spoke only to himself.

"Thank you for letting me see the library," she said, trying not to let her voice betray the strange shakiness that had come over her at the sight of the two figurines. "I should go now. Nine-Lizard will be wanting to start work soon."

"May I come and visit you both later?" asked Huetzin. "I know where your quarters are. I would be eager to see your work, if you don't mind."

His grin was infectious and sunny, almost banishing her unease. She found herself smiling back at him. "I wouldn't mind at all and I am sure that Nine-Lizard would welcome the company of a fellow artist."

She turned and hurried out, leaving Huetzin alone in the library.

* * *

Mixcatl had time to return to her quarters, compose herself and become involved in the painting project once again before Huetzin arrived.

The images in the library had shaken her, not Huetzin himself. She found it easy to greet him and introduce him to Nine-Lizard.

"I am pleased to know you," said the old scribe, rising stiffly from his paintpots to clasp hands with the new arrival. Even though he wiped his hands, he didn't get all the pigment off his fingers and Huetzin ended up with a cobalt-blue streak on his palm.

"No apologies," Wise Coyote's son said, raising one hand before Mixcatl could burst out with an apology for the old man. "We have traded. I wear your paint and you wear my stonedust." It was true, for Nine-Lizard had acquired a jade-colored smudge on the back of his hand. "May I see the work in progress?" Huetzin asked.

Nine-Lizard invited him to bend down over the page. Huetzin studied it with a critical eye. "I am a sculptor, but my father also trained me in the art of interpreting glyphs. It is good work, beautiful, clear and easily read. What are you using as references?"

"Some older books that were sent with us from Ilhuicamina's court. We are coming to the end of what we can do with those, however."

"Then it is fortunate that Mixcatl met me in the library. In my father's name, I am pleased to invite you to make full use of it."

"Then I will accept your gracious offer," said Nine-Lizard, with a sparkle in his eyes that showed that he was greatly pleased. Mixcatl knew that he had been chafing at being restricted to the materials that had been sent with them and he also had grumbled about how far from the truth the Aztec writings strayed.

"I would also like to make another invitation," said

Huetzin. "Would either or both of you like to visit my workshop this afternoon?"

Nine-Lizard declined politely, for he wanted a rest after working so hard that morning. Mixcatl eagerly accepted and soon she was following Huetzin down the path through the garden.

Beneath the wide-spread branches of a huge tree lay a small but well-built house, walled with stone and roofed with tile. Nearby stood a canvas-covered pavillion and inside several workbenches, stools and mats. They were all covered with the gritty dust of stone-carving. Statues in various stages of completion stood on the workbenches, surrounded by stone-chisels and rasps. Mixcatl identified one freestanding figure as the rain god Tlaloc. Others were animals; birds with heads tucked under their wings, a coyote sitting upright, ears pricked forward, tail wrapped about his feet.

Fascinated, Mixcatl put out a hand to touch the statue, then drew it back, fearing that Huetzin might object.

"You may touch and handle anything you like," he said. "You are an artist; you know how to be careful."

Gently she ran her fingers down the smooth slope of the coyote's back. Turning to the workbench, she picked up a small bird carved in serpentine, turned it in her hands, marveling at the shape Huetzin had drawn from the stone. She felt it and smelled it, enjoying the delicate odor arising from the sun-warmed rock. The sight and feel of the piece in her hand reminded her of a dream she had once had, to break free of the boundaries of glyphs and paint the sweep of an entire landscape.

She smiled to herself, a little sadly. To draw a picture that conveyed no specific information was a waste of time. Better that effort be spent in the mastery of difficult glyphs and the ability to combine them. Yet her hand itched for brush and paper with an urge that she knew was foolish. One of the first things she had been taught as a scribe was that beauty alone was useless; true worth must emerge from the flawless execution of a line of glyphs.

Yet was the urge so foolish? She looked around at the statues surrounding her. Huetzin sculpted to serve a purpose; to create temple statuary that honored the Aztec gods. But he also found the freedom to explore shapes in stone, to create beauty for its own sake.

She found Huetzin looking at her, a puzzled expression on his face. "You look unhappy," he said softly. "I did not mean to bring you to a place that would cause you sorrow."

Mixcatl swallowed. How could she explain it all to him? And even worse, how could she admit that the sight of his works had given birth not only to joy and amazement but to a deep envy and a wish to paint as freely as Huetzin sculpted. She fought the urge to turn and run from the workshop, back to the palace where she could shut herself up with the codex and forget anything else.

"Tell me what troubles you," Huetzin said, putting his hand on hers. She looked up, realizing that he had spoken to her not as adult to a child or a master to a novice but as one gifted spirit to another.

She struggled to find the words. "Did anyone ever say to you that it was . . . foolish to use stone just for . . . pretty things?"

"Do you think it is foolish of me?" Huetzin sounded a little disappointed, although Mixcatl thought that it would be impossible for anything to quench his sunny nature for long.

"No," she protested, fearing that she had been rude. "I think your birds and animals are wonderful."

"As a matter of fact, many people have told me that this"—Huetzin took a stone dove in his hand and stroked it with his fingertips—"is nothing but a child's toy and that I should spend all my time working on my commissions.''

Mixcatl touched the dove. He had polished it to silky smoothness.

''But you didn't listen to them, did you?''

Huetzin smiled. ''I did for a while. And I became very unhappy. Then my father came and asked why there were no more little birds and animals in my workshop. Do not be bound by what others say, he told me. Make your creatures again because they are beautiful in my eyes.''

Mixcatl sighed. ''I wish . . .''

''To carve in stone? I could teach you, but it is a long and painstaking art.''

''No, my skill is with the brush, not the chisel. I just wish I could do with paints what you do in stone.''

''Why can't you?''

The question startled Mixcatl. She stared at him, wide-eyed. At last she said, ''I dare not waste the blank pages that we brought with us. They are for the history.''

Huetzin looked thoughtful. ''My father may have some old ones that he has not used. I could ask him.''

Mixcatl protested. ''Paper is too valuable to be used for just . . . scribbling.''

Huetzin took her by the shoulders and looked into her eyes. ''If my animals are not just child's toys, then your painting would be more than 'scribbling.' Still, if you feel uncomfortable about using paper, there are some clay tiles left over from building my little house. They aren't very large, but they are smooth.''

The forbidden dream suddenly seemed within reach. ''I shouldn't,'' she said. ''It would ruin my training as a scribe. That is what Nine-Lizard would say.''

Huetzin laughed, not mockingly but gently. ''I would think the worse of Nine-Lizard if he did. Perhaps it is your own fear that puts such words upon his lips.'' He paused. "And as for destroying your training by allowing yourself a little freedom outside it, well look at me. Have I lost any of the care and precision needed to carve within the forms required by temple statuary?"

Mixcatl gazed at the painstakingly carved figure of Tlaloc and admitted that no, he had not.

"I think now that making my creatures has turned me into a better sculptor than before. I have the discipline if I need it. When I do not, I can put it away."

"So you think that letting myself paint as I want will make me a better scribe, not worse?" She bent her brows at him.

Huetzin shrugged his shoulders, but his eyes sparkled. "It cannot harm. If you fear Nine-Lizard's scolding, you could bring your paints here."

"Perhaps I could," said Mixcatl, half to herself. "I have plenty."

With a warm smile at her, Huetzin drew a stool up to the low bench where the coyote figure was sitting and began work upon it once again. To Mixcatl, his manner spoke more eloquently than words. She was free to accept or reject his offer, but she did not have to make an immediate decision.

She knelt on a nearby mat and watched Huetzin as he dipped a strip of leathery material into a pot of water and set it into a rough-cut groove that marked the junction between the coyote's neck and shoulder. With two hands, he began to work it back and forth. Slowly the leather rasp turned a whitish blue from the stone powder worn away while the cut became smoother and deeper.

"What sort of hide can wear stone?" Mixcatl asked when Huetzin paused to wipe the sweat from his face.

"The skin of a great winged fish that lives in the western sea. It bears a sting so that it is not easily caught, but the rasps I cut from the skin are worth the price I have to pay."

He resumed his work. Mixcatl could see now how the flexible rasp could be drawn through the tightest of gaps or over large areas of stone, grinding and polishing until the worked surface became glossy. The work went very slowly and she could see how one might have to develop a great deal of patience to coax images from stone. But Huetzin seemed supremely happy as his hands shaped the figure. He seemed to fall into a hypnotic state, and Mixcatl along with him.

With a start she realized that the sun was going down and that she had been away from the palace all afternoon. Huetzin rose, dusted off his hands and began putting his tools away.

"Go to your evening meal," he said. "I will be here tomorrow afternoon, if you wish to come."

She said nothing in answer as she turned away, but she found that a smile was on her lips and rejoicing in her heart. She would bring paints tomorrow and sit under the tree.

In the days that followed, Mixcatl spent her mornings with Nine-Lizard, working on the history. Often they visited the library and consulted the books stored there. In the afternoons, Mixcatl took her paints to Huetzin's workshop and experimented on the clay tiles he gave her.

At first she only reproduced glyphs, for despite her impatience with the tightly restricted forms, they were all she knew and she was afraid to abandon them. Then, one day, with her heart beating hard, she deliberately painted color over the black boundary line of a glyph and found herself free on the surface of the tile. At first she wanted to paint Huetzin, but, despite her ability to capture shapes, she knew instinctively that the human face and figure were far too demanding for her at this stage.

Instead she chose a much simpler subject: a large dock leaf that hung down near her mat. Carefully she outlined the shape of the leaf, the veins, the stem. She chose and mixed colors to suggest the changing hues of sunlight and shadow on the leaf. It was so new a task and so difficult for her at first that she took many days to finish the leaf, trying different color blends, discarding tiles when dissatisfied with the results, often putting aside her brush and sighing with frustration.

And then, one day, when she stared at the tile and image on it, she knew that the leaf was finished and that any more work would destroy it. She set it to dry in the sunlight, went for a walk, and when she returned, she looked at it with mixed joy and despair. She compared it with the glyphs she had painted earlier. They were made of black lines, each area filled in with a single flat color, not shaded and blended as she had done with the leaf. She looked at the tile and realized that what she had done could be condemned as perverted, juvenile. Look how she had let the greens and yellows run together, mixing to create a smearing of colors across the dock leaf. No scribe-painter would be permitted such an excess. The colors must be pure, even and contained tightly within the black boundaries.

Her hands trembled and she put the tile over her knee to break it. Something made her gaze once again to the dock leaf and she realized with a shock that the wash of changing hues over the surface was real, that the irregularities in the leaf edge were there, that it had browned a little bit and that there were indeed some shades of violet in the dark veins and in the areas where shadow fell. She had not made an icon of the leaf but an image that was so real it was as if the leaf had grown in the tile.

A shadow fell along the grass near her. She had become so caught up in her painting that she had not noticed that the sounds of carving had ceased. She looked up and saw the sculptor's steady gaze, fixed on her tile.

"Huetzin, I do not know what I have done," she said helplessly. "Should I break it and start again?"

He knelt down beside her, studying the tile and the leaf from which it was drawn. There was a startled look in his eyes, then they narrowed. For an instant Mixcatl felt a cold fear such as the one she had felt when her image of Tezcatlipoca had been discovered long ago in the calmecac. Would he react in disgust, fear, puzzlement, disbelief?

His face showed none of the expressions she feared. Only a look of rapt fascination with perhaps a touch of bewilderment.

"I do not know what you have done, either," he murmured.

"That is what I saw when I looked at the leaf," she said.

"That is why it is so different. You looked at what you painted. You did not make it up out of your mind or from what you have been taught."

"That is what you do when you make your little birds and animals," Mixcatl stated, then halted uncertainly. "Isn't it?"

"Perhaps I do, a little. I watch a coyote and a coyote comes from my hands. But my beast does not look as if he could leap off the pedestal. Your leaf looks as if it could blow right off the tile."

"Is that good or bad?"

Huetzin spread his hands. "There is no good or bad to this. It is what you see."

Mixcatl stared down at her tile. "I should break it."

"No. Give it to me instead," said Huetzin. "Perhaps it will teach me your way of seeing."

Mixcatl stared at him, feeling more confused than

ever. "I think I need to go back and work on the document," she said quickly. "Take the tile, Huetzin. Put it in your house. Perhaps I will look at it again later." She placed the piece in his hands and ran away up the path.

13

WISE COYOTE WAS holding court in Texcoco, his capital city, when word came from his palace at Tezcotzinco that both scribes had settled in. They were progressing well on the history for Ilhuicamina. The young woman Seven-Flower Mixcatl had shown no strange behavior, skin-peeling or anything else that the servants had been told to watch for.

Having finished with the duties of rulership for the day, Wise Coyote retired to his private chambers. He meant to work on the plans for the first temple to Hummingbird on the Left, but he found himself getting distracted by thoughts of Mixcatl.

Her face and that of the Olmec jaguar-baby statuette seemed to drift about in his mind. One was repulsively ugly; the other had a strange, almost compelling beauty. How could they both be the same? Yet gradually the two images came together, as if one mask had been laid atop another. From that fusion emerged the magnificent yet terrifying visage of the great cat.

Wise Coyote broke free of the dreamy trancelike state he had fallen into and sat up, thinking. If the girl had the divine power that he hoped and feared lay within her, she could be a danger not only to him but to his household.

His children were safe, for they either lived in estates of their own or resided in the city. The only exception was his sculptor son, Huetzin, but he didn't live at Tezcot-zinco. His house and workshop stood near the palace grounds, but he rarely set foot beyond. He did come once in a while to use the palace library.

Wise Coyote started to rise from his kneeling position, clenching a fist. He should have sent word to Huetzin, warning him, telling him to stay away.

He sank down again, running a hand across his face. What good would a warning have done? Declaring something to be forbidden always had the opposite effect of increasing interest in it. Better to just let things be. Huetzin had always been totally engrossed in his art, rarely seeing or speaking to anyone other than his immediate family. He was always pleasant, but somehow always preoccupied, and any woman who was attracted to him because of his appearance or his paternity soon turned away.

Woman? Wise Coyote caught himself. Why did he think Mixcatl's womanhood would matter? Her potential power, not her sex, was the real concern. Or was it?

No. The girl herself—the shape of her body, her face, the jungle mystery in her eyes—had kindled a fascination in him. It burned like lust and would not be quenched. He wanted not only the abilities Mixcatl might have, but her body, perhaps even her spirit.

Any man who stood in his way . . . even his own son . . .

Again he caught himself, startled at the surge of possessiveness that knotted his hands once again into fists. Deliberately he opened his palms, stroking them lightly with his fingertips. Even though his queen had turned cold to him, he had many other wives and was used to being able to sate his desires.

He stared down at the documents on the low table

before him. On top was a map of Texcoco, drawn by his own hand on stretched deerskin. It showed the city center, with its many existing buildings and temples. Reluctantly, Wise Coyote laid his forefinger in the most crowded area. Ilhuicamina had demanded that the temple to Hummingbird be raised here. It did not matter how many other houses, public buildings or shrines to other gods had to be demolished in order to clear the site.

He laid his palm up against his forehead, thinking of how much time, aggravation and wealth he would have to spend to mollify the angered priests of other gods, landlords, nobles, shopkeepers and others who would be displaced. He pressed harder. Why, by the love of Tloque Nahaque, was he doing this? Because of an infatuation with an exotic face? Or a hope that was rapidly becoming an obsession.

He sighed, took off his turquoise coronet and ran his fingers through his hair. He might bear the title of tlatoani, but he was as much a slave to Ilhuicamina as the lowest ditch digger in Tenochtitlán. He would be building this temple whether or not he had been granted the loan of the two scribes.

Yet something had compelled him to bargain for the lives of the two painters, especially for Mixcatl's. She was the key to his search for a true god worthy of human devotion. She had to be, or else he would stand alone in the darkness, facing the vicious mockery of godhood raised by a man who had gone insane from his own fears. If there really was no hope, Wise Coyote thought that he too might go mad.

Impatiently he swept the map aside and got out the texts he had brought with him from Tezcotzinco. The words of the ancient Toltec scholars could not lie. The Aztecs might have burned their old books and rewritten their history to glorify their people, but these records, preserved intact from the founding of Texcoco, must hold the truth.

Eagerly he ran one forefinger along the elaborate lines of glyphs, searching again for a passage he had noted once before. Trying to judge the veracity of the tale-teller's stories about the jaguar kings, he had looked for the oldest texts he could find, searching for fragments of information.

There were many such pieces, each tiny, but adding up into a coherent whole. Here for instance, His finger halted as he read. This text claimed that the art of writing glyphs had not originated here in the Valley of Mexico, but had been brought from a people on the eastern coast. The art had already grown highly sophisticated, indicating that it had been developed in a culture that reached its height long before the Aztec state arose.

He unbound another sacred book and searched it. Here, in the myth of the creation story, lay more evidence. Of the four suns that had preceded the present age, the first had been the Jaguar Sun. Tezcatlipoca, shown in the text in the form of a dancing jaguar, had ruled a world of giants. The age had ended when a swarm of voracious jaguars consumed that world and its inhabitants.

Even if the text was not literally true, it seemed to speak of an age even older than the Toltec era that Wise Coyote had learned to revere. Somewhere deep in the past, there had been a first blooming of civilization under the rule of the jaguar kings. Then somehow it had fallen apart, its glories never again to be attained.

In other records, Wise Coyote found many other scattered hints to support the idea. He found more references to Tepeyolotli, Heart-of-the-Mountain, the jaguar aspect of Tezcatlipoca. A series of faces taken from ancient stone carvings seemed to depict the origin of the rain god Tlaloc from a primeval divine jaguar. And there was more.

"Everything points back to the Magicians," Wise Coyote muttered to himself, wiping the sweat from his face before it could drip onto the stiff yellowing pages. "Everything."

In a daze, he sat staring at the swirling glyphs in the text, no longer seeing them. Instead the distant world of the lost jungle cities seemed to come to life in his mind, a time when gods took the shape of the great cats and descended to earth. They took the shape of men and women, as mighty as they were wise. They gave gifts; the knowledge of turning streams to irrigate crops, the art of writing, the calendar, the knowledge of numbers and calculation. Perhaps they had not even wished to be worshipped, but could not turn aside the adulation and the demand that they be made kings.

What tragedy had brought down those first ones? Had it been their jaguar nature and their need to revert to their true shape? How had they been worshipped? Surely such beings would have no need to see human blood poured down their altars; flowers, food and perhaps the beauty of artisanship would have served them. Had it been the blood of the hunt on jaguar claws and teeth that inspired frenzied worshippers or scheming priests to give more of the same? Or was it a need inherent in man to kill his own kind in the name of divinity?

Perhaps the first stream of crimson to spill on those carved altars had spelled the end of that age. A betrayal came in the form of an offering and began a tradition of slaughter that drove away those that it was intended to please and destroyed nearly all that they had built.

Wise Coyote realized that this vision was a fantasy built in part of his own dreams and desires, but at its core, he sensed truth. A beast might shed blood, in feeding or defense, but only men would slay throngs of their own kind and pile the corpses to steam and rot in the name of reverence. Did the jaguar kings flee their cities, horrified at what they had unleashed? Or did they, too, succumb to the bloodlust?

Did it really matter how it had happened? The cities had long since crumbled and their inhabitants become moldy dust. The Magicians had all gone. He would never know the answer, for it lay in the nature of the vanished jaguar kings.

No. The king woke from his vision, blinking. If the girl Mixcatl proved to be a true descendant of those people, her development would tell him if the jaguar heritage inflamed or muted human savagery.

He gathered up the fan-folded texts, bound them and put them aside. Then he pulled the city map before him, wishing that he could put aside this hateful project until he could go to Tezcotzinco. The quarantine period for the two scribes was over, but this duty would keep him away until he had arranged to have the temple site cleared and all occupants of the demolished structures compensated for their loss. And Ilhuicamina would become impatient at any delay.

Wearily Wise Coyote picked up a brush and began to mark off buildings to be removed from the temple site.

The days dragged by at Texcoco. Wise Coyote chafed at a task he hated. He longed to be away from the heat and dust of the capital city and return to the hills of Tezcotzinco. At last his part in the siting, negotiations and financial arrangement for Hummingbird's temple was done. The rest he could leave to lesser officials. He dictated a document detailing his progress and had it sent to Tenochtitlán. Then he ordered his servants to pack in preparation for a well-deserved retreat to Tezcotzinco.

He had no illusions that he was going to the estate for relaxation, however. During the journey by litter from the capital, he thought about Mixcatl and weighed different approaches to dealing with her. He spoke of this to no one, for it would seem absurd that a king should be so concerned over a glyph-painting slave, and a borrowed one at that.

He thought first of meeting her privately in the estate's gardens. The idea tempted him, for the introduction would be less stiff and formal if he could speak to her while strolling about on flowered paths. Reluctantly he put it aside. Perhaps the garden would do for a later encounter, but that setting was too risky for the first.

It would be foolish to assume that the skin-peeling seizure that struck the girl in Tenochtitlán would not happen here. In her beast frenzy, she would have no respect for royalty. She might attack him as savagely as she had the youths who had tormented her. Wise Coyote intended no such provocation, but who knew what might upset or enrage one whom he yet knew so little about?

It would be better to meet the two scribes together, perhaps with the pretext of reviewing the commissioned history. The old man Nine-Lizard might be a bit of a mystery himself, but so far he had proved to be a loyal and useful ally. He could ease the introduction, and if the girl began to transform, he would know how to manage her. Wise Coyote could also have some men positioned discretely outside the chamber so that he could summon assistance if needed.

He arrived in the early evening, settled himself and his entourage and sent a messenger to notify Huetzin of his arrival. He had said that Huetzin need not come for a few days, knowing that the young sculptor was probably in his workshop, ankle-deep in stonedust and chips.

After the evening meal, Wise Coyote had word sent to the two scribes that he wished to visit them in their chambers and examine the document they were preparing. Dressing himself in the simple, comfortable yet regal clothing he usually wore at Tezcotzinco, he straightened his turquoise coronet and ordered a lightly armed escort to accompany him.

Leaving all but two of the men outside, he raised the door flap of the scribes' quarters and entered. A fire burned on the hearth and torches made from twisted pine bark flamed in niches in the wall. He saw at a glance that everything was ready—the completed books of the history were spread for his inspection on a low table and an icpalli laid with cushions had been set out for him.

Motioning the two guardsmen to stand at each side of the doorway, Wise Coyote took his place at the table. The two scribes knelt, touched the floor with their foreheads and then stood quietly by. The king had not intended to devote most of his attention to the document, but his scholar's eye was soon captured by the clarity and beauty of the glyphwork. He noted, with mixed pleasure and alarm, how fast the work had gone.

It was well that the two scribes worked so efficiently, but the completion of the document meant that Nine-Lizard and Mixcatl would have to be delivered back to Ilhuicamina. For the girl, the return would mean death, and he was sure she knew that. He wondered if she had tried to stall or slow the work.

He read one section and glanced at several others. "The quality of this manuscript is excellent, considering how fast you both have worked. You have also blended your styles so well that I cannot say who did most of it."

"Thank you tlatoani," answered Nine-Lizard, dipping his head in acknowledgment. "Seven-Flower Mixcatl and I shared the task."

There was no hint of untruth in the old man's voice or face, nor any indication that he was dissatisfied with Mixcatl's contribution. That the girl evidently had made no attempt to delay the work spoke in her favor.

"Come," said Wise Coyote kindly, beckoning her forward and rising from his icpalli, "let me meet the one who has been so diligent on my behalf."

Mixcatl came slowly, but not timidly, the torchlight flickering in her eyes as she studied him. Her face was as he remembered it from seeing her in Tenochtitlán, with its full bowed lips, short nose and full jaw.

"I am grateful that you have offered me refuge at your court, tlatoani," she answered.

Her plain huipil blouse revealed the shape of her young breasts beneath. Through the rough-woven fabric of her skirt he could see the outlines of her powerful thighs, the curve of her rump, the flowing lines of hips that narrowed to a well-muscled waist.

Wise Coyote could see her heritage in the controlled grace of her walk, the way she held her head and body. She moved with the unconscious suppleness of a great cat. For an instant he could almost see the lines of the divine jungle beast that he hoped and feared lay within her.

As Mixcatl approached him, he noted her height. Most women barely reached his chin. She had cast her gaze down as was proper, but she would only have to lift her head and tilt her chin slightly back to look him full in the face.

His hand twitched at a sudden impulse to place his fingers alongside her jaw, to bring those soft full lips to his . . . Instead he closed his fingers and took his seat once more, indicating that the two scribes should sit nearby.

He became aware of Mixcatl's scent as she knelt down beside him. It was warm, animal, with a humid sweetness like the air of the deep jungle where he had gone to hunt as a young man. Yet her hair was damp and her skin fresh, telling him that she had just bathed.

Yes, he was definitely spoiled in the matter of women, for it was hard to restrain the urge to send Nine-Lizard and the two door guards away and take Mixcatl into his private quarters. But now was not the time to indulge himself, especially under the sharp gaze of Nine-Lizard. He wondered if the old man had already sensed his reaction to the girl. Would Nine-Lizard welcome it, resent it or try to use it?

He swallowed. Gods, he felt like a schoolboy on his first visit to the House of Song.

"Have you had any difficulties in finding sources?" he asked. He expected Nine-Lizard to answer, but it was Mixcatl who spoke.

"Actually, we now have the opposite problem, now that you have so graciously allowed us to use your library," she said. "There are many records and not all agree. I am not sure what to include or what to leave out."

Wise Coyote clasped his hands on the low table. "Where do you find most of the differences?"

"The references we found claim that the Aztecs worshipped other gods before Hummingbird on the Left. The records we brought with us from the House of Scribes claim that Hummingbird has always been supreme."

Wise Coyote watched Mixcatl's face as she puzzled over the disparity between the records at Texcoco and the ones brought from Tenochtitlán. He wondered if she thought that his documents were inaccurate or even the result of heresy. She might be of foreign origin, but she had been raised to believe the Aztec religion.

"Have you any reason to believe one source rather than the other?" he asked softly.

She gave him a sharp look, as if she suspected that he might be questioning her faith.

"The history as related in your records disagrees with what I learned from my teacher, Speaking Quail. Yet these texts"—she paused, laying her hands on the books taken from Tezcotzinco's library—"seem more . . . authentic. I see different styles, different interpretations, as if they were written by many scholars throughout many New Fires." She paused. "I know this may sound strange to you, tlatoani, but I have a very good sense of smell and I have handled many old books. The mixture of odors in the manuscripts from your shelves tells me they are genuinely ancient, and authored by many hands, as the text claims."

"And the ones from the House of Scribes are not?" Wise Coyote asked, growing more intrigued.

Mixcatl shook her head, frowning at the pile of cord-bound books at the end of the low table. "No. Those records are supposed to predate the reign of Itzcoatl, Obsidian Serpent, but they are too new. They do not smell right and the styles are too uniform, as if a small number of scribes produced them over a short interval."

Wise Coyote glanced at Nine-Lizard, who indicated his agreement with Mixcatl's words. Carefully he said, "Perhaps it was done in order to make Hummingbird on the Left appear to occupy a greater place in history than he deserved?"

There was a sharp intake of breath from the girl and her eyes went wide. Wise Coyote wondered if he had pushed her too far too fast. Yet the look in her eyes was not anger or indignation, but wonder touched with a sense of . . . relief? Perhaps she was not as devoted to the bloody god of her adoptive land as he feared.

The king leaned back in his icpalli. "Your observation supports a similar discovery of mine. I came across a text that claimed that Obsidian Serpent had older books burned and rewritten to glorify Hummingbird and his worshippers. Scholars to whom I showed it claimed that it was a lie, written by a disgruntled scribe who had been exiled from Itzcoatl's court. Needless to say, I have not shown it to anyone since."

Mixcatl looked taken aback. "The books that the

House of Scribes has taken great care to preserve and recopy—they cannot be false!" she said indignantly.

"Seven-Flower, remember whose company we are now in," said Nine-Lizard mildly.

Mixcatl swallowed, gave an apologetic dip of the head. "I beg your forgiveness, tlatoani."

"It is given," Wise Coyote answered, and added, "I too would be angered if I found that much of my life's work was devoted to reproducing documents whose truthfulness I later came to doubt."

The girl sat with her eyes shut. "I do not wish to believe what you say, tlatoani, but I cannot turn aside the evidence of my own senses either. I have wondered if those texts . . . were really what they seemed, but I thought it was my own inability to accept what they said. I should have spoken up sooner and told the Master of Scribes."

"And you would have died for it," said Nine-Lizard sharply. "You are not the only one to suspect that those records were forged. I knew too, but I kept quiet."

Mixcatl looked at him, astonished. "Why? If those books are false, all that effort has been wasted to keep alive a lie!"

"The effort was not wasted," said Wise Coyote, with a grim smile. "Altering the story must have served Itzcoatl well, and all those after him, including Ilhuicamina."

"But now, if we have the real story . . ." Mixcatl faltered.

Wise Coyote felt a surge of respect and affection toward the girl. If she valued truth more than religious belief, she had the makings of a true scholar. He regretted what he had to say next.

"It will be recorded, but not in any document intended for Ilhuicamina. I dare not inflame his anger toward me, or I will end up doing Hummingbird a greater favor than just building temples for him." Wise Coyote caught himself, for passion had made him say more than he intended. "Listen," he said to the two scribes in a low voice. "I am enlarging your task to include the preparation of two versions of the history. One will be given to Ilhuicamina; the other will stay here at Texcoco with me. Perhaps someday, when the Aztec state falls of its own weight, the second document can carry the truth to those who live after. Do you agree?"

"You do not need our approval," said Mixcatl, puzzled. "As king, you command us—we were brought here to serve you."

"I can command you, but in truth, I would prefer willing partners in this task."

"Preparation of a second document would allow us to stay longer at Tezcotzinco," added Nine-Lizard.

"That is an additional benefit."

Wise Coyote looked at Mixcatl, who was staring down at her hands, laid flat upon the tabletop. She looked a bit lost and he couldn't blame her, for it was difficult to have the foundation of your religion yanked out from under you. Yet she did not seem as aggrieved as she might over the insult done to the god she had been brought up to worship.

"Seven-Flower," he said, "if you find this painful, please accept my sympathy."

She looked up suddenly and he found himself staring deep into her eyes as she replied, "It is not so much painful as confusing. I . . . I need to think. And I would like to see the other document you referred to, the one by the scribe who was expelled from Itzcoatl's court."

To decide for yourself if it is true or not, thought Wise Coyote. *Well, I will not be insulted if you do not accept it on my word alone.*

"I will have the manuscript brought," he said, getting

up from the table. "This has been a long but fruitful discussion. We will talk more tomorrow—I am tired."

Motioning his men after him, Wise Coyote left the chamber. On his way back to his own quarters, he got the old book out of the library and ordered a servant to take it to Mixcatl.

On his sleeping mat that night, Wise Coyote struggled with sleeplessness. It was an old enemy of his, and lately had been plaguing him more. At last he sat up in the darkened room and wrapped his arms about his knees.

Somehow he could not get Seven-Flower Mixcatl out of his mind. He remembered the sound of her voice and the look in her eyes as she had reluctantly admitted that she also did not trust the truthfulness of the Aztec records from the House of Scribes. There was something else, something that had rung a sympathetic chord in him but had passed away too rapidly. He knitted his brow and pressed his forehead against his knees. Then, her words did come back to him.

I thought it was my own inability to accept what the books said.

Her statement echoed words that he himself had said long ago, not once but many times, as he struggled between the demands of religion and conscience. Last night, had she revealed the signs of a similar inward battle, or had he misinterpreted what she had said? Had he heard only what he wanted to hear?

At last he knew what drew him so strongly to Mixcatl. Not her exotic beauty or the strength in that tall powerful body. Not the titillation of danger remembered from seeing her half-transformed. Not even the frightening promise of seeing her reveal her true nature by taking the shape of the great cat.

It was loneliness. Not solitude, but a wrenching loneliness that first came when he realized that the world about him had become a blood-spewing nightmare and that no one else was sickened by it. Everyone knelt willingly at the temple steps and lapped the red stream trickling down from the altar. And now he, like a reluctant animal, was having his nose forced into the redness and was being forced to drink.

No one cried out. No one rebelled. Even the scholars of Texcoco, whose ideals had shaped his own, accepted it as fate. This is the way the world is, they said, and did not acknowledge his own cry that it did not have to be so. He had begun to wonder over the last year or so, who was really closer to madness—Ilhuicamina or himself.

The most terrible feeling was that he was alone in his inability to bear the world's horror. In blacker moments he wondered if he had perhaps been born into the wrong age. Perhaps the gods, in their cruelty, had taken a spirit destined for the golden light of Quetzalcoatl's reign and thrown it into an abyss.

Even those about whom he cared most deeply could never understand. The women he loved, the many sons he had sired, even the sensitive and sympathetic Huetzin, had all been too well shielded. For them, the pain was dulled, if they felt it at all. For him the pain was sharp and made keener by the inability to share it. Only in his poetry, and perhaps in design, did his desperation emerge.

The thought that he might at last have found in this strange slave girl a spirit whose struggle was akin to his own made the path ahead seem bearable. Perhaps it was ironic that it took someone who was so distant from the rest of humanity to hear what the humanity in him pleaded for. Could one who was born from loins of the predator be sickened by the sanguineous frenzy growing in Tenochtitlán and threatening to engulf Texcoco?

Or was this hope also an illusion? Perhaps she would

kneel and lap with the best of them. Perhaps, in the end, so would he.

Jaguar shapes haunted the king's dreams that night. They prowled the halls of Tezcotzinco, brushing past his thighs as he walked among them. They turned shadowy heads and stared at him. One among them turned noiseless steps toward his chamber and beckoned with a wave of a ghostly tail.

Dreambound, he could only follow.

The powerful sinuous lines of the cat seemed to give way to the sleek curves of a woman, although he could not tell in the dream whether she had become one or the other. It did not matter whatever form she took, for she had ignited a powerful hunger in him. It drew him to where she lay on the sleeping mat, and when he lay down beside her, caressing and being caressed, he did not know if he stroked fur or silken skin. When his desire became heated and the urge to couple strong, he did not know whether hands or teeth ripped away the bindings of his loincloth. And when he buried himself in soft warm flesh, trembling both with dread and ecstasy, the soft sounds that came from her and built to a triumphant cry at his final thrust were both the moans of a woman and the echoing roar of the cat.

He sat up in a cold sweat, the dream falling away like strands of an enfolding shroud. A clammy stickiness beneath his loincloth told him that his body had indeed responded to the illusion that the dream had created. At first he felt a surge of revulsion as he mopped himself up and put on a fresh loincloth. How had he become so degraded to fantasize coupling with a beast?

Perhaps it was the lateness of the night that had stolen away his ability to reason and intensified his despair. He should just pull his cloak over himself once more and lie down on the mat. *If Mixcatl is a child of the divine jaguar, then she is herself a goddess and my desire is not unnatural. The legends say that men united with jaguars to sire the first ancient kings.*

He felt himself relax as sleep approached and his thoughts began to wander. Perhaps it was time for the great cycle of change to renew itself. Perhaps he was the one chosen to bring about the rebirth of mighty people.

If she is indeed the jaguar's daughter, what a son I could breed by her! Texcoco would have an heir, a replacement for my murdered Prodigy, and more.

Wise Coyote lost himself in a vision of a dynasty of jaguar-blooded Texcocan kings. What men such a blending of lineages might produce! The infusion of the jaguar strain into the noble Texcocan descendants of the Toltecs could create a people even greater than any who had previously arisen. Before such warriors, the Aztecs would wither and crumble and Hummingbird on the Left would have the cup of "precious water" struck away from his greedy lips.

How well they would rule and how wisely, for they would have the heritage of their mother's line combined with the gentleness and scholarship of their father's.

Then Wise Coyote remembered Mixcatl in the grip of her beginning transformation.

Would I want any child of mine to have to endure that?

He could create the dynasty he dreamed of and he could watch his progeny struggle with the threat of transformation. What had life been like for the original jaguar-blooded ones? Had they rejoiced in the freedom to run wild as beasts, or had they dreaded the change that seized them?

Perhaps the reward would be great enough to overshadow the cost. Perhaps not.

Wise Coyote knew that the timidity of the Deer had held him back too long. It had cost him his elder son and threatened to cost him his throne. He had to act. Begetting a new heir would not be enough; the boy, if the child was a son, would have no time to come of age. Indeed, he probably would not even have time to be born before the Aztecs took Texcoco.

And there was also the question of legitimacy. If a son by Mixcatl were to be chosen as his heir, she would have to displace Ant Flower as his primary wife and queen. Such a thing could be done, but it would take time and care.

If he displayed her ability to his own people and they accepted her as divine, then the change would be easy. Texcoco would be eager for its ruler to wed a goddess and acclaim her child as a demigod.

As for the Aztecs, witnessing Mixcatl's transformation would convince them of his alliance with a divine power. They would have no choice but to back off or risk divine wrath. The rise of a real goddess could shake Tenochtitlán down to its blood-soaked foundations!

And perhaps the homage paid to one of their own kind would bring others of the Jaguar's Children out of hiding. They might be useful allies if the Aztecs chose to be foolish.

Wise Coyote was starting to smile sleepily to himself when another problem occurred to him.

He had yet to see Mixcatl shed her human skin completely to take on animal shape. Could she really do it?

14

THE BRIGHTNESS OF morning helped to chase the lingering dream shadows from Wise Coyote's mind. Yawning and stretching, he got up from his sleeping mat. He felt a bit foolish about his maunderings the night before. Despair and hope had gotten the best of him.

Now, refreshed and strengthened by sleep, he could examine events with a more detached and scholarly attitude.

As servants laid out his garments and brought his morning meal of amaranth cakes and chocolatl he thought about what he had learned about Mixcatl and decided that it was not enough. He might be better acquainted with her probable background and heritage than she was, but he knew little of her character.

Well, he had given her the book by the outcast scholar who claimed that Obsidian Serpent had deliberately falsified Aztec records. Her reaction to that might give some insight.

With that in mind, the king sent word by his servants that he wished to speak with Mixcatl. This time he would see her in an empty chamber adjacent to the scribes' quarters. Nine-Lizard, working on the history, would not be in the room, but near enough to be summoned. Wise

Coyote decided to have men discretely posted outside the room, but none inside.

As a last precaution, he reluctantly tucked an obsidian-bladed dagger into the band of his loincloth and hid it beneath the folds of his shoulder-cloak. If the young woman should suffer a seizure and turn on him, he wanted protection. It was for her sake as well that he had assumed his own defense. If something did happen and guards were present, they might slay the girl in their haste. He, on the other hand, could wound to disable without killing.

The meeting chamber was much the same as the scribes' quarters, having a low table where manuscripts could be laid out and studied. Mixcatl was there waiting for him, the folded text underneath her arm and a serious look on her face. She also bore slight shadows under her eyes, making Wise Coyote wonder if her sleep had been as delayed or as restless as his.

At his entrance, she greeted him in the formal way, but before she could stoop to touch her forehead to his sandaled feet, he raised her up. Touching her skin and inhaling the musky sweetness of her scent brought back the previous night's dream with a rush. With difficulty, he let her hands go.

As if she sensed his disquiet, she cast her gaze down, although he noticed that she glanced up every once in a while, as if measuring the effect her presence had. For an instant the king wondered if she would dare to entice him. The notion outraged his sense of propriety even as it tempted. A noble might proposition a slave, but he could not imagine the situation being reversed.

Mixcatl broke the awkward moment by kneeling down with the book she carried and unfolding it on the table. "I am grateful that you showed me this, tlatoani."

"I am surprised at your gratitude. If I were you, I

would find this text unsettling. Unless, of course, I did not accept it."

She flushed slightly, color deepening the bronze of her cheeks. He wondered if the cause was anger or embarrassment at being caught in a polite lie. She said, "I might not accept the author's accusation if this text stood alone, but the other evidence supports him." She paused and he could not help hearing a slight sigh in her words. "As you say, Obsidian Serpent must have burned the old books and replaced them with false texts."

"Does knowing this trouble you?"

"I learned glyphs from copying the records in the House of Scribes. I know them well—they are old friends." She shrugged. "If old friends prove false, I will make new ones. It is better to know now than later."

"And your faith?"

"What beliefs I have, lord king, are not changed by this. The sacred books are written by men, not gods. Finding that the texts are false does not mean the gods have lied."

He found himself surprised and oddly pleased by her response.

"You are telling me that your belief does not rest on a foundation so weak that it can be easily undercut," he said.

"No." She eyed him. "Does yours?"

The question was unexpected and caught him off balance. As a king speaking to a subject, he had the right to ignore Mixcatl's inquiry, but somehow there was something about this woman that placed her outside established roles and beyond those boundaries.

"I do not place my faith entirely in the gods," he answered, and was relieved when she accepted that and did not ask him to explain further.

She gathered up the text spread on the table, folded it

and wrapped it with its cord. "I will return this to the library, tlatoani. I am finished with it."

"Wait," he said. She halted, her eyes widening. He took the book from her hands and laid it back on the table.

"The text is safe here. Take my arm. We will walk in the garden."

"I should resume work on the history," she faltered.

"Nine-Lizard is working on it. Come." He offered her his elbow—the one opposite the side where the dagger was hidden in his loincloth. With a hesitant smile, she slid her arm through his.

Together they left the room, going down the tiled hallways, down the bluestone steps and out into the garden.

The trees and bushes were brilliant with flowers, some tiny and delicate, others large and lush. Bumblebees and butterflies flitted above them, through air made rich and hazy by their perfume. As he escorted Mixcatl along the flagstoned walkways, he showed her the plants that he was most proud of, for they had been brought long distances from their native lands and carefully tended so that they might thrive. Here stood a dark-leafed tree bearing aromatic red-brown beans. It had been brought from the far south, a range of hills beyond the borders of the Aztec Empire. There, shaded from harsh sunlight were tiny belled flowers mixed with buds of a glowing orange-gold. Those had been brought from the seacoast far to the west. And those orchids whose roots wove into the bark of a jungle tree had been carefully transported from the hot wet lands to the east.

Wise Coyote watched his companion as she smiled at the flowers, inhaled their fragrance and often touched them gently. Though she was clearly enjoying the walk, she said little. Was she just shy, he wondered. What did she think of him? Did she look upon him as a savior?

After all, he had given her refuge from the dangers in Tenochtitlán. Or did she fear him? Even a benevolent king still had the power of life or death over the subjects of his household if they displeased him.

"Have you found life here pleasant?" he asked, at last.

"Yes. Nine-Lizard and I spend the mornings working on the history. In the afternoon sometimes I go in the gardens near the house. I have never seen so many different flowers." Then she added, with a little daring in her voice, "Someday I will paint them."

Wise Coyote glanced at her, puzzled. He didn't understand. What did she mean by "painting"? Making glyphs for the flowers? As far as he knew, there were none, since signs for exotic flowers were not required for official documents.

"My pictures are not glyphs," said Mixcatl awkwardly and he sensed that she regretted bringing the subject up at all. Yet he was intrigued. The idea of making images that were not part of a document or map, of making lines on paper for the sake of beauty alone, was an idea that had occurred to him, but he had not yet dared to try it. If the girl was dabbling in untried arts, she might have even more to her than he suspected.

"Will you show the pictures to me later?" he asked.

"If you wish, tlatoani." Her answer was guarded, as if she sensed that she was talking of things forbidden to most people. He decided not to push her. He would learn more later.

He noticed that, as Mixcatl walked, she sniffed the air and her brows came together. It was not the expression of someone just enjoying the aroma of the gardens. He tested the air, but could find nothing.

"Is some ill scent spoiling the fragrance?" he asked affably.

"No, tlatoani. It is the absence of a scent that puzzles me."

"What do you find missing? A creeping vine of your homeland, perhaps?"

She demurred, saying that it did not matter, but when he pressed her she said, "I noticed that when you met Nine-Lizard and me, you had guards in the room and outside in the hallway. This morning, when you met me, you brought no guards into the room, but seven armed men stayed in rooms nearby. That is something I expected to find in your royal household," she added hastily. "Here in the garden, there are no men in hiding. That is what I find puzzling."

Wise Coyote felt intrigued, with a tiny warning edge of alarm. How did she know how many warriors he had hidden near the chamber? His household guards were well trained in stealth and moved without making any sound. And even more puzzling, how could she know that hidden watchers were absent from the garden?

"My nose, tlatoani, can do far more than detect the authenticity of a sacred text. I caught the odor of your men. Each is different, so I could tell how many there were."

The king was frankly skeptical that a sense of smell could be so acute. Her pride evidently stung despite her deference to his royal status, Mixcatl suggested that he give her a challenge to prove her claim.

"What does my own smell reveal?" Wise Coyote asked.

"You slept badly, you ate amaranth for breakfast and . . ." She halted, as if her next pronouncement might be too bold.

"What else?" he prompted.

"You are carrying a weapon with an oiled wooden handle."

Slowly Wise Coyote's hand touched the haft of his

dagger. It had been carefully treated with pumpkin-seed oil to prevent splitting, but the smell had long since dissipated. At least to his nose.

"Can you scent the very depths of a man's soul?" he asked, showing her the weapon and trying not to show that he was shaken. She paled as if she feared she had been too bold with him. "Where do you come by this strange gift?"

"I do not know. It is part of me in the same way that my glyph-painting, peeling sickness and strange fits are a part of me." She hesitated. "Is that why you carried the dagger? For fear I would fall into a fit? You are right to do so, for I know I have tried to hurt others when the strangeness seizes me."

Wondering how much she knew about her heritage, he asked, "Do you understand this 'strangeness'?"

She looked away, and when she spoke again, her voice was strained. "No. The only thing I know is that when the peeling sickness happens, I start to feel . . . as if I am becoming something else . . . There is a part of me inside that wants to creep on four feet, to bite and tear and then run away."

There was a desperation in her eyes akin to the feeling that he often had when faced by the threats closing in about him. It made him want to touch her gently, draw her to his breast and comfort her with an embrace.

Why hasn't Nine-Lizard told her more? he wondered. *He must have a reason. Perhaps she already knows, deep down, what she is.*

Mixcatl was speaking again, staring away over the flowers, her voice remote. "Keep your dagger close, lord king, and keep your men always about you when you are with me, in case I should be taken by the strangeness."

Wise Coyote took her hand, holding it firmly when she tried to withdraw. "I do not fear the strangeness," he said, but he was careful to keep his dagger hand free.

Her fingers stayed in his as they continued the walk.

"Huetzin tells me that you and Nine-Lizard have made good use of my library," he said, again trying to break the uneasy quiet that had grown between them.

She turned her head as if she had been distracted by something and had to pull her attention back to him. At the mention of Huetzin, a fleeting smile crossed her lips. "He is nice," she said hesitantly. "He looks very much like you."

"He resembles me in face, but differs from me in temperament," said Wise Coyote lightly.

"He spoke to me one day in the library," she said and her words came easier as if she was feeling more comfortable. "One thing he said puzzled me. He said that he was trying to make an image of a god who has none. He said that it was to be a gift for you."

Wise Coyote chuckled gently. "That is one example of how he differs from me. I only try to do what is nearly impossible. He tries to do what is completely impossible."

"I think he will do it," said Mixcatl stubbornly.

Wise Coyote gave her a sidelong glance. The sudden defense and the loyalty shown in those words suggested that this young woman understood more about his son than a casual encounter would suggest.

"Well, Huetzin has plenty of time yet. The temple that is to house the image has been delayed. I have another project to complete."

"I have never heard of a god that has no image," Mixcatl said. "Since you do not speak of him by name, does he lack that too?"

"You have not heard of Tloque Nahaque, the God of the Near and By, because he has been forgotten in Tenochtitlán. Some religious scholars claim that he is an aspect of Smoking Mirror."

He was surprised at the animation that lighted Mixcatl's face at the mention of Smoking Mirror. It was the same expression he had seen when he had spoken of Huetzin.

Smiling, she said, "I know Smoking Mirror well. I made my first drawing of him while I was a child. To me he looked like a dancing jaguar wearing plumes and gold. I was disappointed when my teacher said that the image was supposed to represent a man clothed in a spotted pelt." She sighed. "I never could bring myself to give up the idea that he really was a great cat, even though I know better."

"Perhaps your first impression was not wrong," said Wise Coyote. "I have searched for the origins of the gods. Smoking Mirror may have arisen from an ancient rain god who was worshipped in the form of a jaguar."

"Would you show me the texts?" Mixcatl asked eagerly. "I would so much like to see them for myself."

Yes, for you are drawn to knowledge of your own kind, the king thought.

He promised her that he would share his sources as they continued their stroll between the lush foliage and exotic flowers of the garden.

Mixcatl spoke thoughtfully. "It is strange that the sacred jaguar has given birth to Smoking Mirror, who has in turn given birth to Tloque Nahaque. He is the one you call your gentle god, isn't he?"

"Yes," Wise Coyote answered, wondering if she had also learned that from Huetzin.

"When will you build his shrine?"

Remembering the bargain that had been struck with Ilhuicamina, he felt an upwelling of grief. "I doubt that I will ever be able to build it."

Mixcatl turned to him, puzzled. "If you wish to raise a temple to your gentle god, why can you not do so?" Within the question he heard another, unspoken. If you are king, why can't you do as you wish? Inwardly he felt a tolerant smile at her ignorance and simplicity as well as a regret that what she assumed was not so. And, unexpectedly, an anger rose at all those who saw him from without and assumed his life as a prince was easy and soft. Many times, he thought bitterly that he would rather be a farmer working in his fields beside a living son who was his legitimate heir, rather than a ruler stripped of his firstborn by weakness and misguided loyalty.

How could he explain this to Mixcatl? Why did he wish to? Would she understand that there were limits to what a head of state could do, especially when he stood in the shadow of one greater. But he did not want to speak to her of Ilhuicamina. Instead he gave another explanation, one that probably had its own truth.

To her he said, "A king must obey the wishes of those he rules, or he finds himself a despot, hated and soon overthrown. Even in my state of Texcoco, where men are encouraged to turn from war to scholarship, people would not accept a god that did not demand death." He paused. "They would think me foolish and a fool is less acceptable than a tyrant."

He saw by the way that Mixcatl looked at him that she heard the pain in his voice and perhaps understood his plight.

"I do not think you are foolish," she said softly.

Her voice was calm, even. He heard and felt the sound of truth in it. *Tell me about your dream of a gentle god*, her eyes said, and somehow, not knowing why, he did.

When he finished, there was not loathing, pity or disgust in her expression. There was amazement, perhaps puzzlement, but beneath a sense of quiet joy that comes when something precious is shared. Wise Coyote felt a growing excitement and a hope that he had at last found a sympathetic spirit.

It made him want to gather her to his breast and hold her tightly, bathe her face with caresses and then combine desire with tenderness to make her his own. Yet he was still uncertain. There was too much at risk to rush ahead.

Deliberately he made his voice neutral. "I am startled that you can even begin to question your religion, much less share my vision of a gentle god."

"Because I was raised in Tenochtitlán?" Her arched brows rose.

"Every child in your city has faith beaten into him through his ears or his backside. Even slaves. No one escapes it and few resist." He found that his voice was getting rough as he remembered his time in the calmecac where his father had placed him for schooling. Two years of that had almost extinguished his own will and spirit. Thank the gods that his father had seen the harm it was doing and pulled him out to study with the priests of Quetzalcoatl.

Mixcatl listened quietly before answering. "While I was in the House of Scribes, Speaking Quail taught me that it was the gods who stand between the world and its ending. Hummingbird on the Left must be kept sated or the sun would be devoured. I believed because I had to, but there was a part of me that said this is not for you, this is not right, that there must be another way." She closed her eyes and he saw the thick black lashes lying against the brown of her skin. "I was ashamed of my doubts. I tried to make them go away, but I could not."

"The House of Scribes is close to the twin pyramids," said Wise Coyote softly. "Could you see the sacrifices from your window?"

"Yes. I could smell them too. I could not bear it. I was sickened and ashamed of my sickness." She faced him, her eyes shimmering. "It is not wrong to love the gods. I have found comfort in Quetzalcoatl and Smoking Mirror. Tlaloc I accepted, for he brings the rain. But I could not love Hummingbird on the Left. I have told no one of this but you." She looked at him steadily, jaguar color flickering in her eyes, her voice strangely distant. "Perhaps speaking to you of this is wrong. If so, punish me."

Wise Coyote felt a surge of joy. Could a woman who bore the soul of the jaguar be repelled by the excesses of the Aztec rites? Did she share with him the same wants and needs that made him turn away from tradition and seek a gentler side to the divine? If that was true, it was more than a miracle.

Wise Coyote put his hands to Mixcatl's shoulders, feeling her flesh warm beneath the fabric of her blouse. "No, it is not wrong. The gods have their rightful place in things and it is well that we should love them, but Hummingbird has stepped out of his rightful place and must be put back." He paused. "I need your help."

"How?" The girl's eyes were wide, her lips parted.

"I have plans, but I think it wise not to tell you yet. Just tell me this. I feel you believe as I do. Is it true?"

"Yes!" The word came out in a rush.

"And you will aid me."

"But what can I do? I am a scribe, but still a slave."

Wise Coyote squeezed her shoulders tighter. "You have gifts that will soon make themselves known. Use them to help me."

"The only things I have are the peeling sickness Nine-Lizard has told you about, and my painting," Mixcatl replied, her brow knitting. "And even Huetzin does not understand the pictures I make, even though he gave me the tiles."

"Huetzin?" Wise Coyote said, feeling his grip loosen on her shoulders. "I know you have met my son, but I did not think that you had become friends."

"Yes. He invited me down to his workshop and showed me his sculptures. Then he suggested that I bring my paints and work while he made his figures."

Wise Coyote felt a thread of uneasiness slip into the

fabric of the new dream he was weaving about Mixcatl. Had Huetzin also been attracted to this girl, drawn by their shared gift of artistry?

Well, it would not matter. Anything that Huetzin had with her could not match the bonds of sympathy and purpose that had just been forged between him and Mixcatl.

Yet this girl was so different. Had he known what sort of uncanny spell she could cast, he would have sent Huetzin away. As much as he loved his son, he wanted nothing to interfere with the plans he had for Mixcatl. If she developed the powers that he suspected lay in her, she would stand by his side, not only as kindred spirit and companion, but as a jaguar queen whose true divinity would bring Tenochtitlán to its knees.

"I think we have spent enough time in the garden," said Wise Coyote, wondering if any of his thoughts had been revealed in his face. He doubted so; long years in the schooling and practice of diplomacy had taught him much.

Together they left the garden paths and returned to the palace.

The day after Mixcatl's walk with the king, Huetzin came to escort her on another afternoon visit to his workshop. Thinking of what had happened between her and Wise Coyote, she hesitated. The king wanted her for a companion, perhaps even a wife. He was a good and gentle man and could give her much. Yet she sensed that he would ask a great deal in return and a part of her felt a vague resentment that she had already become bound to him. Huetzin was fond of her just for herself.

Going with him would not do any harm. Anyway, she had already planned this visit.

Her decision made, she ran down the bluestone steps of Tezcotzinco, paints and brushes clutched against her.

The sun spilled down its light from high overhead, washing the palace and garden in dazzling white and gold. On the garden path, Huetzin waited for her, his arms folded, his head cocked and a smile on his face.

"So, what did Nine-Lizard say about tile-painting?" he asked.

Mixcatl answered happily. "That when I am not painting the history, I may do as I like. You were right. He is not as severe as I feared."

"Will you work on your tile again?"

"I will look at it," said the girl, "but I will probably start a new one, since the one I gave you is finished, I think."

Huetzin nodded agreement and they strolled together on the path. Mixcatl liked the feel of his body against hers. She slipped a hand into his and glanced at his face to see if he minded. The answering look in his eyes and the squeeze he gave her palm told her that he didn't mind at all.

An early afternoon wind blew across the path, bringing smells of the garden. There was another scent among the flowers—a musky, animal odor, the same one that she had smelled when she had first arrived on the palace grounds. Before she knew it, the scent had drawn her off the path and onto the lawn.

"What is this smell in the air?" Mixcatl asked excitedly, turning to him. "Are there animals here? May I see them?"

"Only a few tame deer over in the knoll," said Huetzin. He seemed to be amused and slightly puzzled by her eagerness. Taking her wrist, he urged her back to the path. "I thought you wanted to start painting again."

"Yes, I do, but I want to see the deer first. Please, Huetzin."

The young sculptor gave her an odd look. Mixcatl, caught up as she was in the entrancement of the scent, had to struggle to focus on his face. She realized, with a sharp flash of embarrassment, that she was using the impatient begging tones of a young child. Yet she could not help herself. She felt prickly and excited all over.

Huetzin put one hand on her shoulder and together they walked over a little rise. Below were five small deer, two bucks and three does. He plucked a tuft of new grass and gave a high trilling call. A buck raised his head. Mixcatl could see that he was a youngster, just showing his spikes.

Huetzin called again and held out the grass. The young spike buck tossed his head and began sidling toward them. With one hand Huetzin pushed Mixcatl down into the long grass. For an instant, she pushed back, suddenly angry that she could not stand by him as the deer approached.

Then she remembered a similar anger that had come when she caught this same smell and she remembered the thoughts she had then. She had wanted to break away from Nine-Lizard when he hurried her into the house. She had even wanted to struggle and strike out. She realized to her horror that she was having the same kind of feelings about Huetzin. They made no sense. Huetzin was her friend. Why was she feeling so irritable, so eager and impatient?

"Huetzin," she said, trying to fight the scent that filled her nose, even her mouth, and was tugging away her self-control. "I should not see the deer. I should go and paint."

She looked up, saw that he had moved away from her so that he could not hear. The deer was very close, extending its neck to nibble the fresh grass he held out. Its odor blew all around her, seizing her attention, wrapping her up in a hunger that would admit no other thoughts. Her mouth filled with saliva. Her skin prickled and itched. Impatiently she rubbed her wrists together, felt the skin loosen on both.

Huetzin was turning to her, beckoning, his mouth forming words, but they buzzed strangely in her ears. The deer was eating out of his hand. She could see the delicate black muzzle moving, smell the breath that blew on the youth's hand. Her eyes lingered on the deer's body; the slender legs, the strong haunches, the rounded vulnerable belly. The color in her vision faded to grayed-out tones of blue and yellow.

She crouched low in the grass, saliva starting to seep from the corners of her mouth. She worked her jaws. She was hungry, so hungry. The only thing that would fill her was the deer.

The skin was loose on her face, her arms, as if she were wearing a tunic and mask. The feeling was maddening and she wanted to scratch it off, but she knew the movement would alarm the deer.

Huetzin was looking at her, his face distorting into strange shapes, but she didn't care about him or his face. It was the deer that made up her world now. The scent and sight and taste of it on her tongue. The warmth and blood-sweetness coming from the animal as warmth rises from a sun-heated rock.

She found herself creeping forward on hands and feet, faster and faster, her gaze fixed on the spike buck. Its head jerked up in alarm. She rose on her hind feet as black, white and gray swallowed the colors of her vision. She launched herself, feeling skin split and tear away from her limbs, burst by the growing pressure of the powerful muscles swelling inside.

Past the man she shot, onto the deer. She tried to seize its throat with hands that had gown too clumsy to grasp and instead flung her arms around the beast's neck. She opened her jaws for the throat.

She felt hands on her shoulder, dragging her off the

deer as the animal struggled beneath her. A wild rage surged up inside her as the strong hands broke her grip and dragged her head away from the pulsing place at the deer's throat. Wailing and squalling, she lashed out, but an arm went around her neck and a body was on top of her, rolling her over, grinding her nose in the dirt.

The shouts about her were just noise at first, then her bewildered brain began to hear words in them as the clay pressed into her face blocked the scents of the deer from reaching her nose.

"Hold her down, Huetzin!" came a hoarse shout, almost a croak. Then she realized that she was still hungry and that they were driving the prey beast away. With renewed anger she began struggling again.

She heard the thump of a rock hitting dirt as someone threw it at the deer and missed. Another thump, a bawl, and the sound of hooves striking ground and then fading away. The deer was going. The two men had driven it off. She couldn't get it back. She was seized with a deep sense of loss and grief that sent tears spilling from her eyes and sobs through her body. Her deer. They had no right. She would kill them. Eat them.

Voices again. The sound of another rock, striking and splitting as it missed and hit a boulder.

"Enough, old man," came a voice just above Mixcatl's head. It belonged to the same hands that were holding her down. "I don't want the buck stoned to death. It is bad enough that he will never trust me again."

"You young fool! And your father, too. I warned him that having pet deer on the grounds was a mistake."

Suddenly the voices had names. Huetzin. Nine-Lizard. Mixcatl's vision shivered several times between monochrome and color, then stabilized in color.

"Fill your hand with clay and hold it over her nose," said Nine-Lizard's voice. Mixcatl felt a hand—Huetzin's—dig into the mud where her face was buried and bring up a clump of clay, pressing it hard against her nostrils so that she had to breathe through her mouth.

She felt him lifting her and had to suppress the instinctive urge to struggle. That she did once again have control over her will brought her a strange sort of relief.

"Gods," Huetzin choked. "Look at her face. And her skin too. What happened, old man?"

"Do you want me to take her?" came Nine-Lizard's voice.

"No. You may have the stomach, but you haven't the strength."

"Very well. Bring her into my quarters in the palace," said Nine-Lizard. "Is your father here?"

"No. He is bathing in the high garden."

"Then he will know none of this. Quickly."

Mixcatl felt herself being laid against a strong shoulder and carried back over the lawn, up the steps and into the cool hallways of Tezcotzinco.

15

MIXCATL WOKE TO the feel of salve being rubbed onto her forearm. From the slant of the sun as it warmed her face and the dewy breeze blowing in the window, she could tell that it was dawn even before she opened her eyes.

The hand on her arm paused as if Nine-Lizard had felt her waking. Then the massage began again, old fingers skillfully working the ointment into her skin. She lay, eyes still shut, enjoying the feeling until she woke up enough to remember what had happened. Her eyes flew open and she stiffened as if to sit up.

A pair of gray-brown eyes in a lined and wrinkled face hovered over her. A hand moistened with ointment gently pushed her back down on the pallet. She turned her head and gazed down at her bared arm. From wrist to elbow, the skin was tight and pink, as if she had been burned or scarred.

The old man resumed working salve into the skin. "Do not worry. This ointment will help it soften and soon it will be the same color as the rest."

An odd taut feeling in the skin around her jaw told her that the strange thing had happened there as well. And on her legs, about her calves. Nine-Lizard had rubbed salve on all these places.

"What is this illness?" she whispered to Nine-Lizard, fighting off the sob that was threatening to choke her.

"Your skin—"

"No, it is not just my skin. Whenever this happens, I feel strange. The color goes from my vision. I do not know what is wrong or right and it seems not to matter."

Nine-Lizard sighed heavily and sat down on the pallet beside Mixcatl. "Do you remember what happened yesterday afternoon?"

"I had my paints. I was going to Huetzin's workshop. Somehow I got . . . distracted. There was a smell. I remember an animal. A deer. I wanted the animal." She halted, stared deep into Nine-Lizard's eyes. "I jumped on the deer. I tried to kill it." She began to giggle, not knowing why. "But that is silly, isn't it? I couldn't kill a deer with my teeth and fingernails."

Nine-Lizard was looking at her steadily, with something like sadness behind the ancient gray-brown of his eyes. He smoothed back her hair from her forehead, touched away a frightened tear that had leaked from the corner of her eyes.

"You know what this sickness is," she said, watching as he nodded silently. "Why won't you tell me. Why haven't you told me?"

"It would not help you to know."

She studied his face, quelling the panicked questions that rushed through her mind. She asked only one. The illness seemed to be getting worse each time she had an attack. Would she eventually die from it?

No, he answered. She would not die—not from the attacks themselves. But when she lost her good sense and control, she did things that brought other people's wrath down upon her.

"Such as trying to kill the deer," she said, and again Nine-Lizard nodded.

She chose another question from the flood inside her mind. Was there anything that could help her?

"There are those who understand this . . . sickness. If things were as they should be, you would be with those people."

She asked him to say more, but he only laid a finger on her mouth, hushing her gently. There was a troubled look on his face and a pain behind his eyes, almost an anger as he muttered, "I will speak to Wise Coyote to tell him you must go to your people. To keep you from them now is wrong."

"My people?" she asked, her eyes wide. "Who are my people?"

Nine-Lizard only smoothed her hair once more until she fell back into sleep.

She woke again, telling from the feel and smell of the day that it was late afternoon. Nine-Lizard was sitting across the room from her, mixing paints. She glanced down at her arm again and was surprised to see that the fierce pinkness had faded and the flesh on her arm was almost the same in suppleness and texture as the rest of her skin.

She touched it, wondering why she had healed so rapidly. She had seen other people with burns or wounds and knew that such injuries did not mend in a day. Carefully she got up, feeling her face and her legs. They were also healing. By tomorrow, she guessed, there would be no trace left, not even a slight discoloration.

A tray of food sat on the floor nearby. Tortillas and beans; simple fare but she was famished. Nine-Lizard did not speak until she had finished eating.

"Huetzin came by while you were still asleep. He hopes that in a few days, when you are well enough, you can come down to his workshop."

She swallowed her last mouthful and looked at him in

surprise. "He wants me to come? After I tried to . . . kill one of his pet deer?"

"He knows that what happened to you is not your fault. I spoke to him a bit while you were asleep." Nine-Lizard paused. "It seems that he has grown fond of you."

Mixcatl sat on the floor, staring at the ornate floral pattern on the tray that had been used to serve them. Huetzin had come back.

"He is not disgusted or afraid? If I had been with someone who suddenly began behaving like an animal and peeling off their skin, I wouldn't want to come near them again."

Nine-Lizard raised his eyebrows and chuckled gently. "Well, it is good that he is not you. He did come. And it was as much as I could do to keep him from coming into this room and seeing for himself that you were healing."

The young sculptor was worried about her. He cared about her. Not just about the tile-painting she had done but about herself as well. She remembered his gentle smile and a little happiness made its way up through the uncertainty and gloom that had settled about her. He liked her and wanted her to come back.

"I want to go, Nine-Lizard, but what if it happens to me again? The deer . . ."

"Have been moved to the higher mountain meadows and he has set herders to watch them to be sure none stray near the palace. He told me so himself and I believe he is truthful. I took a walk in the garden this noon and saw no deer."

Mixcatl paused, remembering her times in the outdoor workshop with her paints, her tile and Huetzin quietly chipping a stone figure close by.

"Do you think it is safe for me to go?"

"I think that his companionship is good for you. I have noticed that there are fairly long intervals between your attacks so that you shouldn't have one while you are there. Now that he has moved the deer, you should be free to go outside."

"Could you come with me, Nine-Lizard?" She hesitated. "Not all the way—but far enough so that you can hear if anything does happen."

The old scribe raised his eyebrows. "If you wish me to come, I will. A walk along the paths and a nap beneath the trees would refresh me."

"Do not sleep too soundly," said Mixcatl, trying to make her voice light.

"I have never been a heavy sleeper, although I doubt if there will be need for me. Rest now and we will go tomorrow afternoon."

When the two scribes had put aside their paints on the following day, eaten the noon meal and watched servants clear away the dishes, Mixcatl began to feel eager and anxious. She was restless at having been kept inside and was longing to get out into the warm sun and fresh breezes that teased her through the window. Most of all, she wanted to see Huetzin, smell the odor of carved stone and watch him while he worked his sculptor's magic. Perhaps too he would have a smile for her, a warm clasp for her hand and a gaze that said she was missed and would be welcomed back.

Yet everything would not be as it had been before. He now knew about the strange shadow that hung over her. He had been beside her when the illness struck, had seen the changes that it wrought. Would she see that knowledge in his eyes? Deep inside, would he be frightened or repulsed, even though he tried to cover it with affection?

At the last instant, she almost decided not to go, but Nine-Lizard was already pushing aside the door flap from their chambers into the hall. Mixcatl felt so nervous and unsure that she had to make a quick visit to the little water room before finally setting out with her companion.

Nine-Lizard parted from her a little way before the path reached Huetzin's workshop and Mixcatl went on alone, clutching her paints and brushes to her chest. As she approached the workshop, she heard a high "clink, clink," the sound of Huetzin's horn chisel against greenstone.

When the young man saw her, he put his tools aside and opened his arms. "Mixcatl, I thought you might never come again. My workshop seemed so quiet without you."

She carefully set her paints and brushes on one of his benches, then ran into his embrace. He hugged her, rocking her back and forth. She laid her cheek against his and put her arms about his neck. "I missed you. I was afraid that after what happened to me when you showed me the deer, you might not want to see me again. When Nine-Lizard told me you had come, it made everything bearable."

"Sickness will not make me turn away from people I care about," said Huetzin, releasing her and looking deeply into her eyes. "Besides," he added in a brighter tone, "you are all well again."

Mixcatl glanced down at her arms and saw that her flesh was brown and smooth, the way it had been. Only a light itching that only she could notice marked the site where pieces of her skin had peeled away. Within a few days she had healed completely. Perhaps it might never happen again, she thought, and hoped so.

Huetzin gave her a tile. It was white, smooth and four times the size of the others. She sought about for a suitable subject and finally found it in a stone. Not one of Huetzin's greenstone blocks that stood about his workshop waiting to be transformed by his skill, but a weathered old garden rock that stood in the shade with a cape of moss growing over it. To Mixcatl's eyes, it was rich in shades of color and texture and she wanted to capture those with her brush. She propped the tile before her and began.

The afternoon crept away in a trance of sheer bliss. Somehow there was magic in her brush or in her hands, for the lines she placed and the colors she daubed were somehow just right. She knew she could capture the image of the weathered stone on her tile and do even more. Already the painting was infused with an inward luminosity that was not part of the real stone itself, at least not visible from outside. She wondered if she could dare to capture the intangible essence of the rock, the thing that others called spirit.

She was so engrossed in her work that she barely noticed when the late afternoon wind began to stiffen and blow in strong gusts, sending up swirls of dust and leaves from the ground about the workshop. With it came the scent of the high mountain meadows, swiftly running streams and just a hint of the musky aroma that now meant "deer."

She froze, her brush in her hand. The faint residual itching on her arms had grown more intense. She felt suddenly restless, with an impulse to cast the tile aside. Irritated at the urges that had interrupted her work, she shook off the feelings. The wind died, the smell faded and again she immersed herself in her work.

But she was not left alone for long. The wind came again, first fitful, then steady, bringing her the scent of the creatures she wanted and dreaded. The itching and restlessness seized her again. Her vision flashed briefly, from color and warmth to grayed pastel with hard edges. Again she paused, brush in the air. No. She wanted to concentrate on her painting. By staring at the moss-covered rock—by looking as hard as she could to find the subtle shading and shadowing, the veining and speckling, even the odd red-green halo that seemed to surround the stone when she squinted at it through half-closed eyes—she could drive off the uncanny feeling that was creeping over her.

She glanced over at Huetzin, who was carefully polishing the ribs on his coyote statue. Should she tell him what was happening, ask him for help? No. She could hold off the threatening change by force of will, by seeking refuge in the artistry of her hands and mind.

But the smell of the deer, though faint, continued in her nostrils, making her body tremble with longing. Her brush remained steady, her teeth clenched. She would not give in. The painting was all that mattered. She would not be torn away from it.

In desperation she pinched her nose shut with one hand while the other guided the brush, but it was not enough. The maddening scent crept into her mouth, becoming an equally distracting taste that grew stronger and made her salivate.

Gradually the colors faded from her vision. Everything was edges, movement. It was hard to keep her mind on the moss-covered stone. The images in her mind that she was transferring to tile seemed to lose their clarity. She found herself struggling to capture lines that had, a few instants before, flown effortlessly from her brush. And then, suddenly, she found herself staring at the stone, unable to see it with the artist's eye, and even worse, wondering why she had even been trying.

Gods, what was happening to her? What kind of sickness was this that would steal from her not only her will and her good sense, but even the wish and the impulse to create beauty?

"No!" she hissed fiercely under her breath and stared at the stone she had been painting. With force of will, she brought back the richness of color and detail into her vision, regained the need to paint and taught her hand once again the mastery of brush and line.

A shadow fell across the half-completed tile, startling her and nearly making her vision slip once again into grayness and edges. It was Huetzin, stooping down beside her.

"Are you all right?" he asked softly.

She found it hard to force words from her tongue. "It is happening again. I can smell the deer in the wind from the meadow."

"I can take you back to the palace," he said, laying a hand on her arm. She felt the skin loosen where he had grasped and felt a pang of dismay.

"No. If I stay here and paint, I can fight it off. Nine-Lizard is nearby. I asked him to come with me, just in case this should happen."

Huetzin asked if he should summon Nine-Lizard.

"No," Mixcatl answered. "Just sit down beside me, upwind so that I can smell you instead of the deer. Do not speak. Just let me paint."

Silently Huetzin did as she asked. The scent of stone-dust on his garments mixed with the sweat of his working helped turn her mind from the deer smell, although it created distracting thoughts of a different nature. But she was too shaken and wary to explore her feelings about the man sitting near her. Instead she turned back to the tile, struggling for the same depth of concentration she had reached earlier, searching for the same will to create that had been so strong in her only a short time before. She made a line, frowned. No. It wasn't working. It wasn't right. Whatever strangeness was possessing her, it was stealing her gift as well as her self.

"Mixcatl," came Huetzin's voice. "You asked me not to speak, but you look so troubled that I must. What is happening to you?"

Brokenly, she told him, fearing that her words were clumsy and that he wouldn't understand.

"We must summon Nine-Lizard," he said. "This is not something you can fight alone." He stood up beside her and gave a long high whistle.

Soon the figure of the old scribe appeared on the path. He was brushing leaves from his cape and was blinking as if he had been asleep. Huetzin gave an impatient gesture with his hand.

Nine-Lizard stooped down beside Mixcatl. She spared her attention from the tile just long enough to give him one agonized look and to see that he understood.

"It is coming on you again," said Nine-Lizard. "But why?" He turned to Huetzin. "Did you not send the deer all up to the hills."

"I can still catch their scent," Mixcatl whispered.

"From that distance?"

Numbly she nodded.

Nine-Lizard muttered to himself. "This is ominous. She is much more sensitive than I expected and the beast nature less willing to be confined." To Mixcatl he said, "Can you hold off the changes you feel coming?"

"If I think only about this," she answered, touching her brush to the tile. "But it is getting so much harder." The brush faltered as she felt a bout of trembling take her and her vision flashed again, losing color. She saw both Huetzin and Nine-Lizard move toward her, but she held out her hand, warning them off.

Whatever this evil is within me, I will not let it free.

She bit her lip until blood came as she willed her attention to her work. She asked Nine-Lizard to hold clay to her nose to block out all smells but that of the earth. But the restless thing that circled within would not be defeated. She could see this by the looks on her companions' faces when she shuddered in the grip of spasms that grew stronger each time she fought them off.

Yet, in the end, it was exhaustion that ultimately won. A weariness so deep that it seemed to grind her bones to dust made the brush slide from her hand and she felt herself toppling sideways. She felt the tile and brush being taken from her, tried to grab for it and realized that she had won, that the piece still had meaning for her and she felt alarm.

She felt herself being gently taken into someone's lap. From the sweet, dusty stoneworker's scent, she knew that it was Huetzin. His arms went around her, cradling her. From a dimness far away, she heard his voice and fought to stay close enough so that she could still make out his words.

"Is she asleep, Nine-Lizard?"

"Yes." The old man's tone was weary. "You can carry her back to her quarters."

"Let me just hold her here for a while." He paused and Mixcatl thought he had faded into silence, then he spoke again in a low voice. "When I saw her, I thought she was only a gifted child, but she has grown into my heart like a woman."

"Huetzin," began Nine-Lizard in his aged rasp.

"What are these strange fits that ail her? What is it that rips her art away from her? If there was a torment worse, I could not imagine it. Did you watch her? It seemed to me as though a part of her died each time, then was reborn only to die again." Huetzin paused and though his voice wavered in Mixcatl's ears, she still could make sense of his words. A new coldness came into them. "Old man, I feel that you know what this sickness is and you have known all along. Why have you withheld answers from her and from me?"

"I felt that she was not ready to understand or accept. To tell her would only frighten her and make it worse. As for you, young sculptor, your entry into this has come about much faster than I had anticipated. I feared and still fear that the truth will turn you from her."

"Then you do not know me well enough, old man," said Huetzin fiercely. "Tell me."

"She looks asleep, but she may be listening," began Nine-Lizard.

"All the better if she is. Whatever this affliction, it is wrong to keep the knowledge from her. Or from me and my father."

"Your father already knows," said Nine-Lizard, and Mixcatl heard Huetzin draw a breath. "That is why she and I are here. The history that we are writing is not the real reason."

There was another silence. Mixcatl could feel Huetzin's arms tense about her and she knew he was waiting.

"You are right," said Nine-Lizard. "You deserve an explanation. So does she, but I would rather that she be awake enough to grapple with the fears it will raise." There was a rustle of cloth as the old scribe got to his feet. Huetzin shifted his weight and Mixcatl felt herself being lifted.

"Can you manage her?"

Huetzin grunted with effort and surprise. "She is heavy! The last time I carried her to the palace, I thought it was my imagination." Mixcatl could feel the youth struggling with her and wished she could shake off enough of the weariness and lassitude to walk. "But I have lugged stone blocks to my workshop. I can carry her. Lead the way, old scribe."

Later that evening, the three sat together in the scribes' guest quarters at Tezcotzinco. Mixcatl lay on a pallet, still feeling drained by the struggle she had gone through that afternoon. She had managed to eat after resting and now was awake enough to take part in the conversation. Huetzin sat on the pallet with her, holding her head in his lap.

Gently he stroked her hair as Nine-Lizard spoke. Beside him, on the floor, stood the greenstone statue of the kneeling jaguar man. Nine-Lizard had asked Huetzin to bring it from Wise Coyote's library.

Mixcatl cast a cautious glance at the figurine and recalled how the sight of both it and its companion had so unnerved her. Perhaps she sensed somehow that it held a clue to what she was and why these strange episodes were coming down on her.

Nine-Lizard picked up the figurine and cradled it between his two hands. The look in his eyes was an unreadable mixture of emotions as he looked at it. Suddenly Mixcatl knew that the statuette unsettled him as much as it did her, and not only because it held the explanation to the mystery of her peeling sickness.

Her lips moved almost soundlessly. "What is it?"

"An Olmec jaguar shaman. The image of a man casting off his human skin to free the jaguar beneath." Nine-Lizard paused. "You are a descendant of the Olmeca, Mixcatl, as am I. There is nothing of the Aztec in your face, which is why to many men, you are ugly."

Huetzin slowly touched the statue as if it might spring to life. "My father showed me this in the library. I thought that it was just an image, a metaphor of the savagery inside men. I never thought to take it literally."

"You saw its literalness when Mixcatl's skin peeled at the sight of the deer."

"Give me the statue," said Mixcatl, a cold calm seeping through her. Wordlessly Huetzin gave it to her. She ran her fingers over the greenstone face, then touched her own. "Is this what I am?"

"Yes."

"Why I get the peeling sickness and other things as well?"

The old scribe nodded.

Mixcatl felt fear strike her. She was different, as she

had long suspected. Now that it had come into the open, she would be looked at with suspicion, cast aside, driven away. Yet at the same time, she felt a strange sort of relief. Now she had at least the beginning of an answer.

"The jaguar beneath," she mused, feeling strangely distant. She turned her face to Nine-Lizard. "But I have never peeled off all my skin. When that happens will the . . . thing inside . . . come out?"

"In time, yes."

Huetzin broke in, shaking his head angrily "I can't believe this. People do not become animals. Perhaps in myths or in tales of the gods, but those are only ways to tell certain truths. Yes, part of me can believe when a priest dons the skin of a beast that he has become the creature, but part of me knows that the body of a man lies beneath."

"Perhaps I am the opposite," said Mixcatl, feeling oddly calm. "A beast wearing the skin of a woman. It would explain so many things." She lay quietly, thinking of how the deer smell excited her and no one else, how her skin loosened and peeled when she became excited, how the intensity of her art had diminished as the change came closer. A beast cares nothing about beauty, she thought, and felt cold.

"I still do not believe," said Huetzin, stroking Mixcatl's hair. "The eyes that look at me, the hand that holds the brush; they speak of a woman's spirit, not a slit-eyed cat's."

"The beast is there," said Nine-Lizard. "And it will emerge. Trust me. I know. And that is why Mixcatl must go back to the land of her birth and be among the people whose gift she carries."

Again Mixcatl stared into the old scribe's eyes and saw the remains of an ancient agony that might have once matched her own. She sensed that he did know what would happen to her. And not just from reading about it in a book of glyphs.

"Then if it is important that she go, take her," said Huetzin. "I will miss her, but it is better if she can experience this with people who understand it. And surely she will come back to me?"

Mixcatl reached up to Huetzin's arm. "Yes, I will come back," she said softly, but her mind was in confusion. Suppose the jaguar within became free? If it had no care for art, would it care about Huetzin?

"I would take her at once, if your father were not standing in the way," said Nine-Lizard, with a steady gaze at Huetzin.

The young sculptor shook his head in a puzzled manner. "This is what grieves and frightens me most about this. The change in my father. He has never before kept things from me. He has never let his desires overrule his wisdom and he has never hurt anyone willingly. But perhaps he has only misunderstood," Huetzin said, his mood brightening. "If he knows that sending Mixcatl to these people will help her, surely he will not oppose that." His manner grew more determined. "I will speak to him. I know he will listen."

"I hope for her sake and yours that he will," said Nine-Lizard softly.

Wise Coyote sat in his chambers across from his son Huetzin and the slave-scribe Nine-Lizard. Out of courtesy he had given them both reed icpallis to sit on, but he also kept his turquoise crown on his head.

He saw that Huetzin noticed that he did not put the crown aside, as he often did when meeting with his sons. The young sculptor's face stiffened, yet he did not hesitate to speak.

Taking a deep breath he said, "My father, these words come hard because I have never had to say anything like this to you before." Huetzin gulped and clenched his fists to still his trembling. "I have always admired your wisdom and it disappoints me to see that you have departed from it."

Wise Coyote waited, thinking, *this is not the first time, Huetzin, but you were too young to know the others.*

"When you brought the girl Mixcatl here, why did you not tell me about the illness that causes her so much torment? And now, why do you not allow her to be sent to those people who can offer her help?"

"I did not tell you about her because I had no idea that you would become involved," said Wise Coyote mildly. "You are always at your workshop; you have shown little interest in the company of women or the arts of courtship. Perhaps I should have foreseen that the gift of craftsmanship that you both share would have drawn you together."

"It was not only that," said Huetzin slowly. "When you see someone in pain, your heart goes out to them, father."

Wise Coyote remembered how Huetzin had come to comfort him as he stood alone on the hill after his eldest son's death.

"What is this thing that possesses her? Why does she start sniffing like a beast and scratching off her skin when she sees or smells my pet deer? Is it true, as Nine-Lizard says, that she will transform into a jaguar?"

Under the steady but guileless gaze of his son's eyes, Wise Coyote had no course but to retreat. "You have seen her—during one of those times?"

"Twice," said Nine-Lizard. "Lord king, I think it would be simpler if the young man were told the full story."

Wise Coyote sent the old scribe a sharp glance, but Nine-Lizard did not flinch or quail. The king sensed that he was being faced by two wills as strong as his own. He also felt a strange aching jealousy. He thought he was the only one who had gotten close to the strange young woman whom he had taken under his protection. He remembered how she had walked with him in the garden and shared his hopes and his quest for a gentle god that would be worthy of his devotion.

"Wait here," he said abruptly. "I must go to the library."

When he returned, he carried the second of the two statues, the Olmec carrying the snarling jaguar-baby. He put it down beside the kneeling jaguar man and said to Huetzin, "We spoke about these once before."

"You said that they were from an ancient tradition that has gone."

Wise Coyote smiled tiredly. "Not entirely, Huetzin. Look closely at the kneeling man. It was you yourself that said that his skin was peeling off, revealing the animal beneath."

Wide-eyed, Huetzin stared at the statue, then at Wise Coyote's face. "So you really believe it," he said, and Wise Coyote saw him glance at Nine-Lizard in amazement.

"Huetzin, listen to me," Wise Coyote said. "It is not an illness that Mixcatl has. It is her nature, struggling to surface. And it is a savage, dangerous, vengeful nature. I know, for I saw it emerge."

Briefly he told Huetzin what he had seen when Mixcatl had been cornered and teased by the children in Tenochtitlán. He watched as the young man's pupils grew wide with fear and uncertainty. "She was going to rip out the boy's entrails, Huetzin. It was only luck that weariness overpowered her in time. As it was, the youth escaped, but he still bears deep scars on his thighs. And his memory."

"No," Huetzin whispered. "In my workshop, I could see her spirit. She is a gentle and gifted artist."

"She is both, Huetzin," said Nine-Lizard sadly. "It would be better if she were not graced with an artist's soul, for it wars with that of the beast and makes the struggle even harder."

"I have seen that struggle," said Huetzin, then added defiantly, "and the artist won. You saw, Nine-Lizard. When she concentrated on painting, she held the beast away. She does not need to give in to that side of her nature. She can fight it and I will help her."

"Do you think she can suppress it indefinitely?" asked Wise Coyote harshly. "Huetzin, she is not of the same flesh as we. We may have a beast inside, but it only emerges through our words and acts. Never does it cast off our flesh and all humanity with it. Mixcatl is of a different breed. The cat within will rule her. She will turn on you." He sighed. "Give your affection to another, my son. She is too dangerous for you."

Softly, Huetzin asked, "Then why do you keep her, father?"

Wise Coyote sat and looked at his son's face while the reasons poured through his mind like the rushing water of the Chaultapec aqueduct. In the beginning he had brought the girl to Tezcotzinco out of concern for her safety. There was also the hope that she, as a living link to the ancient Olmec tradition, might be able to help him find a path through the maze of false gods to true divinity. And buried deep in his heart was the hope that when this jaguar queen arose to her full power, he would sire upon her sons that infused the proud blood of Texcoco with the ancient power and glory of the mythical rulers. But the rational part of him said that it was a dangerous dream and he dare not speak it aloud to Huetzin or any other.

And the dream would be shattered if it was Huetzin to whom Mixcatl's heart turned and not to him. Suddenly the anger and jealously flared up again, putting an edge on Wise Coyote's voice, even though he tried to speak in tones of patience and reason.

"You say that Mixcatl can fight the beast inside her by using her art. Is it wise, my son, or even right, to aid her in denying her own nature? You, as a creator, know that most of all. One must be true to oneself. Until she knows and accepts what she is, her pain will not end. It will only be delayed and made worse in the end."

"That is a strong argument for sending her to the people who know her and who will aid her," Huetzin pointed out.

Wise Coyote shot another glance at Nine-Lizard. "I cannot do that. Not yet."

"Why, father? If it is the wise thing to do . . ."

"The history must be completed. Ilhuicamina is already getting impatient." Wise Coyote knew he was only stalling and he felt a stab of disgust at himself when he saw Huetzin's eyes narrow.

"The history is not the real reason. You have another purpose for keeping her," said Huetzin, his voice flat. He stared hard at Wise Coyote, and the king knew he was remembering those conversations in the library when Wise Coyote had shared his longing for an alternative to a bloody god and the hope that one might lie within the tradition of the Olmec statuettes.

"My reasons are mine and I will share them with you when I deem it proper." Wise Coyote sat up and touched his hand to his coronet.

There was a sudden bitter laugh from Huetzin. "Father, it is not reason but obsession. You see her as some sort of demon or demigoddess who can lead you to what you seek. Whatever she is, she is not that."

Wise Coyote had half risen from his icpalli. He made himself sit down again and folded his arms. "Mixcatl will no longer concern you. She will stay here at the palace and you will remain in your workshop. You are my son, but I will accept no interference from you. If you disobey, I will have you sent far away and the workshop dismantled. Do you understand?"

Huetzin paled. His mouth hung open for several instants, then slowly closed. "Father, this is not worthy of you," he began in a choked whisper.

"You are not the one to judge. Obey me or depart. That is the choice I give you."

Huetzin swallowed and his eyes grew hard. "I cannot bear to watch what you are doing. I will leave and take my tools with me."

Wise Coyote felt his heart sinking. Of all his sons, he had been closest to Huetzin and now he was being forced to drive him away.

"May I ask one favor?" Huetzin's voice startled Wise Coyote from his reverie. "May I see the girl before I go and explain to her?"

"Yes. I see no harm in that."

Huetzin bowed his head, rose from the icpalli and left the room. Nine-Lizard, however, stayed.

"Your son is right," the scribe said in a husky voice. "This action is not worthy of you."

Wise Coyote looked across at Nine-Lizard and clenched his fists. "Nothing must stand in the way of Mixcatl developing her full powers. With her beside me, the Aztec will not dare to crush Texcoco. And if she becomes as powerful as you have said, the masses of Tenochtitlán will flock to her, deserting the temples of the blood gods. Is that unworthy of me?"

Nine-Lizard rose from the icpalli. "That judgment you can only make for yourself. And you will, in time."

Gathering his robes about him, the old man walked from the room, leaving Wise Coyote alone.

16

THE DAY AFTER his disturbing meeting with Huetzin and Nine-Lizard, Wise Coyote began a new building project. It was not to be a great public-works feat, such as the aqueduct to Tenochtitlán, nor a religious monument, such as the temple he had planned. This, he thought, as he put the final strokes to paper with a fine-tipped brush, was a project as unworthy of his skills as his refusal to listen to his son was unworthy of his better nature.

He summoned craftsmen and gave their leader his instructions. The construction was to be of the best quality, as stout and strong as possible. And it was to be built as rapidly as possible.

The project was a chamber, to be fitted into a corner of the palace near his own quarters. It was made of wood, of heavy planks butted and lashed together. The floor was made in the same way, and the ceiling, so that it was essentially a room-sized box. Inside was a low, wide shelf for a pallet and higher shelves and brackets so that lights could be placed inside.

He had it built in sections, then carried into the hallway inside the palace where workmen assembled it. Then he inspected it carefully, making sure that there was no weakness that would yield to a woman's fists or a beast's claws. Once he was satisfied that his creation would hold its intended occupant, he furnished the interior as richly and pleasantly as he could, putting tapestries on the walls and fine blankets on the low bed shelf. There were mats and a low table laid with ink and paintpots for scribing or painting.

But, as the king left his creation and eased down the heavy leather-hinged door behind him, he had no illusions that what he had built was anything but a cage.

He knew that Huetzin, Nine-Lizard and the girl herself suspected what was going on, even though he took pains to keep the two scribes confined in their quarters. The coming and going of workers, foremen and large pieces of lumber wasn't something that could be hidden long. Even care and muffling could not disguise the noises that echoed down the stone hallways.

He had hoped that both scribes would turn all of their energies to working on the history. He assigned one of his servants the task of getting them anything they needed from the library, although they were no longer permitted to visit it freely.

Each time Wise Coyote inspected the day's work, he noticed that Mixcatl was starting to lag behind Nine-Lizard in the amount she produced. He thought at first that it was resentment, but soon Nine-Lizard told him the truth. Even though the girl stayed indoors and the deer were far away, she still had bouts of her peeling sickness. She fought them off by painting, on the tiles that Huetzin had given Nine-Lizard to take to her. At first she had tried to drive off the attacks by concentrating on making glyphs, but somehow that did not release the intensity of feeling she needed to stave off the threatened change.

While the cage was being built, Wise Coyote wanted her to suppress her ability, for he did not know what he would do with her if she changed before he was ready. But after the box was prepared and ready, he began to feel impatient. If the girl learned to contain her nature and never release it, she might be safe, but useless.

After several days had passed, with the box standing open and empty, Wise Coyote visited the scribes' quarters. He chose to come in the late afternoon, for that was when the two glyph-painters rested from their efforts and turned their attention to other things. For Mixcatl that was tile-painting, and she was sitting, working intently, trying to capture the form and shading of an earthenware pot that stood on the table before her.

So absorbed was she that when Wise Coyote entered the room she did not turn her head. He glanced at her subject. It was not an especially pretty pot, shaped for utility rather than elegance. Then he glanced at her painting and was astonished at how she had transformed the crude everyday object into an image on the tile. No, it was more than an image. She had caught the gleam of sunlight on the glaze, the shadow under the earthenware handle. She had put in colors that seemed ridiculous on first glance, yet when he looked at the pot again, he could see that they were there.

As he watched, he almost forgot the reason that he had come. Somehow this girl had managed to capture the very pot-ness of the pot and express it in a unique and startling way. To some eyes, he knew, the attempt would be ugly; to others, juvenile. But Wise Coyote had strayed often enough from the paths of established tradition in many arts to recognize the gift of genius, even if he did not understand the form it took.

He made himself wait until she rested her brush. "Mixcatl, I have prepared a better place for you to paint," he said. "Bring your work with you and come."

Gathering up brushes, paints, pot and tile, she obeyed, walking after him down the hall. He saw her slow her pace at the sight of the box.

"Here you can work without interruption," he said,

beckoning her through the propped-open hatch. He followed her inside and watched as she studied the interior. "You see, there is plenty of space, mats to sit on. Put your pot on here"—he tapped a low table—"and see if you have enough light to paint by."

With a doubtful glance at him, she began working on the tile once again. He sat down nearby.

"Tlatoani, this will be difficult. I was working by the sun and the torch gives a different kind of light. But I will try."

Her first brushstrokes were tentative and unsure, but as she kept working, she became absorbed. As he stayed, watching her, he saw that it was more than just the expression of her gift that made her work so intensely. Whenever her concentration or her brush faltered, the change began to creep over her again. When she caught the inspiration once more, the change retreated.

Despite himself, Wise Coyote could not help but admire the strength of will and the power of art that pushed away the beast's savagery. Yet he knew by the shaking of Mixcatl's body that her mind had become a battleground in a war between her innermost nature and her artist's soul.

He knew what he must do, even though he hated himself for it.

Taking hold of the tile, he pulled it from her hands.

Her eyes turned to him, unbelieving, accusing, panic growing in their depths. Her voice was shaky. "No! This is the only way I can keep it from happening."

She grabbed for another tile in the stack behind her, but Wise Coyote caught her wrist. "No. Do not fight the change. Let it come."

"No! I will run wild. I am afraid of what I might do."

"You are safe in this chamber."

"No! Give me back my tile. Please. It is the only way. I am afraid. I will lose myself. Please."

"You will not lose yourself. You will find your true nature, which you have been fighting for so long."

"You do not understand," she whispered, her eyes wide and staring. "A beast knows no beauty."

"That does not matter now," said Wise Coyote, forcing the words from his mouth. "I need the beast."

He took away the brush she clutched, tossed the tile with a clatter onto a low table. She lunged after it, but he caught her. "Mixcatl, I will not let you hide any longer," he hissed.

She went rigid, staring at him in terrified disbelief while rage kindled in her eyes. Suddenly she drew back her lips in a snarl. "Then, curse you, have it!"

The change came on much faster than he had ever seen it. Before she finished speaking, her canine teeth had elongated, the entire shape of her face seemed to go fluid and start shifting. The hand that struck him was already welding itself into a paw.

He spun her, wrapped both arms around her in an armlock, but he could feel her body already expanding, pushing out against his grasp with a steely new strength.

Pulling her arms up behind her, he grabbed a blanket from a nearby pallet and flung it over her head, bundling her in it. She struggled wildly and he knew that she could overcome him. In a burst of panic, he thrust her away, scrambled through the hatch, knocked away the prop and slammed the door down.

Fierce scratching and shrieking came from within as he fumbled frantically with the clumsy wooden latch. It fastened and he backed away, clapping both his hands against his ears to block out the muffled screaming. There were crashing and shattering sounds from inside and he knew she had destroyed the pot and her tile painting.

Trying not to think about what he had done, the king hurried away.

* * *

Much later, Wise Coyote returned, walking down the halls of blue tile that darkness had changed to slate. He halted as he neared the chamber, for his mind would not call it a cage. The drop-hatch lifted and Nine-Lizard climbed out. The old man's cloak and loincloth were soaked with sweat and pink smears that were a mixture of salve and blood. Through the hatchway, Wise Coyote could hear the girl's cries, made hoarse by exhaustion. Nine-Lizard let the door fall and slam, cutting off the sounds.

The old scribe straightened up, tried to take a step and nearly fell from weakness and shaking. Wise Coyote went to him, escorted him to a nearby mat, despite his protests that he was able to walk. The king lit a brazier overhead and then sat down opposite, watching red and slate shadows play across the ugly bearded face. Nine-Lizard mopped his forehead and cheeks with a corner of his soiled robe, then lifted his gaze to Wise Coyote. His eyes, the king saw, were rimmed with red and bruised with exhaustion.

"How does she fare?" he asked quietly.

"I cannot ease the pain of the change as I have done before," Nine-Lizard answered in a croaking voice.

"The ointment?"

"Does no good when there is almost no skin left on which to smear it."

Wise Coyote felt a shiver run through him, too strong to suppress. He started to his feet, wanting, yet dreading, to peer through the peephole he had made in the box so that he could watch what happened to Mixcatl.

Despite his weakness and trembling, Nine-Lizard reached out and halted him. "Do not try, my king. She looks like the priests of Xipe have flayed her."

"I have already seen . . . ," Wise Coyote began, then fell silent. "So it is much worse."

Nine-Lizard gave him an unreadable look. "For her,

worse. For you, perhaps . . . better." He paused. "This is what you wanted, wasn't it?"

The king glowered across at the wizened, almost monkeylike, face before him. He wanted to grab Nine-Lizard by his curly stained beard and shake him until what was left of his teeth fell out. Instead, he only clenched his fists. "Yes," he said in a low voice. "Only I wish that she would not have to suffer so for it."

"If you had truly felt that way, my king, you would have given her to the Jaguar's Children before the change worked its full power on her. I have no doubt that they could have eased her through it. I have not the skill."

Again anger surged in Wise Coyote, but he held it back, knowing that the bitterness that Nine-Lizard spoke was only the truth. Instead he only said, "You know my reasons for what I do. I will take responsibility for whatever happens. I only ask that you do not cease your efforts until . . ."

"Mixcatl is dead or you have a jaguar goddess to parade before the tyrant of Tenochtitlán," retorted Nine-Lizard. He gave a deep, shuddering sigh and put a hand to his forehead. "I will not abandon her, tlatoani, but I do need a little time to recover from the task." He slumped, burying his face in his hands. Wise Coyote touched him lightly on the shoulder and rose from the mat.

He could not make himself walk back down the shadowed halls and away from the chamber. He stood, staring at the heavy drop-door and hearing the muffled groans that seeped between the massive boards he had used to build the box. He put a hand on the bar that raised the door. "Let me go in," he found himself saying, and the urgency in his voice startled him. "If she is exhausted, she is no longer dangerous. Perhaps I may be able to soothe her into sleep."

He had already raised and propped the door and was

ducking through it when Nine-Lizard's cry came from behind him. "Tlatoani, no!"

The interior of the wood-sided chamber had been cushioned and padded with rugs and blankets. Several clay lamps burned, high up in brackets, where Mixcatl could not reach them in her frenzies of throwing herself against the walls.

She lay hunched on her side upon a pallet of blankets. Shuddering, she faced the wall. Her back was deeply raw and oozing. A long curled sheet of white parchmentlike material—was it her own skin?—lay alongside her on the bed. It must have just come off, Wise Coyote realized, feeling nausea claim his stomach and rise in his throat. Otherwise Nine-Lizard would have taken it away.

Hoping that shadows from the flickering lamps would hide the rest of her, Wise Coyote bent over the pallet. He had meant to come in, take the girl in his arms and soothe her as best he could, but he realized that much of her body was like raw meat and that it would cause unbearable pain to touch her. Faltering, uncertain, sickened, he instead took the piece of skin off the bed and dropped it into a basket where similar parchmentlike curls rested.

She stirred. The motion was abrupt, animal-like. Instinctively he backed away, knowing that seeing this was too much for even a warrior hardened in battle or a king used to witnessing sacrifices. She came up and off the bed in a fluid, feral move and flung herself on him.

Whether it was a maddened attack or desperate embrace, he did not know. He had only fragmented impressions; teeth gleaming beneath a split, swollen upper lip, patches of stubble growing in the stripped and oozing flesh, hands whose fingers seemed to have become grotesquely shortened and thickened while the nails narrowed and curved, an entire torso that seemed to have deepened through the chest. Then he was down, his hands slipping and sliding on the raw flesh as he struggled to keep the clawlike nails from his face. For an instant he was literally face to face with her, his cheek thrust against hers in the parody of an embrace. With a horror that threatened to turn to gibbering madness, he felt as well as saw the change continue, the bones of her jaws thrusting forward, her nose widening and flattening.

But when he pulled away, he saw the worst sight of all—her eyes. They were not distorted or bloody, as he might have feared by witnessing what else the change had wrought in her. He thought—he almost hoped—to see eyes blank with unknowing, staring with fever or colored with the savage amber flame of the jaguar.

Though the color had changed and the pupils had begun to narrow into slits, they were still a woman's eyes. And he knew that those eyes saw; they knew; they cried out in mute pain and fixed him with the desperate question he could not answer.

Why did you force this to happen?

Rage born of shame gave his arms the strength to thrust her away. Shedding flecks of blood and shreds of skin, she came at him again as he scrambled back toward the hatchway. His hand went for the obsidian dagger at his waistband, but he had only half drawn it when she was across him. The drop-door started to fall, and he thought Nine-Lizard had knocked the prop away from outside, but before it was down, she forced herself into the gap and wiggled through.

A hoarse shout and thump from outside showed that she had got past Nine-Lizard; then there was the sound of running feet echoing down the corridor.

Shaking as he had seldom done since childhood, Wise Coyote stumbled to his feet and pushed his way through the hatch, his hand tight on the hilt of the dagger.

He found Nine-Lizard on his back, bruised and winded, but not seriously hurt.

"She's gone," the old scribe said tightly. "She knew I tried to drop the door on her."

Wise Coyote looked down the hall, where the echoes of those footsteps still rang.

"No!" Nine-Lizard clutched his arm.

"I said I would take responsibility for whatever happened," Wise Coyote said harshly. "If I must kill her myself, I will. Perhaps that will be my punishment. Stay here, old man. You have endured enough tonight."

Flinging his cloak about him, Wise Coyote strode down the shadowed hall after the footsteps.

17

HEEDLESS OF THE pain from her skin-stripped limbs, Mix-catl reeled down the stone hallways of Tezcotzinco. She staggered and crashed into the walls, fighting to stay upright and make her legs carry her, even though they had somehow shifted so that her feet were becoming longer, her upper thighs shorter and more powerful, her shins elongated. In the black and white images of her memory, Wise Coyote's face loomed, grimacing with surprise, then repulsion. Then Nine-Lizard, crying out with despair as she rushed him, then shot past him. The images whirled and swung, making her clasp her head with strangely clumsy hands and howl aloud.

Then came the prey smell. It enveloped her, seized her, dragged her down the hallway as if a chain had been cast around her neck. It should have been gone, she thought. Had not Huetzin said he would move the deer? But, outside this great cage of stone, prey wandered on the wide lawns. The scent crept through the chinks, beneath the hangings to entrance her with its blood-richness.

It was this smell, she knew, that had tormented and teased her until she could no longer withstand the urgency of the transformation. Saliva ran in her mouth, her belly cramped in the demands of hunger. Finding no exit from the cage of stone that had once been the palace, she flung herself angrily against the walls, as if she could batter a way through. The dull burning in her flesh sharpened to knifing pain each time she collided, but the intensity of her need swallowed up the pain.

And then she halted, going down on still-changing hands and feet, feeling the slight pressure of a breeze on the sensitized flesh of her face. Creeping, she rounded a corner and her night-keen eyes caught the edge of moonlight falling between a doorhanging and the stone threshold it covered. With one bound she was through.

The rough fabric against her raw flesh made her cry aloud with pain as it slid from her back and along the beginnings of a tail growing from the base of her spine. She tumbled from the patio down into the garden, came up into a crouch. Ahead, outlined in the hazy moonlight, were two long-legged shapes. Two heads lifted and two pairs of ears spread wide.

With taut slowness, she began the stalk, keeping the wind that blew from the deer at the side of her face so that the intoxicating smell kept coming to her. Now she could see the glint of their eyes, the sheen of moonlight off their coats, outline of proudly lifted heads, muzzles swiveling suspiciously.

They were stupid. Tame. So easy. So easy. She quivered and something behind her lashed as she crept forward in the first steps of her final rush at the deer.

A hoarse man-cry froze her in midleap. A heavy blow struck her back, sending her crashing back down onto the lawn. Whirling, she reared upright, forelimbs lifted, teeth bared. Again Wise Coyote's face loomed in her memory, now strangely blurred and distorted. But the face before her was not the man she had struggled with a short time ago.

Huetzin!

It was not his name that sounded in her mind now, for she had lost all names and their meaning, even her own. It was the smell of him, the memory of his touch and his voice that came forward to battle the wild rage that sent her charging toward him for daring to interrupt her kill.

The realization only slowed her leap, for the animal in her was now dominant. She landed on the man, bearing him to the ground. She saw his face as he caught sight of her, his eyes staring in terror, his mouth wide open. Again came the instinct to take him by the throat and squeeze hard until no breath was left.

The eyes rolled up, the face went slack, the limbs flaccid. The human fear smell that had added to her intoxication faded. It would be easy now to tear into his belly and sate the growing tyranny of her hunger. But, as with the boy in the plaza, something that had been forced into a corner inside her now screamed out in protest and she backed away, circling in confusion.

Her gaze traveled to the man's face and she knew, in a distant way, that he had been overcome not by the power of her attack but the shock of her appearance. Miserably she put out a forelimb and tried to stroke his cheek, but her fingers had become too blunt and immobile for her to do much more than paw him, like a beast.

This man . . . meant . . . something to her, something murky that she could no longer understand but that still echoed in the remembered kindness of his voice, the gentle lightness of his touch. With a great effort to move beyond the trance of animal thought, she wished that he would wake again and stroke her with the same gentleness, but she knew that if he did wake, he would cry out in terror and flee screaming.

Panting in great shuddering gasps, she clutched Huetzin's head into the circle of her forelimbs and laid her face against his.

Another shout, above and behind her, made her start,

but she would not release the man from her embrace. Looking up, she felt her ears flatten and saw the shadow of a club descend upon her head.

Wise Coyote let the club fall from his hand as he stood over his son Huetzin and the creature that had been Mixcatl. He had dealt the thing enough blows to kill it, yet it still breathed and kept its hateful embrace about Huetzin's neck.

The moonlight spilled over his shoulder onto the two bodies on the lawn. He did not want to recognize Mixcatl in the shape of the beast that lay on her side in front of him, but enough of her face was left in the cat muzzle that he could not help but know her. And the forelimbs, wrapped tightly about Huetzin's neck, told what Wise Coyote did not want to know.

Though he had saved her from sacrifice by bringing her into his household, nurtured her talents, fed her hunger for knowledge and her need for guidance, she had turned from him to Huetzin. Though she might still serve as an ally against the Aztecs, his hopes of a loving sympathetic partner were destroyed. Gone too were the dreams of a jaguar queen who would bear him sons that carried the strength of the ancient blood. He had always been the builder, but now his plans had fallen into dust.

His hands closed about the dagger, lifting it high to plunge into the cat ribs of the creature. One stroke would end an accursed life and free both him and Huetzin from the web of fear and madness in which they had been caught. One stroke, and Wise Coyote could not make it.

Tears of rage and grief burned in his eyes. It was not pity or love that made him lower the dagger but a more complex blend of emotions that seethed in him as he looked at Huetzin. *Fool! Betrayer!* He wanted to shout the words aloud. All love for his son fled as he stared down at the youth, who lay as if peacefully sleeping within the embrace of the creature.

So you would love her, Huetzin. Then bear the wounds of that love.

Another thing was there, a creature of vengeance that took over Wise Coyote's body, closed his hands on the obsidian dagger as he bent over Huetzin. The dagger's shadow fell on the youth's face as the point descended.

No. It would be too easy to just kill you.

With five short deep dagger-strokes that lay together like the claws of a jaguar, Wise Coyote ripped Huetzin's cheek from eye to jaw. As Huetzin cried out, waking from the pain, Wise Coyote plunged his knife twice into the back of Huetzin's hand, then yanked it free and stepped back quickly as the youth writhed.

He saw, too late, that his knife had struck Huetzin's right hand, the one that guided the chisel. As he stared down at the blood welling from the wound, he realized what he had done. The rage seething in him turned to shock and then remorse.

He cursed the blind fury that had made him strike the youth's sculpting hand.

When he wakes and sees his hand destroyed . . . I would have been more merciful to have slain him.

A hoarse cry broke the trance of anger and grief that held Wise Coyote. He glanced back, saw Nine-Lizard stumble down the steps of the patio. Lights flared in the palace windows, telling him that servants had been roused by the noise.

The king tossed his knife into the waters of one of the fast-running streams that cut across the lawn. The current would sweep it far down from Tezcotzinco and wash it clean of his son's blood.

He took a hempen rope from his waist, knotted it into a noose and slipped it about the Mixcatl-creature's neck. With a yank, he broke her hold on Huetzin and dragged her away. Convulsively the youth sat up and stared with terrified eyes at the creature, a scream bubbling in his throat.

Nine-Lizard reached them. Wise Coyote thrust the rope end into the old man's hand.

"Hold her while I see to my son," the king said brusquely. He took Huetzin into his arms, cradling him, shielding him from the sight of the thing.

"It was the deer, wasn't it," Nine-Lizard whispered, kneeling beside him. The old scribe sounded puzzled. "I thought Huetzin had them taken away."

"Some must have escaped or were missed," Wise Coyote answered, feeling dead inside. "I saw one near the house. Huetzin tried to stop her from attacking it and she savaged him." He looked back over his shoulder and hissed, "Servants are coming. I want them to know nothing of this. Drag her into the bushes while I carry my son to his room. To them the story will be that Huetzin was attacked by a mountain cat but it was driven off."

He saw Nine-Lizard nod mutely, then haul the unconscious form of the half-transformed thing behind an oleander bush.

The youth in his arms was panting and moaning, with occasional small terrified cries.

"Hush," the king said softly, though the words caught in his throat. "You are wounded, my son, but you will live."

The youth's head lolled and moonlight gleamed on his blood-smeared cheek. Tears were rolling down and mixing with the welling crimson as Huetzin moaned, "It wasn't Mixcatl. Tell me that she did not turn on me."

But silence was the only answer Wise Coyote could give as he bore his son into the palace.

After Wise Coyote had seen to Huetzin, he went to another chamber where the form of a young woman lay on a pallet. Perhaps it was the shock of the attack that made Mixcatl's transformation reverse itself, but whatever the reason, he was grateful.

Inside, Nine-Lizard knelt by Mixcatl, rubbing salve on her limbs and dabbing fever sweat from her brow. The king hesitated on the threshold, remembering the enraged, distorted creature she had become.

With a gesture, Nine-Lizard invited him in. "She will be too weak to transform for several days. It is safe."

Wise Coyote sat down near the pallet. He had known that leaving Mixcatl unconfined was risky, but he could not bear the thought of putting her back in the wooden cage.

"How fares Huetzin?" Nine-Lizard asked.

"I have given him into the care of his mother. She is skilled at nursing the wounded. I myself have lain under her care."

"Did she ask what happened?"

"I gave her the explanation we agreed on—that the youth startled a great cat who was stalking his deer," Wise Coyote answered.

"Those facial wounds will not heal without scars. Be grateful that the young man is not prey to vanity. The bite wounds on his hand . . ." Nine-Lizard shook his head.

The old man did not have to finish his sentence for Wise Coyote to know what he meant. It would be many seasons before the young sculptor's maimed right hand could again hold a stone-chisel, if ever. And Wise Coyote would have to look upon his son as Huetzin struggled, knowing that it was his knife that had crippled the youth, not Mixcatl's teeth.

For an instant he wanted to confess to Nine-Lizard what had happened out on the darkened lawn, then he closed his eyes. No. To admit to the act would be to admit the savagery in his own soul and a cruelty that rivaled that of the Aztecs.

Instead he thrust the thought from his mind and seized upon another.

"She nearly completed the transformation this time," he whispered, fixing his eyes on the girl, who moved restlessly on her pallet. He could see that his eyes and tone of voice betrayed a feverish eagerness that he strove to conceal. He could also see that it disgusted Nine-Lizard, although the old scribe said nothing.

"Tlatoani, you know what should be done," Nine-Lizard said in a low voice, looking away. "The Jaguar's Children are ready to take Mixcatl and train her properly in the use of her gifts. I have asked them to send someone for her."

"I did not give you permission to do so," Wise Coyote said tightly.

"Then what will you do? Keep the girl imprisoned until the full power of her heritage comes through? Each time she transforms, she will be stronger and more dangerous. The tragedy that happened tonight will pale beside that yet to come. My king, I beg you to give up this ill-fated plan. Let Mixcatl go back to her people who are ready to reclaim her. For her sake . . . and yours as well."

"If I do release her back to those who call themselves the Jaguar's Children, will they return her to me when she is able to perform the role that I have asked of her?"

Nine-Lizard met Wise Coyote's eyes with the same unsettling steady gaze that the king had come to hate over the past few days.

"I cannot speak for them," he said coldly. "I doubt that they would want her to engage in such a charade as you propose. How can I make you understand that Mixcatl and others like her are not gods; at least not the kind you seek."

"That may be true, but what matters is that Ilhuicamina and those blood-smeared priests of his will believe." Wise Coyote paced the floor beside Mixcatl's pallet.

"And you would turn him aside by walking before his people with a woman who can turn into a jaguar at the snap of your fingers."

Wise Coyote felt anger flare, but he kept his voice level. "To them she will be a goddess, and I her favored one. Other kings have risen to rule the Triple Alliance on less that that."

"She will be but a performing animal," Nine-Lizard snapped back. "And you, though you may not intend it, will become a tyrant. Neither one of you deserves such a fate."

At this Wise Coyote lost his temper. "Be quiet, old man, or I will have your tongue cut out!"

He saw Nine-Lizard pale in shock and anger.

O Tloque Nahaque, I am becoming everything that I hate in other kings.

He put his hand to his forehead, wishing he could somehow undo everything that had happened.

"Tlatoani?" Nine-Lizard asked softly. "Am I dismissed?"

"No. Stay. Your tongue is safe if you use it wisely."

Nine-Lizard was silent while Wise Coyote gathered his rage-scattered wits.

"Texcoco deserves better than to become a province of Tenochtitlán," the king said harshly. "I know of no other way. I know Ilhuicamina's weakness, and in this girl I have a weapon I can use to strike him to the heart. I would be a fool if I failed to use it."

"Tlatoani, will you not believe that there are other alternatives?"

"What? An alliance with the Jaguar's Children? I would do so gladly, if they would come forth, show themselves and speak to me. I have made it well known.

And what do I hear? Nothing. If you really wish to aid me, use your influence to bring their leaders here."

"I have tried."

"What do they say?"

"That their previous experience with royal houses such as yours has made them very wary. They will decide when and how to act. I have made them aware of the danger you are in. I cannot do more."

"Then they are useless," said the king impatiently. "Mixcatl, at least, can serve my purpose. Now that I have her, I will not let her go." Wise Coyote found that he was again on the brink of shouting. He took a deep breath. "Now leave, old man. She is waking. I must speak to her alone."

Nine-Lizard rose and went to the doorway, his head bent, his feet dragging.

"I pray to the gods that you do not destroy her," he whispered. "Or yourself, either."

Mixcatl slept for several more hours while Wise Coyote stayed beside her. At last, when dawn announced itself by creeping under the edges of door hangings, he saw the girl stir, yawn and open her eyes. Her gaze was mild and dreamy, as if she had woken from a night that included only the most restful of slumbers. Not until she felt the ointment on her arms and the healing skin beneath did a haunted look come into her eyes as she lay on her pallet.

"I dreamed that I changed again. That it hurt so much that I went wild and attacked someone. Then I got out of my chamber and tried to stalk a deer and someone else made me stop." She lifted her eyes to Wise Coyote. "It was not a dream, was it? I know I tried to hurt someone."

"Huetzin," Wise Coyote said as gently as he could.

Mixcatl lifted herself on her elbows, breathing hard, eyes staring. With an abrupt start, she tried to rise from the pallet. Wise Coyote put a hand on her chest and pushed her back. He could feel the drumming of her heart beneath his palm and knew that she was terribly afraid that she had slain Huetzin.

"I could not have," she said, her eyes grown feverish. "I remember now—his face. I fought to hold myself back. I could not have killed him—I . . ." Her voice faded. Despite her pleading words, Wise Coyote knew that she did not remember and he could say the words that already felt like filth in his mouth.

"You attacked him, but you did not kill him. I pulled you off in time. He lives, but his face is scarred and his right hand is badly bitten."

Her heart slowed; he could feel it beneath his palm.

"May I see him?" she asked.

"I think it better not to. I left him in the care of his mother. Now lie back."

She let herself be pushed back down onto the pallet.

"You are right," she said savagely. "If he sees me, he will shrink away in terror. It is better that I never see him again."

Wise Coyote ached with the wish to comfort the girl, but another part of him whispered that her pain served his purpose.

She wept, softly, her face turned toward the wall. She grimaced, too, with pain and he could see that the salty tears were stinging the still-tender skin of her face.

"Mixcatl," he said softly, and when she did finally turn her head toward him, he dabbed the welling tears away.

"I wish," she said, "that I will never change again."

"I do not think that wishing will alter what you are," said Wise Coyote.

"And what am I?"

"Nine-Lizard calls you Tepeyolotli, Heart-of-the-Mountain. He believes that you will be a great queen of your people when you develop your full powers." He paused. "Mixcatl, I know this is hard. You have wished to be only a human woman, an artist and a scribe. But you are not. By your gift, you are set apart. You will change again and nothing you or I can do will stop it from happening. Do not fight against your nature. Each time, you will become stronger, more powerful. Then you will be able to stand against the enemies that threaten both of us."

The tears slowed their trickle as the hardness of anger replaced the sorrow in her eyes.

"That is better," said Wise Coyote. "A jaguar does not weep."

A strange bitter smile came onto her face. "It is you who wishes to be the jaguar, tlatoani. If I could, I would give you my gift."

Her words tore at the weak place in his heart but he said only, "That is something you cannot do. Use it for me instead of casting it away."

She was silent for a long time, staring up at nothing. On the pallet, in the chamber, she looked lost and alone. Wise Coyote wanted to take her in his arms and hold her close, but his memory of seeing Huetzin in her embrace stopped him.

Let her be alone. Let her find the armor that is built from sorrow. Only then will she be fit for the purpose I plan. Softness only rots the bowstring, warps the spear, chips the glass-edged sword. Let her be hard.

"Will you see Huetzin?" Her voice was flat.

"I will be paying him a visit." He kept his voice neutral. "Have you a message for him?"

"Tell him I wish I could have pulled my teeth out by the roots before they closed on his hand. Give him all the best healers so that he may sculpt again."

"I have sent out word for healers who specialize in such wounds," Wise Coyote answered.

She looked up at him and suddenly he saw her as a

woman still close to childhood, her face crisscrossed by wide pink swaths, as if she had been burned badly but was now miraculously healing.

"You speak as if you understand," she said softly. "But you do not. No one can know what it is like to have become a beast, to have turned on someone you thought you loved."

Wise Coyote opened his mouth, then closed it, but the words echoed in his mind. *I know it too well.*

"I must go, Mixcatl. Rest and prepare yourself."

"For the next time."

He nodded tightly as he left the room, not trusting himself to speak.

Much later, the king of Texcoco sat on his sleeping mat, his head cradled between his two hands. He had been to see Huetzin. The boy's wounds had been anointed and wrapped. Potions had been given to dull the pain, but they could do nothing about the madness that threatened in the youth's eyes.

The concubine with the golden skin had accosted Wise Coyote in the outer chamber that led to the room where the youth lay. She looked at him with grief and bewilderment in her eyes.

"What happened to my son?" she asked, her melodic voice hoarse with weeping. "The wounds on his face and hand do not explain his staring and raving. Would a mountain cat be such a fearful thing? He cries and whimpers like an infant and will not speak."

"To one not trained as a hunter or warrior, such an encounter can be devastating," Wise Coyote said. "A gentle nature is often vulnerable to shocks like this. Please do not worry. He will come to himself again soon."

"Well, there will be no temptation for wild beasts to

prowl the grounds of Tezcotzinco," said the woman. "I sent house servants to kill the deer."

Wise Coyote nodded silently. He did not tell her that a few of the tame herd still survived, kept in a hidden pen and cared for by a servant that he had sworn to secrecy. He had done so as soon as he suspected that Huetzin's mother might destroy the animals. He had not saved the buck and two does out of compassion; he had observed that the smell of prey excited Mixcatl and stimulated her transformation.

After more words that he hoped would be reassuring, he left Huetzin's mother in the outer rooms and was admitted, alone, into his son's chamber.

Huetzin sat on an icpalli, his bandaged hand cradled in his lap, the five parallel gashes on his face now crusted and scabbed over. Wise Coyote felt remorse sweep through him like a strong tide, threatening to wash out the truth. The sight of those brutal wounds on what had been a handsome and sensitive young face, a face that many said was a reflection of his own, was almost too much to bear. Wise Coyote had to steel himself before he could kneel down beside his son.

"Huetzin," he said, but the shocked eyes stared straight ahead without recognizing Wise Coyote. "Huetzin, I'm here. Your father. It is over. You are safe. You will be healed."

Slowly the youth's gaze turned to Wise Coyote, the pupils wide with a grief that could not be banished. The eyes seemed to be windows through which Wise Coyote could glimpse a deeply riven soul. He knew then that the words he had spoken to the youth's mother were lies.

"You are safe here," he said, grasping his son by the arms. "It is over. She is far away. She will never come near you again."

Great tears rolled out the corners of the agonized eyes, then, abruptly, Huetzin's gaze focused in a moment of lucidity. "You told me what she was, how she would change. But it never meant anything to me until I saw her there in the moonlight."

"Now you do understand," Wise Coyote whispered.

"Her face—it was bleeding and horrible, yet my lips still longed to kiss it. Her eyes—I could see that she knew me, yet . . ." Huetzin's voice trailed off as he touched the gashes on his face. The glassiness came back into his eyes and suddenly he screamed. "Gods, no! Get it away! Bleeding on me, dropping horrible bits of skin on me. Hot breath, woman's eyes, yet I love, I still love . . ."

"Put it all from your mind, Huetzin."

"Oh, father, I cannot. Every stab of pain in my hand reminds me. I thought she loved me." He lifted his maimed hand, his arm shaking. "She is an artist; she knows what it feels to have her gift torn away, yet she has done this to me. Why?"

The last word came out as an agonized cry.

"She lost herself," Wise Coyote tried to say, but Huetzin only cradled his wounded hand against his breast like a dead child and rocked back and forth, weeping.

At last Huetzin subsided, staring dully at nothing, a few tears still seeping from his eyes. He was caught in a maze of love, terror and loss, each one warring against the other and making the sensitive artist's soul the battleground. The wounds on his face would heal, but unless his hand regained its ability, the torture that had descended upon the young man's mind would never end.

Watching him, Wise Coyote thought, *My war has started. Huetzin and Mixcatl are the first casualties. How many more will there be?*

"Rest and try to find peace, Huetzin," he had said, kissing the youth on the brow before rising.

Now, sitting on his sleeping mat, remembering all that had happened, he feared he might never find peace until he sought it with the point of a dagger aimed at his own heart.

No. His death, without a legitimate heir to carry on the line of Texcoco, would spell the end of his city as an independent state. He must carry through on his plans, whether or not he had the heart. With a heaviness in his breast, he rolled over and at last managed to find sleep.

18

When mixcatl woke from her healing sleep again, she found that she had been moved back into the wooden chamber originally used to confine her. Torches in their brackets cast a low shadowed light over the heavy plank walls and floor. The room had been scrubbed with agave wash and the sweat and bloodstained bedding replaced with fresh blankets. She rolled her head wearily.

At least he has cleaned my cage before putting me back in it.

The thought began as irony and ended in despair. She wondered if the drop-door was barred again on the outside.

She knew she had regained her strength and could rise from her pallet to see if the door would give when she pushed outward, but somehow she didn't want to try. The heaviness and lassitude of grief weighed her down and kept her lying there, staring up at nothing.

She wanted to wipe her mind of all feelings or memories, leaving it gray and featureless as a shroud. For a while she managed it, but gradually the painful thoughts crept back. Huetzin. She had attacked him, slashed his face and driven her fangs into his hand. Yet she didn't remember. The last image in her mind was of the youth's face as he lay in a faint before her. The last thing she remembered was drawing him close in a clumsy embrace. She knew him, loved him, even while the jaguar wildness was raging inside her.

But after that moment, she remembered nothing. Was this lack of recollection also a legacy of her nature? Did the transformation steal her memory as it did her need to create beauty? If so, she was doubly cursed.

The grinding creak of the door as it lifted made her start and sit up. For a moment she thought her visitor was Wise Coyote; then she recognized the bald pate and paint-stained cloak of her fellow scribe.

Nine-Lizard clambered through awkwardly, for the door was heavy and not made for easy opening. Then he came over to Mixcatl, knelt beside her pallet. The torchlight made his watery eyes seem to shimmer and there was a graveness in his face that spoke of more grief to come.

Yet he only sat silently and stroked her hand.

"I did not maim Huetzin. Please. Tell me that I did not." She seized his robes, hands clutching in desperation.

The graveness in his face grew deeper. "Mixcatl, I cannot tell you that. The young man bears wounds made by teeth and claws."

She squeezed her eyes shut, ducked her head in shame. "If I did it, why do I not remember?" The next question was even harder to ask. She lifted her face to his and stared into his eyes. "Did you . . . see . . . me attack Huetzin?"

"I did not arrive until Wise Coyote had pulled you off the youth," Nine-Lizard said, and she felt him gently trying to disentangle her fingers from his robes.

"Huetzin was . . . he *is* my friend," she choked as he eased her back down upon the pallet. "I would not have hurt him. If I did, why can I not remember feeling his hand in my mouth when I bit or the skin of his cheek open beneath my claws?''

Nine-Lizard tried to soothe her. "You were confused, pain-maddened. You did not know what you were doing. Do not try to live it again, Mixcatl."

She lay, feeling defeated. Bitterly she said, "I will live it again. Whether or not that is my wish." She paused. "Is that what this change does to a person? When I wake up after having been an animal, will I be unaware of what I have done, whom I have killed?''

He leaned over her, the wattles on his neck shaking, and startled her with the violence of his reply. "No! It must not happen that way!''

"Must not?'' Mixcatl asked quietly after a long pause.

Nine-Lizard was trembling, one fist in the air. Slowly he lowered his hand. "I am an old fool, shouting at empty air. My words do not matter. What has happened cannot be changed."

There was a change in his eyes as he looked down at her. The sudden rage shrank away. In its place crept pity and then a strange dispassionate gaze as if he were forced to admit that something he had done was a failure and that now he had to put it aside.

That frightened her more than anything he had said, even his shouting. Again she felt the impulse to clutch at him as if to save herself from falling into a pit that was opening beneath her. Instead the panic came in hurried words.

"When I changed before, I was aware of myself. I was confused, but I knew what I did. This time was no different. I knew what I did. Until . . ." She faltered.

"The time that you cannot remember," said Nine-Lizard.

"Why should this time have been different from the others?''

"You went further into the transformation," Nine-

Lizard answered. She felt his dry, callused fingers as he clasped her hands between his, yet the distance that had come between them was still there. "Mixcatl, I do not know what happened. The likelihood is that you did lose yourself in the shock of change and that you did not recognize Huetzin."

"If you were not there . . . ," she began.

"Are you asking me to doubt Wise Coyote's words? How else could the boy have been so wounded?"

"I do not know. Huetzin was angry at his father for the same reason that you are."

"Anger may beget anger," said Nine-Lizard, "but it would take more than that to make a man like Wise Coyote speak untrue words or turn against his son." He paused. "Is there anything that you can recall to suggest otherwise?"

Mixcatl closed her eyes. The last moments of the scene were so clear. She could still see Huetzin's face, bathed in moonlight. And then the memory became murky.

"No," she answered.

The truth is that I do not know what happened. I am only accusing Wise Coyote because I cannot face what must lie within myself.

Nine-Lizard asked, "Then there is no reason for me to doubt him, is there?"

Again, she felt her lips form a soft "No."

"It does us no good to turn away from the probable truth. However," he added, as Mixcatl felt despair begin to choke her, "you are not to blame. How could you be if you were in the grip of something beyond your control?"

Whether or not I am to blame does not matter. You know that the thing within me is evil and must be destroyed. That is why you look at me so.

She let the words speak only inside her head, for they were, like the beast that had torn Huetzin, too dangerous to let free. Nine-Lizard would have no answer. He would only turn and walk away, leaving her even more alone.

There was a silence between them until she felt him shift his weight on her bed. Perhaps he was feeling that he could say no more or give her no more comfort. Even if that was true, she could not bear for him to go.

"Nine-Lizard," she said after a long time. "I was fighting the change. When I painted on the tiles Huetzin gave me, I could keep the strange feelings away. If Wise Coyote hadn't taken the tile from me, I would not have lost myself."

The old scribe made a chuckle that turned into a sigh. "How long do you think you would have been able to hold off the transformation?"

"As long as I had to."

"Yes, and when the tiles ran out, you would have covered Tezcotzinco's walls with frenzied pictures." Nine-Lizard gave her a sad smile.

"It would have been better than . . ."

He smoothed her brow. "Whatever mistakes Wise Coyote made, he was right about one thing. One cannot deny one's own nature. It must and will emerge."

"No. It must not," said Mixcatl in a low, shaking voice. "You do not know what this thing is. It has no wish for art or beauty or love. It is all hate and hunger."

Again the intensity came to Nine-Lizard's face. "That is not all. That cannot be all. Give yourself time to understand."

Mixcatl looked away. After another long silence she asked, "Is there any way to rid me of this curse?"

Nine-Lizard's voice was sharp. "It is not a curse. It is your heritage and history. You were born with the jaguar in your blood. It will be with you until you die."

"Then perhaps I should return to Tenochtitlán and accept the death that awaits me there."

"Feeding the blood gods that you despise?" Nine-

Lizard leaned over her fiercely. "No! Neither I nor Wise Coyote will permit you to be sacrificed."

"Then what will you do? Keep me shut up in this cage until I go so mad that I no longer care what I do?" She wanted to shout the words, but she felt too weary.

"No. I have sent word to the Jaguar's Children. I have told them what you are and what you need. They are sending someone to take you."

"Where?"

Nine Lizard shook his head. "Where I do not know. The Jaguar's Children have a refuge for those of their own kind. A canoe will arrive to take you to their settlement. They will teach you how to deal with the transformation."

Mixcatl folded her arms. She did not want to learn how to manage her jaguar nature. She wanted only to be rid of it.

"When their contact comes, go with him."

"You will not be here?"

"Perhaps. Perhaps not."

"How will I know who he is?"

"I can only say that when you see him, you will know."

"If you want me to go to these people, why do you not take me?"

He stared away into the shadows. "My connection with the Jaguar's Children is tenuous. They will allow me only so close and that is not enough to get you to where you must be." He paused, leaning over her, grasping one shoulder. "You must promise me that when you see and recognize the contact, you will go with him without resisting or questioning."

"Very well, I will go." She rolled her head restlessly. "I no longer want to stay here. I cannot bear to be close to Huetzin without being able to see him, and Wise Coyote . . ." She stopped, fighting a sob. "I thought he was a good and gentle man. I was growing fond of him; perhaps as much as I was of Huetzin. He is right when he tries to struggle against such gods as Hummingbird on the Left." Her voice grew low and angry. "But that does not justify his trying to make me into a weapon or a goddess."

"You will find," said Nine-Lizard softly, "that men have a strange attitude to those who are different. They will cast themselves at your feet and worship you, or they will condemn you as the blackest demon. It will not be first time nor will it be the last." The shelf supporting the pallet creaked as he shifted his weight and stood up.

"Do not go, Nine-Lizard," she said as she felt her hand slip from between his callused palms.

"You must sleep. I have work to complete."

"When will the boat be here?"

"Soon enough, I hope," he said and moved toward the door. When he had gone through, he poked his head back in and said, "I regret that I must bar it again on the outside, Mixcatl."

She let her head fall back on the blankets. If he had left the door unblocked, she might have been able to escape. And what then? Try to see Huetzin and risk frightening him into deeper madness? Try to flee Tezcotzinco and be seized again by the transformation? Run to the cliffs overlooking Lake Texcoco and fling herself down?

She felt her lips curve in a bitter smile. Wise Coyote might have barred the door for the first two reasons, but Nine-Lizard had done it for the last.

None of those things would probably happen. As soon as she came out of the door, she would be stabbed or speared by one of Wise Coyote's guards. It would be a stupid way to die. And it would do nothing to help Huetzin.

And perhaps, just perhaps, the mysterious people

Nine-Lizard called the Jaguar's Children might be able to help her find a compromise between the demands of her beast nature and the needs of her art.

The next morning, Wise Coyote knelt at the same low worktable that he had used to draw plans for the aqueduct to Tenochtitlán and many other building projects. This time, however, two documents were spread before him and he was not the executor but only the judge of how well the work had been done.

Behind him, the old scribe Nine-Lizard Iguana Tongue waited patiently. Wise Coyote knew that the last part of each history had been completed rapidly, in the cold hours of the night. He examined the final sections closely, but could find not even the most subtle flaw.

He studied the old man's haggard face, the darkened flesh beneath the eyes. Yes, he had done what he claimed, even though Wise Coyote could scarcely believe that so much work of such quality could be done in one night. He wasn't sure why the scribe had put forth so much effort. Was it to make up for what the girl could not do, or had Nine-Lizard decided that it was best to complete their obligation so that he and the girl could leave Texcoco?

He reached for his stone seal, dipped it in a shallow bowl of blue pigment and affixed it to the end of the book. "I will send a messenger to notify him that it is complete and he can send an escort to fetch it. Once he has examined it for himself and declared it satisfactory, your obligation to me is ended."

Carefully he folded up the rigid pages of the book and bound it with a richly woven strap before setting it aside.

"Thank you, Speaker-King," said Nine-Lizard formally. "Is there anything else, or am I dismissed?"

Wise Coyote rose from the table, straightened his shoulders. Was there anything else? Only a life that was coming down around him like a collapsing temple. Only the rumors that had spread from his palace retreat to his capital city and then around the countryside—rumors that the king of Texcoco had dabbled in sorcery and was now paying for his folly by the maiming and madness that afflicted his son. As soon as those rumors reached Tenochtitlán, its ruler's wrath would build and not even the completion of the history would be enough to compensate for Texcoco's misdoings.

That was his own responsibility, not Nine-Lizard's.

"Will you be returning to the House of Scribes?" Wise Coyote asked.

"For a short time. I was loaned from the court of Tlacopan and I will soon be recalled there."

Tlacopan. A small, powerless kingdom. A member of the Triple Alliance in name only, its ruler only a figurehead. Ilhuicamina had swallowed it completely, as he soon would Texcoco. Nine-Lizard would find refuge there, away from the gathering storm.

"What of the girl?" Wise Coyote asked.

"According to orders from the House of Scribes, she is to return with me. Those orders are meaningless now; you hold her within the cage you built. If you choose to keep her, there is nothing I can do, except repeat the warning I have already given."

Even if I do keep her, Wise Coyote thought, *I will have only her body and the beast that lies within it. Huetzin has her love, though it will do him no good. I wanted her affection and loyalty, but I have earned only her hatred.*

He saw Nine-Lizard eyeing him, as if the old scribe could read the thoughts on his face.

Nine-Lizard spoke softly. "Let her go, my king. The Jaguar's Children can help her and they need her. And now, it is more important than ever that she be sent to her own people."

"Why?"

"Her attack on Huetzin has revealed something new about her. It is something I did not know at first. Even now, I am not sure."

Wise Coyote waited, wondering what this revelation would be.

The scribe was studying him again. "Before I tell you what I suspect, I must ask you again about the attack. It is, of course, your privilege, as king, not to answer."

Wise Coyote felt a tendril of cold start to creep up his back toward a point between his shoulders. Did Nine-Lizard suspect he had lied in his account of the incident? Had the old man found evidence, perhaps even the knife that he had used to slash Huetzin's face? No, that could not be. The streams that poured down from the hills through the grounds of Tezcotzinco would have carried the weapon far away.

He let nothing show on his face, which he kept in a relaxed and pleasant expression. "If my answers will aid you in helping Mixcatl, I am willing to give them." He indicated a sitting-mat and he sat down cross-legged opposite the scribe.

"I will make this brief," said the scribe. "I know that you pulled Mixcatl away from Huetzin. Did you actually see her wound him?"

"Why else would I have wrenched her away with a rope about her neck," Wise Coyote said. "I nearly throttled her—she collapsed in a faint."

"Then you did see the attack."

Wise Coyote knew that he could choose to stay with his lie or abandon it. To confess the truth now meant admitting to both Nine-Lizard and himself that he was not the gentle scholar-king that both his subject and he had come to believe. In Nine-Lizard's eyes and his own, he would be no less cruel and ruthless than Ilhuicamina. It would not matter that his intent was more noble; it would make no difference. Somehow he could not bear the thought.

Whatever gods there are in this world, give me strength, he thought. To Nine-Lizard he said calmly, "Yes. She leaped on him, slashed his face and then bit his right hand when he raised it to defend himself."

At his words, Nine-Lizard seemed to slump. "Did she even check herself when she ran at him? Did she show any signs that she recognized him?"

"No," Wise Coyote said, baffled by the question and wondering what all this was leading up to.

"Then my fears are true." Nine-Lizard closed his eyes, as if in pain.

Wise Coyote started to ask what he meant, but abruptly the old scribe opened his eyes again and began to speak. "I have told you a little about the Jaguar's Children. Now I must tell you more. You already know that Mixcatl is one of that line. The power of her gift is greater than any I have ever seen. She is the leader that they have been waiting for.

"But the strength of her gift opens a danger that only the most powerful among the Jaguar's Children face. This is a flaw inherent in their natures, the reason why they have remained few and almost powerless."

Nine-Lizard paused, as if measuring his listener. Slowly he said, "You would think that someone who transforms into an animal would lose all memory of their humanity and act only upon their animal impulses. Such is not true. When the Jaguar's Children take the shape of the beast, they retain the guiding and directing ability of the human mind.

"Yet the more powerful and dominant the animal side becomes, the stronger the personality needed to control it. For some among the Jaguar's Children, the animal is too strong. For them, transformation is a descent into unknowing savagery."

Wise Coyote stared at Nine-Lizard. "How do you know this?"

The scribe's answering gaze was level. "I have studied these people all my life."

"And you fear that Mixcatl is flawed in the way that you describe."

Wise Coyote saw the veined old fist close in helpless anger. "She felt strongly about your son. Even if she was driven wild by pain, she should have recognized him."

"There was no light. She could not have seen him well enough," the king protested.

"I or you could not have seen him, but her eyes were becoming a jaguar's. Even if she could not see him, she would have known him by smell." Nine-Lizard brought his fist down on his bony knee. "No. The fact that she attacked someone she should have known is a bad sign."

"She attacked me inside the cage before escaping," Wise Coyote said, remembering. "But her rage was human . . . and I cannot claim that I did not deserve it."

"Everything indicates that her power rules her, which it should not." Nine-Lizard gave a heavy sigh. "Too many times I have seen this. The young ones are rare enough, especially when they show such promise as she. But then the taint shows itself and strikes the gifted aside before they can rise to leadership. So many times and now, again!" He shook his head. "Thus those who carry the ancient blood dwindle and die out."

Wise Coyote felt as if he had unwillingly been given a part in an ancient tragedy that well might condemn Mixcatl. By giving up his lie, he could reverse Nine-Lizard's conclusion, but at what cost to himself? No. Though his conscience pained him, he could not take down the fortress of untruth which was starting to rise higher about him. The first sacrifice was the hardest. The second might be easier.

"It is possible that I might have misjudged her," said

Nine-Lizard solemnly. "That is another reason why she must go. The people at the refuge can test her and evaluate her. Perhaps even if she does have the flaw I fear, they have some way to deal with it."

The last words sounded faint, as though Nine-Lizard had no real hope.

In a warning voice, Wise Coyote said, "I have many misgivings about this, old man. Nevertheless, what I have learned from you requires thought. I will let you know of my decision whether to release Mixcatl if and when anyone comes for her. Until then, she will remain where she is."

"Then I can ask no more of you, lord king," said Nine-Lizard. Bowing once, he departed.

That may be the last that anyone can ask of me once Ilhuicamina hears what has happened, Wise Coyote thought gloomily.

He remembered the spears and swords that his slain elder son had stored at his palace. He should go and look them over. If he was any judge of Tenochtitlán's reaction to the charge that he was meddling in forbidden things, he would soon have use for the weapons.

Three days after he had dispatched a messenger via boat to Tenochtitlán to let the Aztec ruler know that the history had been completed, the answer returned.

Wise Coyote brought the envoy into his private chambers and gave him refreshment. Then he sat in his reed icpalli and listened as the messenger spoke.

Ilhuicamina was eager to inspect the completed document and was dispatching an escort to fetch it back along with the two borrowed scribes. But, as Wise Coyote feared, there was more. The escort would contain not only scribes charged with transporting the document and warriors to guard it but a party of high priests and all their attendants. Among their tasks was to oversee the construction of the temple to Hummingbird on the Left, which Wise Coyote was ordered to commence at once.

In order to begin the project on an auspicious note, Ilhuicamina added, the priests would bless the ground-breaking by a sacrifice to the war god. In accordance with Ilhuicamina's tolerance and leniency toward his fellow sovereign in Texcoco, only one victim would be needed and she had been chosen. Indeed, the priests of Hummingbird had already requested this particular victim, for it was thought that her sorcerous gift would make her a powerful offering. It would be most convenient for everyone involved.

The envoy's voice and face carried the same arrogance as the message, but Wise Coyote only nodded at appropriate intervals and sent the man away, saying that he had heard and understood.

Then, as soon as the envoy was safely away from Tezcotzinco, Wise Coyote clenched his fist in rage. Tenochtitlán assumed he would crumple at once; he would show them otherwise. That Ilhuicamina did not anticipate any real resistance showed in the fact that he had made his intentions clear.

He thinks so little of me and my nation that he cares nothing for what I might do.

He sat and pondered. There was always the swift and brutal method of surrounding the party of priests with warriors once the escort had departed with the document. The priests could die swiftly and silently and their orders could be forgotten.

Such an act would bring retribution on Texcoco before Wise Coyote had prepared himself and his people for war. No. Better to take another, more devious road. He already had much practice in such doings. He would welcome the priests, make them comfortable in his palace and cheerfully embark upon the plans for their temple. But the sacrificial victim they required for the ground-breaking ceremony would be spirited away, hidden in one of the secret chinks of Tezcotzinco.

However much Mixcatl had angered Wise Coyote by refusing to aid him with her powers, and however much grief she had caused by abandoning him for Huetzin, he was not yet ready to give her up. Better the misty uncertainties of the Jaguar's Children than the bloody altar of Hummingbird.

And, although he would not dare admit it, buried deep within him was the hope that she might, once her life had been preserved, change her affection back to him.

When the bluestone palace had first been built, Wise Coyote had foreseen the need for hidden chambers and passageways. There was one small bolthole located under the floor in the water room. Ostensibly it had been built as an extra cistern, but it had a false bottom beneath the water chamber. No one dabbling their fingers and peering down into the water had any idea that beneath the shallow basin might lie another chamber large enough for a young woman to lie in. And the sounds of the stream rushing past would drown out any sound she might make.

Wise Coyote told Mixcatl about the priests' intent and showed her the refuge beneath the false bottom of the cistern. It could be padded and carefully vented. She could have food, water and even a cautious amount of light if she so wished. It was certain that a party of priests and their assistants would not be able to find her once she was hidden here.

She had shrugged, saying that one cage was no different than another. If the messenger from the Jaguar's Children arrived, she would go with them, but until that time she would stay in hiding and be quiet. It would help, she said, if she could once again have paints and tiles, for if the change threatened again while she was entombed in the cistern's false chamber, the noise she might make would lead the searchers to her.

Wise Coyote agreed and handled all the arrangements himself. Not even Nine-Lizard was to know where Mixcatl was hidden, lest the priests become impatient and try to extract information by torture. The only ones immune from their interrogations would be Wise Coyote himself and his family. This, thankfully, included Huetzin, even though Wise Coyote knew that the wounded youth's ravings would be of little aid to the priests. He would have to move rapidly, however. Once Hummingbird's priesthood arrived, he did not know how long his own immunity might last.

The high priests and the escort for the completed document arrived in a high-prowed barge nearly as splendid as the one used by Ilhuicamina on his previous journey to Tezcotzinco. Wise Coyote was on the stone quay beneath the cliffs to receive the party.

He wore full royal regalia, shimmering gold and green cloak, a plume of quetzal feathers. He had donned gold ear and nose plugs along with his traditional turquoise circlet. Nine-Lizard too was dressed more splendidly than usual, though not so much so that he might be accused of dressing above his station as a slave-scribe.

Nine-Lizard carried the bound volume of the official history, ready to accompany it back to the House of Scribes in Tenochtitlán. The other version had been hidden in the library.

Wise Coyote was reluctant to let Nine-Lizard depart, but he could see no alternative. Keeping Mixcatl by trickery would cause enough provocation, but her life was endangered. There had been no such threat against Nine-Lizard. He should be allowed to return peacefully to Tlacopan.

The king smelled the party before their barge reached

his quay. The onshore wind from the lake brought the stink of tangled and filthy hair mingling with the blood that still stiffened their robes. He tried to judge how many men were in the boat to be sure that his own escort was large enough to counter any threat the priests might bring. From a distance the party appeared small.

As the barge neared the quay, he caught the smell again. It angered him that they would step ashore onto his land with the stains of sacrifice tainting their garments. The leader, who was dressed in gold pectoral, wristlets and black bodypaint, addressed Wise Coyote in the formal words of greeting; but they were tossed off with such carelessness that it was as if the priest were addressing one of his minions, not the king of an allied state.

"You have a great reputation as an engineer and builder," said the high priest as he stepped from the barge onto the quay. "I will look forward to seeing the temple rise under your guidance. Have you chosen the land on which it will be sited?"

"A site has been chosen. It is the center of the city, which should please you." Wise Coyote refrained from mentioning that his choice for a site would be a place where refuse was carted from the city and dumped. The air about the dump already stank and carrion birds frequented it; they would not have to move if the charnel house of Hummingbird was erected there.

"And of course, the victim for the ground-breaking sacrifice," said the high priest, as others of his party disembarked and stood in a group about him. "I trust you are preparing her well."

"With great regret, I must tell you that the girl has already been slain and her corpse burned. It was, of course, the eagerness of my men in following Il-huicamina's edict that suspected sorcerers must be utterly destroyed."

"But there will be no sacrifice for the ground-breaking," the high priest fumed. "This is not what we had been led to expect."

"I assume that a suitable replacement can be found, even if it means postponing the ceremony by a few days," said Wise Coyote smoothly. "Unless you wish to omit the shedding of blood into the first trenches."

The high priest's brow darkened. "That would be sacrilege. It would cast ill favor on the work. The god would not be pleased."

"Then you will allow the time necessary to please him." Wise Coyote caught himself before the cultivated smoothness in his voice became mocking. He shot a quick glance at Nine-Lizard to see how the scribe was reacting. Of course the old man had been told about the ruse, but he did not know where Mixcatl was hidden so that torture would be of no use, should the priests decide to examine him. Nine-Lizard was also not aware of the exact details, since Wise Coyote was improvising them a bit as he went along.

He was finding, to his dismay, that he had a distinct talent for lying.

The priests gathered into a little huddle on the quay, muttering among themselves. Then they motioned several scribes and their warrior escort into the conference. Wise Coyote and Nine-Lizard were pointedly left out.

At last the impromptu meeting ended, just as Wise Coyote was getting ready to clear his throat in an irritated manner to remind them of whose territory they were now on.

Abruptly the high priest stepped forward, flanked by two armed warriors. "Bind that man," he ordered, gesturing at Nine-Lizard. "He has been a companion to the girl since they were both in the House of Scribes. He can tell us what has happened."

The warriors seized Nine-Lizard, pulled his arms behind his back and began wrapping his crossed wrists with rawhide strips. The old man sent an alarmed and bewildered look to the king of Texcoco. This surely was not part of the ruse.

"Release the scribe," said Wise Coyote sharply.

The high priest raised his eyebrows in surprise. "I did not think you would see fit to object, King of Texcoco. You promised our lord that you would return this man once his service was complete."

"I will return him to the House of Scribes in a manner befitting his status as a scholar. To be sure that he arrives there safely I will send him in my own barge with my own men. If necessary, I will have my men take him directly to Tlacopan."

"I fear the matter is out of your hands."

"He will prove useless to you. He knows nothing," Wise Coyote argued.

"We will discover that for ourselves when we question him in Tenochtitlán," said the high priest, both his eyes and his voice hardening. "If you expect us to be fooled by your claim that the girl has been killed, you insult us. Produce her at once, or we take the old man now."

"You are asking for the impossible. She was slain and the corpse burned. I can show you what remains."

"What you have could be the bones of any woman taken from your household. No." The high priest folded his arms and gave the king a withering look. "Put the old man in the boat," he snapped sharply over his shoulder. He whirled to face Wise Coyote as the king strode forward, his glass-edged sword drawn, his own warriors close behind him.

The high priest made a swift hand motion to a man near the barge. To Wise Coyote's dismay, more warriors, armed with swords and lances, rose up from beneath hides laid in the bottom of the boat.

Now the opposing force outnumbered his. Wise Coyote knew he could summon help, but before enough men could rush down the narrow stairway cut into the cliffs, he would be overwhelmed, perhaps slain.

The king gave a sharp hand signal to his men, moving back with them along the quay. He cursed himself for not scenting treachery.

"So you show the wisdom for which you are so well known," said the high priest, lapsing back into that unctuous tone that Wise Coyote had already begun to hate. "That is well. Had you attacked me or any of my party, your beautiful retreat in the hills above would have been destroyed before the day ended. Our lord in Tenochtitlán is eager to strike. All he needs is sufficient provocation."

Wise Coyote had no doubt of that. Already Ilhuicamina must be gathering forces to march against him. Behind the islands dotting the lake, there might be war canoes, filled with archers and Eagle Knights, eager to taste blood in combat.

And if he died here on the quay in a skirmish, Tenochtitlán would only have to walk in and take his lands. He must not be such a fool.

He lowered and sheathed his weapon, signaling his men to do the same. "I do not wish to provide such provocation."

The high priest laughed, showing teeth that had been hollowed and then filled with precious jewels.

Wise Coyote put a rein on his temper, knowing that the high priest was deliberately trying to goad him into rash action.

Nine-Lizard rose to his feet in the rocking barge. "I think it best to do as the high priest wishes, tlatoani. Doing otherwise could cause my death and yours."

Wise Coyote lifted his voice to speak in reply, then fell silent. Nine-Lizard was right. The king stepped back, breathing heavily, swearing at himself for a fool. He should have known that the high priest would not be easily duped and that he would have men hidden in the barge. That would have made no difference up in the palace or the city, where Wise Coyote could outnumber the high priest's men with warriors of his own. But here, on the narrow dock beneath the cliffs, he had placed himself at a disadvantage.

He wondered if he was perhaps too numb from what had already happened to think straight. Several warriors and lesser priests boarded the barge with Nine-Lizard, leaving the high priest with a smaller but sufficient party on the quay. Wise Coyote watched the barge pull away, knowing that he had made a costly mistake.

"Now that the misunderstanding is over," said the high priest archly, "you may show us to our quarters. Put down your weapons," he added to the warriors who still surrounded him as a cloud of disturbed bees swarms about the hive. "The Speaker-King of Texcoco expects us to behave as guests."

Wise Coyote saw the old scribe raise one hand to him as if in salutation. Slowly he waved back, then let his hand drop to his side. Without Nine-Lizard, it was going to be much more difficult to handle Mixcatl. And how would he know who the contact from the Jaguar's Children would be? How would they find Mixcatl since he now had her so well hidden beneath the false bottom of the cistern? Would they even come at all, now that Nine-Lizard was no longer there to act as liaison?

Too many questions and no answers. For now he had the high priest and his retinue to deal with. Surrounded by his own party to make sure that no one from the high priest's men would try a quick assassination stroke, he led the way back up the stone stairs toward his palace.

19

DURING THE LONG hours of hiding, Mixcatl could only paint by fluttering lamplight with a tile on her knees, curl up and sleep on her blankets or eat the food stored with her. Though she knew that less than a day had passed since she had entered her refuge, it felt much longer. In the cramped space beneath the false bottom of the cistern, she had barely enough room to sit up and she found herself thinking almost longingly of her wooden cage.

Often she felt herself growing angry. Wise Coyote had said she was being hidden for her own safety, but he had said that her imprisonment in the wooden chamber was also for her own good. That was in part a lie—he had caged her like a young beast and waited for her to grow the talents that he could use. But it was also in part the truth. By attacking Huetzin, she had wounded herself.

No, she should not think of Huetzin now. The grief would return, with its pain, making her want to scream aloud. And that, surely, would lead the priests to her. And the anger too was dangerous, for if she gave herself to rage, she felt the transformation creeping over her. So far she had managed to fend it off by painting, but she had already run out of tiles.

She glanced at the curved ceramic walls of the cistern,

where she had begun her mural. If Wise Coyote did not let her out soon, he would lift the false bottom to find the chamber filled with wild figures and rioting colors. The only blank space would be where she sat or lay.

He did not come and soon the need to fight the threatening change seized her again. She was painting in a frenzy of brushstrokes when she heard the sound of water being drained away from above. She went rigid and extinguished her lamp. Had Wise Coyote returned to free her, or had other searchers discovered her refuge? Then it came, three raps, a pause and another rap. Again she hesitated before answering in kind. The priests might have also wrung that code from Wise Coyote as well.

There was nothing she could do except curl herself at the bottom of the chamber and wait as the false-bottomed clay basin was drained and lifted. She breathed, openmouthed, feeling sweat crawl down her forehead and back, despite the clammy cold of the chamber. If an unfamiliar face peered over the lip she would lunge and strike, calling on the jaguar within to possess her.

Even as that fierce hope surged up in her, she felt it sink back down again. She knew that the change wouldn't be fast enough. She would still be in its grip when the lid was lifted.

The rough ceramic grated as it rose above her head. She squinted for a glimpse of the one who was freeing her and strained for the sound of familiar or unfamiliar voices. The echoes in the stone room and the sound of running water below distorted the whisper when it came, but Mixcatl was sure that it had been Wise Coyote's.

"Out," he said. Ignoring her stiffness, she scrambled up and over the lip of the cistern. She badly needed to use the water room for its intended purpose, for she had restrained herself from using the pisspot that had been provided. The smell, in such a confined space, would have been unbearable.

But before allowing herself even that small luxury, she turned a questioning gaze on Wise Coyote.

"Yes, we are safe now. I sent the party of priests on to the city, where they are quartered in my other palace."

She cleared the chamber of all her belongings; paints, tiles, blankets, food bundles, empty pisspot. He helped her in her task, glancing in amazement at the decorated inner walls.

"I ran out of tiles," Mixcatl said, feeling awkward.

"The work is beautiful! I only wish you had done it in a more accessible place. Try not to mar it as you climb out," he added.

He went outside while she relieved herself through the opening in the water room floor. Then she helped him slide the false bottom back into the cistern. They lowered it so that it again fit snugly on a ridge that ran around the inside wall of the water tank.

He moved a trough so that the water cascading down from a higher basin would refill the cistern. She noticed that he arranged it so that the flow would run silently down the side of the ceramic wall, not fall and splash noisily.

Leaning against the outside wall of the tank, the king gave a weary sigh. "Those arrogant wretches are gone, but before they left they went over every stone of this palace. I thought they would tear apart my library. They even forced their way into Huetzin's chambers, but when they saw that he was lost in despair, they quickly left."

"So we are safe," said Mixcatl, trying not to think of Huetzin. She wanted to see him so badly, yet she feared it would only harm him more.

"For the moment." The torchlight flickered across Wise Coyote's face, deepening the lines that worry had already created. "Come," he said, leading the way out.

"I thought Nine-Lizard would be with you," she said. Did his face twitch suddenly in a spasm of pain or regret? His voice, when he spoke, was level, even, controlled. "He is no longer in Texcoco. That is why we need to talk."

He hurried her along the shadowed corridors to his own chambers. There a fire was burning on an open hearth and Mixcatl leaned gratefully toward it to warm her hands, which had become stiff from the clammy cold beneath the cistern. He draped a cloak about her shoulders and wrapped one about his own before inviting her to sit on a mat before the welcome blaze.

"Nine-Lizard was removed this morning by the priests when they arrived," he said before Mixcatl could ask any questions. "I did not foresee that when they could not find you, they would take him for questioning."

Nine-Lizard taken! Despite her closeness to the fire, cold began to seep through Mixcatl, fear for the old scribe who had been her mentor and friend.

"Do they hold him now? Will they kill him at the temple ground-breaking just as you said they would kill me?"

"No. They put him on the barge under armed guard, along with the historical document you both prepared. The barge departed for Tenochtitlán."

"And you . . . just let him go?" The words slipped out, angry, accusing.

Wise Coyote sighed. In that breath, Mixcatl heard the weariness of a man who had been pushed nearly to his limit and who knew he would be asked for even more. She also understood that as ruler he did not have to justify his actions to anyone. For an instant, she thought he would use that privilege as a shield and stay silent.

Then, as she looked into his face, she realized that he wanted her understanding if not her support. Behind his calmness, he was frightened, shaken, and most of all lonely. Nine-Lizard might not have been his friend, but the old man had been a companion during the terrible events over the last few days. She did not want to remember that she had played a key part in those events.

"I am sorry," she said. "I did not mean it to sound so harsh."

He gave her an odd steady look. "Only one such as you could scold a king. Perhaps I deserve it." Then he too put his hands out to the fire. "Perhaps this is wishful thinking, but I do not believe that Nine-Lizard is in any immediate danger. Though the priests told me he was to be interrogated, I believe he is a hostage. Ilhuicamina will treat Nine-Lizard carefully until the old man has fulfilled his purpose."

"And that purpose?" Mixcatl asked carefully.

"To lure me out of my burrow and into the halls of Tenochtitlán. The Aztec knows that I will attempt to intercede to save Nine-Lizard. My family is known for our loyalty to those of my household, even those who are not permanent members. With the rumors of sorcery at my court now flying about Tenochtitlán, it is likely that I will be charged with heresy and given to the priests of Hummingbird. With the stroke that opens my breast, he will have Texcoco without having to fight a troublesome war." Wise Coyote spoke in a flat voice, as if it were someone else's fate that he was reciting.

"Since you are clever enough to see the trap, you will not walk into it."

"Is that a kind way of saying that I will choose to preserve my own skin by casting Nine-Lizard to the vultures?" Wise Coyote asked bitterly. "There was once a time when I upheld the family tradition of loyalty to the household." He sighed and buried his face in his hands. "I swear by Tloque Nahaque and Quetzalcoatl that I wish I could bring those days back again, those days before my deer's heart deprived me of my eldest son and then the respect of all around me." He lifted his face from his hands and gazed steadily at Mixcatl. "I would bring those days back again. I will put my fear aside and go to Tenochtitlán for Nine-Lizard's sake. I only wish I had some hope of success."

Mixcatl stared at him in surprise. This was a move she had not expected from him. She could see at once that it was no feint or lie. There was a naked openness on his face that would allow no more lies. If he said he would risk his life to save Nine-Lizard's, he would do so.

Her feelings were in turmoil. Once she had been prepared to hate and despise him for forcing her jaguar power on her before she was ready, and using her for his own purposes. Now she was beginning to understand why he had done so—even a noble-spirited man would turn ruthless if backed far enough into a corner. She could already see in his eyes the mute agony of having to watch the blood of his own nation being spilled on the steps of a hated temple that would soon be rising in his city.

She had to struggle to put aside her fear for Nine-Lizard, a fear that made her impatient. But urging Wise Coyote to undertake a foolhardy rescue mission would do no good to her or Nine-Lizard.

Choosing her words carefully, she said, "Nine-Lizard is probably safe for the moment and for many days to come. The fisherman will not throw away the bait until he is convinced the fish will not come to the hook. Send messengers and letters making promises and setting up arrangements. Make him think you will come soon."

Wise Coyote gave a tight smile. "I have already done so. I am glad you made the suggestion, however. From my lips it might have had the taint of cowardly reluctance."

"It is you who make that judgment upon yourself, tlatoani," she answered softly. "It is a wise move and it will give us much-needed time."

"Time for the Jaguar's Children to come for you." His smile softened, the light in his eyes became gentler. He took her hands and she found that she did not wish to pull away. "I do not regret . . . everything . . . that has happened, Mixcatl. Those walks in the garden, when I discovered that you shared my dream of a gentle god; they lifted up my soul in a way that not even the darkness about me now can make me forget."

She closed her eyes. "I wish, for your sake . . . and Huetzin's, that I had been just an ordinary woman. I think it would have been easier to share your dream and help you find it."

"Most likely you would have died with me in the struggle for it." He shrugged his shoulders. "That does not matter now. I have lost. The priests are in my city; the paper for the temple plans is on my worktable and I will draw the first lines tomorrow. I have lost, yet I must lift up my head and stand as my father did, even when he realized that he was defeated."

"You have not lost yet," Mixcatl said. "You can still fight."

Wise Coyote laughed hollowly. "By my doing, Texcoco has become a state where learning, manners and scholarship are more esteemed than skill in battle. Yes, I will fight if I am forced to, but I have no illusions about winning."

She watched him, wishing she could somehow reach out and give him some comfort, not knowing why. He, her jailer, the one who wanted the beast inside her, the one whose jealousy had parted her from Huetzin—why did she want to offer him anything, let alone hope?

If the Jaguar's Children came for her, she would start a new life in a new place with new people. What had happened here would drift into the past. When the dust of battle rose over Wise Coyote's city, she would not be there to see it. When the temple stood and started to claim its victims from among Wise Coyote's people, she would be far away. Why did she still care?

Because he is right. A part of me does share his dream of a god worthy of human devotion. A part of me will weep when the light of Texcoco's promise is extinguished by the bloodstained hand of Hummingbird.

And then another thought came. He need not lose. If she changed her mind, if she used her jaguar powers to aid him, the ominous vision might be turned aside.

The words were on her lips. It would be so easy to say them.

But what would the price be if she gave herself to his cause? Waking from the entrancement of beasthood, not knowing what she had done, whom she might have killed or maimed? She could never forget what she had done to Huetzin.

Her power was too strong, too uncontrollable. Even if she wanted to help Wise Coyote, her ability was so unpredictable that she might be unable to do what he wanted. In the frenzy of transformation, she might turn upon the king himself. If she could be trained, if she could understand and use her gift, then she could aid him. But there was no time.

And there was another fear that cut deeply into her. She remembered again the feeling of her art being torn from her as the change approached. She could never forget how the skill had drained from her fingers and the joy of creation had faded from her mind as the jaguar nature threatened. The loss of her art would be little sacrifice, another might say, perhaps even Wise Coyote himself. What is daubing with paints compared to saving a king and his nation?

A little sacrifice . . . but one far greater than she could give.

It was Wise Coyote who said that she could not turn away from her true nature. This gift of the mind, the heart and the hands, to see beauty and attempt to capture it; that ran as deeply in her nature as her heritage from the jaguar. She must find a way to reconcile the two. If not with the Jaguar's Children, then somewhere else.

"If you are fearing for Huetzin's safety," he said, evidently misreading her long silence, "do not worry. I have sent him to healers in the south, far beyond the effects of a war between Texcoco and Tenochtitlán."

He sat up, stretching his back and shoulders. "It is late. I have much to do tomorrow."

"Do you wish me to return to the hiding place?"

He shook his head. "No. The priests have made their inspection. They will not return. Take the chamber that you and Nine-Lizard used, or if you fear that the transformation might come upon you again, sleep in the box that I built you. It will block out all scents." He hesitated. "And I will not have the door latched from the outside unless you ask it of me."

With those last words, she realized, he had freed her. Was it that he recognized the futility of keeping her body captive while her will fought against him? Or was it that he did understand and was starting to respect her for her choice.

She asked, "If . . . anyone . . . does come tonight, will you wake me?"

"Yes," Wise Coyote answered and she knew he would keep the promise. Slowly she went out of the room and let the door flap drop behind her.

As she lay on her pallet in the wooden box that night, her thoughts were a tangle. As she thought of Nine-Lizard, she clenched her fists. It was not only anger at Wise Coyote for having let the old man fall into unfriendly hands; it was anger at Nine-Lizard himself for meddling in her life and then disappearing and leaving her a difficult choice. And no one to counsel her in making it.

It was by Nine-Lizard's doing that she had come to Wise Coyote's court. His inability or unwillingness to stand up to Wise Coyote when the king had tried to turn her gifts to his own uses had contributed to her escape and her frenzied attack on Huetzin. Her rage flared, making her wish that she had never seen the old man's wrinkled face or heard his scratchy reproving voice.

If you hadn't, you would probably be dead, a more sensible part of her replied. It was true. Had Nine-Lizard not stopped the enraged young priest who had run at her with his dagger that day in the House of Scribes, she would have been slain. If he hadn't managed to smooth over the incident and then persuade Wise Coyote to give her refuge, she would have been given to the priests of Hummingbird. It was Nine-Lizard who contacted the elusive Jaguar's Children in hopes of finding her a better life among her own kind. Even if they did not come, or they were not what she wished, she owed Nine-Lizard far more than she wished to admit.

With her chin between her hands and her elbows propped up on her knees, she thought hard. She could not turn her back on Nine-Lizard and go off with the Jaguar's Children, even if it was what he wished.

Wise Coyote had said that he would attempt to save Nine-Lizard from the priests of Hummingbird, even if it meant walking into the trap set by Tenochtitlán's ruler. Mixcatl knew that if the king of Texcoco went, it would be to his death. Wise Coyote had already been accused of sorcery and heresy because of her. It would be easy for Ilhuicamina to make the charges official, subject Wise Coyote to a mock court and then have him sacrificed.

The image of Texcoco's king bent back over the stone altar while the priests tore out his heart made Mixcatl freeze even in the warmth of her blankets. She might have locked wills with Wise Coyote, even hated him at times, but she could not condemn him to that fate.

Even if he wishes to die as punishment or an escape from what he has done.

And there was more. As little as she had known the people of Texcoco, she sensed in them a certain liveliness and love of freedom and life that had been stripped from the citizens of the Aztec state. A young man such as Huetzin could not have grown up in Tenochtitlán. Art, literature, poetry, sculpture; all flourished here, nurtured by a leader who would not let fear of the gods extinguish the human spirit.

All that would be threatened in the coming war against the Aztecs. If the last free city-state within the empire lost its ruler, then all certainly would be destroyed.

So then. It was clear. Wise Coyote could not go. She would have to act in his place; otherwise the old scribe who was her friend and mentor would be slain.

Mixcatl wondered how long Ilhuicamina would wait before deciding that the fish was too wary to take the hook. And she—how long did she have before the Jaguar's Children came to fetch her away?

"Well, with Nine-Lizard gone, they may not come at all," she muttered, but the thought gave her little comfort and even less sleep.

Mixcatl saw red through her eyelids and heard the low crackle of a torch. Someone shook her shoulder.

A voice that she knew as Wise Coyote's whispered above her head. "I have done as you asked me. The messenger from the Jaguar's Children has arrived."

She blinked and pushed herself up on her hands, feeling cross and grumpy, for she knew she had not gotten enough sleep. Her irritability made her suspicious.

"How do you know he is really from the Jaguar's Children? It could be a trick, and he could have been sent by those priests who were trying to find me."

"He said that you would know him when you saw him. And, if you were reluctant to come along, he told me to show you this." Wise Coyote opened his palm, revealing a tooth. It was as large as the first joint of his thumb and it had sharp jagged edges for scissoring meat. Mixcatl recognized it at once, for her own back teeth had taken on the same shape even before the rest of her body transformed. She remembered how the reshaped teeth felt as her tongue rasped against them.

Even so, the priests could have sent a man with a jaguar tooth.

"The messenger told me to tell you that he could answer the question of why you would not float in the canal."

Hurriedly she slipped her feet into her sandals and drew a cloak about her shoulders.

Wise Coyote watched her quizzically. "I told him that to me the question was meaningless. He replied that you would certainly understand."

"I do. It means—"

Wise Coyote held up a hand. "Do not explain it to me now. The messenger waits in my chambers."

He held the heavy door of her chamber open for her as she scrambled out of the wooden room. She knew her face was flushed with anticipation as she walked down the torchlit halls of Tezcotzinco. This messenger was no dupe of the priests if he knew that secret about her. There was only one place he could have learned it, only one other person who knew.

She rounded a corner, hurrying to catch up with Wise Coyote's longer stride. And then they were through a door flap and into the chamber where the messenger sat waiting.

Mixcatl knew the messenger even before he shrugged back the hood of his rough cloak. There was no mistaking that spare loose-limbed body, even if it was now that of a man instead of a boy.

The lean brown face was stronger, the eyes deeper, though just as mischievous. But the black patch above the upper lip was still there. She saw Wise Coyote's eyes widen as he also recognized Latosl.

"You see, nobleman," Latosl said to Wise Coyote. "She came, just as I said she would." He turned to Mixcatl. "And you, who have grown from a little stone statue to a great one, do you now know what you are?"

She held up the jaguar's tooth that Wise Coyote had given her. She swallowed hard. How much did Latosl know about what had happened here; her transformation, the attack on Huetzin, the threat from the priests of Hummingbird?

And then a new question formed in her mind, prompted by the flickering of yellow in Latosl's eyes and the easy grace of his movements.

"Are you . . . the same as me?" she asked, wondering if she was at last looking upon a man of her own kind.

"You are you and can be no other. I am the same."

"That's no answer. It can be taken two ways."

"Take either one you wish," he answered lightly and his eyes danced like sunlight on the canal.

She was determined not to let him elude her. "Are you one of the Jaguar's Children? Do you change?"

"I am what you might call a helper. And you will find that all things change."

Mixcatl felt her lack of sleep build her irritability into annoyance. She was about to say something sharp when Wise Coyote gently interposed. "I think she means to ask if you are also a were-jaguar."

Latosl made a face. "Ugh. What an ugly word, even in your sweet-tongued language. It sounds like an imitation of an animal, which I am not, thank goodness."

Mixcatl felt herself glower, while Wise Coyote looked

at her and shrugged his shoulders as if to say "I did try."
"The night passes quickly," he said. "You said that your
boat is moored at the quay below. I will come with you."

"You need not," she said. "I trust this messenger,
even if I cannot get any straight answers from him."

"I will escort you to the quayside," said Wise Coyote
firmly, reminding her that he still was a king.

He took a blanket from among those folded on the
floor and wrapped it about her. Then he shouldered into
a hooded cloak and beckoned both of them out the door.

It was misty outside as she half trotted between her
two companions along the paths that wound through the
gardens to the cliff and the steep stairway down to the
quay. The wind that blew during the day had slackened,
leaving the night heavy and still. Moisture beaded on
late-blooming flowers and fell with a sound like a deer's
footsteps.

Mixcatl found herself testing the air about her, all
senses sharpening for the signs of prey. She caught herself, recognizing the first signs of change. It must not
happen! Not here, not now.

She clamped her hand across her nose, even though
she had not actually caught any prey scent, and hurried
ahead, nearly dragging her two companions with her.

Down the stone stair they went, single file. Mixcatl
found it harder to balance with just one hand, but she
dared not take the other from her face. And then, finally,
they were at the bottom and on the stone quay.

She had half expected to be greeted by the smell and
shape of the old refuse barge, but instead a sleek high-
sided canoe rode at its mooring. Several cloaked and
hooded men sat in it, and as the party approached, she
saw the glint of eyes and the flash of moonlight on wet
paddles. Somehow she had thought Latosl had come
alone. Now she saw that he had not and it made the
thought of the coming journey more real to her. Yes, he

would have to have companions, for one man could not paddle the breadth of Lake Texcoco. Were they from the Jaguar's Children? Perhaps they would answer the questions that Latosl evaded.

Mixcatl wondered if the canoe would go directly to the settlement without making any other stops. She had thought of escaping from the settlement and making her way back to the Aztec capital in order to free Nine-Lizard. If the canoe touched land anywhere else, she could slip away and walk overland to the city. Or, if the landing place was another harbor, she could hide aboard a boat bound for the open market in Tenochtitlán.

She glanced at Latosl, who was talking with Wise Coyote. *If he knew what I intend, he would have me heavily guarded during the journey.* She wondered if Wise Coyote had any suspicions. No, she decided. The king would never guess that she would try to free Nine-Lizard before he made his own attempt. Would he even wait? If so, how long?

If I fail, he may have to intercede for both of us. Or perhaps not—I will probably be dead.

She shivered despite the blanket and the cloak, then yawned. She was not looking forward to the task she had set herself. It would be so much easier just to stay on the canoe and let Latosl take her to the settlement and a new life.

She jumped when Latosl tapped her on the shoulder. "The king wishes a few words with you before you board."

She looked over to the figure of Wise Coyote, outlined by the shimmering surface of the lake. He looked very much alone.

Mixcatl went to him. He seemed distracted, staring out across the lake waters. Then abruptly he jerked his head back to her.

"Men have spoken of my poetic eloquence," he said,

"but tonight, I have none. This is where we part, Mixcatl, with many things still unspoken, and feelings unexpressed." He took her hand, stroked it softly, looked down. The gleaming black of his hair shone beneath the circlet of shadowed turquoise that was his crown. "For any harm I have done you, please forgive me. I thought a wise man would be immune to obsession. I have found that it is not true."

Mixcatl found the corners of her eyes stinging. For an instant she wished she were not leaving him to face what he knew was coming—the war with the Aztecs and the temple that would soon be rising in his city. Many conflicts already pulled at her and this was one more.

"For any harm I have done you, please forgive me," she said, echoing his own words. "I thought once that I loved Huetzin and only resented you. Now things no longer seem so clear. I know you better now and I do not hate you."

"To know that lightens my heart," he said, laying his hands on her shoulders. "For your sake, I will do the best I can for Huetzin and for Nine-Lizard."

"Do not forget yourself," said Mixcatl softly, and found herself raising one hand to touch his face. He drew her to him slowly and placed a light kiss on her brow.

"May you find what you are seeking," he whispered.

"May you find peace," she answered, then turned quickly and strode to Latosl, who was waiting to help her into the canoe.

As she took her place on the thwarts, she felt the craft moving, the thump as the mooring rope was cast aboard and then the rocking as Latosl swung himself aboard.

As the canoe turned, she lifted her head for a last look at Wise Coyote. He was there, not standing and looking out after her as she half feared but striding down the quay. His shadow melted into that cast by the overhang of the cliff and he was gone.

She ducked her head into her hood and pulled her blanket tightly around her against the damp cold rising off the lake.

For a long time, she heard no sound except the rush of water past the canoe and the steady dip of paddles. Then there were footsteps in the bottom of the canoe and a creak as someone came to sit beside her.

Despite the damp chill and the wind of their motion, he put back his hood.

"The king has an elegant palace, doesn't he? I wonder how many slaves died to build it."

Mixcatl glanced sideways at Latosl from the edge of her hood. How Tezcotzinco had been raised was not something she had wondered about. She did not like the thought that Wise Coyote had probably given orders that had resulted in death or injury for workers. Erecting such structures was no easy job. A block or beam could shift and tumble down on the gangs that raised it.

No. He would be careful. He knows how to build. He would take precautions to protect even slaves, for he would know that men are not just beasts to be used . . . Her thought cut off abruptly and bitterly as another took its place. *Not just beasts to be used . . . as he tried to use me.*

"You do not like Wise Coyote." Her voice was sharper than she intended, perhaps because he was somehow echoing the part of her that would not forget what had happened at Tezcotzinco.

"I do not like any of those who call themselves kings. If a real war comes, as rumors say, my hope is that the kings will kill each other off and their hosts of priests as well."

Mixcatl felt a yawn overwhelm her reply and she realized that she was too weary to argue politics. She wondered a bit about Latosl. He was acting for the Jaguar's Children, but he implied that he wasn't one of them. Or had he? His words had been slippery and sleepiness was making them even harder to recall.

She gave up trying to remember and concentrated on her plan to rescue Nine-Lizard. The priests of Hummingbird would probably take him to their own temple complex, near the huge pyramid at the center of the sacred precinct. That part of the city was surrounded by the Snake Wall that barred intruders. However, the House of Scribes lay inside the wall. If she were to go there, perhaps on a pretext of a visit, she could get inside the wall. The next task would be to find Nine-Lizard. It would be difficult, but not impossible. She knew his scent well and her nose would aid her. How she would get him out, she didn't yet know.

First, however, she needed to know if the canoe planned any stops during the trip.

"What route are we taking?" she asked Latosl.

"West, across the lake. We put into Tenochtitlán at dawn for supplies, then turn south to the settlement."

"Tenochtitlán!" Mixcatl blurted.

Evidently mistaking her startled reaction for fear, Latosl added, "You will be in no danger. I will hide you under blankets and baskets. Two men will stay with you. They know what to do should you start to change."

"Why do you need to stop there?"

"We need certain rare medicines and herbs that are only sold in the large market."

Knowing now that Latosl's first destination was the Aztec capital, she quickly changed her plans. Latosl and his companions would be weary after a night's journey across the lake. The two watchers would be guarding their passenger against anyone who might enter the boat and take her. They would not expect an escape attempt, especially after she had appeared anxious about the danger within the city. As soon as the two men relaxed their watch, she would leap out and disappear into the city streets.

She knew she should get what sleep she could. Soon after the craft reached the Aztec capital, she would need all her strength and speed for escape.

But as soon as she tried to rest, Latosl started muttering to himself. She tried to ignore it, but suddenly the voice spoke a name she knew—one that had long been preying on her mind.

She sat up quickly. "What did you say about Nine-Lizard?" she asked, trying to keep the edge from her voice.

"Oh, don't worry about that old renegade?"

"Renegade?" It puzzled Mixcatl to hear Nine-Lizard described in such terms.

Latosl laughed. "I forget. To anyone outside our little circle, he is just an ugly-faced glyph-painter."

She felt her face growing warm. "What do you mean?"

"Oh, Tlaloc's hair! Haven't you figured it out yet, girl, or will the Jaguar's Children have to turn you away for being impossibly slow witted?"

She stared at him, at first angrily and then thoughtfully as her mind began to put all the pieces in place. How else would the old scribe have known what to do for her when she began to change? And some of the things he had said—they had made no sense unless . . .

"Nine-Lizard is one of the Jaguar's Children." She said it aloud.

"If I threw you and him overboard, you would sink like statues." Latosl grinned. "Until you changed. Have you never noticed that you are larger as a cat than you are as a woman? All that extra flesh must go somewhere. When it is squeezed into your human skin, it is denser, so if you fall into water, down you go."

She blinked. "Did you know that when you were teaching me to swim in the canal?"

"No. Otherwise I would have known the uselessness of attempting."

Suddenly another idea rose in her head and quickly turned to a hope. "Latosl, if Nine-Lizard was . . . in trouble . . ."

The youth's sharp features turned toward her. "Is he?"

"Yes. He was taken from Wise Coyote's quay when the party of priests landed. I cannot explain it all to you now, but he is in Tenochtitlán, in the hands of Il-huicamina and the priests of Hummingbird."

"So one king tired of his toy and passed it to another," said Latosl.

She repressed an urge to stamp, knowing she might put her foot right through the bottom of the canoe. "No! Wise Coyote would not do such a thing. He was taken by surprise. He couldn't do anything except let Nine-Lizard go!"

"Well, I did not know that. I will certainly report it when we arrive."

"And then the Jaguar's Children will rescue him?" She tried not to let her eagerness show in her voice.

"No."

"Why not? If he is one of them . . ."

"He was," said Latosl laconically. "When he was a young man, he did a few unwise things and got himself exiled. I do not think that anyone will raise a hand to help him. You were lucky that they were even willing to listen when he told them about you."

Mixcatl was quiet, feeling her hopes sink once again. She realized that she knew very little about Nine-Lizard. There was the irascible old man, the disciplined glyph-painter and the surprisingly gifted artist. But beyond that, she knew nothing. What had he done to make his own kind turn their backs on him?

She was going to ask Latosl, but decided against it. The youth's words had a way of running around in circles and making her dizzy. She wasn't sure she believed everything else he had said either. If Nine-Lizard was also a were-jaguar, why hadn't he said something. Surely he must have been terribly lonely, especially if he had been cut off from his own people since his youth. How could he have stood it, being beside her all the time and keeping his true nature a secret? And why?

Mixcatl gave up. She was accumulating more mysteries than she had answers. Well, she knew at least one thing. When the canoe reached Tenochtitlán, she would do all she could to find the old man and, if possible, gain his freedom.

She glanced at Latosl. Had the things she mentioned made him suspect what she planned?

With a deep sigh, she said, "I wish we could go directly to the settlement."

"Do not worry," Latosl said indulgently. "You will be safe in the canoe."

She hunched up, drawing her cloak and blanket close about her against the predawn cold. Latosl got up and went to the bow. She let her head fall forward and slipped into a doze.

20

THE SCRAPE AND shudder of wood against stone jolted Mixcatl from sleep. She raised the blankets that had been laid over her to conceal her and keep out the lake's chill. The craft rocked as Latosl and the other hooded crewmen went to the stern and prow to toss ropes over stone blocks. She knuckled her eyes, peered into the pink glow and long shadows of dawn, then tensed as she recognized the canals and quays of the market square where she had been sold as a slave.

Tenochtitlán! They were here already and she was still muzzy from slumber. She had assumed that when the craft moved from the lake into a canal, the change in motion might wake her, but she had been too deeply asleep to notice.

She huddled back under the mats and blankets, lifting one corner to glance up at Latosl, who was maneuvering the boat's stern to dock by hauling on the line he had cast. Another man at the bow coiled his rope, tossed, caught and began hauling. The canoe drifted sideways, rocking gently. Mixcatl watched as the span of dark-green canal water between the hull and the dock narrowed.

When the side of the canoe touched the quay, she felt an urge to throw off the coverings, leap out and disappear into the city. She stayed where she was. It would be easier to escape later, when Latosl and his crew were at the market, leaving only two men to watch her.

It seemed to take an agonizingly long time for Latosl to get the canoe secured, choose who was to accompany him and who would stay behind, and finally to depart. When Mixcatl peeked out and saw the market party finally disappearing, she felt relieved. She was anxious and eager to find Nine-Lizard and she had at least part of a plan.

She was wearing the same huipil blouse and skirt that she had worn in the House of Scribes. She had on a short mantle, tied with the knot commonly used by scribes. She also had a bundle containing her paints, brushes and a blank folded book. Even if the guards at the precinct's gate did not recognize her face, her costume and the contents of the bundle should get her inside.

The two men assigned to guard her were at either end of the boat, alert for anyone who might approach. Soon one began to doze, lulled perhaps by the canoe's rocking. The other made some sharp comments to rouse his companion, but when he saw that no one seemed interested in the boat or its passengers, he gave up.

Mixcatl's fingers tightened around her bundle as she pulled the coverings slightly aside to spy on the two. She waited until one man was snoring and the other was looking away. Then, with a scramble and a bound, she was out from under the blankets, on the quay and running.

Ignoring the startled shouts from behind her, she fled down the docks and then into the open-air market, hoping to lose herself among the stalls and vendors who had already set up shop in the predawn hours and who were now crying their wares. Fearing pursuit, she zigzagged up and down the aisles, making her way through the growing crowd of customers who had come out to enjoy the morning's cool air and get the best selection of the goods being offered.

Panting, she crouched behind a pile of sweet potatoes, whose damp skins and streaks of muddy soil indicated they had just been dug. She inhaled the earthy smell, letting it calm her. Then she peered out from behind, looking to see if anyone had followed her. She caught a glimpse of a gangly figure in a hooded cloak and prepared to flee again, but after peering about in several directions, the man lifted his hands helplessly at the confusion of the marketplace.

Mixcatl felt a slight sting of guilt as she watched him disappear toward the quay area. He would be scolded for failing to keep her safe. She wished she could have told him why she had to desert the boat.

She knew that the crestfallen guard would find Latosl and soon the entire party might be searching for her. These men from the Jaguar's Children might be able to detect one of their own, even when hidden in a crowd. If she was any judge of Latosl's tenacity, her interval of freedom would be short.

Keeping an eye out for Latosl or any of the canoe's other crew, she came out from behind the pile of sweet potatoes and walked quickly out of the market toward the center of the city.

Mixcatl soon came to the ceremonial temple district where the House of Scribes stood among other religious and official buildings. As she neared the high crenelated Snake Wall, she felt a mixture of relief and apprehension. She was now on familiar ground; she had walked this way many times on errands while living in the House of Scribes. Once she passed through a gate into the great plaza, Latosl and his companions couldn't reach her. The warrior-guards would turn away anyone not dressed as a noble, priest or scholar. She was unsure, however, if she could indeed get in. Although she still wore the appropriate dress, it had been a long time since the warrior-guards at the entrances had seen her.

She might get in by the smaller opening that was used by occupants from the House of Scribes. It was seldom guarded, but it led directly into the courtyard of the House. She would be in trouble if she were to be seen there, for everyone thought she was in Texcoco. Reluctantly she decided to enter by the main ceremonial entrance and hoped that her clothing and the contents of her bundle would get her through.

Once inside the Snake Wall, she would have to cross the plaza in the shadow of the great stepped temple-pyramid of Hummingbird. Venturing near the pyramid gave Mixcatl cold chills. She would end her life on Hummingbird's altar if she was caught. Remembering the smoke from the burning offerings that had sickened her so, she was grateful that no offerings were being made today.

Thoughts raced around in her mind, and her heart thudded as she hurried along the wide walkway just outside the sacred precinct. To her right stood the Snake Wall, to her left a canal. At the base of the wall stood huge carved serpent heads, spaced evenly five or six paces apart. She passed the last stone serpent face and mounted the wide steps leading up to the brightly painted triple archway that led out onto the sacred plaza.

She wished she could hide amid a throng of people, but on a nonceremonial day such as this, only a thin stream of visitors entered and left through the gate. High-ranking warriors strutted about in their plumed head-dresses and eagle-feather costumes. Nobles' capes were ablaze with fierce orange, black, yellow and green, in spiral designs or intricate interlocking shapes. Sunlight sparkled on jewels set into bronzed faces.

Even though bright sunlight spilled down around her, the first steps felt clammy beneath her bare feet. She stared at the colorful facade of the entryway, not wanting to watch the expressions of the guards. She knew that her plain scribe's dress would set her apart from the richly arrayed visitors. Perhaps if she looked as though she had a perfect right to enter, she could pass through without being questioned.

She was just stepping into the cool shadow of the center tunnel when the challenge came.

"You, slave. What is your business?"

She forced herself not to flinch, freeze or run at the sound of the guard's gruff voice. Instead she turned around slowly. She faced two warrior-guards, who were almost as well garbed as the high-ranking warriors passing in and out of the portal. Even their spears bore tassels and collars of plumes, but the obsidian tips looked sharp.

She glanced at the one who had spoken, then averted her eyes, as was proper for a slave. "I am from the House of Scribes. I have been summoned by the priests of Hummingbird."

"Why?" the warrior asked, scowling. He was a powerfully muscled, big-bellied man. A jagged scar went down the outside of one thigh and his face was hardened by battle. His companion was thinner and his face looked less severe.

"To compose a document," she answered.

"I have never seen the scribes send a young woman. You are just another slave who wishes to gawk at the sights in the plaza."

Mixcatl felt the pavement begin to grow moist beneath her feet. Her mouth went dry and her tongue felt sticky. "I have official business with the temple of Hummingbird." She took her bundle of paints, brushes and the blank folded book from her shoulder and opened it, displaying the contents.

"She is wearing the garb of a glyph-painter as well,"

said the other warrior-guard, but the first one refused to abandon his suspicions.

"What is the content of your document?"

Mixcatl took a deep breath and summoned all her dignity. "I am to prepare an account of the upcoming sacrifice."

"Oh, the animal-witch," said the second warrior-guard. "I have heard gossip about such an offering. This victim must be a powerful sacrifice, since the priests are holding him for an auspicious day."

So Nine-Lizard has not been killed, she thought. But I cannot depend on rumors.

"What is your name?" the first guard asked.

"Seven-Flower," she answered.

"Who is the Master of Scribes?"

Mixcatl gave the name, hoping that nothing had changed in the time that she had been away. She saw by the expression in his face that her answer was correct.

"They have never sent a woman," he growled, still unsatisfied.

"I think I have seen her before, Twelve-Monkey," the second man said to his companion. "I was posted at a smaller gate used by the scribes and I recognize her face."

The first warrior-guard lowered his spear. "Be about your business, glyph-painter. But if I see you loitering and gawking, I will seize you by the hair and throw you into the canal."

Slinging her carry-bundle over her shoulder, Mixcatl walked swiftly through the entryway before the man could change his mind. She felt nervous sweat crawl between her breasts and down her ribs beneath her blouse. Tension made the beast in her start to wake.

No, not now, she thought, trying to calm herself by breathing evenly and concentrating on the beauty of the feathered banners and gaily colored tiling of the plaza. From a distance she caught the white flash of bone against the dark timbers of the rack where the priests displayed the skulls of sacrificial victims. To her left the great pyramid reared up toward the sky, but she dared not turn her head to look at it, fearing she might lose either her nerve or her resistance to transformation. The beast inside had been growing more restive ever since she had left Latosl's canoe.

Going past the skull rack would not be pleasant, but from it she could learn if Nine-Lizard had already been sacrificed. The possibility of his death had haunted her ever since Wise Coyote had told her of the old man's capture. The king of Texcoco believed that Nine-Lizard would not be offered immediately, but Mixcatl wasn't so sure.

She passed a low stone dais with wide steps leading up to a raised platform. Beyond it stood a higher pedestal that supported a horizontal carved disk of stone. Here, she knew, prisoners of war were sacrificed by being tethered to the center of the disk and forced to battle Jaguar and Eagle Knights until wounds or exhaustion ended their lives. Again she gave silent thanks that no captives were fighting today.

Mixcatl chose a path that led her directly to the front of the rack. She might not be able to find Nine-Lizard's head among so many others, but if his scent were among those swirling in the fetid air, she could abandon any useless attempt at rescue. Perhaps she might even be able to return to the dock and reboard Latosl's canoe so that she could continue her journey to the settlement. Only then would she mourn the old man. And she would also send word to Wise Coyote that it was too late for him to come to Tenochtitlán.

Without pausing in her stride, she searched the rows, dreading to find Nine-Lizard's head among them. At the same time, she sought for traces of the old man's scent. It was easier if she allowed the beast in her to come forth a little, for it was not as sickened by carrion as the human part of her. The unnatural odor of burning flesh was what the jaguar could not bear.

She tried to rest her gaze on each only long enough to see that it was not the old man's, but she could not help seeing details.

The heads were impaled through the ear region, strung side by side on a slender pole and placed horizontally on the rack. Some skulls were clean, polished either by scavengers or exposure. Others had shreds hanging from cheekbones or eye sockets. Many had enough dried and shrunken flesh left to see the remains of features. Some were horrifyingly fresh, enough to attract a cloud of flies.

To her profound relief, Mixcatl found no trace of Nine-Lizard anywhere.

"Slave, what are you doing lingering about?" The voice came from so close behind her that she gasped and whirled.

The voice was not that of the entryway guard, as she feared. Instead she stared at a black-smeared figure whose tangled, soot-caked hair proclaimed his membership in the priesthood of Hummingbird. For an instant she was too frightened to speak and the beast threatened to possess her. Then she found her voice.

"I am from the House of Scribes," she said, and repeated the same story she had previously given. She had little hope that he would accept it, for surely all who served Hummingbird would be on the lookout for one who had escaped the altar.

The priest eyed her suspiciously. "If you have been summoned by my superiors, why are you dawdling near the skull rack?"

She felt a start of surprise, having expected the man to seize her and shout loudly that a sought fugitive had been found. Gathering her wits, she stammered, "It is my first

time in the sacred plaza, honored one. I was over-
awed . . .''

"More likely you were indulging frivolous curiosity,"
said the priest severely.

Mixcatl closed her eyes meekly. "Yes, honored one."

"I will escort you, scribe, to see that you do not waste
any more time." He turned on a sandaled heel, demanding that she follow.

Though she hated the priest's harsh manner and the
rancid stink of his hair, she soon realized that his presence kept her from being intercepted by other people.
Beside him, she appeared more legitimate.

"This is where the high officials work," he said, indicating a windowless building ahead. "You must have
been summoned by one of them."

He walked her inside.

Fearing that he would insist on showing her right to
the official whose request she was supposedly answering,
she said, "I have inconvenienced you enough, honored
one. I will find my own way."

"Very well, but if I see you where you are not supposed to be, I will call upon the House of Scribes and
demand that you be punished."

"Yes, honored one." She turned and began to walk
briskly away, not letting the priest have a chance to
change his mind.

She was in a massive pillared hallway, its sandstone
facings lit by torches. A few white-mantled officials and
other priests walked past her in both directions, but none
questioned her.

*Thanks to that priest, I got in; but I am not sure that this
is really the right place.*

When she saw an intersecting hallway ahead, she felt
more uncertain but she dared not slow her pace and thus
reveal her lack of confidence. Just as she was about to
make an arbitrary choice, a man dressed as a temple

servant walked past her and went down the opposite way. In the breeze of his passing, she caught a trace of the scent she had desperately hoped to find, the smell of an old man mixed with the faint yet lingering aroma of brushes and paints. Nine-Lizard!

Quickly she checked to make sure she was not being fooled by the smell of her own paints and brushes. No. She turned around and followed the servant, whose footsteps were fading down the hallway.

She trailed the man through several corridors, always being careful to keep her distance and not arouse suspicion. The servant disappeared through a portal lit not by torchlight but by bright sun. The odor of fresh flowers and leaves told her that he had gone into a garden or courtyard.

Pausing before the threshold, she peered through, not wanting to emerge blindly into the open. The sound of voices ahead made her more cautious, but she did not want to lose track of the servant. She saw him skirt a crowd of priests and officials gathered in the courtyard. To her relief, he paused to speak to someone else. She was about to enter the courtyard when she spotted the priest who had escorted her.

She halted, knowing that if he saw her wandering around, he would probably descend wrathfully on her and she would certainly lose track of the man she was trying to follow. Frantically she searched both sides of the courtyard, hoping to find either a shadowed walkway or a parallel passage she could use without having to cross the open area.

Nothing. The gathering crowd stood as a barrier between her and the man she trailed. Soon he would finish his conversation and leave. She would be stuck here until the crowd broke up and by then the servant would be long gone.

Gnawing her lip, she stood just inside the doorway,

wondering what had drawn all these people into the
courtyard and hoping that they would soon disperse.
Then, as she stared harder, she saw that the focus of
attention was a cloth spread on the ground. Near it sat a
merchant dressed more elegantly than the vendors she
had seen in the open-air market. In between the black-
painted legs of the priests gathered around, she caught a
glimpse of the merchandise.

The goods appeared to be religious or ceremonial
items. Necklaces made of animal claws, feathers and
glazed clay beads strung onto leather things lay beside
carved statuettes and bone flutes. As she watched, she
felt the ghost of a tingle. It reminded her of the sensation
she had felt in the House of Scribes, when she had been
drawn by the presence of a jaguar skin and had stumbled
into its wearer. She closed her eyes, letting the cat within
her search for remnants of its kin, but she found nothing.

She searched the assembled priests and officials who
might be wearing jaguar regalia, but found nothing she
could identify. Again the sensation touched her. Was
someone perhaps wearing a small belt or wristlet? No.
The feeling came from the items in the display.

No one was glancing her way. They were all absorbed
by the merchant's patter. Quickly she slipped from the
doorway into the courtyard and hid behind a large pot
containing an agave plant. Just in time. Two priests were
detaching themselves from the group and walking back
toward the door through which she had come. From the
way one glared and turned his back on the merchant and
his customers, she could see that he resented the use of
the courtyard as a marketplace. He spoke to his companion as the two passed Mixcatl's agave and their voices
drifted back to her.

"I do not care if he brought the items for our convenience," the angered cleric said to his fellow priest.

"Trade belongs in the outdoor market, not the sacred precinct!"

"But our superior gave his approval," said the other.

"That does not make it acceptable in my eyes," retorted the first. "I will buy nothing—things sold in such a sinful way are likely to be cursed."

The voices faded as they moved beyond Mixcatl and disappeared into the shadowed doorway. She used the opportunity to flit to another hiding place behind a bush. The strange tingle was definitely stronger. It must be coming from the items laid out on the cloth.

Mixcatl felt her power stir and cautiously sent it into the claws on the necklace. When she felt them tremble, she knew that they had been stripped from a dead jaguar. At the thought, she felt a sudden surge of anger and outrage that made the claws jerk. What right had the Aztecs to slay the magnificent cats of the jungle so that nobles might adorn themselves with claws, teeth and skins?

The anger strengthened the beast and she felt it struggle to break free. Again transformation threatened, and with it, discovery and capture. She knew that she was losing the struggle to keep the beast contained.

Somehow she had to tap off the wild energy that fed her jaguar spirit. Perhaps she could redirect it into something else. She let more of her power into the claws, firmly holding the rest back, and sidled around the bush so that she could see the effect on the necklace. The rigid material was much harder to manipulate than the softer skin and fur of a pelt. She had to concentrate harder, use her ability more precisely.

So he thinks that the merchandise might be cursed, she thought. *If it was, the courtyard would clear out in a hurry and I could get through.*

She made one claw move forward on its string, then hook into the display cloth, pulling the rest along. The neighboring claw moved past the first, slowly, like the leg of an insect. Soon she was able to control all the claws on the necklace. It began to creep along the table, dragging its thong.

The customers and the vendor were so busy in another transaction that they did not notice. The seated merchant glanced down briefly, saw the necklace was out of place and brusquely swept it back into position before resuming his haggling with the two would-be purchasers.

Carefully Mixcatl made the necklace creep again while she considered what she could do with the other items laid out in the display. Funneling the power of the jaguar into the necklace was helping; she felt less pressure from the threatening change, but she knew she would have to do more. She was close enough to see the flutes and whistles, and sense that they were made of jaguar bone. They felt quite light and she found that she could manipulate them easily.

Continuing to animate the necklace, she began to play with the other items. Moving several objects at once was tricky. At first she could only give them light "taps" that rocked them slightly, then a steady push that made them move.

The merchant did notice when a little carved whistle mysteriously rolled to the end of the table, but he only muttered under his breath and replaced it beside its fellows. When a bone flute gave a sharp jerk and skittered sideways, everyone, startled, stared down at the display.

"The wind," said the vendor impatiently, grabbing at the flute, but he froze and snatched back his hand when he saw the claw necklace moving like a scorpion across the display cloth. With growing glee, Mixcatl made two whistles stand up and twirl on their ends.

Now the merchant and his customers stared in horrified fascination at the sudden and unexpected behavior of the goods. Mixcatl grinned to herself as two more little whistles stood up to join the dance. They fell over as she lost control from trying to handle too many different objects, but she was learning rapidly. The whistles soon obeyed her command. What else could she do?

She spared a glance beyond the table to the temple servant. He was still by the opposite door, so absorbed in his discussion with another man that he had not yet noticed.

Controlling multiple objects was becoming easier. She decided to get creative. Four additional bone instruments hopped up and sprang atop the first ones, forming four bending dancing legs without a body. Once she had them operating, she decided that the lack could easily be remedied and quickly rounded up some bone seal-cylinders, arranging them in a line as a backbone and neck. Bone stickpins formed a lashing tail while a small carved cup formed the head and a U-shaped hairpin fastener formed the lower jaw. It took fierce concentration to keep everything together and moving, but as she gained experience, the task became easier. A stack of bone bracelets did nicely for the ribs and then Mixcatl had the entire skeleton of a miniature jaguar marionette bouncing and jumping around on the display cloth as if it were a tiny stage.

"Witchcraft! Sorcery!" bellowed the vendor, trying to swat down his gleefully rebellious merchandise. The cry was taken up by others and quickly spread. Some people shoved their way out of the crowd to flee, others edged close to peer at the uncanny show. The jaguar skeleton continued its dance, sometimes leaping up to bite the nose of a fascinated official who got too close, or the merchant's finger when he tried to grab the crawling necklace.

Mixcatl concentrated harder. She sent her power into every jaguar-bone item until combs, pins and statuettes were rioting around with the rest.

"Witchcraft!" shrieked the merchant again. "Make it

stop! I refuse to have my goods meddled with. I refuse, do you hear?''

The young priest who had been Mixcatl's escort stepped up and slashed his palm deliberately with an obsidian chip, calling upon Hummingbird to give him power against evil. Blood dripped onto the display cloth, but the objects only increased the frenzy of their dance.

A collective moan broke from the crowd as the merchant fled. A clatter of sandals sounded as other people lost their nerve and ran from the courtyard.

The priest's voice sounded above the crowd. ''It is the doing of the sorcerer imprisoned here! Drag him out and sacrifice him now!''

The temple servant, startled from his conversation, stood and stared, frozen by disbelief as panicked priests and officials poured around him. The young priest, his palm still bleeding, pulled a knife from his loincloth, grabbed the temple servant and said, ''I have seen you carrying food to the prisoner. Lead me to him and I will put an end to this witchery.''

He forced the protesting man through the opposite door as everyone else scattered. The courtyard was empty.

Mixcatl broke from her hiding place, letting all the bone articles fall in a heap. She ran to the door where the priest had gone with the temple servant. Nine-Lizard was here after all, and with luck she would be led right to him. If he wasn't killed first.

She found herself in another sandstone hall. Far ahead, the knife-wielding priest was forcing the temple servant to lead him. Stealthily, Mixcatl followed.

She heard sounds of a scuffle, then a sharp cry as the terrified temple servant broke away from the priest and scurried away down the torchlit corridor. With a curse, the priest went after him. Mixcatl saw her chance. They had been moving toward a door flap that covered a smaller passageway and, she guessed, one that led to Nine-Lizard. She dashed toward it, threw the flap aside and nearly fell down a steep flight of steps that descended abruptly.

A hoarse yell from behind told her that the young priest had spotted her and the drumming of footsteps confirmed the fear. She ran down a dank narrow corridor, fighting off the fear that she might be seized or stabbed from behind. Where was Nine-Lizard? Was he guarded?

Her answer came in the sound of footsteps ahead of her. She halted, listened carefully. One man. Good.

In the clammy wind blowing down the passageway, she caught the scent of the old scribe that she was seeking. It was sharpened and distorted by his fear and pain.

The footsteps grew louder and she could see the figure of an Aztec warrior backlit by distant torchlight.

Shrinking back against the wall, she inched along it, begging silently for some sort of refuge. To her astonishment, she spotted a small niche, where she could crouch just out of the way. There she waited, feeling her heart thud, as the warrior stalked down the hallway, peering suspiciously about him. He stumbled, cursing the poor light and rough floor of the passageway.

Mixcatl was puzzled by the guard's difficulty. There was plenty of light for her. Then she realized that she could see much better than he could. She felt a stab of relief, then alarm. If her vision was starting to shift, the transformation was again creeping up on her. She had relieved its pressure by animating the bone articles, but it was building again. Once her skin began to loosen, the jaguar would be free.

No. She had to reach Nine-Lizard first. She could not retreat either, for she could hear the sound of sandals clattering on the stair. The priest was still chasing her.

The warrior-guard blocked the way.

She felt her body sink into a crouch, ready to attack.

Even as her muscles tensed, she could envision herself leaping, striking, seizing the throat with a sharp twist of her head. She trembled, feeling the skin on both hands loosen and slip off as her fingers shortened and her nails narrowed into claws.

Time seemed to slow as the change accelerated. The footfalls of the priest grew louder, but the interval between them seemed to stretch. She focused on the man ahead. She could smell his weapons, but they did not matter. She would move faster than he could react.

The man would fall before her . . . the way Huetzin had fallen. He would bleed . . . as Huetzin had bled. And he would die . . . the way that Huetzin had not, for there was no one to fend her off.

The jaguar within her knew only the needs of survival, of hunt and defense. The human knew that and more; outrage at the cruelty of those who served Hummingbird, fear for one she loved, revenge for the hurt already done, and hatred for what she felt was evil.

It would be easy for both the human and the jaguar to take the warrior's life.

But the blood that pooled on the passage floor would be the same blood that spilled down from Hummingbird's altar. In her mind she saw again the grim pyramid that overshadowed the plaza and the city, but the figure enthroned at the top was no longer Hummingbird. It was herself.

The guard had become the sacrifice, bent back over the altar to stare helplessly at the sky. No longer was he an impersonal barrier between her and Nine-Lizard. He had become a man who cried out in terror and pain. And he was no longer alone but surrounded by his children, his parents, his wife, his brothers and his friends who all mourned.

As she had wept for a life that she had nearly taken and certainly had destroyed. Huetzin's.

The trembling of the beast eager for the hunt mingled with shivers of revulsion. Even as her teeth sharpened, her face shifted, her legs started to change in proportion, she forced herself back against the wall, back into the niche. Mentally she pulled the jaguar back, putting forth as much effort as if she were actually dragging a struggling animal.

Sweating, trying not to pant, she forced herself into the niche, hoping desperately that the warrior-guard would go by without seeing her. If he found her, she knew that her self-control would not hold. The beast, cornered, would kill.

Then it would turn and rend the priest whose perception-slowed footsteps were slowly getting louder.

Mixcatl made herself wait until the warrior-guard had gone several paces past, then, as quietly as she could, crept from the niche. Fighting hard not to fall on all fours, she stole along the passage. That door flap. It must be the chamber.

Throwing the curtain aside, she dashed through. A single torch mounted low on the wall shone on a bearded figure in a ragged loincloth, his neck yoked and tethered to the wall.

His head jerked up as Mixcatl entered and the torch-light fell on a familiar ugly face. She wanted to fall on his neck and embrace him in a flood of joy and tears, but she had no time. He looked frightened. She knew he could not see her well enough to tell how far she was into the change, or if she recognized him.

Nine-Lizard cried out in alarm as she felt the thong that tethered him. She had no knife; she would have to bite through it. Hampered by the clumsiness of her paw-hands, she used the back of her wrists to lift the tether to her mouth. Taking advantage of her sharpening back teeth, she sheared through the heavy leather and snapped the thong apart.

The thudding of footsteps outside, a crash and two startled yells told her that the priest who pursued her had run into the guard.

"The side gate at the House of Scribes is unguarded. Run!" Mixcatl shouted, her voice growing hoarse. She did not know how much longer she would be able to speak. Nine-Lizard needed no further urging. Though shaking with age and weakness, he lunged for the door flap and ducked through it. She came after him, struggling to keep to a two-legged run.

The clatter of sandals told her that the two men had regained their feet and resumed the pursuit. She had the animal swiftness that could outdistance the men, but Nine-Lizard's weakness and the narrow hall hampered her. She was also still fighting her transformation and the changing proportions of her legs.

As she stumbled around a corner after the old man, she caught a glimpse of a square of light far down the passageway. Her heart leaped. A way of escape.

Just as they seemed only strides from the escape route, her legs betrayed her. She crashed down on the floor, losing her breath. She felt Nine-Lizard's fingers wrap about her wrist, trying to help her to her feet, but she could no longer stand.

Knowing that she could not go on, she tried to shake free of the old man so that he would have a chance. His grip only tightened. With an upsurge of relief and dismay, she realized that he would not abandon her.

"No!" she rasped and pushed him away, but he would not run. Instead, he crouched down, wrapping her in his bony arms.

She struggled to make the now-alien flesh of her face and her lips form words. Her voice wavered, running away into a strange nasal whine and then dropping into a harsh rumble. "The two men . . . if I change, I . . .

will kill them. I . . . do not want to . . . but I will. For you . . . Nine-Lizard, to . . . save you . . .

"No," said the old man softly. He clutched the back of her head, pushing her face against his chest. She knew that he was trying to hide the strange sight of her half-animal face. "I know why you do not want to."

Huddling in Nine-Lizard's arms and seized by the immediacy and intensity of the transformation, she only dimly heard the clatter of sandals slow as the two men reached them.

"Gods! The sorcerer has conjured up a demon to aid him," said the breathless voice of the warrior. Nine-Lizard's grip hardened on her and the emerging beast struggled wildly, expecting the agonizing thrust of the spear.

"Use caution," she heard the priest say. "Take the elder alive, if possible. Hummingbird will be angered if such powerful sacrifices are wasted." In a stronger voice, he said, "Sorcerer, cast that demon back into the foul air it came from. If you give yourself into our hands, you will live until the day of sacrifice."

" 'It' is 'she' and she is one of my own kind, not a demon," Nine-Lizard answered quietly. "I cannot banish her with a wave of my hand."

"You did not conjure her up to free you?" the priest asked.

"I have no such powers, as I have told you before." Nine-Lizard's voice was patient.

"But she has," said the warrior. "Or do you now embrace a beast?"

"I can keep her harmless so that she cannot attack you. But I suggest you both back away."

Both men laughed scornfully and the warrior-guard said, "You must think us fools! You would escape."

"Guard, step past the two and take up a stand between them and the exit," the priest ordered. There was a pause and he added, "Old man, if either you or she makes any move, you are dead."

There was the sound of someone sliding against the wall and a shadow crossed Mixcatl's face as the warrior sidled gingerly past them.

"Both of you, move away from us now," Nine-Lizard said, as anger and dread goaded Mixcatl into another struggle. "Hurry!" His voice sharpened. "I do not know how long I can hold her. And if any others come, hold them away."

Two sets of sandals made several steps down the hallway.

"Mixcatl," Nine-Lizard said, as she writhed against the strength in his wiry arms. "Stop fighting."

Her mouth stretched wide as she tried to speak, but the transformation had gone too far.

"I am grateful for what you tried to do even if it was foolish," Nine-Lizard whispered. His voice started to buzz in her ear and she lost some of the words. "Help me now, in a different way. Stop fighting. Let yourself grow calm."

I should have killed those men. Then you could have escaped, she thought sullenly, but she obeyed, growing limp. An overwhelming weariness lay upon her like a great heavy blanket, pushing her down to the edge of consciousness.

She felt herself twitching something that wasn't her limbs or her body. Had she really grown a complete tail? She wanted to raise her head and look, but she was much too tired. It was a shame. She had almost made the complete change, but she was too terribly sleepy to do much more than wonder if Nine-Lizard was cradling a jungle cat now draped across his lap. Then her thoughts grew fuzzy and faded out completely.

21

To MIXCATL, WAKING was like a long slow dream. She didn't know where she was, or even what she was. At times she thought she still had the body of a jungle cat; at other times she felt as if she were something in between. Toward the end of the dream, she opened and closed her hands and knew that she had fingers again.

The only thing that seemed to stay the same was Nine-Lizard. The old man's scent lingered in the room, touched with the smell of glyph-painter's colors. He would probably keep that odor for the rest of his life, Mixcatl thought as she lay in a half-awake doze on a pile of rough mats, covered by a tattered cloth. He had mixed so much paint that it had worn into his skin.

She felt his touch as he moved about her makeshift pallet. He tended her, soothed her, spoke to her. Often he seemed to be cleaning up hair or bits of skin that came off her. With a cloth dipped in a water bowl, he sponged the raw areas left by skin that had peeled away during the change from woman to beast.

It was the stinging and burning of her skin that finally ended the dreamlike state. She sat up abruptly, crying out and pushing away the old man's hands. Then she stared at her companion and at the room, at last able to see without having a strange film across her vision. Looking down at herself, she realized that she had regained the shape of a woman.

"So you have returned to yourself at last," said Nine-Lizard.

Then the memory flooded back into her mind of her failed attempt at rescue. It had come so close to success. If she had slain the two men who stopped her, Nine-Lizard might be free.

But she had learned something from the attempt. Even in the shock of transformation, she had recognized Nine-Lizard. Perhaps that showed that she did not have the defect that blighted others of the Jaguar's Children.

When she pointed this out, he only smiled sadly. "I do not know how far you were into the change. As for the fact that you recognized and did not harm me; it means little. I am a special case.

"Because I know you so well." Mixcatl felt disappointed.

"Yes, it could be said that way. As well as . . ."

"My attack on Huetzin," Mixcatl said, her voice flat. "Nothing can outweigh that."

Nine-Lizard only sighed. He did not seem inclined to say any more and she didn't want to push him. She should have known better than to hope.

"Here are your clothes," he said, offering a torn and stained bundle.

Mixcatl accepted the skirt, blouse and mantle. Not only were the garments soiled, but several of the hand-sewn seams had parted. She remembered how the transformation enlarged her flesh, causing not only her skin to give way but her garments as well.

"I managed to salvage them, but I could not repair the damage."

She slipped the blouse over her head. There were several gaps, but it would do to preserve modesty. The skirt was a wraparound, but one of the ties had ripped off. She secured it as best she could. The mantle she gave to Nine-Lizard, who had little more than a loincloth.

Then she asked him how much time had passed.

He sat down on the pallet beside her, stroking the yellow-white curls of his beard. "It is hard to tell without seeing the sun. Two days, perhaps. Maybe three."

She looked about the windowless cell. It was larger than the one where she had found Nine-Lizard. Instead of a door flap, it had a barrier made of planked wood lashed to a frame.

"The priests think we, or rather, you, are far too dangerous to rely on guards alone," said Nine-Lizard dryly. "The barrier is a clumsy thing—several men are needed to shove it aside when anyone enters or leaves."

Mixcatl got up. Her legs were a little shaky, but the shaking subsided after a few moments of standing. She crossed to the plank barrier and pushed. She didn't expect to feel anything give and it didn't.

Nine-Lizard said, "It is braced from outside and tied. A suitable cage for a beast."

Sourly she kicked the bottom board with her bare toes. Instantly she regretted it. The toes were as tender as the rest of her new skin and had lost their calluses.

Wincing, she said, "Wise Coyote did a better job. His cage door was not as hard to open." She went back to her pallet and eased down on it.

Nine-Lizard gave a noisy sigh. "Well, I am glad that you are yourself again and that your skin seems to be healing. I only regret that when the priests see that you no longer require me to tend you, they will separate us."

Mixcatl paled. She scolded herself for getting up, then lay back down on the mat, trying to look as sick as she could. She still felt weak, so that playing malingerer was easy.

"I doubt you will fool our captors," Nine-Lizard said. "You are no longer showing any physical changes."

"What happened to . . . my pelt?" Mixcatl looked about the room, thinking that she had shed her jaguar exterior to return to human form in the same manner that she cast off her human skin to become a beast.

"You did not really have a full coat, just scattered patches of fur. Your beast skin shrank back down and became human skin; you did not need to cast it off. You shed your fur, your whiskers and even the dead part of your claws. The live portion became your fingernails. The priests were fascinated," he added. "They kept pushing the barricade aside and peering in until I threatened to make you into a great cat again and tell you to scratch out their eyes."

Mixcatl grimaced. She disliked the idea of anyone observing watching her in the midst of transformation, especially the cruel priests of Hummingbird.

"How soon will they separate us?" she asked.

"I imagine they will give you a little time for full recovery. Other than that, I do not know," Nine-Lizard answered and then fell quiet.

As Nine-Lizard predicted, the priests of Hummingbird gave Mixcatl several additional days before moving her to a separate room down the passageway. The guards made Nine-Lizard escort her to the new quarters. As the old glyph-painter walked beside her, she fought to keep back tears. This was the last time she would see him until the day of the sacrifice. She spoke to him frantically all the way down the passage and flung her arms about him for a final embrace before the guards tore him away and shoved a barrier across the door.

Later she was fed; an earthenware dish with beans and tortillas was slid through the crack when the barrier was pulled slightly aside. They also gave her a jug of water. Despite the despair that choked her throat, she found that she was ravenously hungry from the ordeal of the change. She ate and then, when she placed the bowl back by the door to indicate that she wanted more food, the bowl was refilled. As she finished the second portion, she was relieved that she would not be left to starve. That made sense. Hummingbird would want his victims in good condition.

She found some mats and arranged them into a pallet, then curled up and slept.

The following morning she was roused by the grinding sound of the barricade being pushed back. Four warriors entered the room, one holding a wooden slave yoke and the others some stout leather thongs. They all held spears with points leveled at her as she submitted to having the yoke placed about her neck. Thongs were tied to the yoke and to her wrists as well. She was backed up against the wall and tethered, more tightly than Nine-Lizard had been. The guards left.

She shivered with fear and cold, wondering what they planned for her now and wishing she could be back with Nine-Lizard. They had not stripped off her clothes for beating, torture or other bodily insult. Probably she was to be questioned and then, hopefully, left alone.

The guards returned, escorting a middle-aged man with a solemn but not unkind face. He reminded her of her teacher, Speaking Quail. As soon as she had made the comparison, she regretted noticing the similarity. It was Speaking Quail's way of teaching that had helped her understand the Aztec religion and aided her to accept as much as she could of it. She remembered his voice speaking to her as a child, gentle, yet serious.

Nothing exists, nothing endures, without sacrifice.

She suddenly wished she could hate this priest.

"Have you come to condemn me as a demon?" she asked, making her voice hard.

"I do not see a demon before me today." The priest smiled. "I have come to ask you why you attempted to escape the fate that was decreed for you."

Mixcatl eyed him. "Why bother? You have me. You can just drag me to the altar."

The priest's expression was still pleasant. "Yes, but surely you are aware that gods are better nourished by blood given willingly. You are such a powerful sacrifice that your cooperation does make a large difference." He paused, rubbing his palms together. "Certainly you will," he went on, as if talking to himself. "Resistance is very rare."

Despite her fear and anger, Mixcatl was curious.

"No one else has ever tried?"

"Very few and they were deranged. Most who are chosen welcome an opportunity to feed the sun." The priest paused. "You appear to be quite lucid. In fact you speak more intelligently than I would have thought."

"I am a glyph-painter. I was trained in the House of Scribes," Mixcatl answered.

"And, as I understand it, you received religious instruction from a colleague of mine, Three-House Speaking Quail. Did he fail in his task?"

"He did not fail."

"Then I find it difficult to believe that you deliberately rejected the duty that is the most important of all. Speaking Quail told you that our world only moves from one moment to the next because men give up their lives before the altar."

"He did."

"Yet you do not believe."

"I . . ." Mixcatl faltered. She forced certainty back into her voice. "No. I do not believe that people have to die to keep the sun in the heavens. Your world may be such a fragile thing, priest, but mine is not."

She expected harsh words or even blows for her reply,

but her inquisitor only kept smiling, although a coldness glittered behind his eyes. "Your words are well chosen for defiance, young woman, but your hesitation and your voice cannot hide uncertainty." He stroked his chin reflectively. "Tell me, if you had the power, would you starve the gods and risk the deaths of millions of innocent people for your heresy?"

Mixcatl swallowed. It had been easy enough to cast aside her beliefs while she was in Texcoco or while speaking with Nine-Lizard. Yet here, the religious indoctrination she had undergone in childhood and adolescence was harder to reject. Perhaps the truth was that she had not really examined her beliefs when Wise Coyote and Nine-Lizard challenged them. Instead she had shelved her religion for convenience' sake. Yes, the blood of burning flesh revolted her, but did that mean the entire religious structure was wrong? If so, what could replace it? The world could not be completely empty, without gods or meanings.

Did she really have the conviction or the strength to rebel against the order and way of the world, as it had been taught to her?

Not alone, she thought. Not without Wise Coyote and Nine-Lizard.

"I see that you hesitate," said the priest, his smile widening. "That is an excellent sign. In it lies your salvation. I will leave you now."

As he left, Mixcatl cursed him inwardly. She would rather have been beaten.

When the priest had departed, the guards brought in a bowl of food and loosed her from the wall before backing out and sliding the barricade shut.

The interviews continued over the next few days. Each time the priest came, accompanied by guards, or sometimes by other members of the clergy who asked their own questions. The interrogation was not harsh, but unceasing and relentless. They hammered at the uncertainty that was the weak point in Mixcatl's defense.

She grew weary, her head began to spin and her resistance began to erode. She began to wonder what she did believe. If she rejected Hummingbird on the Left, must Tlaloc go too? And what of Smoking Mirror, the dancing jaguar of her childhood, the image from which she had drawn needed comfort? Both asked for blood, although not in such rivers as Hummingbird demanded.

"You believe," said one voice after another. "You do not wish to, but you believe."

And behind all the voices was the soft but insistent tone of Speaking Quail, telling her again of his experience of the New Fire and his joy that the world had been reborn once again.

Nothing is born, nothing can endure, without sacrifice.

Did she have the right, the arrogance, to throw such wisdom away?

The jaguar, too, must kill to survive.

In the few intervals when the priests let her alone, she curled up on the pallet, trying to find refuge in sleep. More often she found exhaustion that ended in tears.

She was panicked by the knowledge that her denial was falling apart and that her captors could see it crumbling. The guards only tightened her thongs and the priests kept up their quiet but unrelenting pressure.

Then, they began to offer her hope. She would redeem a useless life. The sun was in danger. She could give her heart to avert the terrible doom. She was more powerful than other victims, her willing sacrifice would mean so much more. She was special. Surely she could not deny the god such nutritious sustenance.

And so it went, day after day, until she no longer knew what she believed and felt as lost as a child.

It was an easy path that the priests were laying before

her and she would be a fool not to take it, she often thought to herself. When she had acted on her own, refusing to accept guidance, she had only caused disaster. Perhaps she was too headstrong, too impulsive. Perhaps she needed outside voices to tell her who she was, what she believed and how she must act.

Her attempt to free Nine-Lizard was an example. What she had done was worse than useless. She and Nine-Lizard would both die on Hummingbird's altar. And there was another life at risk. The priests often gossiped among themselves, thinking they were beyond reach of her hearing, but that sense was keener than they assumed. She could hear conversations in the passageway, even through the heavy planks of the barricade. And what she heard cast her deeper into gloom.

Wise Coyote would soon arrive at Ilhuicamina's court, in a vain attempt to trade the freedom of the two imprisoned scribes for more of his service as an architect and builder. He would construct whatever Ilhuicamina wanted; another dike across Lake Texcoco to keep the briny water of the south from mixing with the fresh water of the north, an extension of the aqueduct, more new temples . . .

She was sure that the Aztec would pretend to agree, perhaps even promising to abide by the agreement, before turning on his fellow king and giving him over to the priests. She could only hope that the Chichimec's caution and cunning could keep him from getting too far into the trap before it closed upon him.

Each day the knowledge ground more deeply into her, aiding the priests in their effort to wear her down. It made an aching hollow of remorse. Her jaguar powers were no gift, but instead a curse, blighting or endangering everyone about her.

She had barely been able to restrain herself from slaughtering the two men who had caught her in the passageway, and then only with Nine-Lizard's aid. Those closest to her had paid dearly. Huetzin, Wise Coyote, Nine-Lizard—they had all suffered.

They would be the last, Mixcatl vowed, for she would resist the beast within. Never would she allow it to take over her body and swallow her soul. Even though her captors had forbidden her the paints she used to fend off the transformation, she held the change away. Under the weight of her despair, she buried the jaguar.

Many days later, Mixcatl stood in a chamber near the pyramid of Hummingbird and listened to the boom of the snakeskin drum echoing over the city.

Though at first Mixcatl had defied the priest's doctrines, religion and the need for blood sacrifice was something ingrained more deeply in her than she wanted to admit. As the days of her imprisonment passed and her gloom deepened, she could not help but think that her life might be redeemed after all. Hummingbird might be the sanguine god of war, but he was also the aspect of the sun at its height, when its rays spilled down on the world, giving warmth and life.

If the sun was really in danger and her death would help to save it, perhaps her life would not be as purposeless as it now seemed. The question had gnawed at her, gradually breaking down her resistance, for it offered her one hope, tenuous as it might be. She became resigned to death, hoping the offering of her heart could preserve the sun.

Now she spread her hands on the wooden barrier that had been dragged across the entrance and braced to imprison her. Her gaze lingered on her hands, pressed against the heavy planks. Her hands were wide and powerful, her fingers stumpy almost to the point of deformity. No one, just looking at her hands, could see the skill that had produced many pages of elegant glyphs and had started to explore beyond the bounds of traditional painting.

She laid her forehead against the wood. The sound of the snakeskin drum vibrated the heavy timbers and the bones in her skull. It beat the message of hunger and thirst, of the god's need and the end of her life.

Mixcatl knew that more lives than hers and Nine-Lizard's would end on this day. Though she could not see outside, she imagined the lines of captives who must now be marching steadily to the drumbeat toward the twin stepped pyramids. And from what she had overheard of the priests' conversations, Wise Coyote had already arrived in the city.

Pushing herself away from the door, she paced restlessly in the chamber. Usually the priests of Hummingbird used the windowless stone room for costuming and ceremonial preparation. She had been moved here from her previous prison so that she would be closer to the altar.

She knew her time was growing short. Soon the priests would come to paint her skin white and then cover her with eagle down before clothing her for the sacrifice.

She sat down on a bench carved from scarlet nephrite, formed in the shape of a jaguar whose back was flattened to form the seat. It stood with paws defiantly spread, head lifted and growling, tail lashing along its flank. High priests and kings had taken their place here, to be draped with feathered robes, gold chestpieces, jade, and quetzal feathers.

Mixcatl fingered the spots, inlaid with a green jade in a pattern of rosettes that closely imitated the true markings of a jaguar. She touched the head of the stone cat. There was a certain irony about sitting here. Though the jaguar statue spoke of reverence to the animal's spirit, its creators were preparing to destroy one in whose veins its blood still ran.

A wave of anger and grief swept through her and she buried her face in her hands. Again her acute sense of touch brutally reminded her of her birth-curse and she remembered what she had done to Huetzin. Her finger-tips touched her temples, then slid up into her hair, tracing the shallow cleft that depressed the crown of her skull.

She felt the lengths of her slanted eyes, her narrow ears laid close to the sides of her head. Her palms cupped her cheeks and her deep jaw, felt the bowed recurve of her lips and the flared nostrils of her short flattened nose.

She closed her eyes, remembering a voice that sounded only faintly in her mind. Wise Coyote. She had walked beside the tlatoani in the gardens surrounding his palace and listened to him. Now the words were distant and quavery in her memory, but still there.

The sun is no bloodthirsty god, Mixcatl, he had said. It is something greater and more powerful than any god could be. And the sun does not need to have the heart torn from your body in sacrifice. That demand is made by men.

Did you lie to me? Mixcatl silently asked the memory of Wise Coyote. Perhaps he had only spoken such words to persuade her to join his own revolt against the gods.

There came the clink and grind of stone against stone and then the scraping of stone against timber. A crack appeared as the barrier was pulled aside to admit a weak shaft of light that backlit a figure who stepped into the chamber. Mixcatl's throat caught, then she was able to swallow again when she saw that it was not one of the black-smeared, wild-haired priests of Hummingbird on the Left, but the Aztec warrior Six-Wind, who had been assigned to guard her.

He had replaced one of the original complement of guards on the second day of her captivity in the preparation room. It was a shock to see the young boy she had known in the calmecac now grown to handsome and sturdy manhood. Though she had not been able to speak with him on that day, they did manage to trade glances. His look told Mixcatl that his assignment here was no coincidence; and hints that he dropped later implied that her old teacher, Speaking Quail, had come up in position since his days at the school and had been able to influence the choice of guards.

It was also very possible that Wise Coyote, working through the network of spies he had in Tenochtitlán, had contacted Speaking Quail and notified the ex-tutor that one of his former charges was being held for sacrifice. She doubted that she would know how or why Six-Wind had been maneuvered into this position, but the fact that he was with her offered some comfort, if not hope.

Six-Wind stood aside, letting pale light stream in past the barrier. "They have kept you away from the sun for many days. You may come out now if you wish."

She emerged from the cave of her chamber, squinting against the hazy light and the wind that blew her hair across her face. For a moment she turned, studying Six-Wind as he drew his sword, a wooden shaft set with glass-sharp blades of obsidian. An impulse from the fiercer part of her mind urged her to attack and overwhelm him, but with his sword ready and other warriors nearby to be summoned at his call, she had no chance. Such a death would be a waste.

And it would be a betrayal of her vow never to let the transformation make her kill.

The warrior seemed to measure her, reading that flash of intent that must have shone in her eyes. "Do not betray me, Mixcatl," he said in the tone of a man much older.

She walked along the carved-stone balcony in front of the preparation chamber, grateful that Six-Wind would allow her this interval of freedom at his own risk. If she had turned on him and he were forced to slay her, he would have been judged as having failed in his task of keeping her safe for the sacrifice. He would join the lines of the victims.

As part of the temple complex, the preparation chamber was set atop its own pyramid. From where Mixcatl stood on the balcony, she could look out over the city, seeing the lime-washed walls of palaces and temples that dazzled unshaded eyes, as if to challenge the brilliance of the sun. Between the massive buildings ran canals which carried more traffic than did the narrow streets. Beyond the solemn grandness of the city's heart, she could see the spread of adobe houses that ended at the lake surrounding the island that held Tenochtitlán. In the distance, the five great causeways to the mainland appeared like white threads against the midnight-blue of the lake.

She was grateful that the back side of the temple of Hummingbird on the Left blocked her view of the sacrificial ceremonies and that the snakeskin drum drowned the victim's cries.

"So at last they are coming," she said, with her back to Six-Wind.

"I wish I could kill you myself," he said in a rush of words. "I know the swiftest, most painless ways. Those who wield the altar knife . . ." He could not say more and turned away, his handsome face working. "They should not have chosen me for this, Mixcatl. I have known you too long." Abruptly he straightened. "Do you want octli? I will have it brought and you may drink as much as you need."

Mixcatl thought about taking the draught he offered. Octli, made of the fermented pulp of the agave, was strong enough to dull awareness. But dying with her wits muddled like a common drunkard would not be right.

"No," she said quietly. "I do not want octli."

She had made her choice and she would go with clear eyes and a steady pace. But the priests had not yet come.

"Is there anything else you wish?" Six-Wind asked.

"I wish to see my friend Nine-Lizard. It is my last request before I am taken."

She knew that even the Aztecs would honor requests from those who were facing their last hours of life.

"I will do all that I can to bring him," Six-Wind replied. "You may stay out on the balcony while I am gone."

She leaned on the balcony, felt the wind on her face, saw the distant shimmer of the lake. With his respect, Six-Wind had given her a small but important gift. For a short time she could be alone beneath the sky and taste freedom.

Wise Coyote followed the two warriors as they led the way down a cramped and lightless corridor. In the torch-light he could see moisture seeping through the stone, telling him that the den holding Nine-Lizard had been sunk underground, in the marshy soil about Lake Tex-coco.

The flaming brand lit a doorway that differed from the rest. Instead of a moldering door flap, this one had a rectangular frame of stoutly woven reed and rattan lashed across it. Wise Coyote had never seen such a contrivance used to block a doorway. The thought occurred to him that the chamber was being used as a cage, the same sort of cage as the wooden box that had held Mixcatl.

The guards grumbled as they undid the bindings that fastened the barrier, and slid it aside. Inside the chamber, a stone niche held another torch. Its light fell on the prisoner, an old, balding white-bearded man dressed in a ragged tunic and paint-stained mantle. Nine-Lizard.

He saw the old glyph-painter's eyes widen with sur-prise, joy and then dismay when he lifted his head. But Nine-Lizard's expression quickly changed as he took in the situation. About his neck was a filthy wooden yoke, which was tethered by two ropes to a carved stone ring on the wall.

Wise Coyote thought to himself as he entered that Ilhuicamina must consider Nine-Lizard a dangerous man indeed if he had to be barricaded into his chamber as well as being yoked and tied to the wall.

The guards stood in the doorway, staring at both of them.

"Leave us," Wise Coyote commanded.

They exchanged glances, reluctant to depart.

"Ilhuicamina said I was to have privacy while speaking to this man. Barricade me inside, if you wish, but leave us alone."

The rattan frame was once more bound across the doorway and Wise Coyote heard the guards' footsteps diminish, then fade. He reached at once to the tethers that held Nine-Lizard to the stone wall, thinking to give the old man the comfort of some freedom.

"No, tlatoani," the old scribe said softly, laying his hand on Wise Coyote's. "You do not know how far down the corridor those two have gone. They may still be listening. If I am kept bound against this far wall, it is less likely they will hear."

Wise Coyote nodded, then knelt down beside the prisoner.

"When I saw you at first I feared . . . ," Nine-Lizard began.

"No. I have walked into the trap, but its jaws have not closed about me . . . yet."

"How did you persuade him to let you see me?"

Wise Coyote couldn't help a grimace. "My suddenly discovered enthusiasm for building monuments to Hummingbird has brought me once again into his favor."

"You know that Mixcatl has been taken," said Nine-Lizard. "Foolish girl! She sought my freedom. If the transformation had not come upon her, she might have succeeded."

"Mixcatl is why I came."

"Why did you ask to see me then, instead of her?"

"I need your help."

Nine-Lizard gave a bitter laugh. "It is a little late now, tlatoani. I imagine that you saw the preparations being made for the ceremony. Soon the priests will come for me and Mixcatl as well."

"It is not too late. Listen." Wise Coyote said and put his face close to Nine-Lizard's. "If Mixcatl were to use her abilities, would she be able to escape?"

"Yes. She is the most powerful child I have seen born to the Jaguar's Children. If she were to transform, no bonds would hold her." Nine-Lizard closed his eyes. "But she will not, tlatoani."

"How do you know? Perhaps she has not tried to escape because she fears her power is not great enough."

"She knows all too well how strong her gift is. And how much pain comes from using it. Only her own judgment on herself keeps her in that cell."

Wise Coyote felt his fists clench. "Nine-Lizard, I want you to talk to her. Persuade her to rebel, use her ability to get away."

The old man regarded him steadily, the torchlight touching red sparks from the brown of his eyes. "Why?"

"What do you mean?" Wise Coyote felt taken aback.

"Why? Is it for her own sake that you want her freed, or your own?" Nine-Lizard's stare became hard. "You have never given up your mistaken idea that she is some sort of goddess."

"Is my idea so mistaken? What is a god, or goddess, Nine-Lizard, except an individual who has abilities beyond those of men? How do I know that her gift is not a flickering of true divinity? Even if it is not, it far surpasses any of the poor imitations that have so far been raised."

"Will it always be so, that you men misunderstand and misuse those who differ?" Nine-Lizard hissed. "What do you really want? To raise her up in opposition to Hummingbird on the Left? To use the fear that men will have of her to topple Ilhuicamina from his throne? To breed by her an army of jaguar-blooded sons who can overwhelm the Aztecs?"

"Why does it matter what I want?" Wise Coyote said, trying to keep his voice low. "You said that the Jaguar's Children need her badly. If she dies, they will have lost a queen and a leader. One like her will not be born again for many New Fires."

Again he received the steady gaze, undulled by the weariness that marked the rest of the old man's face. Softly Nine-Lizard said, "Perhaps then it is better that they wait."

Wise Coyote felt his mouth fall open in disbelief. "You struggled to save the girl, to bring her to Texcoco. Why would you now let the chance to save her slip away?"

Nine-Lizard paused. "Do you remember when I spoke to you of the taint that lies within the most powerful of the Jaguar's Children?"

Wise Coyote recalled the old scribe's words; how he had described a flaw in the nature of those who bore the jaguar's blood; a flaw that let the animal nature overwhelm and distort the human when the individual transformed.

"That is the reason?" He swallowed. "You were not certain that she has it. You were willing to send her to that hidden settlement in the south to be trained."

"I told you that the people there could test and evaluate her for the defect," Nine-Lizard said quietly. "I did not tell you that if they found her to be so flawed, they would kill her quickly and painlessly."

Again, Wise Coyote found himself without words to reply. Finally he said, "How do you know that this . . . flaw . . . is so deadly that those who bear it must be killed?"

There was a long silence as Nine-Lizard looked up. "I know because I bear it myself." He gave Wise Coyote a strange grin, half savage, half sad. "I think you have long suspected the truth, tlatoani, but have never been able to accept it."

"You are one of the Jaguar's Children."

"No. I was once, for I have the same heritage as Mixcatl, but I am now outcast. I have never been able to tell anyone my story, tlatoani. Perhaps now that my life is closing, it is time for the truth."

Slowly Wise Coyote let himself sink from his kneeling position in front of Nine-Lizard to sitting cross-legged on the floor, ignoring the clammy cold of the stone. The old man began to speak.

"When I was a youth, I was as powerful as Mixcatl. As I grew, my people rejoiced. I was the leader they had waited for; I would bring them out of the long decline they had been in since the fall of the great eastern cities. Under my guidance, they would rise again and throw off the rule of mere men.

"A glorious life lay ahead of me. My people awaited my maturity and my first full transformation. But as I approached that time, I found that the beast within threatened to overwhelm me each time transformation approached. I should have spoken of this to my teachers. Instead I kept silent.

"There was a young girl in my village. Her name no longer matters, but to me it outshone every other word. I was not alone in seeking her, for I had a rival, another of the Jaguar's Children, but not as powerful as I. He watched me keenly, eager to learn anything he could use to discredit me or make me seem an unfit mate to the one I cared for.

"At last, watching with jealousy-sharpened eyes, he learned the secret, the hidden flaw. He accused me of it and I would not admit his words were true. Had they been, I would have been forbidden ever to transform again and barred from the leadership I desired as much as the woman.

"After that meeting, I found myself consumed by fear and rage. I think I went mad, for how else can I explain my decision to kill my rival and get rid of him before he could speak the truth to my teachers and my people?"

"You killed him," said Wise Coyote.

"When I found him, I was so filled with rage that the transformation threatened. Instead of holding it back, I let it come on with full force. All was blood and rage and confusion." Nine-Lizard faltered, then found his voice again, sadly shaking his head as he said, "I am told that the strongest among my people had to bind me and drug me heavily to drag me from my last victim and restore me to my human form."

"Your last victim? How many did you slay?"

"It does not matter. My rival and my love were among them. The elders of my people decreed death for me, but one spoke up and asked for mercy. I was not responsible for what I had done; it was the flaw in my nature. No, I do not know why I was not killed then. Instead I was exiled. I have sworn never again to allow the change and I devoted myself to ways of fighting it back.

"I had been training in glyph-painting while among my people. I used that skill to find a place in the world. It was easy, for the glyphs the Aztecs use are far less elaborate than the ones we had. I found a position at the court of Tlacopan. The rest you know."

Wise Coyote sat up feeling dazed.

"If Mixcatl is one such as I, it is better that she die on Hummingbird's altar than transform and lose herself in savagery," said Nine-Lizard softly.

"But you do not know that she has the same flaw," Wise Coyote said, feeling panic start to thin his voice.

"I know enough so that I am almost certain. Why else would she have blindly attacked your son Huetzin?"

You have only my testimony to prove that she did, thought Wise Coyote. He closed his eyes. So it had come to this. His lie would condemn the girl, for she had rejected the powers that could save her. And Nine-Lizard would say or do nothing, for he believed that she had the fatal taint.

What if he gave up his lie? What if he told Nine-Lizard that he, not Mixcatl, had gashed Huetzin's cheek and maimed the young man's sculpting hand? Would such a confession turn everything around, or was it too late?

As there had been a price for the lie, so there would be a price for the confession. Once Nine-Lizard—and Mixcatl—knew, they would draw back from him, their faces filled with bewilderment, disgust and, worst of all, pity. His image would be shattered, both to them and to himself. The illusion of a gentle scholarly ruler would crumble and reveal a hardened tyrant, no better than the one who ruled Tenochtitlán.

Perhaps the image should crumble. The thought came to Wise Coyote, but he did not push it away as he had so many others.

I am just as obsessed and driven by fear as Ilhuicamina. As he seeks to raise up his god, so do I seek to raise up mine. Who am I to condemn the cruelty of his methods when mine have caused equal pain?

Wise Coyote shuddered and buried his face in his

hands. *I acted in the name of the ideal of gentleness I believe in. But Ilhuicamina also acts to serve his ideal. Are we two, after all, that far apart? No. If that recognition is a bitter draught for me to swallow, it is a fit punishment.*

He felt a touch on his shoulder just as the sound of footsteps grew louder in the hall outside.

Nine-Lizard's voice came, soft and urgent. "Tlatoani, I do not know whether you ponder or grieve, but there is no time left. Guards are coming."

Wise Coyote stumbled to his feet. The scrape of the barrier as it was drawn aside drowned out his words. The two warriors who brought him to the chamber stood in the doorway, but there was a third, a younger man in noble dress with an open, handsome face and a straight-forward manner. By the richness of the embroidery on his cloak and loincloth, he clearly outranked the two.

Stepping into the chamber, the young officer ordered the others to untether the old man from the wall. Then he turned, regarded Wise Coyote, and his eyes widened.

"I did not know that Nine-Lizard had such honored visitors," he said. "Forgive my intrusion, King of Tex-coco. My name is Six-Wind. I have been ordered to take this man to the chamber of the girl Mixcatl. She has asked to see him and her wish has been granted, as a ritual favor to the condemned."

When Nine-Lizard's tether had been loosened, the young officer Six-Wind turned to the king, indicating the two other warriors. "They will provide your escort back to your quarters, tlatoani."

"It is my wish to accompany Nine-Lizard to Mixcatl's chamber," Wise Coyote said. He saw the scribe start, then catch himself.

Six-Wind hesitated. "My orders were . . ."

"She would ask to see me if she knew I were here. She was a glyph-painter at my court." Wise Coyote used his most reasonable tone. "I am sure that your master will not be displeased when he learns that you have obeyed my request.''

"I see no harm in it," said the young commander, at last. "Very well, then. Come."

22

THE GRINDING SCRAPE of the barrier outside drew Mixcatl from the balcony back inside the preparation chamber. Six-Wind entered, as she expected, and then Nine-Lizard, as she had hoped. She stifled a gasp as a third man appeared and she recognized Wise Coyote.

She turned to both men, trying to damp down the anger that had risen at the sight of Texcoco's ruler. Why was he here, endangering his own life? Hadn't he interfered enough? Yet he was a king—she could not ask him to leave.

She went to Nine-Lizard and took his wrinkled hands between hers. "I do not remember my father or my grandfather, but it does not matter. You have been more than a teacher to me. Perhaps it is right that we go to Hummingbird's altar together."

The grinding sound came again as Six-Wind left the chamber and the guards outside pulled the barrier closed.

"You are not afraid, Mixcatl?" the old man asked.

She paused. "If you would know the truth, Nine-Lizard, I am less afraid of the priest's knife than I am of living. Each time the beast in me slays the painter, the pain is worse. There is no way for me to live with what I am and no way to reconcile the two sides of my nature."

She let Nine-Lizard's hands slip from between her own and tried to say the words gently. "If it is true that Hummingbird needs the strength of my heart, it is best that I give it."

Nine-Lizard started to speak, then shook his head, as if he dared not say what was on his lips.

"Mixcatl." The voice was Wise Coyote's. She turned to face him, narrowing her eyes and folding her arms as he said, "After all we said during your time in Texcoco, do you still believe the Aztecs' religion?"

"Does it matter what I believe?" she retorted. "My life has done little good. If there is even a chance that my death will serve a need, then I welcome it."

"You do not have to die," said Wise Coyote and Mixcatl was startled by the passion in his voice. "You can save yourself if you wish." He alarmed her by grasping the old scribe by the upper arms and crying out, "Speak to her. Persuade her. I beg you!"

"I cannot, tlatoani," Mixcatl heard Nine-Lizard reply in a low voice. "I have told you why."

She stared at both men, bewildered.

Again the king turned to her, something akin to desperation in his deepset eyes. Why was he asking her to release the monster in her that nearly destroyed his son? Before he could speak, she held up her hands, curled her fingers like claws and said softly, "Huctzin."

Wise Coyote shut his eyes tightly. "The time has come for the truth. I have too much blood on my hands. I will not add yours as well."

Mixcatl stared at him dumbly. She heard a sharp intake of breath from Nine-Lizard. She felt the king's hands grasp her wrists, and before she could pull away, he said, "Your hands became claws, but they never touched my son.

"Tlatoani," Nine-Lizard began.

"No, listen to me," Wise Coyote said in a choked

voice. "I lied to you. Mixcatl never attacked Huetzin. I did."

A shock ran through Mixcatl as she stared into the king's tortured face. Could it have been true? Could Wise Coyote have struck down his own flesh and blood out of desperation or jealousy? Yet his words made all the inconsistencies fall into place. She had often wondered why she couldn't recall the attack.

"But I thought that you pulled her off your son," began Nine-Lizard, his brow wrinkling in confusion.

"I did. Not because she was attacking him, but because she was embracing him. Something in me broke. I struck her with a club. I cut his face and hand with a dagger. My son had fainted from fright, so he would not know who maimed him."

Staring at him, Mixcatl remembered. The blurred, wavering images suddenly became clear. Huetzin had fallen, out of shock and fright. And she, despite the pain and wildness of transformation, had known him and put her forelimbs about him. Not to ravage, but to comfort.

"I loved him," she whispered. "I could not believe that I had hurt him."

"My lie made you believe that," said Wise Coyote.

Nine-Lizard cleared his throat, eyeing the king suspiciously. "How can I be certain that your words now are not another untruth? You are twisting and turning to save your life as well as ours."

"If I am not believed now, I will understand," answered Wise Coyote sadly.

Mixcatl felt as if a warm light had been kindled inside her, clearing out all the half-truths, lies and fears. "He is speaking the truth," she said to Nine-Lizard. "I know."

"Then if she recognized the youth, she did not lose herself during the transformation," Nine-Lizard said to the king, his voice rising with excitement. "Which means that she has the power without the taint."

Wise Coyote nodded.

Mixcatl stared at both, utterly bewildered. What were they saying? That she was not the evil creature she imagined herself to be for so long? Could the jaguar blood within bring aid as well as harm? Was it even possible that the artist and the beast might find a common purpose? She felt suddenly dizzy with renewed hope.

"I know now that you of the Jaguar's Children are not the only ones who risk losing themselves to the savagery of your own natures," said the king sorrowfully. "We men have a beast inside far more ruthless and ferocious than the jungle cat." He turned to Mixcatl. "The lie is ended. You do not need to die. Free yourself and live."

Mixcatl felt her heart begin to hammer. Dare she reach down inside herself and bring forth the jaguar? She was still afraid. And she had pushed that side away for so long, she wondered if she could even reach it. All the transformations she had gone through had been incomplete, reversing themselves before the jaguar could emerge.

As she stood at the edge of decision, Wise Coyote undid a sash that bound a flat package to his side beneath his cloak. He brought out a bundle and handed it to her. It was unexpectedly heavy. She had to use two hands.

"I brought these," he said. "I thought you might want to see them again."

He withdrew to one side of the room, taking Nine-Lizard with him so that Mixcatl could have some privacy.

With a puzzled glance at him, she accepted the bundle and undid the wrappings. Nestled together in a bed of soft cloth were the two Olmec statuettes from his library. She knew that they represented different aspects of the Jaguar's Children.

First, she picked up the solemn guardian who held the grimacing jaguar-human infant. She touched the cleft in the baby's head and ran her finger along the side of its face. Was this what she had looked like at birth? Had she been ritually carried in and presented to her people by a grave-faced guardian, such as the man depicted in the statue? She shook her head. She would never know unless she found her grandmother or other surviving relatives still living among the Jaguar's Children.

As she turned the piece over between her hands, she wondered who had shaped it. Though the carving was beautifully done, there was a coldness and a sense of distance to it, as if the artist had looked from afar at something he did not understand and thus feared. The baby had been made demonic in its ugliness while the figure who bore it was stiff and grim, its face empty of any humanity. Was this a true image of the ancients whose descendants were the Jaguar's Children? Something inside Mixcatl said no.

She replaced the guardian-infant statue and picked up the carving of the Olmec shaman shown in the midst of the change. Now she could see that the shaman's head was thrown back in a rapture of mixed joy and terror as the skin peeled away showing the emerging beast. Mixcatl wondered if her face had shown the same expression when she transformed. Whoever had sculpted the little figurine knew intimately what the change was like, had experienced the heights and the depths of the dual existence that she had only begun to understand.

She turned the statuette around in her hands as the realization struck her. The unknown hand that had made the figurine belonged to a gifted artist who was also a shape-changer. Someone else had lived with the same conflict between art and animal nature that she now faced. Had that individual managed to reconcile the two?

For a while she doubted the possibility as she held the statuette. The gap between the opposing sides of her own self appeared far too wide to ever be united. Perhaps the unknown artist's life had been an unending struggle between the two sides and he or she had died early, worn out by the warring within their soul. If so, there was little hope for her.

Yet as she touched the shaman's face, she felt that this answer was not the truth. The carving showed a controlled grace and dignity that spoke of a mature hand, a life that had been long and well lived. It also spoke of a rejoicing in life and form that showed a spirit still child-like and fresh, undulled by bitterness. The longer she gazed at the piece, the more she became convinced that its creator had found a way to blend what was best in the animal and the human without sacrificing either.

With a deep yearning, she wished she could speak to the long-vanished carver and beg them to reveal their secret. Fate had played a cruel trick on her, to let her be born so long after the flower of her people had faded. What she would have given to be the pupil of this artisan, even if the medium was that of stone and not paint.

Yet she understood that the unknown ancient had given her the most necessary knowledge of all; the fact that one gifted with the jaguar heritage and the artist's spirit could not only survive but triumph. Even if the path was not laid out for her, she knew that someone else had found or made their way.

Gently she placed the statues back in their cloth wrappings, giving the shaman one last touch.

"I am grateful, tlatoani," she said softly, returning the bundle to the king. "I did need to see them again."

Instead of binding the package to his side again, he laid it carefully beneath the jaguar-bench. Precious as the statuettes were, he could not risk being encumbered by the extra weight. The bundle would be safe here and he would return for it when and if he could.

Mixcatl felt Nine-Lizard and Wise Coyote watching her, the same question in their eyes. Could she bring the beast forth and use it to free herself and her companions?

She felt herself begin to shake. The barriers had begun to fall, now that she had learned what had really happened to Huetzin. From the statues, she had gained hope that her art and her jaguar gift might be reconciled. But it was too soon for anyone to ask her to transform. "I do not know if I can. I still do not trust my power. It is too unreliable."

She saw Wise Coyote look at Nine-Lizard. "Then it is up to you, after all," the king said.

The old scribe seemed to stand straighter and a fire lit in his eyes. "Once I swore never again to take on the form of the cat, but I will break that oath for Mixcatl's sake. Now that I am old, I do not fear death and I am tainted by my own nature and bloodied with killing."

Mixcatl stared at the old scribe. "You *are* the same as I am."

"Not exactly," Nine-Lizard answered wryly, "for you are the queen our people have been waiting for. Your gift may be erratic now, but it will develop. I am only a failed hope. There is no time to tell the full story," he said, interrupting her next question. "We must plan what to do next. Six-Wind and the priests will soon be arriving."

"We may be able to sway Six-Wind to our side," said Mixcatl. "I knew him at the calmecac, and he is fond of me."

"Perhaps," muttered Nine-Lizard, "but his aid is not something we dare depend upon." He turned to Wise Coyote. "It has been a long time since I took on animal shape, my king. I do not know how fast I can change."

The king touched a sheathed dagger at his side. "Begin as soon as the guards free us from these walls. I have this and I may be able to take a sword from an unwary warrior."

Mixcatl could not help staring at Wise Coyote in open amazement. He had caused her so much pain, yet he was willing to fight for her life.

"You court death, tlatoani," she said.

"Better the clean stroke of a sword than the many pinpricks of betrayal and cowardice," Wise Coyote answered and added, "if you want my help."

"Now that I know the truth, I want my life."

"Then ready yourselves," said Nine-Lizard sharply, as the sound of footsteps outside began and grew louder.

Again the barrier slid aside, letting bright sun spill into the preparation chamber. Mixcatl saw Six-Wind appear, his face solemn, his sword drawn. Behind him stood a semicircle of blackened, wild-haired priests. Their putrid smell, compounded of dried blood and rank hair and skin oils, made her shiver.

Wise Coyote left the chamber first. She heard his voice as he asked Six-Wind to let him accompany the party. The warrior argued, but in the end, he gave in. Nine-Lizard was the next to step out into the sunlight. She saw him tense as he went out and she wondered if he was preparing for transformation. Could he do it and would the distraction he provided be enough to let them escape? She followed Nine-Lizard and stood nervously by him as the priests surrounded the two. Wise Coyote stood outside the escort, near Six-Wind.

The black-smeared figures seemed to caper like monkeys as they danced about in triumph and peered into Mixcatl's face. She shot a quick glance at Nine-Lizard. His eyes were closed, his fists clenched, the veins starting to swell on his neck. She watched in hope and dread, remembering the horror of her own uncompleted transformations, yet knowing that Nine-Lizard would offer her a chance to escape—if he could do it.

She felt a spearpoint in her back and heard the order to move. Nine-Lizard fell into step beside her, his eyes now open, but his gaze turned strangely inward. Wise Coyote had told him to begin the change as soon as they

were free of the chamber, yet he was showing no signs
other than intense concentration. She turned her head
and saw that the king too was sending Nine-Lizard fur-
tive worried glances.

Mixcatl felt her hopes sinking. *He is too old. He has
suppressed the beast for too long.*

The escort marched the sacrificial victims from the
preparation chamber into the huge plaza, full of people.
She saw surprised glances as Wise Coyote was recognized and pointed out. Whispers ran through the crowd,
questions such as why the king of the neighboring state
was in procession with the sacrificial victims. Was he
also to be given to Hummingbird?

*He probably will be the next one dragged up the steps after
Nine-Lizard and I have died,* Mixcatl thought. *Ilhuicamina
will not waste such an opportunity.*

She cast another glance at Nine-Lizard, who was
swallowing so hard and panting so heavily that the wattles on his neck trembled. Six-Wind and the others in the
escort were starting to notice. Several men moved closer
to the old scribe, as if fearing that he might be in the
throes of some strange illness and would collapse. She
watched his struggle with growing alarm.

Nine-Lizard cannot do it.

Mixcatl searched inside herself for the beast that had
once been all too eager to emerge. Perhaps the erratic
nature of her power was the cause, but her jaguar side
seemed distant and lost, as if she had at last managed to
drive it from her. Even the fear coursing through her and
the blood smell coming from the priests failed to wake it.

The crowd's roar swelled as the priests brought their
captives through. Shouting throngs of people crowded
about the base of Hummingbird's temple-pyramid and
overflowed onto the steps. More fingers pointed at Wise
Coyote and more mutters came. She feared that he too
would be seized and offered if he did not escape.

"Go!" she mouthed at the king when she caught a glimpse of him from between the sweating blackened bodies of the priests. Wise Coyote shook his head tightly. No. Even if Nine-Lizard failed, he would not desert them.

The clamor and deathlust of the crowd swirled around Mixcatl, making her dizzy. The smells and the fears touched the beast inside and she felt it stir. Half in hope, half in dread, she silently coaxed the beast, but it was slow to rise . . .

Now the priests and their captives ascended the lower steps of the pyramid. Mixcatl looked down and saw an endless tapestry of faces, all looking to her. Although a long queue of victims stood in line to give their hearts, the Aztecs had begun with their most powerful offering; an old man and a young woman of the Jaguar's blood.

Above her the drums beat, the chanting started, the plumes waved on the fantastic headdresses worn by the priests. High above, haloed by the blazing noon sun, she could see the tiny silhouette of Ilhuicamina. The Aztec was arrayed as a High Priest, holding a dagger. His command came down, thundering over the noise of the crowd.

"Ascend, first of the blessed!"

The priests grabbed Nine-Lizard to send him staggering up the stone steps, but he shoved them away with surprising strength. He flung his head back, the tendons cording in his wattled neck. He inhaled and expelled his breath in sharp coughing grunts. His mouth opened, exposing weathered sharpened teeth. His face writhed and seemed to shift as he shouted, "If the High Priest would feed his god with the Jaguar's Children, then let him see his victims!"

A moan went up from the priests in the escort. They drew away. Others, made brave from frenzy, seized the old man to drag him up to the altar.

Mixcatl lunged to break free of her captors but she fell

against clasped hands that held her back. Again she sought her own jaguar spirit, but it would not come forth, as if it sensed that she could not really trust it. Everything was all happening too fast, she thought in despair. Nine-Lizard would die and she could do nothing.

Her lunge had brought her close enough to see Nine-Lizard's eyes bulge, his cheeks quiver. His skin turned from weathered bronze to white, then went transparent and fell from his limbs as if he were shedding an unwanted garment. His flesh yellowed and black rosettes bloomed all over his body.

Just as she feared that he might burst his heart from the effort, his form expanded, lengthened, his snarling face becoming the jaws of the spotted cat. The increased bulk of his muscled body stretched his garments until they tore and fell off. The yoke about his neck cracked and dropped on the temple steps.

She saw the glint of astonishment and triumph in the rheumy green eyes of the old jaguar as he whirled to fling himself on his enemies. And there was something else in those eyes as well, the fire of madness.

In the sudden panic that sent the priests scrambling back, releasing her, Mixcatl found Wise Coyote by her side, whispering, "Gods, he has damned himself to save us."

In a bound the great cat was halfway up the steps, yet he swayed and seemed to falter. The warriors and priests on the temple steps, who had shrunk back from him, closed in again. The old jaguar made one clumsy lunge and then fell heavily.

Mixcatl knew then that the transformation had taken too much out of Nine-Lizard. Again she called the beast within, trying to put aside the sight of madness in the old jaguar's eyes and forget that she had heard Wise Coyote's whispered words. Nine-Lizard and Wise Coyote had both said she was free from the taint, but did they really know enough to judge? Huetzin's maimed face rose up in her memory and she knew that she was still afraid of what she might become.

She turned sharply at the sound of a scuffle beside her and saw Wise Coyote wrench a glass-edged sword from a startled warrior. Even as he leaped up the stone steps, the fallen jaguar shuddered and then shrank back into the shape of a naked, ugly old man crawling on his hands and knees.

"Demon power cannot prevail before Hummingbird on the Left!" came Ilhuicamina's thundering cry from above.

The boldest priests descended on Nine-Lizard to bear him up to the stone altar. They were met by the gleam and flash of Wise Coyote's sword and the greasy black of bodypaint was stained with flowing crimson.

Mixcatl scrambled up the stone steps and dropped on her knees beside Nine-Lizard. Above her, Wise Coyote stood, guarding the old man. At first she feared that Nine-Lizard was dead, but she gasped when he touched her and made a clutch at her arm.

"It has been . . . too long for me. You must . . . save yourself . . ."

Above her head, the glass edge of Wise Coyote's blade hissed as he swept it in a circle, fending off the priests closing in about him.

In the crowd that pressed about her, she saw a familiar face. Six-Wind!

"Help us!" she cried, hoping that her childhood friendship with the young warrior and the sympathy he had already showed her would sway him. She could see in his face that this sacrifice disgusted and revolted him. He also bore a greater respect for Wise Coyote than he did for the ruler of his own city. He had always been eager to step in on the side of the outnumbered. Would he do so now?

A determined look came across Six-Wind's face and he used his powerful shoulders to push his way through the crowd. Mixcatl could not read his intentions in his face until the last moment, when he broke through the ranks of the priests and leaped to Wise Coyote's side, his own sword ready.

As he passed Mixcatl, he pulled an obsidian dagger from his belt and tossed it to her.

Even with the weapon in her fist and this unexpected ally, Mixcatl knew that her party was hopelessly outnumbered. Daggers and spears were appearing in the enemies' hands. Soon Wise Coyote and Six-Wind would fall. Unless she could call forth the power of the beast that lay inside her.

Her jaguar was rising, but so slowly, as if fighting its way through the heavy jungle. She knew what that barrier was. She was still afraid of losing herself, her soul, her art.

Now two glass-edged blades swept in circles, keeping the crowd at bay. Six-Wind and Wise Coyote stood back to back while Nine-Lizard sprawled at their feet. Mixcatl crouched beside the old man, lashing out with the dagger at anyone trying to grab him or drag him away. When she was not fending off enemies, she tried to rouse Nine-Lizard from his exhausted stupor.

"Priests of Hummingbird, stop!" The same voice that had roared from above was now closer. Mixcatl jerked her head around to see the Aztec ruler, arrayed as High Priest, descending the steps. Ilhuicamina folded his arms and glowered down at Wise Coyote. The spearpoints menacing the king of Texcoco drew back.

"So have you changed your mind once again, my false ally?" Ilhuicamina asked. "Or have you decided to give a greater gift to Hummingbird than your skills at temple-building? Your heart, perhaps?"

Wise Coyote held his sword level. "You speak of gifts

to your god, Ilhuicamina. You have already given him your own heart, soul and mind.''

The Aztec ruler's face twisted and Mixcatl could see that Wise Coyote's words had struck home.

''I am tempted to deny you the honor of being sacrificed,'' Ilhuicamina replied. ''Death by drowning, like a common thief, and no tomb. Who then will remember the king of Texcoco?''

''I would sooner be forgotten than hated the way that you will be.''

The Aztec's face darkened. ''Hummingbird is angered by the delay. Seize the old man and bring the girl to the altar. And bring the heretic so that he may observe closely as she dies.''

Before Mixcatl could scramble to her feet, strong hands wrenched the dagger from her grasp and pinned her arms. Wise Coyote's sword was knocked from his grasp by a spear. Beside him, Six-Wind lowered his weapon, defeat showing in his face. Two warriors hoisted Nine-Lizard between them. Two more took her and began to march her up the stone stairs. Beside her, Wise Coyote climbed, prodded on by spears behind him.

At every step, the jaguar spirit rose inside Mixcatl, but it was still distant. The weight of fear, the unwillingness to give in to that side of her nature enmeshed the jaguar and dragged it down. Huetzin's maimed face still haunted her.

No! She hadn't wounded him. She hadn't lost herself to savagery, even in the pain of partial transformation. But what would happen in the full change? She still remembered the madness she had glimpsed briefly in the old jaguar's eyes.

And then the choice stood forth, as stark as the outline of the altar atop the pyramid. Only her heritage could save her and the men who were her companions. She had to trust in it or dic.

A strange calm settled on her. The barrier inside turned to feathers and the jaguar leaped through. She felt the skin of her arms begin to loosen in the grasp of her captors. Ilhuicamina, resplendent in his feathered cape and headdress, stepped back as she was dragged past. She caught a glimpse of his eyes and knew a moment of pity for him, for she knew that he was caught in the jaws of a beast far more savage than the jungle cat.

The smell of rotted blood drenched the air at the top of the pyramid. Here stood the image of Hummingbird within the stone alcove of his temple. She fixed her eyes on the altar, which was carved with strange forms and marked with ancient stains. It was a block of stone with a rounded top where she would be spread with her back arched, her face up toward the sun. Beside the altar, on a bronze tripod, stood the casket of lava where her heart would be burned.

A mixture of terror and triumph bounded up inside her. She planted her feet firmly on the bloodied top step, resisting the pull of the two men to either side of her. With a shrill cry, she jerked both elbows out of their grasp. The skin came off her arms like a severed sleeve. The change rushed upon her with a fever and intensity that she had never felt before. Eagerly she gave herself to the new strength swelling her limbs, bursting her skin.

She shed both skin and garments as she leaped high, pushing off with hind legs that were already reshaping themselves into powerful hindquarters. A cry of dismay went through the priests surrounding her and they scuttled away. Time seemed to slow for her as the transformation surged through her body, changing, resculpting and shaping her form even as she rose above the heads of her captors, clawing triumphantly at the sky.

When she plunged down again, she landed on all fours, the still-growing tail lashing her flanks. As she turned her head to the awed crowd upon the steps, the rich ceremonial colors of their garments paled in her vision, letting edges and movement dominate. She was almost grateful as the terrible beauty of the temple and the priest's costumes dissolved into meaningless patterns. A high, hollow whispering and keening filled her ears and she realized that she was hearing sounds that were much higher and softer than those her human ears could detect.

Yet even as she felt her senses become those of the cat, the loss of self that she dreaded did not come. Yes, the cat mind was there, guiding and controlling with its powerful instincts, but she, Mixcatl, was there as well. To the cat, there was no individuality in the wall of human faces that surrounded her. For an instant they all seemed enemies and instinct urged her to go wild, slashing and clawing a path through the hateful gibbering things that pressed so closely about her. Yet when her gaze found the features of Wise Coyote, she knew him, as well as Ilhuicamina.

And she could understand words that the Aztec emperor spoke, although they buzzed strangely in her ears and were contradicted by the smell of hate and fear coming from the man.

"The power of evil cannot stand against Hummingbird on the Left!" the Aztec cried, his voice growing shriller. He raised his hands to the heavens. "Hummingbird, strip the animal shape from this woman to show your divinity. Let her fall and grovel like the old man did before her!"

The jaguar felt the sun beating down on her back, watched the crowd and heard many breaths being drawn and held. If Hummingbird had any power, she would feel it. The moment seemed suspended, drawn into the endless "now" of animal awareness that she was beginning to experience. And then, as the crowd breathed out again, she knew that the Aztec god had no sway over her except through her own belief. Only if she saw Hummingbird for what he was, an empty wooden idol animated by myths and hatred, only if she cast aside completely the religion that had been drummed into her for so many years, only if she put her faith completely in her own nature, would she keep the form and power of the cat.

She felt a triumphant joy and knew the crowd would see no god-miracle. She wanted to shout out her victory but it emerged in a roar that shook the air and vibrated the stones beneath her feet.

Slowly she turned to the men who held Wise Coyote. Beneath their bodypaint, the warriors paled and she could smell the growing terror. She knew that every instant that she remained in cat form increased their fear.

With a snarl and lunge she scattered them, placing herself before the tlatoani of Texcoco.

"Seize the she-demon and sacrifice her as she is!" Ilhuicamina commanded. "Hummingbird's warriors have hunted jungle cats. Her pelt shall lay upon his shoulders as the pelts of those animals lie upon ours!"

Wise Coyote interrupted him, shouting, "Your god is worthless! Not only your people but the true powers in the heavens have tired of pouring out blood for him." The jaguar caught the motion of his hand, his finger pointing at her. "She is the sign they have sent."

About him people were starting to kneel on the stone stairs, moaning prayers. The jaguar heard it with mixed relief and despair.

I am not a goddess. Do not try to set me up as one.

She whirled around and faced Wise Coyote, forgetting in her haste that she could not speak. All that came out was a whine and a coughing grunt.

"Cry and whimper before the might of Hummingbird," Ilhuicamina shouted, taking a spear from his escort of warriors. "I will slay you and strip off your pelt.

To me, all those who believe. Death to heretics and their pet demons!"

The Aztec's defiance emboldened the priests. They seized javelins. One advanced on Wise Coyote. The jaguar blocked the attacker, growling.

Baring his teeth, the man flung the spear at her. It struck at the side of her neck and fell aside, doing no real injury. But even as the spear clattered onto the stones, the jaguar felt the blood well and drip from the flesh wound. She knew that it showed brightly against the white fur on the underside of her neck. It was a badge to her enemy, showing that she could be wounded or slain.

Wise Coyote sensed it too, for he stooped beside her long enough to wipe away the thin trickle of crimson, but it was too late. Again there was a circle of spears about her and her companion. She felt Wise Coyote's hand touch her back, as if saying farewell before the final battle.

"Stand aside," came a voice that she now knew well and hated. Above the heads of the priests she saw the plumed headdress and the turquoise band of the Aztec ruler. The jaguar crouched as the spears around her opened. She saw two figures. One was Ilhuicamina, the other a tall, plumed Eagle Knight. His javelin was raised, and his mouth grinned within the open beak of his eagle mask. He wore a jaguar skin draped across his shoulders and tied by the forelegs.

Even as the jaguar sprang at him with flattened ears and open jaws, she felt the animal spirit within her grow in power, seeking another outlet. She felt it expand from her own body into the spotted pelt on the Eagle Knight's shoulders. The skin billowed and lifted, with more than the power of the wind behind it. It expanded to become a live, clawing animal on the man's back. He shrieked, cast his javelin aside and leaped from the tier to land far below among the crowd.

Ilhuicamina, in his High Priest's costume, wheeled, striking at her with the sacrificial blade from the altar. He had forgotten that he also wore the jaguar pelt draped down his chest. The skin writhed. The hanging head snapped up, fire flaring in its empty eye sockets. The Aztec fell to his knees, wrestling for his life with a jungle cat savaging his chest and throat.

She let Ilhuicamina struggle wildly with the jaguar skin before she withdrew her power. Bleeding from deep scratches on chest and throat, the Aztec tore away the skin and called for help. No one answered. Their attention was fixed on her.

Scornfully she turned her back on Ilhuicamina and forced her way down the closely packed stairs, Wise Coyote behind her. Nobles and commoners alike gave way, their features writhing in fear. She made her way to where guards held Six-Wind and Nine-Lizard.

At the sight and sound of the jaguar, the press of people shrank away. She could see Nine-Lizard's head turn and his eye gleam as he caught sight of her. He looked haggard and weak and she wished once again that her throat and jaws could form human speech, for she wanted to tell him that the flaw he feared in her nature was not there, that she could guide and use the instincts of her cat body without being overwhelmed.

Trying to clear a path down the stairs, she made a short charge at the crowd, snarling. Lashing out with a paw made people leap back, but they only fell against and over their neighbors. The mass was so tightly packed that she and her friends were trapped almost as effectively as if they had been caged.

Roaring in frustration, she pivoted and charged in a different direction, widening the clear area on the temple steps, but again, unable to break through. She began to circle, feeling panic, both human and animal, begin to grow. She broke from a fast pace into a trot, trying one side of the human wall, then the other, seeking a weakness. Sweat broke from the bottom of her pads and panic crawled like a parasite beneath her skin. It was becoming difficult to suppress the cat nature that urged her to leap on the nearest person, drag them down and savage their throat.

Both Six-Wind and Wise Coyote were trying frantically to shove a way out through the throng, but neither could do it without abandoning Nine-Lizard. The jaguar bounded up and down the steps, clawing and snapping at bared legs or feet as she went by. The tension built in her until she feared she would go into a frenzy, but just as she found herself charging with intent to leap and kill, the power inside her broke free and scattered, like a handful of flung dust, into the crowd.

As she skidded to a puzzled halt, she felt every piece of jaguar regalia in the entire crowd suddenly come to life, animated by her frustration and rage. Pendants of jaguar claws trembled on their wearers' breasts and then began to hop and pierce the skin like ferocious insects. Necklaces of jaguar teeth twisted and writhed, rattling the fangs together. Some strung teeth jumped off their owners' necks altogether and sought others of their escaping fellows so that the renegade molars and fangs took their places as if in the ghostly jaws of a cat's mouth. Once assembled, the teeth took on a life of their own, bouncing around on the stone steps and biting at exposed heels or calves.

Armbands, wristlets, belts, sashes, headbands; anything made of jaguar skin, fur, teeth or bone came to life with startling ferocity, attacking the privileged wearer. Carved combs buried themselves in scalps and drew blood before they were jerked out and flung down. Belts and sashes were wrenched off and thrown as if they had become rattlesnakes. And even the unlucky noble who had taken a pinch of ground jaguar bone as a preventative to poison experienced a raging commotion in his guts which was relieved only when the man vomited and expelled the rebellious powder.

Panic washed through the crowd like a flood. The sensitive hairs in the jaguar's ears trembled to a strange noise that grew like thunder. It was the sound of thousands of people falling on their knees, moaning in terror before a new and angry god.

The jaguar stood watching as the gesture rippled through the crowd. It began on the pyramid, in the area surrounding her, but quickly spread down the stairs into the plaza until the entire crowd was huddled on its knees.

Someone said a name and it was picked up and spread.

"Tepeyolotli! Heart-of-the-Mountain!"

It grew from a whisper to a mutter and then to a moaned supplication.

"Tepeyolotli!"

Whether or not the jaguar wished it, to these people she was divine.

She had a strong urge to flee, to gallop down the stairs, away from the groveling mass, and free herself from the terrified adulation that now seized them as strongly as had bloodlust. It was a mockery, a charade. She was no goddess. Yet if she abandoned them now, disappearing into the city as her conscience urged her to do, she would abandon her companions and lose a chance that might never come again. If the new deity deserted her worshippers, they would turn, with renewed intensity, back to the old god and the old ways.

The jaguar looked out over the crowd. Thousands of bare or cloak-draped backs formed a huge tapestry of humility that now covered the pyramid. Underfoot she trod all the objects of jaguar bone, hide and teeth that they had cast off in their terrified frenzy.

Wise Coyote still stood upright amid an ocean of crouching, praying people.

"Hummingbird's rule is over!" he shouted. "People of Tenochtitlán, a new power has risen, a true divinity. You have no need for idols of painted wood now that Heart-of-the-Mountain walks among you!"

"Heart-of-the-Mountain," the crowd intoned, dread and hope mixed in their voices.

She felt a flash of anger at Wise Coyote for seizing the situation and pushing her into a role that she did not want. Yet she could see that he had little choice. He had to master the crowd and take control away from Ilhuicamina.

I will play the goddess now, but there will be a reckoning later.

A short distance away, Six-Wind knelt, supporting Nine-Lizard. Their guards had fled.

She saw the old man's limbs move and his chest heave as he drew breath. A part of her sighed in relief that his attempt at transformation had not cost his life.

Tail swinging, she approached Wise Coyote. A wave of tension swept through the crowd. She sensed their fears and their secret hopes. Would Tepeyolotli show herself to be as arbitrary and bloody as Hummingbird by savaging the man who stood up on the temple steps, as if defying her? Even Wise Coyote did not know what she would do, for he had seen her snarling at the people in the crowd. She could smell his uncertainty.

She wished that the jaguar lips and tongue had the ability to form words so that she could sooth the nervousness that danced in his eyes. She heard and saw him whisper her old name and longed to tell him that she still knew it.

She looked up at him, trying to make the cat eyes carry the message and warmth of recognition that her human gaze had been able to do. And, somehow, either she reached him or he took a leap of faith, for he cast aside the dagger hidden in his loincloth and came to her.

The crowd took a long, indrawn breath as the king and the jaguar met on the pyramid steps. He extended the back of his hand. She licked it, raising her tail. She could feel his growing confidence as he caressed her head and the crowd let out their breaths again in a long sigh.

Tepeyolotli had chosen her consort.

She stood beside the king of Texcoco as he spoke to the crowd. He was living his dream of ending Hummingbird's tyranny. The stained altar and tiles would be scrubbed clean, he said, for no more victims would die. The burden of blood demand and endless war would be lifted.

A figure moved against the sun. The only other man still standing. Ilhuicamina.

The jaguar spun around.

The Aztec stood with a spear set into a spearthrower, ready to cast it. He was backlit by the sun, brilliance glowing about his outline, as if he too had revealed divinity. She could not tell if he aimed the spear at her or Wise Coyote. In the white sun glare, she could not see his face or his features, but his scent spoke of the deadly terror that filled him.

Trepidation filled her as well, for she had already been hit once by a spear. A glancing blow, but one that showed she was vulnerable. She reached, almost instinctively, for the jaguar skin he had worn before, but it was gone, thrown aside.

Her ears flattened, her tail began to lash. One swift rush up the steps and she would be on him before the cast spear could reach her. Her nose wrinkled, her lips pulled back, baring her fangs. One swift rush and pounce and she would feed the meat-hunger growing in her belly as well as the revenge-hunger growing in her mind.

Kill him, came the demand, beating in her mind. It

came also from the onlooking crowd, whose smell in her nostrils spoke of anticipation of a new sacrifice, despite the message they had heard. Kill him, came the message in Wise Coyote's scent. End the savagery of the Aztec Empire and the threat to Texcoco.

The jaguar circled her chosen victim, feeling her eyes burn, her muscles grow taut with anticipation. This was what she wanted. It was good. It was right.

The spearpoint followed her as she circled. Now Ilhuicamina was no longer bathed in the sun's halo. She could see his face, gray-white in her cat vision, beads of blood like black jewels on his wounds.

With a roar she lunged. The spear shot overhead, clattered uselessly on the steps. With a shriek, Ilhuicamina turned and fled, scrambling up the pyramid steps with a speed given by mortal fear. Feeling the fever of the chase rise in her, the jaguar bounded after her prey.

23

As the jaguar pursued the Aztec king, she saw that no man among the many huddling on the temple steps moved to aid him. Even the high priests and officials only watched, fearful of the new god and hungry for a new sacrifice.

Ilhuicamina reached the top step and was fleeing into the temple containing the image of Hummingbird when the jaguar brought him down. Her claws caught and tore the feathered cloak on his shoulders, sinking into the flesh beneath. He fell, striking his head on the lava urn where the offered hearts were burned, and rolled limply across the stain-darkened tile.

With a surge of triumph she pounced on him, tongue and jaws aching for the feel of flesh yielding to her teeth.

And then she saw a shadow across the body that made her look up. The image of Hummingbird loomed above. In her jaguar sight, the color was drained from it, leaving only grays, whites and pale blues. The god rose like a pale triumphant ghost over her and Hummingbird's cruel mouth seemed to grin, as if he knew that when she ate, he would be fed.

The shock of that realization seemed to cast the jaguar into another world, one where Ilhuicamina lay as a sacrifice, bent back over the altar. Above her, face twisted and mocking, stood the image of Hummingbird. He was no longer wood and paint but a malevolent, hungering being. Hummingbird had become the real god and she his servant, slaying yet another sacrifice in the endless line of victims . . .

No!

The jaguar staggered back from her prey as if she had been struck. The blood from Ilhuicamina's wounds cast a scent that intoxicated her, but she resisted it, wrenching her head from side to side as if fighting a noose that had been thrown and tightened about her neck.

Sandals slapped on tile, making her start. Her ears twitched back, then she recognized Wise Coyote as he entered Hummingbird's shrine. He looked down at Ilhuicamina with an expression of grim triumph, as if he expected the body to be lifeless.

Then he came closer and with a gasp of surprise dropped down on his knees beside the Aztec. Quickly he rolled the man over, wiped away the blood from many gashes about the face and shoulders. Almost reverently he touched the chest that still rose and fell.

Bewildered, he stared at the jaguar. "I thought you would kill him," he whispered.

I could not, she thought, wishing she could speak. With alarm, she saw Wise Coyote pluck a dagger from the band of Ilhuicamina's loincloth. His face hardened. Holding the haft in his fist, he raised the blade over the Aztec's throat.

As she started to growl, Ilhuicamina's eyelids fluttered. Wise Coyote made an abortive stab downward, then bit his lip and lowered the weapon.

"Help me," the Aztec moaned, his head lolling. Then his eyes opened and he stared up at Wise Coyote. "You were once my friend. Help me, please."

The jaguar came and crouched beside the king of Texcoco. Gently but firmly she fastened her teeth on the dagger and drew it from his grasp.

If you make me a goddess, then this temple is mine. I will not allow any more blood to be spilled within it.

Ilhuicamina had caught sight of her. His eyes went glassy and his lips trembled so that he could barely form words. "That . . . that . . ."

"That is your savior," said Wise Coyote, and she heard a trace of irony in his voice. He made a hand motion at the jaguar, silently asking her to back off. She obeyed, taking the dagger with her.

In a chamber inside Ilhuicamina's palace, the jaguar lay in a corner, looking down at herself. In front of her lay her massive paws, now veleveted. She raised one and licked it, exploring the shape and feel of her pads with her sensitive tongue. Craning her head over her shoulder, she gazed at the sweep of thick gold rosette-dotted fur that swept over her back, down her ribs and over her crouching hindquarters. She brought the tip of her tail around and examined it closely before it twitched out of her paws. Playfully she swatted it, then lay back and yawned.

Laying her head on her paws, she stared at the seat that had been prepared for her in the center of the room. It was a wicker frame heaped with cushions, surrounded by braziers that stood on tripods, fire flickering inside them. All around were spread objects of gold and silver, rich cloaks of quetzal feathers and bowls heaped with precious stones.

It might be a fine seat for a goddess, but the jaguar had found it uncomfortable. She had perched there while priests and officials had brought in the gifts, but once the ceremony was over, she had retreated to the corner. The smoky smell of the braziers bothered her and the glint of flame on polished gold pained her sensitive eyes.

Amid all the fuss and pomp, no one had thought to provide her with what she really needed; a bowl of water, some fresh meat and . . .

The door flap to the chamber was pulled aside and Wise Coyote entered. She saw him stop and shake his head at the sight of the ornate luxury piled up before Tepeyolotli's empty throne.

"Mixcatl," he called softly.

It wasn't until he called a second time that she recognized the name and got up. She felt oddly distanced from the part of herself that had once been called Mixcatl. With a grunt and a disgusted look at the useless finery, she padded to Wise Coyote.

He ran a hand along her back and scratched her behind the ears. She licked his hand, enjoying the salt taste, but it made her thirsty. She grimaced and lolled her tongue out.

Wise Coyote walked to the chamber entrance, summoned a servant and spoke briefly to the man before sending him away. The conversation was a meaningless buzz in the jaguar's ears. She knew that if she really tried, she could understand, but she did not want to make the effort. Restless and resentful at being confined, she paced back and forth. Glancing at Wise Coyote, she gave him a jaguar scowl.

"You are lucky that you did not end up on display in the priests' quarters. They had a special room prepared for you and facilities for your anticipated throngs of worshippers. It was all I could do to persuade them to keep you here in the palace."

She halted in her pacing, feeling a sensation that meant that she needed to relieve herself. Squatting, she raised her tail without even thinking about it. Only when the warm flow of urine trickled to an end did she notice Wise Coyote's grimace and felt a belated embarrassment.

"If I had known you were going to do that, I would have taken you outside," he grumbled.

Ignoring him, she sniffed the puddle. It didn't smell offensive to her, but she remembered that creatures like Wise Coyote did not appreciate such pungent aromas. She grunted and made scraping motions with her paw. The instinct in her made her want to bury the offending evidence, even though she could see clearly that there was a tiled floor and no dirt. She whined and shook her head, perplexed.

Wise Coyote glanced around the room. "Those idiot priests forgot to give you a basket of sand. They are so used to dealing with divine needs that they cannot cope with real ones."

The servant returned to the room, bearing a tray. From it Wise Coyote plucked the dish of water and the platter of raw venison, set them down on the floor and quickly escorted the servant out. Again the jaguar heard the buzz of voices, but the scent of raw venison wafting to her nostrils stole her attention. She lunged, grabbed and swallowed before she really even tasted the food. With her front fangs, she took more, backing away from the platter and holding the meat between her forepaws as she sliced it with her side teeth.

"Easy," said Wise Coyote, putting his hand down on her muzzle. "Nine-Lizard said that if you eat too much of that and then change, you will have a terrible bellyache."

The jaguar's ears flicked in irritation, for the demands of her belly were still strong. The more sensible part of her mind understood that Wise Coyote was probably right. She sighed, exhaling a long breath. There were so many things to learn about a life where one could exist as a human or an animal.

Servants brought in a large shallow basket filled with sandy soil and set it down where Wise Coyote directed. One also used a small wooden trowel to spade sand over the urine puddle, then scooped up the damp sand and dumped it back in the basket.

When they had gone, Wise Coyote said, "Nine-Lizard is relaxing. The palace healers have told me he will be fine—he just needs rest."

Although part of the jaguar's mind was concerned about Nine-Lizard and the other things that Wise Coyote had to say, she found herself growing restless and the words kept turning to meaningless buzzing. Abruptly she got up and walked away.

"Mixcatl?" He frowned. "Are you . . . all right?"

She sat down and scratched herself, feeling grumpy and short-tempered. She was fed up with all this fuss and chatter. She wanted to curl up somewhere and have a long nap.

"You are tired. I think you are probably going to change back again and Nine-Lizard said that it would be best if that happened while you were asleep."

She shook her head. No. It was fun being a jaguar. At least it had been. She yawned, feeling the sides of her mouth stretch. She didn't want to change back. Well, maybe she did. She wanted to talk to Nine-Lizard and make sure that he was all right. And there was someone else that she needed to see. A young man's face came into her mind, followed by a warm feeling of affection. Yes. Someone she loved. Someone she needed to see. Huetzin.

For an instant she felt ashamed that all thoughts of the young sculptor had slipped from her mind. Perhaps she was so convinced that she had wounded him that she could not bear to think of him. And then, after Wise Coyote had confessed and lifted the guilt from her, there had been too many distractions, the least of which was her transformation.

I must see him. I know that Wise Coyote will tell him the truth now, but I must also be there.

* * *

The misty light of early morning leaked through Mix-catl's closed eyelids. She knew, even before she was fully awake, that she had changed shape once again. This time the reverse transformation had been much easier and she had slept through it. As she opened her eyes, the blush-ing colors of sunrise streaming in her window made her blink in wonder. The jaguar had little ability to see colors, especially reds and oranges, but to renewed human vi-sion, those hues were intense.

She yawned and stretched, exploring the other changes in her senses. Her sense of smell was lessened, although still strong. Her stomach felt a little unsettled and she recalled what Wise Coyote had said about eating too much raw meat before returning to human form.

With a start, she realized that she was no longer in the chamber where she had fallen asleep as a jaguar. Some-one had covered her with a mantle and had clean clothes laid nearby.

"Good morning," said a familiar voice. Wise Coyote came through a nearby doorhanging. Mixcatl realized that she was in his quarters.

"I thought it prudent to move you in here. The palace servants have enough amusement without being able to watch Tepeyolotli become an unclothed young woman."

Mixcatl imagined what that might have been like and felt grateful that he had moved her. He left the room, giving her privacy to dress.

As she reached for her huipil blouse and wraparound skirt, her hands and arms felt strange after having been a great cat's forelimbs. She wiggled her fingers, glad to have them back. With a twinge of regret, she saw that all her gold and spotted fur had fallen off, making a nest about her as she slept.

Wrapped in her mantle, she stepped out of the nest of fur. Poor Wise Coyote. He had already coped with the results of jaguar behavior in Tepeyolotli's throne room. Or at least his servants had. Now there was all this shed fur.

I may have to go to the Jaguar's Children just to learn how to clean up after myself. She caught herself, thinking about the events that had happened the previous day. *Considering everything that has happened, I probably will not go, at least for a while.*

She was sweeping up handfuls of the fur when Wise Coyote came in, told her not to worry about the mess and invited her to share his breakfast.

The honeyed amaranth cakes were tasty and helped soothe her uncertain stomach. Her temper felt a bit uncertain too. How many times had she said that she would refuse to play the role of a goddess; and now . . .

"How long was I asleep?" she asked.

"A little more than a day, but worship of the Jaguar is already growing. You already have a number of new shrines in Tenochtitlán and an image of the Jaguar is being carved to stand atop the pyramid."

At his use of the word "your," Mixcatl grimaced. "Those shrines are not mine, tlatoani. Tepeyolotli was worshipped long before I came to Tenochtitlán."

"The divine jaguar underlies much of Aztec religion. By becoming Tepeyolotli, you have tapped that undercurrent and brought it to the surface."

"But is it right to pretend to be something I am really not? It is as if I am misusing my gift."

Wise Coyote stroked his chin. "What you are really saying is that *I* am misusing your ability. Am I right?"

Mixcatl sighed. "I am sorry, tlatoani. I do not wish to seem ungrateful, but I do feel that way. If you had not shouted to the crowd about a new god, I would not have felt compelled to become one."

"I admit that I took some advantage of the situation.

I did not have much choice. We had to destroy Hummingbird or he would have devoured us."

"And Texcoco as well."

His eyes became intense. "I have never disguised my love for my city, Mixcatl. To preserve Texcoco, I have done a great many harmful things in my life. Both you and Huetzin are witness to that." He drew a breath. "I will take responsibility for what has happened, although I must point out that your decision to transform was the event that sparked all the others."

"If I had not, you and Nine-Lizard would have died along with me. All right, I agree that it is useless to argue. We are both responsible. What bothers me is the question of whether what we did outweighs the way we did it."

"It is not only a question of what we have done," said Wise Coyote seriously, "but what we must continue to do in order to keep the gains we have won."

"Is that a way of asking if I will keep becoming Tepeyolotli? For now, yes, as well as I can. Remember that my ability is still unpredictable."

"But you are still not comfortable with the idea."

"To be honest with you, no."

The king got up. "Come with me."

She joined him, letting him lead her out of the room, across the hallway and into another chamber. The room had a large open window that looked out toward the sacred plaza and the stepped pyramid. She leaned beside him on the wide sill.

"Smell the air," he said softly. "There is no taint. No smoke rises from the burning of flesh."

She breathed in the air, still fresh with dew. Across the sacred plaza, the huge pyramid stood without its usual pall of black smoke.

"The priests of Hummingbird have been put to work scouring out the stains of their excesses." Gently he put his hands on her shoulders. "Ilhuicamina sent out orders yesterday that all wars for captives are to be stopped. What we have both longed for is happening. And we are not the only ones. Many people in the city are rejoicing because the burden has been lifted."

"You are trying to seduce me with the good we have done," she said, feeling herself weaken.

"I am not trying to persuade you that the end justifies the means. I am saying that this end is good and worthy. Perhaps a way might be found to make the means less onerous."

He let his hands slide down her shoulders to her arms. They felt warm and kind and she let herself lean against him.

"Ilhuicamina," she said softly, watching the sun cast a brilliant glow on the pyramid.

She turned her head to look Wise Coyote in the face. He bit his lip. "I wanted to kill that man. Badly. You stopped me when you took the blade from my hand."

She chuckled. "King of Texcoco, you are a clumsy liar. And you underestimate the keenness of jaguar sight. You put down the knife when he opened his eyes and stared at you. Not when I took it."

There was a silence. "I plead guilty as charged," he said finally. "I am finding it harder to kill these days. Perhaps it is because my aim is bad. When I wield the knife, I strike myself."

And those wounds still bleed, she thought, knowing he would always have to live with what he had done to Huetzin.

"Do you regret that Ilhuicamina is still alive?" she asked.

"No. We took the wiser course in sparing him. His death would have thrown everything into chaos. This way we can work through him. I have no wish to destroy the Aztec state. I only want to turn it to a new path."

Again she fell into a puzzled silence. When Wise

Coyote asked what was troubling her, she said, "I am just thinking about what a contradiction I am. I turn into a jungle beast, yet when I have been faced with killing, I have drawn back from it."

"Perhaps when you are a beast, you cannot kill the way men do."

"Perhaps," she answered, wondering what would happen if she were in cat form and had to hunt for food. She imagined that was one of the things she could learn from the Jaguar's Children. Somehow she would have to get the training she needed, but how?

She could not leave Wise Coyote. Wise and clever as he was, he could never accomplish the changes he wanted without Tepeyolotli's presence to back him up. Perhaps Latosl or some others of the Jaguar's Children might come here in order to teach her. However, having other shape-changers around might bring its own problems. Tepeyolotli's power at this point depended in part on her uniqueness.

"We cannot stay here long," said Wise Coyote regretfully as he slackened his embrace. "We have much to do. I need to speak to Ilhuicamina this morning."

Mixcatl leaned on the window ledge, feeling the wind stroke her hair. "I find it difficult to believe that he has come completely over to our side."

"I share your skepticism. I am not sure that he really has."

"Then how . . ."

"Remember his fear of gods, Mixcatl. Now that Tepeyolotli has proved more powerful than Hummingbird, Ilhuicamina bows to the Jaguar."

"And my role is to make sure that he keeps doing so." She tried to keep the distaste out of her voice.

"For the present, yes," said Wise Coyote. "I think he actually is relieved that he does not have to provide such huge sacrifices, but he is fearful that lesser offerings will fail to satisfy divine hunger. Until he and those about him become comfortable with the changes, Tepeyolotli's presence will be needed."

Mixcatl frowned, remembering what Speaking Quail had taught her.

Nothing is born, nothing endures, without sacrifice.

Even though the hungry sun god had been thrown down, this truth still stood at the center of belief.

"You do not wish to abolish the giving of 'precious water,' completely, do you?" she asked, feeling uncomfortable.

"No," Wise Coyote answered. "Our people would not accept that. I am not sure that I could accept it either. Although I worship Tloque Nahaque, I believe that giving life to other gods is necessary to maintain our world. Perhaps the world will change, and then there will no longer be a need, but many New Fires will pass before that happens."

Perhaps it will be the nature of the sacrifice that changes, Mixcatl mused. *Maybe it will no longer be the spilling of blood at the altar, but something else.*

A name whispered softly in her mind and the image of a young man's face came into her memory. Huetzin. She closed her eyes, feeling the ache of a familiar pain. She wanted to see Huetzin again, but did not know if she could bear it. Besides, he was far away across Lake Texcoco, being tended by healers.

"Are you thinking of my son, Mixcatl?" Wise Coyote asked softly.

"Yes," she admitted.

"I have sent for Huetzin. I meant to tell you," he added as she stared up at him in astonishment. "The healers who are tending him will bring him to Tenochtitlán in a few days." He paused and said softly, "You are not the only one who needs to speak with him."

"Are you afraid . . . to tell him . . . what really happened?"

"Yes. Very much afraid."

"I am too," Mixcatl said, looking into Wise Coyote's eyes. "Even if he knows I did not attack him, he won't be able to forget the horrible thing that I was that night. And even though the change will not be as terrible, it will still happen. What will he think when I walk before him as an animal?"

"He will know us as the beasts we truly are, both inside and out," said Wise Coyote, his gaze steady. "And if he turns away in fear or distrust, we must bear that pain."

Mixcatl looked at the man with whom she had come to share such a strange kinship. Silently she slipped her hand into his and they walked together from the room.

A few days later, she sat on a finely made mat in the quarters that had been given to her. They were located near the throne room where she, as Tepeyolotli, had received adoration and offerings. Now that the image of the Jaguar was complete and in place within the temple that had housed Hummingbird, she hoped that the faithful would take their gifts there.

Between her hands, she held the statuette of the transforming Olmec shaman. Wise Coyote had rescued both Olmec images from the preparation room and had put them on a low table in her chamber.

She stared at the statue, wishing it had answers for her. Huetzin had arrived earlier that day, but stayed in seclusion, attended only by his healers. Soon Wise Coyote would come by to take her to see him.

She started to replace the statue on the low table, then hesitated. At the sound of the door cloth being drawn aside, she turned her head. Wise Coyote beckoned silently. Huetzin was ready to see them.

Carrying the Olmec carving in her hands, Mixcatl joined him. She glanced at the king as she walked beside him to the chamber where the youth and his healers were staying. He had noticed the statuette, but he did not object or ask why she had taken it.

Nor did he ask if she wanted to go in before or after him. She felt the unspoken but powerful agreement between the two. They would go in together.

"This is the chamber," said Wise Coyote quietly, but she already knew from the scent of unguents and medicinal ointments drifting out from behind the door flap.

As she walked in she saw several white-robed elderly men sitting together to one side, the healers to whom Wise Coyote had entrusted the care of his son.

Huetzin was sitting cross-legged on a mat, his bound right hand lying in his lap. His head was up, but the gaze of his deepset eyes was cast down, as if he refused to pay attention to a world that had turned on him so savagely. He looked thinner than when Mixcatl had last seen him and the rich bronze of his skin had paled. The carefree openness of his face that had drawn her to him was gone, replaced by the shadow of pain and defeat.

At first Mixcatl thought Huetzin would not even look at her, but slowly his head turned, bringing the scars on his right cheek into view. Mixcatl felt a jolt of shame at the sight, even though, she reminded herself fiercely, she was not the one who had made the wounds. She glanced at Wise Coyote for his reaction, but saw only a twitch of bruised skin beneath the king's eyes.

Then Huetzin's blank gaze sharpened. A flicker of fear crept across his face, his body stiffened, his shoulders hunched. Mixcatl felt an upsurge of dismay that nearly sent her running from the chamber. He remembered her . . . and was afraid.

She stood stiffly, not wanting to watch as Wise Coyote

approached his son, knelt before him and took both of Huetzin's hands in his own.

The youth lifted his head slowly, as if he found it difficult to rise from the despair that claimed him.

"Your wounds are healing," the king of Texcoco said, touching Huetzin's cheek and running his fingertips lightly along the youth's jaw. "Have you tried using your right hand?"

Huetzin only answered dully, "It is a useless lump of clay."

"No, it is your hand and it is healing," said Wise Coyote, and Mixcatl could not help hearing the helplessness in his voice. "Here. Perhaps if I unbandage it, you will see."

At this point, an old healer, who had been sitting to one side, shuffled over to the king. "Lord, I would not advise that."

"Why? You told me that the wound was mending well."

"That is true," answered the healer, "but the hand has lost ability that we have not been able to restore. When the young man discovered that his fingers would not close about a stone chisel, he could no longer bear to look upon his hand."

Mixcatl bit her lip hard to keep it from trembling. Huetzin had been so strong, so full of life's joy. To see him broken like this was more than she could stand.

She listened as Wise Coyote tried to use reason to convince Huetzin that he could learn to use his hand again. The king's words grew more desperate in the face of his son's tortured gaze, then his voice grew husky and fell silent.

Again Mixcatl felt the urge to flee from the room, an urge so strong that she had started to move. She forced herself to turn back.

She saw that her motion had caught Huetzin's attention. His gaze fixed on her. Again fright crossed his face, but it warred with a remembered tenderness.

Huetzin swallowed, touching the scars on his cheek. Then, with the fingers of his left hand, he raised the bandaged and useless right one and cried, "Where is my hand?"

"No, Huetzin!" Wise Coyote tried to interrupt, but Mixcatl quickly strode in front of him and knelt down before the youth. In the background she heard Wise Coyote asking the healers to leave the room. Again memory lit Huetzin's face and he reached out for her, then drew back. Love and fear fought in the depths of his eyes.

He murmured, "Looking upon you is like turning my face to the noon sun, with its golden warmth. Yet it can turn so black. You were the flayed thing that ran at me—I know because it had your eyes. Or was it not you at all, but another nightmare?"

"Huetzin," said Mixcatl, trying to keep control of her voice. "What you saw that night is the truth. I was that creature. I could not control the change. When you saw me, my skin had fallen away and I was only half-transformed."

"No wonder your eyes were maddened with pain and you did not know me," Huetzin muttered. "If I touched you now, would my fingers go right through? Are you goddess or demon?"

"I am neither. I am just . . . different. And I swear that I did not attack you. I ran at you and frightened you into a faint, but then I turned away."

Huetzin lifted his bandaged hand. "Then if you did not do this, who did?"

The silence became long and empty. For an instant, Mixcatl feared that Wise Coyote would not speak. Then she heard the king's voice, weighted with sorrow.

"I did, my son."

Huetzin turned his head slowly. Shock and disbelief

filled his eyes. "You . . . no, you are my father, you could not . . ."

Wise Coyote struggled to speak. "Huetzin, listen to me."

"No," Huetzin said, but his protest was growing weaker, as if the unwanted knowledge were forcing itself upon him. He stared at Wise Coyote as if he could not bear to take his eyes from his father's face.

Mixcatl heard the king's voice harden. "When I came upon you lying in her embrace, I could not bear the sight. I slashed your face five times with my knife, as if a jaguar had clawed you. Twice I stabbed down in anger, not looking at which hand I struck. And then, when the knife had gone into flesh, I saw; but then it was too late."

Huetzin's gaze turned to Mixcatl.

"You . . . were not the one who hurt me . . . ," he whispered.

"No," she answered. "I was not."

Huetzin's stare turned to his father and she watched the young man struggle with a truth that seemed more terrible than any punishment decreed by gods. At last he asked, "Why do you tell me . . . now?"

"Because when I look upon you, it seems as if my knife has pierced your heart, not your hand."

Mixcatl knew that Wise Coyote's self-accusation was bitterly true. Crippling the hand of another man—a farmer, a fisherman, even a warrior—would not have caused such a steep decline. They would have raged, wept and then struggled to make do with what they had left. But for Huetzin, life was centered about his ability to draw shape from stone.

I understand the pain, she thought, as if speaking to him. *I know what it feels like to have that part of your soul wrenched from you.*

Huetzin blinked, as if coming out of a daze. "It is so hard to believe that you could . . ." He faltered, then his voice steadied as he stared at Wise Coyote. He seemed to be gathering strength from hearing the truth.

The king tried to reach out to his son, but Huetzin shrank away, putting up a hand to guard his face, as if fearing he would be struck again.

His expression suddenly bleak, Wise Coyote backed away, then turned sharply toward the door. Mixcatl jumped up and hurried after him.

"Wait," she called.

The king halted, his back to her, his hands clenched. "You no longer need me. Now that Huetzin knows the truth . . ."

"He needs you more than ever," she said fiercely. "If you walk out of this room with another lie in your heart, you have learned nothing from all this!"

Wise Coyote swung around, his cloak billowing out behind him, his eyes flashing. For an instant Mixcatl thought she had pushed him too hard and that he was turning on her, but he rushed past and fell on his knees before Huetzin.

He drew his son forward. For an instant Huetzin resisted, then he let Wise Coyote embrace him. The king wept in great hoarse sobs, his shoulders heaving. Huetzin, his emotions numbed by shock, sat stiffly, eyes closed.

Mixcatl approached them and put a hand on each. How different yet how alike the two men were, each striving with intensity to reach for something above themselves; Wise Coyote in his search for true divinity and Huetzin in the working of his art. Because of that, they were both terribly vulnerable. She realized that she had indeed loved them both. Love for Huetzin had been easy and open. What she felt for Wise Coyote was mixed up with many more emotions and clouded with doubt, but she could not deny the love.

When Wise Coyote's storm of grief was over, he drew

away. "Huetzin," he said, his voice husky. "You may never forgive me. I accept that. I ask only that you believe in yourself. You will heal and you will sculpt again."

"Please go now," Huetzin said softly to his father without opening his eyes.

With a last glance at his son, Wise Coyote rose and left the chamber.

Mixcatl wanted to go after him, but she knew Huetzin needed her more. When he reached for her hand, she gave it, and when he pulled her close, she came.

"You are not afraid to be alone with me?" she asked, surprised by his trust.

"No, not any longer," he murmured. "My sweet tile-painter, I have longed for you, but I dared not see you. I feared that you might become the beast again."

"Even when I was, I did not harm you. I will never harm you." She put her arms around Huetzin, cradling his head against her breast. "Does it help to know that?"

"Yes. Even though it was my father who . . ." He choked, unable to finish.

"Do not think about it now," she said gently and held him in silence.

After a while he said, "Mixcatl, I have your tile with me. The one you painted with the dock leaf. It is wrapped up in cloth, over by the healers' bundles." He faltered, then managed a faint smile. "I have kept it with me. Looking at it helped me through the worst days. Do you want to see it again?"

"No, not now, although I am glad that it gave you comfort."

That Huetzin would stay with her alone in this room even after he knew what she was lifted her spirits. She knew that he was far from complete understanding and acceptance; she herself had barely begun to understand what her heritage meant.

She thought of her tile painting. Even though he could

not understand the work, he had recognized its value, even though it was something far outside the limits that either one of them knew.

If he understood and accepted the painting, could he do the same with its maker? Could he overcome the memory of seeing her in the agonizing transition? Even if he did, what would happen if she changed shape in front of him? It was true that now that she had better control, the transition was far shorter than it had been, but even so . . .

Gently she pulled free of his embrace, picked up the jaguar-shaman statuette that she had placed to one side and gave it to him. In answer to his questioning look, she said, "You saw this statue before, in Tezcotzinco. I brought it here to try and explain . . ." She trailed off, finding it difficult to speak. "Even with it, I find I have no words . . . to . . . tell you what I really am."

She saw him swallow and knew that he was remembering the skin-stripped apparition that had run at him out of the night.

"You will not have to endure the sight of me as *that*," she said quickly. "The change comes rapidly enough now so that stage is very brief."

"So you have actually transformed completely into a great cat," Huetzin said.

"Well, I feel as though I have become one and all the people around me react as if I were. If it is a delusion or madness, I do not know the difference."

"I suppose I will soon see for myself," Huetzin answered.

Mixcatl shook her head. "No. It is one thing to hear such a thing described and quite another to face it. I would not want to scare you into another faint, nor have you turn away because you cannot bear it."

"But if you cannot control when you change . . . ," Huetzin started.

"I have better control now, but it is not complete. I need training or someone else might be injured because of me."

"I do not want you to go away, Mixcatl." Huetzin pulled her close into an embrace that was made clumsy by his bandaged right hand. "No one else could have brought me out of the dark I cast myself into. Even if you are this," he tapped the statue, "I will still care for you."

As she felt his hands cradling her against his breast, she felt a great rush of warmth and hope. She wanted to stay with him always and feel like this. But she felt the statue that had become pressed between the two of them and knew that she could not accept any man as a partner until her gift was no longer a danger or temptation to those about her.

"What is it like, being a jaguar?" Huetzin's voice startled her out of her reverie.

"Strange, confusing, funny and sometimes embarrassing," she said thoughtfully, then couldn't help a giggle as she remembered what happened in Tepeyolotli's throne room.

"Tell me," he coaxed. She did and soon both of them were chuckling.

She ended by saying, "That is just a silly example, but it shows that I need to handle myself better. There are people who can teach me."

"Are they all jaguars and do they piss on palace floors when they aren't thinking?" Huetzin asked, sending Mixcatl off into a fit of laughter.

"I do not know. I need to find out more. Perhaps when things here settle down, I can go to them."

Huetzin tried to stifle a yawn. Mixcatl could see that he was growing tired. She told him to lie down and got him a cushion for his head. Soon he grew drowsy.

"There is a rumor that Ilhuicamina has stopped the mass sacrifices," he said sleepily.

"It is true."

"That is what my father wanted. I am glad that he has it." He closed his eyes again. Soon he was breathing regularly in a deep slumber.

I wish I could do more for him, Mixcatl thought. *He is still hurting from two losses—his hand and the knowledge of his father's betrayal. It will take much time for those wounds to heal. At least I am here and I will stay as long as I can.*

She stayed with him until the healers returned, then left him in their care and quietly departed from the room.

On her way back to her quarters, Mixcatl was startled when she was hailed by someone in the dress of a temple servant. She eyed him doubtfully, remembering her experiences with the priests of Hummingbird and their retainers. Even though the priesthood had been given over to the worship of Tepeyolotli, she felt uneasy when any of them approached.

The servant prostrated himself before Mixcatl, which made her feel more uncomfortable than ever.

"Seven-Flower Mixcatl, honored lady and vessel of the divine Tepeyolotli, a message has come for you."

"A message? Who sent it?"

"This humble piece of earth does not know, sacred one. It was given to the king of Texcoco and he awaits you in his chambers."

Without waiting for the servant to rise, she hurried down the hallway to Wise Coyote's quarters. There she found him gazing with undisguised curiosity at a bound document that lay on a low table. She noticed that he had also restrained himself from opening it until she arrived.

Carefully she picked up the document. It was much less bulky than anything she had seen before, though it retained the general shape and the fan-fold design. It was about half the size of Wise Coyote's books, with only three thin, fine pages. On the outside her calendar name was written in standard Aztec glyphs—seven round dots and an iconographic flower.

She undid the cord and unfolded the document, then stared at the first page, puzzled. The pictographic script inside was one entirely unfamiliar to her.

"What is wrong?" Wise Coyote asked.

"Can you read this?" She showed him the page, watched him study it, frowning.

"This is more complex than anything I have seen before. I can decipher a few simple glyphs, but the rest, no."

"Who would send me a message I cannot read?" Mixcatl asked, baffled.

Wise Coyote looked up from the elaborate curls and forms of the strange glyphs. "I think Nine-Lizard may be able to decipher this," he said, giving it back to her.

Mixcatl shook her head doubtfully, but the king was already striding toward the door. Holding the odd document, she followed him to Nine-Lizard's quarters.

She began to feel guilty. Various duties and distractions had kept her from seeing very much of the old scribe. He had also spent much time asleep, recovering from his failed transformation. Wise Coyote had also said that Nine-Lizard had helped to tend her during her reverse change. All that had probably taken much out of him and she had not said or done anything in return.

When she slipped through a doorhanging that Wise Coyote held aside, she saw a raised pallet, and on it, the old slave-scribe. She was relieved to see that he was sitting up and eating beans rolled in a tortilla, although there was a certain fragility and paleness about him that she had not seen before.

When he saw her, he put aside the remains of his meal and held out his arms. Mixcatl came into his bony embrace. "Child, I feared that my failure had destroyed everything, but you did what I could not."

"You did all you could," Mixcatl answered softly. "I would not call that a failure."

Over her shoulder, she heard Wise Coyote say, "Nine-Lizard, in that moment on the temple steps, you gave more than any man could expect. I know that you risked losing much more than just your life when you attempted the change. Perhaps it is better that you could not sustain it, otherwise you would have been lost to us." He paused and added, "It is not a choice most men could have made. Honor yourself for it."

The lines in Nine-Lizard's face seemed to relax as he looked up at the king of Texcoco. "Thank you, tlatoani. My attempt may have been worthwhile if it aided you in bringing down Hummingbird. Also if Mixcatl can get the training she needs from the Jaguar's Children."

"That is what we have come to see you about. We have received a message that might be from them. Do you recognize the script?" Wise Coyote asked as Mixcatl unbound the document and put it into Nine-Lizard's veined hands.

"Yes. It is the writing I learned in my youth. Be patient, for it will take me a little time to recall how to interpret it."

Mixcatl leaned forward in anticipation as Nine-Lizard peered at the document and muttered to himself.

"Here, I will summarize it for you," said Nine-Lizard when he had completed his reading. "It is from the Jaguar's Children. With all the flowery language deleted, it says:

"To Seven-Flower Mixcatl: We rejoice at the changes now taking place in Tenochtitlán and wish to honor your part in them. Although the events occurred in a manner we did not expect and cannot entirely condone, we acknowledge the good that has been done by ending the religious excesses of the Aztec state.

"We understand why you had to abandon the escort

taking you to our settlement. However, your youth and the strength of your power makes it important that your instruction not be delayed any more than necessary. We can either send someone to instruct you or have you come to us. The latter would be a better alternative, but we recognize that your situation may not allow you to do so.

"To this end, we invite you to meet again with our emissary on the auspicious day of One-Jaguar of the next month in the city of Texcoco. Nine-Lizard Iguana Tongue and Wise Coyote of Texcoco are the only others to be included. We await your response."

The old man slowly lowered the document, a stunned look on his face. "They are inviting me to come with you? I cannot believe it."

Mixcatl found her voice. "Of course you are coming. We will all go together. Nine-Lizard, can you write in this script?"

When the old man said that he would try, Wise Coyote requisitioned paints, brushes and several small pages suitable for a reply. They sat together on Nine-Lizard's pallet while she dictated and Nine-Lizard alternately scratched his head, bit the end of his brush and carefully made the very difficult glyphs that he had known in his youth.

"There," he said at last, when the message was complete and the document left to dry. "I will take care of sending it. Now, with due respect, Wise Coyote, I am still very tired, so if you both would not mind . . ."

Mixcatl gave him one last hug and then left with the king.

Later that day, she went with Wise Coyote on a palace balcony that overlooked the city. All about them Tenochtitlán spread out, gleaming in the strong afternoon sunlight. In the distance, Lake Texcoco glimmered.

Wise Coyote rested his elbows on the carved parapet

edge. The afternoon wind off the lake blew strands of hair from his face and made his cloak billow.

"I never wanted to admit that this city can be beautiful," he said, "but today it is."

Mixcatl shook back her own hair. "Sometimes this all feels like a dream."

"Or a nightmare, when I look at Huetzin." Wise Coyote sighed deeply.

Struck by the pain in his face, Mixcatl tried to offer comfort. "Tlatoani, I know that it hurt when he asked you to leave, but do not take it as rejection. He needs time to come to terms with what has happened."

"Do you think he will ever sculpt again?" Wise Coyote's anxious gaze turned to her.

"I think his spirit has been wounded more badly than his hand. If he can be encouraged to try, he will regain the skill."

"Then you can do more for him than the healers. You can use the gift of art you share with him. Creating beauty can be healing in itself, I have found."

"That is so," answered Mixcatl, "but the road back for him will be long and slow." She hesitated. "Tlatoani, I may not be able to remain here. When we meet with the Jaguar's Children, they will offer me training. I know that you need me as Tepeyolotli and I want to stay by Huetzin, but I must learn to control my gift. Otherwise I could harm someone else."

Wise Coyote stroked his chin thoughtfully. "We have some time before we meet with their emissary."

"I do not know how long I would be gone. How could you manage?"

"Without Tepeyolotli? Well, considering that most gods never do show themselves to their worshippers and yet attract a devoted following, I believe it can be done. I am starting to assemble a group of men who wish to see their state take a different path than that of blood and fire.'' The king paused. ''I might need to recall you if Ilhuicamina becomes balky, but that is the only difficulty I can foresee.''

''I would agree to that, although I do not know about the Jaguar's Children.''

''I imagine that we will have to do some negotiation, which is a skill at which I have some ability. It will be . . . interesting to finally meet these people.'' He paused, eyed Mixcatl and asked, ''How do you feel about returning to your own tribe?''

She felt a shiver of excitement mixed with anxiety. What would the People of the Jaguar be like? How did they live? How would they think of her? How would they judge her? The message had said they had mixed feelings about what she had done, although they approved of the result.

''I do not know,'' she said at last. ''It would be easier if I were not faced with leaving you and Huetzin in order to be trained.''

''You were taken from your family. You never knew any parents. I would find it astonishing if you were not excited by the prospect. You may even have surviving relatives among them.''

''I might. I never thought about that. Or, perhaps I never wanted to think about that because there was little chance that I would see them.'' She felt the shiver up her back again and then a surge of impatience. How could she bear to wait for the meeting? ''So many changes, tlatoani!'' she said aloud, gazing at the smokeless blue sky over the city. ''How will we survive them all?''

''By using what we have. Foresight, perseverance, a sense of what is right. And hope.''

''Bravery as well, tlatoani,'' Mixcatl said, wondering why he had forgotten it.

Though he smiled, an old sadness crept into his eyes. ''No. That is a quality I may not lay claim to. One-Deer, the day of my birth, has always shadowed me. I have always been a reluctant warrior."

"I am not speaking about the courage of war, tlatoani," Mixcatl replied. "You said that we are beasts, both inside and out, you as well as I. What I speak of is the strength needed to face that beast."

"I did not face it. I turned away. I lied. Both to you and Huetzin." Wise Coyote closed his eyes.

"But when the choice came between ending the lie or letting me go on believing that I was too flawed to live, you ended the lie. I know how much that choice has cost you and how much it will still take."

"Mixcatl . . ."

She continued. "You told Nine-Lizard to honor himself for the choice he made on the temple steps. Those words helped him. I saw it in his face. Your wisdom comforts others, tlatoani. Why deny it to yourself?"

As he looked at her, something shifted within his eyes and the sunlight was at last able to brighten them. "By Tloque Nahaque, you must be right." His smile became warmer, then he laughed.

"You are braver than anyone," she teased.

His eyebrows went up beneath the turquoise band of his coronet. "What makes you think so?"

Mixcatl smiled, for she knew that the answer would come easily to her lips. And with it a sense that she had begun to accept herself and her ability. It was the first in a long series of steps she needed to take.

Taking Wise Coyote's hand, she asked, "Who else would walk alone with a jaguar?"

ABOUT THE AUTHOR

Clare Bell has always loved big cats. This interest, coupled with her interest in prehistoric mammals led to her first novel, *Ratha's Creature,* a young adult work that was an A.L.A. and PEN award-winner. Since then she's written three more young adult novels, two in the Ratha series, and one science fiction novel, *People of the Sky* (Tor, 1990).

She has also co-written three Polynesian prehistoric novels, under the name Clare Coleman. The first novel, *Daughter of the Reef,* was published early this year; the second, *Sister of the Sun,* is currently being published.

Before and during her writing career, the author analyzed seawater aboard the USGS San Francisco Bay research ship *Polaris,* clerked in a bookstore, hauled fish on a tuna boat, nursed cats in a veterinary clinic and worked for twelve years as an IBM manufacturing equipment engineer. She belongs to the Electric Auto Association, contributes to its newsletter, *Current Events,* and drives a VW Baja Bug that she converted from gasoline to battery power. Recently she bought a '76 Porsche 914 that she intends to convert to electric and hopes to run the car in the 1994 Solar-Electric 500 race in Phoenix, Arizona.

She lives amid "creative clutter" in San Jose, California.